Gift of the Fallen

S. B. Richter

Copyright © 2024 S. B. Richter

All rights reserved.

No part of this publication may be reproduced, distributed, or transmitted in any form or by any means, including photocopying, recording, or other electronic or mechanical methods, without the prior written permission of the publisher, except as permitted by U.S. copyright law. For permission requests, email richterbrooke404@gmail.com

The story, all names, characters, and incidents portrayed in this production are fictitious. No identification with actual persons (living or deceased), places, buildings, and products is intended or should be inferred.

Book Cover by Saturniidae Guethler

Library of Congress Control Number: 2024905107

ISBN 979-8-9900783-0-7

To the most supportive family I could ever have

Gift of the Fallen

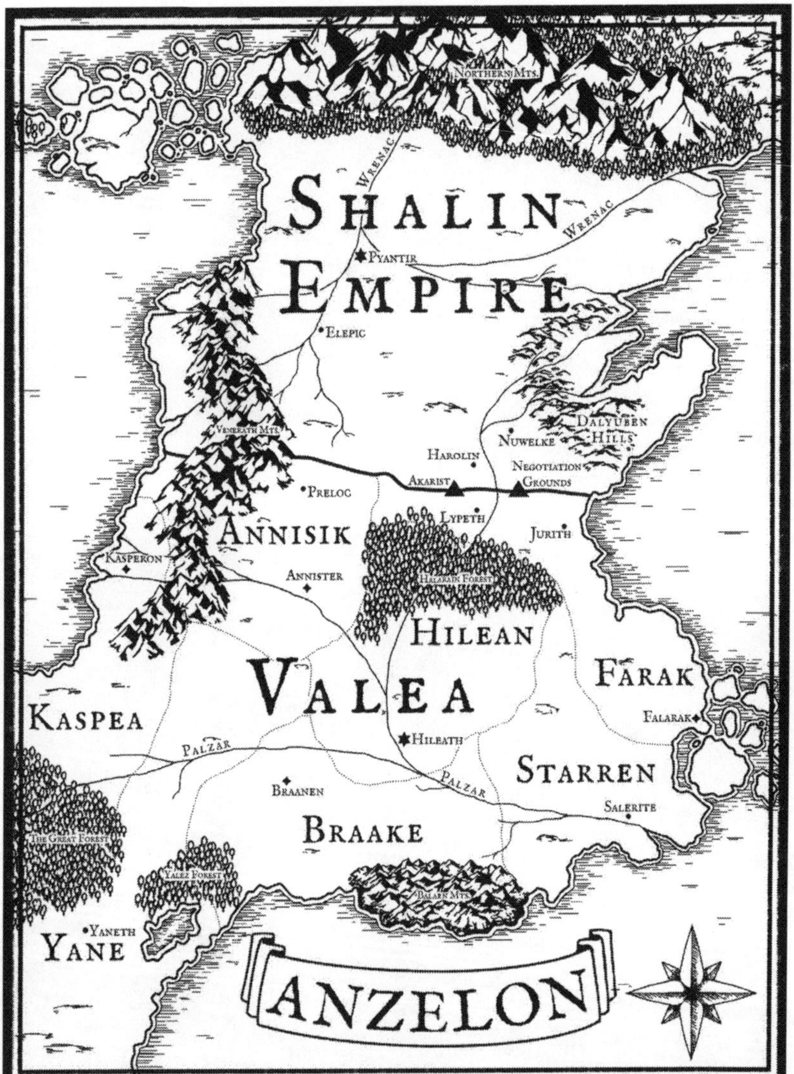

Northern Mts.
Wrenac
Shalin
Empire
Wrenac
Pyantir
Elepic
Venerath Mts.
Dalyuben
Hills
Nuwelke
Harolin
Negotiation
Grounds
Akarist
Preloc
Lypeth
Annisik
Jurith
Kasperon
Annister
Halarain Forest
Hilean
Valea
Farak
Kaspea
Falarak
Palzar
Hileath
Starren
Palzar
Braanen
Salerite
Braake
The Great Forest
Yalez Forest
Balarn Mts.
Yaneth
Yane
Anzelon

1

Thalen

Lord Thalen strode across the clean stone floors of his new castle, refusing to glance back at his guests. If he did, another wave of revulsion and anger might strike him, and he might no longer be able to contain the tempest of anger straining to break free from the confines of his excellent manners. To distract himself from the surrounding commotion, he approached one of the many tall glass windows lining the dining hall and gazed at the intricacies of the hand-carved ceiling.

Only a few more hours. He yearned to lounge in his opulent throne room—this ridiculous opening celebration might be the death of him. A chorus of cheerful laughter echoed through the massive hall, grating against his ears as he stared out the window, admiring all that he could see of Annisik Castle's grounds, the new symbol of Annisik Province's power. *His* province. *His* power.

Despite his current frustration, Thalen smirked. Ten years of hard work had finally paid off. He had submitted forged paperwork to the queen's advisors, bragging about the declining poverty levels and high earnings throughout Annisik Province. He'd gathered laborers from every corner of his lands, providing jobs for those in need. And although his vault was now nearly empty, here stood Annisik Castle.

Thalen's men would tear down the old castle shortly; a spectacle he was quite eager to witness. It had been a dinky, run down thing plagued by rats and dirt. The gate to the grounds had not been ten yards from the castle entrance; he could still hear the endless pounding and screaming of the peasants, begging for food or money, or cursing his name. But no more. His new jet-black fence never came closer than thirty yards to any point on the castle and was tall enough to keep out even the cleverest of stupid peasants. Peace and quiet. *At last.* Except for this repulsive party.

Thalen glanced across the room to see the giant oak doors ajar. He rolled his eyes as even more guests piled into the great hall. Cursing under his breath, Thalen pulled his black robe tighter against the passing chill sweeping through the room. The luxurious robe, sewn with the highest quality silk, was his one comfort in this horrid party. He curled his upper lip in disdain as the crowd's obnoxious voices rang in his ears. Maybe if he stood here long enough, away from the party, they would all leave. He turned away from the throng again, making the highest effort to ignore them.

"Lord Thalen, are you well?" asked an unfamiliar voice from behind, intruding on his thoughts.

"Yes, perfectly fine, thank you," Thalen said, clenching his jaw in irritation. There was a slim chance the man was important to his coffers; it would not do to upset him.

"Join your guests by the table, won't you, my lord? Your distance has puzzled them." Thalen closed his eyes, hoping the man would disappear before he opened them again. "I suppose I shall." It would be a miracle if he could keep this welcoming façade up until his guests departed. Being lord of a province truly had its downsides.

Stiffly, he turned around and began walking toward the tables of food, wine, and chatter. He supposed the queen did not take well to his distance from the party and had sent this man to fetch him. The man, who he now recognized as a servant, stayed by his side, as if he were equal to Thalen.

"You've done such a magnificent job on this castle, Lord Thalen," said the servant, breaking the lingering silence. Thalen glanced over to see a disgusting grin on his servant's face.

"Indeed," he eventually replied, turning back to face the party. Satisfaction filled him as he realized he needn't act amiable anymore. "The servants of my castle ought to reflect its magnificence, don't you think?" he asked, a smirk playing on his lips.

"Ah . . . yes, of course, my lord."

"Well unfortunately, that's the one aspect that falls short." He watched with pleasure as the servant understood Thalen's insinuation, and the grin dropped from his face.

The servant's step faltered. "I—I apologize, my lord. It won't happen again, I swear." His face was flushed, and his wild eyes darted around the room as if looking for an escape.

Thalen considered firing him, but he was already short on servants. He chose instead to remain silent, leaving the servant to anticipate Thalen's retribution. The pair resumed walking toward the rest of the crowd in awkward silence, the servant staying two paces behind him now. *Perfect.* He resisted the urge to scowl at the waiting crowd of servants, guards, and government officials. The boisterous crowd of drunkards disgusted him, all indulging in the food and wine prepared by his servants.

"A glass of wine for you, my lord?" another servant asked, grinning as he held a glass of dark red wine inches from Thalen's face.

"No," spat Thalen, jerking his head back and waving the glass away.

"Ahem!" The intoxicated crowd was coerced to silence by the commanding voice of Queen Gladia. "Now that our esteemed lord has joined our celebrations, I'd like to make a small toast to the construction and opening of this new castle. Under Lord Thalen, laborers completed this endeavor in just under ten years, an incredible feat. No doubt the lives lost along the way were worth this new, pristine building."

Thalen's pulse accelerated. Blood rushed to his cheeks as dread and anger welled up inside of him. Against his better judgment, he glanced around at the faces of his servants and guests—they were all rapt.

A venomous smile formed on the Queen's lips. "I'm positive that the money in Annisik's vault could not have gone to a better place, and that this magnificent structure will benefit all equally," she said, her words dripping with poison. "Fortunately, when I reviewed the fairness of this new castle, I found that the general standard of living in Annisik Province permitted the expense." Her piercing eyes found his own, and though she was a great deal shorter than him, he nearly cowered beneath her accusing gaze. "But then I found something strange, Thalen. When I sent my informants to confirm the information was valid, they found that the true standard of living was ten times lower than your report showed."

No! His fate was nearly sealed, he knew. Each of her words was a dagger slice to Thalen, shredding his meticulously crafted reputation into ribbons. He swallowed, racing to counter her evil ramblings. "Unfortunate, Queen Gladia. But if I'm not mistaken, your jurisdiction does not extend to the province's expenses." His booming voice filled the room, making it clear that the queen had no place in his castle. She would not demean him.

"Ah, of course, you are correct." She flashed a conciliatory smile before raising her head and locking eyes with servants and nobles alike. "It is, however, my jurisdiction to protect the people of Valea. To ensure that they are not being forced into *slavery*, for example. But I'm sure everything you've done was in the best interest of all your citizens, isn't that right, Thalen?" she asked, turning back to him. "Your admirable legacy will surely continue once you convince your wife to bear your children."

There was an audible gasp and the crowd attempted to conceal their laughter, but the damage was done. She had undermined him in his own castle, in only a few moments. Partygoers glared at him as though he were a trespasser, a lost man who stumbled in on an exclusive gathering he was not invited to.

"What kind words, Queen Gladia." He needed an escape. A way to save face. "How unfortunate that all this excitement has made me rather overheated. I think I shall take a walk . . . A breath of fresh air will revive my appetite for the festivities."

He hurried away, muttering curse after curse on Gladia, the guests, and whomever had exposed him. How could she have wiped away his superiority in an instant? The laughter from the guests resumed, now without a hint of suppression. He pushed on one of the massive double doors to exit the castle, but they wouldn't budge. As a servant appeared from behind to lift the latch, Thalen heard even more laughter and felt his cheeks grow even hotter. Finally wrestling the doors open, he shivered as the frigid air struck his skin. He neglected to close the doors behind him, but the sound of a servant slamming them shut only worsened his resentment. He'd have that servant executed. No, he'd have the entire castle staff replaced. The brain-dead nobles and barons would soon forget this incident amidst new, menial gossip, and he would never invite them back to his castle. Then, only he and the queen, however long *she* lasted, would remember this ordeal.

After walking aimlessly for a few minutes, Thalen decided to sit for a while in the spacious front garden of his castle, well within the safety of the fence. He relished the silence; at least he could wait out his guests. Thalen swept the autumn leaves from a bench and took a seat, facing Annisik's capital city, Annister. Gazing at the city through the thick fence posts, he couldn't help wrinkling his nose. He'd been so keen to distance his castle from the city, yet his advisors had convinced him otherwise. The fools! Why did he ever listen to them?

Without warning, a thunderous explosion shattered the silence.

He sprang to his feet as tremors reverberated through the ground, shaking the earth and trees around him. Thalen watched in horror as the eastern tower, his throne room, crumbled to the ground. He stood frozen for the second time that night, consumed by shock. Even as an enormous cloud of fire and dust burst from the dining hall, he could not move an inch. The explosion threw shrapnel in every direction—pain shot through his leg as a shard of stone embedded itself in his thigh and he collapsed to the ground. He cowered and shut his eyes while a shower of debris fell around him. Vague figures ran from the ruined castle, screaming in terror and pain. Guards soon appeared, arriving from the grounds and nearby streets.

"No, my castle, my poor castle," whimpered Thalen.

He hadn't seen the queen emerge from the castle yet. Could she be dead? Thalen raised his head and squinted to see a figure emerge from the rubble, carrying her. Again, his hopes were crushed. The man placed the queen on the grass and opened a pack of what he had to assume were medical supplies. *Strange . . . is he a doctor?*

Pain lanced through Thalen, and he looked down at his leg. With alarm, he saw blood pooling on the grass and felt himself growing faint. Taking a breath, he tried to move his leg, but the pain was overwhelming.

One of his servants saw him and rushed forward. "Lord Thalen is injured!" he called.

Another explosion rang out, and another section of his treasured castle fell. Screams echoed around him once again. More orange fire burst from the remains of his prized home. Distraught and frightened, his devoted servants abandoned him. Thalen attempted to call out, but no words left his lips. Fighting against the black void threatening to consume him, he tried in vain to move, to scream, to do anything. *Please, someone help.* Raising his head now brought intense dizziness and nausea, leaving him helplessly splayed out on the grass. His world went black.

2

Melkin

Melkin gazed at the papers on his desk, unable to focus on any single page. There was a complete lack of identifying information in the dozens of bombing reports sprawled out before him. Months of incidents, yet no evidence as to whom the perpetrators might be. He almost regretted asking for copies; they were all useless. The same story repeated itself over and over: no one looked suspicious, and nothing was out of place before any of the explosions.

However, this new attack was unique in one way. The recent explosion had been of unprecedented magnitude and had caused irreparable destruction. The castle spies were now poring over the longest report yet, with nothing to show for it. They had taken on the responsibility alone; Queen Gladia hadn't been able to oversee the investigation, injured as she was. Melkin sighed and dipped his goose feather pen into an inkwell. Perhaps if he put pen to paper, an idea or two might form in his mind. But as the ink pooled and soaked into the page, he found it impossible to move his hand, to think a single coherent thought. His mind was occupied, sifting through the abundance of useless information. A knock on the door finally broke his trance. He laid the pen down and shut his eyes, ridding himself of the impossible work.

"Enter."

"Queen Gladia requests you. Meeting room." Barely finishing his words, the servant left the door open and hurried away.

Melkin frowned. Given the severity of Queen Gladia's injuries, he thought she might take at least another few days to recover. It had been so close; if he had reacted a fraction of a second later, she'd be dead. He cleared his head of the thought. All was well now—at least in that regard.

That she had called a meeting was good news. Gladia knew her limits; he wouldn't complain about her efficiency. With a sigh, he stood from his chair and followed the retreating servant up the two flights of stairs to the meeting room.

Melkin walked through the grand double doors into the dimly lit room, eyes falling upon the injured Queen Gladia. She sat at the head of the table, arms in bandages and her leg in a splint. Her olive skin was marked with bruises and blemishes, and her wavy black hair looked unkempt. The seven other meeting attendees looked rather uncomfortable, as if they had expected Gladia to ignore her duties as a monarch in favor of recovery.

To the queen's left sat her two sons, Fareod and Galdur Ravinyk. Three commanders sat to Gladia's right, none of whom Melkin knew personally. A few empty chairs down from Galdur sat fellow castle spy, Leina Kierth, and a medic with whom he was unfamiliar. Melkin scrunched his brow; it was certainly an odd gathering.

Queen Gladia flashed him a pleasant smile. "Please, take a seat."

He did as requested, taking the furthest of the twelve empty chairs around the stone table.

The queen glanced at her audience of eight, grimacing. "The visit to Annisik Castle did not go quite as planned... The cost in lives is only one of the many concerning aspects of the tragedy. It is imperative that we find and eradicate the source. Leina, do you have any information of use?"

"There were traces of explosive powder near the bombing site, of course, but I have never seen a bomb inflict so much damage. I found no other chemicals, but any specific testing would require that I know what to look for. My plan is to research the remnants of the explosion further, to find out how such a destructive thing came to be. Whoever created it must have had access to some sort of hitherto unknown explosive substance."

"Any information on who that might be?" Gladia placed her hands on the table, lacing her fingers together. Eagerness showed from behind her pained, exhausted face.

"No witnesses reported any strange behavior before, during, or after the event."

Gladia leaned back, the corners of her mouth turning down. "I thought much the same. Commander Geral, has anything come up during the recovery effort?"

The commander closest to Gladia was pensive for a moment, staring at the table. He shook his head. "My guards don't know every face in the city, but none of them saw anything unusual."

Melkin began tapping his foot against the ground. They were only restating the bombing reports; did these people not check them beforehand? A quick glance from Galdur reminded him that he was surrounded by the kingdom's most important people. He willed himself to remain still, to not let his impatience show.

Gladia glanced at the table for a moment, pressing her lips together. "Hmph. If only Thalen knew the faces of his servants, he may have seen an odd one out."

"We investigated the castle staff, both living and dead, and found that everything aligned perfectly with the records—"

"Why have none of you considered that the Shalin Empire is obviously behind this?" said Fareod, a sneer on his face. Melkin resisted smirking at the smug expression; it seemed like the prince thought he had real power in this meeting.

"Patience," said Queen Gladia, turning to glare at her eldest son. "It is our duty to explore all options first."

Fareod spread his hands in a gesture of incredulity and raised his voice. "If we're weak about blaming them, they'll continue to kill our people!"

"And if we're too hasty, we'll spark another unnecessary conflict, or worse," said Queen Gladia, her tone unchanged from when she was conversing with Geral. She looked back at the rest of the table. "Thalen survived the incident, so perhaps he may report something."

Geral sighed, resting his head in his hands. "We already questioned him. He saw nothing."

The queen nodded with a sigh. "Well, I figured as much. How is he, anyway?"

"We predict he'll make a full recovery," said the medic, grimacing.

A wave of deep disappointment washed over Melkin. Someday, that man would reap what he had been sowing for his twenty-five years of rule. The shared looks of disgust around the table told Melkin that the feeling was mutual. They had all hoped he wouldn't make it.

Queen Gladia nodded slowly. "Unfortunate, but not important right now. We need to keep our people safe and—"

"So, what are you going to do about the Shalin Empire?" Fareod looked between the meeting attendees. "We ought to declare war for this atrocity!"

Queen Gladia glared at him. "Don't be rash, my child. People die in wars. They are not to be declared without at least proof of wronging."

Fareod opened his mouth but must have reconsidered his words, for the room went silent. Still, Fareod bounced his leg, his impatience obvious.

Geral leaned forward, hesitating for a second before he spoke. "The simplest answer is usually the correct one, Your Majesty. The Shalin Empire—"

"I don't need a lecture about the Shalin Empire, Commander. I was just hoping that we could finally make peace."

"Peace would be incredible, Your Majesty, but history is too red to repair."

Her stern face turned toward Geral's sheepish one. "That is not your judgment to make." Melkin admired her respectful tone, free of anger or annoyance. She faced the rest of the table, glancing at each of the eight she had gathered. "I have a plan to investigate the Shalin Empire's involvement in this. It does not leave the room except by my word and my word alone. Is that understood?"

The room fell silent again as they all nodded.

"Wonderful. Our delegation of soldiers, servants, and advisors depart for the Akistaria in a week. Melkin, I want you to go with them disguised as a servant."

Melkin nodded, his mind racing furiously to remember anything about the subject matter. He vaguely recalled the Akistaria being a sacred meeting between Valea and the Shalin Empire. It took place at the Akarist, a castle on the border between the two countries. He'd long lost interest in them after years of failed peace agreements and de-escalation policies.

"At the Akarist castle, you'll attempt to gain knowledge concerning the Shalin Empire's plans. Don't interrupt the actual Akistaria meeting but find out as much as you can. Be wary, for if the Shalin Empire catches you, they may not forgive such an infiltration. Consequences worse than your own execution may follow."

"Your Majesty," spoke the commander closest to Melkin, "why not send this spy in as a soldier? In the hundred that I bring, he will blend in."

"In any other year, I would agree with you, Commander Taleek. This year, I am limiting you to twenty soldiers. I cannot send so many of our men and women to a peaceful negotiation. We must aid Annister after the castle's collapse, prepare relief efforts for any more bombings, and resolve increasing border skirmishes with the Shalin Empire. You may choose who you would like to bring from your brigade."

Commander Taleek nodded and gave a quick glance at Melkin as if to size up his capability or his trustworthiness. Melkin resisted rolling his eyes at the gesture and instead ignored the commander.

"Until the Akistaria party returns," the queen continued, "we will refrain from antagonizing the Shalin Empire any further. Leina, commit all your resources to understanding the cause of the explosion. Hire an alchemist, replicate this bomb, do whatever you must. You'll be reimbursed for all your expenses."

"Yes, Your Majesty," said Leina. Though she seemed delighted with the assignment, Melkin wondered if there *was* anything for her to find.

"Good. Now, Commander Balan, you have other news?" Gladia caught the eye of the third commander from her right.

"Indeed. My brigade is suffering at the border, as are others. I know resources are scarce, but we need more supplies and more soldiers. General Yorela sent me here from the border of Farak Province to report." Balan swallowed, averting his gaze from the queen's. His next words were a soft mutter. "The Shalin Empire gained a mile of land on the seventeenth of last month. They're occupying it, claiming it as a part of the empire."

Queen Gladia sighed. "Given their past tendencies, they'll retreat before too long. I have no desire to grant General Yorela more supplies; it only prolongs the skirmishes."

"They will continue with or without your help. The only difference it makes is who will win," said Geral, matching Gladia's diplomatic tone but remaining firm in his assertion.

"I understand, but we must—"

"Supply them! We must hold our ground! Those magic-wielding bastards will never relent!" yelled Fareod, springing to his feet. In an imprudent show of power, he planted his hands firmly on the table. Melkin smirked, watching Fareod's face contort from anger to fear as Gladia turned toward him, her eyes narrowed.

"Know your place! You may be the prince, but I am your mother and your queen! Guards, escort him out."

As the queen's raised voice echoed throughout the room, everyone suddenly seemed quite interested in the floor. With a huff, Fareod allowed himself to be led out. Melkin welcomed the coming silence with open arms; it gave him time to think. He glanced at Leina, who had a mildly amused expression on her face. He couldn't blame her. Watching Fareod face consequences for running his mouth never got old.

"His opinions do not echo mine, your Majesty..." said Geral, averting his gaze from the Queen's. "Or at least... his attitude does not."

"I know. I'm thankful for our courteous debates, Commander. This... this I must think upon for some time, though," responded Queen Gladia.

"Please, do not think too long, your Majesty. I am under pressure from my general and soldiers. Every day, I receive letters of this sort, begging for supplies," said Balan.

"I apologize, Commander, but this decision is of the utmost importance. I cannot give a resolute verdict without proper consideration," said Gladia. "If you wish, you may stay at the castle until I decide. If anyone has further questions or news, we may meet again in the coming few days. For today, we are concluded."

Swiftly, Melkin stood from his chair and left the room. *What to do?* Halfway down the stairs, he paused and turned back, but Commander Taleek was now engaged in deep conversation with Commander Balan at the top of the staircase. With reluctance, he returned to his study, wishing he could have asked Taleek a few questions about the Akistaria party he was joining. Melkin filed away the bombing reports cluttering his desk and stood by the window, considering his next move. He knew little about the customs of the Akistaria or how he should act as a servant. Before long, the sound of footsteps interrupted Melkin's thoughts and grew louder until they stopped in his open doorway.

"What are your thoughts on your assignment?" asked Leina from behind.

"I'm not sure," replied Melkin, still staring out the window.

"Any hunches you neglected to share with Queen Gladia?"

"The idea of Thalen's involvement crossed my mind. I obviously have no evidence, though. Ooh! If you want, I can forge some to get him executed!"

Melkin shook his head, trying not to find humor in her impertinent joke. "He can't be behind it; he'd never put himself at risk."

Leina's voice became serious once again. "Well then, the culprits are obvious. The Shalin Empire."

He turned to face Leina, resisting the urge to roll his eyes at her grand assertion. "What evidence do you have?"

"I have logic. Thirty-three bombings, Melkin, and no one has seen them. Only with the funding of a government could the bombers accomplish that."

"There are other ways to obtain funds. . . . Plus, one couldn't control such a tightly run operation from hundreds of miles away."

"They could sponsor a leader to pull it off from within Valea. Why do you defend the Shalin Empire?"

"Like you said, logic. Anyway, I need some time to figure out . . . everything about the Akistaria."

"Do you want any help?"

"No, I need to be alone with my thoughts for now." He turned his head back to the window. After Leina left, he heard another set of footsteps approaching and again refused to glance back at the doorway. He knew who it was by the gait, anyway.

"How are you on this splendid day, Melkin?" asked the prince of Valea.

"Don't you know the condition of your mother?" He'd expected Galdur to be in a more solemn mood; after all, his mother had come quite close to dying.

"Why do you think I'm so cheerful? Thanks to you, she's alive and well."

He faced Galdur, whose grin was unwavering beneath Melkin's glare. "What can I do for you?"

"Just wanted to have a little chat with my friend, that's all."

Melkin pressed his lips, glancing at his desk. "I don't really have time for such levity right now."

"I know. You must be under a lot of stress from your assignment. But I'm positive you'll succeed in every way possible."

Melkin kept his expression flat—did Galdur understand the peril he faced? "Thanks. You know, you should really be the heir instead of that fool you call a brother."

Galdur grinned wildly. "Watch your language in the royal castle."

Melkin rolled his eyes. "You know I've said worse."

"Indeed. Anyway, you've been to the Shalin Empire before, right?"

Melkin paused. If he insisted, Galdur would leave him to his devices, but a part of him wished for the prince to remain. A distraction of sorts. "A few times. Mostly rural areas where the chance of detection was low."

"So, you've seen the faul race, the people who live there?"

Melkin nodded. "Yes. Only a few, and from quite a distance."

"You blend in with their height." Galdur's grin widened upon seeing Melkin's scowl. "Anyway, I was doing some research on their magic and other characteristics."

"Their magic is always light, heat, or air pressure. They're physically weak, have pale skin and hair, and as you so politely pointed out, are quite short. What more is there to know?"

"Will it surprise you to learn that not all faul are a part of those three magic categories? About five percent have a mutation that lets them do . . . other magic."

"Like what?"

"Mind reading, invisibility, tidal control—many things."

Melkin swallowed, a pit forming in his stomach. "So . . . I could see one of these faul at the Akarist?"

"Not likely. Mutated or strong powers often kill their hosts before they reach adulthood. They're physically weaker than the other faul."

"Alright, so what?"

"Well, even if they're not very powerful, you *will* be around a lot of faul at the Akarist. They'll have their natural weapons while you won't."

"Why not?" asked Melkin, fearing he knew the answer.

"All humans must leave their weapons in their tower, and all faul in theirs. No plate armor or chainmail either. The Akarist is a sacred castle, you know. The Akistaria meeting itself is even more secure. I'm not too familiar with the specifics myself, though."

"No one told me any of this," muttered Melkin, glancing at his storage chest of comforting weapons. "I have to research this further."

"You know, I could just stay here . . . follow you around . . ." Galdur's grin spread further across his youthful face.

"Don't." Melkin strode out of his study, leaving Galdur standing in the doorway.

The prince shook his head in disbelief. "How is it you have the authority to disrespect both me and the crown prince?"

Melkin didn't respond. He made his way down to the library, cursing his lack of knowledge and the short notice of the mission. Queen Gladia hardly ever sanctioned espionage against the Shalin Empire, and certainly nothing ever as outrageous as this. He had expected an assignment to investigate the bombings like the other castle spies. Instead, he would infiltrate the most sacred building on the entire continent of Anzelon. There would be no weapons, no room for error, and no help.

Which was better, boredom or terror?

3

MELKIN

On the twenty-third, Melkin rose before dawn and dressed in his modified traveling servant outfit: brown boots, brown trousers, a black long-sleeved tunic, a brown leather jerkin, and a black hood. Not a horrible outfit—it was actually quite inconspicuous, he thought. He glanced out his window, fearing that he was late, but no one was in the training yard. Typical. At least he could use the extra time to train until the others arrived.

In all the times he'd stepped foot onto the training grounds, he'd never seen another soul there. He suspected no one else used them. Guards and spies practiced at their respective academies, never at the castle. The almost perfectly intact target dummies and old, rusted weapons proved how useless the grounds were. Melkin stood around five yards away from his chosen dummy and reached down to his boot, drawing the only knife he carried.

It had been simple, altering the servant boots to accommodate a six-inch knife. He also carried a slim shard of flint in his other boot and two thin coils of rope for emergencies. If Shalin guards discovered either the flint or the rope on him at the Akarist, he'd be alright.

A knot of fear formed at the thought of being caught with the knife though. Turning his attention back to the dummy, he spent almost half an hour throwing the knife, getting a feel for how this particular blade flew through the air.

Eventually, Melkin heard soldiers marching toward the grounds. It was tiny for a brigade; a fifth of its normal size, Melkin estimated. He had intended to speak with Taleek before departure, but the commander had been busy preparing for the journey. By their tardiness, Melkin guessed Taleek was the sort of commander to let his soldiers run amok. Each soldier carried a spear and was clad in either chainmail or plate armor over their padded gambeson. Many had daggers or swords hanging at their sides, only used when the spear was not viable.

Melkin slipped the knife back in his boot before anyone could see it. He was eager to finally leave. Scanning the boisterous soldiers, he found Commander Taleek and walked over to the tall, muscular man.

"Little late, aren't we?" he asked, unable to resist the sarcasm. "Your messenger told me we would depart before sunrise."

The commander chuckled. "Oh, I tell that to everyone. Now you know I mean, 'a little after sunrise.'" Presumably noting Melkin's scowl, the commander sighed. "Alright, I'm sorry, but it's really the ambassadors and their servants we're waiting on. I tell them every year and yet . . ." He shook his head. "Believe me, I'd love to get moving."

Melkin nodded. "They'd better arrive soon. I thought they were the royal council, though. Advisors."

"For this mission, they take the title of ambassador. It's Melkin, correct?"

"You'll address me by my surname, Evarith."

Taleek extended his hand, a friendly smile on his face. "Will do. It's a pleasure to officially meet you." Melkin shook it, having to physically look up to meet the eyes of this much taller, larger man. No doubt the soldiers thought Melkin looked ridiculous next to him.

"You know my position is to remain as secret as possible, right?" asked Melkin in a low voice. Taleek nodded and winked before retreating to speak with one of his soldiers. The strange interaction between commander and servant had already garnered a bit of attention from the soldiers, who were surely speculating about the cause. Melkin walked to a rack of training weapons and reached for some throwing knives. He paused, glancing back at the group of soldiers, and took two spears instead. Though they were hardly more than blunt-tipped staffs, their strikes could leave a mark. He knew that from experience.

"Would anyone like to spar with me?" he asked a few soldiers, interrupting their conversation.

"Sure," responded one of them, smirking at his friends. He was over six feet tall and far broader than Melkin. Speed, then, would be Melkin's greatest advantage, he thought.

Melkin handed the soldier a practice spear, and the two moved to a deserted patch of the training grounds. As they took their places a few yards from each other, some of the soldiers gathered around. They watched as the two circled each other, waiting to see who would make the first strike. Then, quick as a fox, Melkin stabbed his spear toward the other man's side. He dodged with ease and lunged to counterstrike. Melkin barely got his spear shaft up in time to block it; he staggered back a pace to dodge the next stab before again moving in and aiming for the soldier's torso. Melkin's spear was pushed to the side, throwing him off balance for a split second before he regained control and ducked under the next strike. He widened his grip on the spear and used the leverage to match the man's strength in his next parry. Caught off guard, the man backed up, and the two once again circled, searching for an opening.

Melkin's pulse quickened, excitement coursing through his veins. Though the nature of his missions typically left him with only a mere dagger to protect himself, spear-fighting had always been a passion of his. The years of training at the intelligence academy rushed back to him, filling him with the energy and heightened senses needed to beat this soldier. His opponents in the academy had never taken more than ten seconds to best, but the man before him was infinitely more skilled than any of them ever were.

As the soldier tensed, Melkin foresaw the incoming stab and easily deflected it. He pressed his advantage, moving with agility as he stabbed again and again. But as each of his blows were easily evaded, he felt his arms grow heavy and soon found himself on the defense. *Please, make a mistake!* In a last-ditch effort, Melkin made a wild feint—to his great surprise, the man fell for it and was caught off-balance. He drew his spear back and thrust at the man's ankle, successfully grazing it as his opponent's spear slammed into Melkin's shoulder. Too late, Melkin realized that the soldier had feinted in turn, thus tricking Melkin instead. The surrounding soldiers laughed and cheered good-naturedly. Though he hoped for another chance to duel the soldier, Melkin figured he'd attracted enough attention already.

"Better than most of my soldiers could have done!" laughed Commander Taleek. Though the commander had a wild grin on his face, a pit of dread formed as Melkin realized just how strange a duel between a servant and a soldier must have looked. "Watch out, I'm going to replace one of you!"

The soldiers laughed comfortably at the jest, glancing at Melkin with a mixture of amusement and bewilderment. Melkin presumed Taleek had chosen these nineteen men because they were his best—he wondered how many of them he could defeat in a duel.

Noticing movement to his side, Melkin turned to see his opponent extend his hand, which he quickly shook, easing the subconscious scowl that had spread across his face. Commander Taleek approached the pair and waved away the soldier with a grin.

"Why didn't you join the military, Evarith?"

Melkin stared deadpan into the commander's eyes. "I get paid more."

Taleek laughed and slapped Melkin on the back, making him awkwardly stumble forward. "I'm sure you do!" Taking no notice of Melkin's chagrin, the muscular commander continued to laugh as he walked away.

Melkin hurriedly left the crowd of soldiers and returned to the training weapons rack, searching for anything else he could pass the time with. *Where in Anzelon are those ambassadors?* After selecting a few throwing knives, his sparring partner sauntered up to him.

"It's been some time since someone came that close to beating me. In a proper fight, I would have had to live with that injury, unlike you."

"I've survived worse than that stab." He examined the knives he chose, caked with rust and dirt, and frowned at their treatment.

The man stood, arms crossed, as he stared at Melkin with a raised eyebrow. "Tell me this tale."

"Another time."

"Well then, perhaps you could explain why a servant arrived earlier than any of their advisors or companions. Or, why they fight like a trained soldier."

Melkin glanced at him, wishing he'd thought of that beforehand. He cursed himself, pretending to clean the knife while he fabricated a story. "When I was too poor to buy meat, I would hunt. One must be prepared should they come across a wild boar. Crime was always a worry where I lived, as well."

"Surely you've been a servant for some time now, though."

Melkin shrugged. "Of course. But the years of practice have not left me, and the queen has never denied my use of the training grounds." He turned to leave the nosey man alone with his questions.

"Wait! What do I call you?"

"Evarith," he said cautiously, turning back. "And you?"

"I'm Vallec, Commander Taleek's right-hand man. A pleasure to meet you." The soldier extended his hand, and Melkin shook it after a moment of reluctance. The earlier shake had been one of etiquette. This one indicated... trust? Friendship? Melkin couldn't afford either of those things with Vallec.

Together, they turned at the sound of horses and the creaking of wood approaching. Melkin shielded his eyes from the rising sun. Silently, he counted five ambassadors on horseback and nineteen servants on foot emerging from around a castle wall.

"Ah, our company has arrived," said the commander. "Soldiers, to attention!"

Despite the eyerolls that Melkin noticed from a few of the soldiers, they followed the instructions of their commander. Standing off to the side, Melkin felt incredibly out of place. *This wouldn't be a problem if the ambassadors arrived on time.* He tried to slide into the missing servant's position without being noticed. Thankfully, the servants were well organized in packs of four and the incomplete group was easy to spot.

"We are at your service, members of the royal council," said Commander Taleek.

"I apologize for the wait, Commander, but we encountered a few delays," responded one ambassador, without a hint of sorrow. Melkin held back a laugh at the ambassadors' clothes. The men wore long fur cloaks around leather jerkins secured with belts, while the women wore their cloaks over corsets and thick, ankle-length dresses. Such heavy clothing had no place this early in autumn. The coddled government officials wouldn't last a day in the dead of winter.

"Strange how that occurs each year," remarked Taleek.

"Four years ago, it didn't," said the same ambassador, raising his voice slightly.

"Hence why we must arrive early each year in case that happens again," said Taleek. "But what am I saying? We shan't get anywhere by bickering. Let us depart."

They took the main road out from the royal castle, assuming a formation in which the soldiers surrounded the party of ambassadors and servants.

Around a mile into their journey, the soldier next to Melkin looked up at the ambassador on horseback. "Sir, forgive me, but where is our usual fourth member?" Melkin glanced quickly at him, but the servant's face showed only innocent curiosity. *Was he suggesting something, or not?*

The ambassador glanced at the servant, an untroubled expression on his face. "Yesterday he woke up quite ill and I excused him from the mission. Though our ... new member has only recently joined the Hilean servant corps, I assure you he is qualified."

"Ah, is that why we saw you on the training grounds before the correct time?" asked another servant. "We always meet with our advisor, prepare for the journey, and head out together."

Melkin nodded, giving a quick smile through gritted teeth. "How foolish of me. I must have been misinformed. The name is Evarith, by the way."

The first servant nodded his understanding. "I'm Cirel."

With that, the conversation stopped. Melkin couldn't tell if this group usually traveled in silence on the way to the Akarist or if his presence stifled any talk. He suspected it was the latter, noticing the ample chatter in the other groups of ambassadors and servants. He enjoyed the silence though, content to think upon various matters for hours rather than engage in petty discussion or gossip.

Melkin missed traveling at a pace faster than two miles per hour, the speed required by the encumbered horses and unconditioned servants. After covering only a fraction of the ground Melkin or the soldiers would have on their own, the company stopped for lunch. Bags of dried food were retrieved from a cart, then rationed out to each member of the company.

"Oh my, each year I suffer new disgust at the food we must eat on this journey," complained his ambassador, nibbling on a piece of dried meat. The other three servants nodded and mumbled in agreement. Melkin had no aversion to such food, but wished he could forage for something fresh without drawing attention. With each passing hour of inefficiency, his heart sank more and more. He would have preferred to spy on Emperor Orwic of the Shalin Empire himself than travel with this slothful party.

Only fifteen miles into the journey, Commander Taleek called for camp to be set. While the soldiers patrolled the perimeter of the campsite, it was the servants' job to turn the grassy plain into a camp fit for the delegates of Queen Gladia's court. First, all twenty servants were needed to unload and set up their ambassadors' individual tents, followed by the four-person tents for the soldiers and servants. The servants then split up, with some going to fetch water, and others tending to the horses and gathering wood for small cooking fires. With the sun now edging closer to the horizon, one servant from each group of four made a sort of stew with water, dried meat, and foraged vegetables. Despite more grumbling from the ambassadors, all seemed to appreciate the hot meal after what they likely considered a hard day's work.

After all the tasks were done, Melkin sat back against a tree. Some servants had brought their instruments and were now entertaining the traveling party before nightfall. He missed his usual, much more efficient, camping practices. Everything took far longer with forty-four companions.

"Time to rest!" ordered Commander Taleek after a while. "You six are taking watch tonight." He pointed to several soldiers in turn. "Two per shift."

Melkin lay down in his tent but could not relax and let sleep overtake him. After the other three in his tent had long since fallen asleep, he donned his boots once more and sat outside. Embers from the fire still smoldered, dimly illuminating the campsite. Though they were only a few miles from the road, both soldiers taking watch looked inattentive and unconcerned about potential attackers. Any exhaustion he felt from the day's journey was immediately swept away, replaced by alertness. *These are Taleek's best men?* The moon rose a considerable distance before fatigue finally crept back into Melkin's mind, causing his eyelids to droop and senses to dull. He crawled back into his tent, careful not to wake the others, and wondered if they might all be massacred in the middle of the night.

The next four days of the journey were much like the first, except conversation became more frequent. The three servants seemed to grow more comfortable talking with and around Melkin, which mildly irritated him.

"When were you employed by the castle?" Cirel asked on day three.

After a second or two, Melkin realized the question was aimed at him. "I worked five years in Annister as a servant for Lord Thalen. I ah . . . left and found work here. Around a month ago."

The servants nodded, continuing the conversation amongst themselves whilst Melkin resumed his fruitless endeavors sorting through information stored in his mind about the Valea bombings. There had to be something he had missed.

"So, did you grow up in Annister?" asked Cirel on day five.

He shook his head. "A small town on the western border."

"Do you have any stories about Lord Thalen?"

The advisor gave his servant a disapproving look. "It's unwise and impolite to insult the lords and ladies of Valea."

Melkin thought the fact that the ambassador assumed any story told about Thalen would shed an unsavory light on the man spoke volumes in and of itself. If not for the horrible truth of the assumption, it would even be amusing.

"Well, any stories about Annister?" amended Cirel.

Perhaps they were getting suspicious. "Not really. It's what you've heard, I'm sure. Poor and dirty. Not much more to say about it, I'm afraid."

Again, Cirel nodded and resumed conversing with the others. Melkin took a silent breath, calming himself after the conversation. He didn't think any servant would betray him willingly to the Shalin Empire, but accidentally was another matter altogether. As far as he knew, only his ambassador and Commander Taleek knew his purposes. At least Taleek seemed relatively competent, even if he kept assigning inept soldiers as nightwatchmen.

That night, Melkin found it difficult to sleep. Again. He sat against a tree by his tent, keeping watch for the fifth night in a row. On his solo journeys, he never needed to keep watch at night, but with such a conspicuous campsite, everyone for miles might see them if not for the trees. Alone, he would sleep in ditches, behind bushes, anywhere he was concealed from view. In what Melkin thought to be a gross oversight, Taleek had the Akistaria party camp near the main road cutting through Halarain forest, a road often traveled by brigands and bandits.

At a quiet hissing sound, he whipped his head around, only to find that two of the guards were whispering to each other, sitting on a log around ten yards from him. He rolled his eyes at the absurdity of it all. It was beyond irritating that his highly trained instincts were now leading him to false conclusions. He relaxed back against the tree again, scanning around the campsite for any intruders, as usual. Another sound from the two guards. He looked over and saw a darting shadow behind them—his heartbeat quickened, and he raced to think of possible plans of action should the shadow be of any threat. It was almost pitch-black outside, yet the shape of a figure appeared behind the guards. Perhaps an animal—but no—it was much too large.

Making no sudden movements, Melkin drew his boot knife and narrowed his eyes. The slow, silent figure was clearly intent on taking out the two guards on watch. He could alert the campsite, but the figure might take a guard hostage or escape before other soldiers were roused. However idiotic these two were, Melkin knew he wouldn't forgive himself if he didn't at least try to protect them. He brought his arm back, shifting a bit to have a better angle. The figure jerked its head in Melkin's direction, and he froze. Once the eyes of the figure moved on from him, he released the knife, hoping his aim was true and the guards didn't make any sudden movements. The figure released a shriek of pain, breaking the silence of the night.

Melkin sprang to his feet, sucking in a breath. "Intruder! Intruder!"

The two guards leapt up and readied their spears. One of them bound their would-be-assailant, while the other pivoted on his feet, looking for other attackers. Melkin grabbed a spear from the ground and circled the camp, yet he saw no one else. Awakened by the shouts, more of Taleek's men crawled out of their tents. Melkin's attention snapped back to his immediate surroundings as a man appeared in front of him, thrusting a spear toward his side. He narrowly avoided the strike, grabbing the spear shaft and tripping his attacker with his foot. The man, now sprawled on the ground, was helpless to resist as Melkin put a foot on his right hand and aimed his spear at his throat.

"Do not pursue!" shouted Commander Taleek. "Guard the camp!"

Shouts echoed from around the campsite, giving way to the shuffling of feet and rustling of branches as the attackers retreated into the darkness of the forest.

"I'll tie him up," said Vallec, appearing beside Melkin.

Melkin nodded, panting from exhilaration. After the prisoner was restrained, he looked around to see what had happened. One soldier was wounded by an attacker, but no one had been killed. Soldiers had already tied the first intruder to a tree and Vallec was carrying the one Melkin had detained to a neighboring one. He crouched down near the spot where he'd hit the first attacker, but it was too dark to find his knife; he would have to wait until morning came. Gazing out into the darkness from the edge of the campsite, he saw no more figures, yet rest was inconceivable now that he knew how close danger lurked tonight.

"The campsite is secure!" announced Commander Taleek. "We'll deal with the prisoners in the morning, but in case our attackers come back, I'm assigning half the soldiers to watch for the next few hours."

Melkin heard the shuffling of feet and cloth as the startled servants and half of the guards crawled back into their tents.

Taleek's voice boomed across the campsite once more. "Morran, Heathe, how come you two missed the intruders? Evarith shouldn't have to alert the campsite, and you know it! Next time you're on watch, I want full attention on your surroundings!"

"Yes sir!"

At least now they might pay attention. Melkin sat at the edge of camp again, feeling increasingly exhausted as the exhilaration left his veins. Just as he began to relax his guard, footsteps sounded from behind him. It was a different gait than the shuffling guards—and far closer. Alarmed, he remembered his knife was missing. He whirled around but breathed a sigh of relief—it was only Commander Taleek.

He approached wordlessly, standing beside Melkin. Taleek held out a familiar knife, offering it to him. "Go to sleep, Evarith. You need rest."

Melkin turned the forbidden knife over in his hands, amazed that Taleek had found it in the dark. He had even cleaned off the blood. "I'm not tired."

"Yes, you are. We walk all day, and I've seen you stay up for hours, taking watch alongside my soldiers every night. You need to rest."

Melkin shifted, cornered by the imposing commander standing over him. "Your soldiers failed today. I don't trust them. At least one, if not more, would be dead if I didn't spot our attackers."

"If you exhaust yourself, you'll be more likely to slip up at the Akarist. Though I hate to say it, that would be far worse than the death of one soldier, or even of us all."

Melkin sighed, meeting Taleek's gaze. "Fine. If we die, I blame you. Wake me up before sunrise."

"Deal. Now go to sleep."

Melkin slipped the knife in his boot but paused before walking away. "How did you know it was my knife?"

"I saw you with it on the training grounds. I'm not sure how I feel about it, by the way. It did some good today, I suppose, but..."

Melkin looked down, unable to meet Taleek's eyes. "I don't plan to use it in the Akarist." He walked back to his tent and took off his boots before crawling inside. Almost before he closed his eyes, he fell into a deep sleep.

4

LOTHAR

"Soldiers, listen up!" ordered Sergeant Lothar Raiken in a low voice. "We don't know how many are in that cave. Prepare yourself. If we must retreat, we will, but ... this might be it." He willed his hammering heart to slow. His regiment was hiding behind a rock formation not too far from the cave they were about to invade. They didn't expect too many enemies, but he had to prepare himself for anything.

One soldier stepped forward. "Should we retreat if we can't take them prisoner?"

Lothar closed his eyes for a brief moment, pondering the question. "Kill if you must. I don't want to retreat unless it's our last resort." He edged out from behind the rock and signaled for his soldiers to follow. He and his regiment moved toward the cave, pressing against the rugged mountainside. He gestured for absolute silence as they approached the entrance. Lothar peered around the corner; no one was directly outside the cave. The only sound Lothar could discern was the gentle whistling of the wind.

Lothar raised a hand, waiting another second before giving the signal. They burst out from their hiding place and into the entrance of the cave. Five faul sprinted to meet them, weapons at the ready. Panic struck, but it was soon quelled by the feeling of magic throughout his body as he summoned heat to burn the hands of the closest attacker, whose daggers clattered to the stone ground. One enemy stood further back, muttering the call of magic before darkness settled over the cave. Thankfully, in only a moment the attacker lay on the ground, knocked unconscious by one of Lothar's faul. With their vision cleared, his regiment charged the remaining three, wielding their daggers with non-lethal intent. The first was blown off balance by a gust of wind summoned by one of Lothar's soldiers, and easily disarmed. Five soldiers cornered and fought the last two bandits, winning the skirmish within seconds. By the time the regiment had restrained all five faul, only one of his soldiers needed tending to.

Lothar crouched beside the injured soldier. The faul's face was calm, but Lothar had seen a grimace of pain before he'd approached. "Are you alright?"

The soldier had one hand clamped over his right shoulder, but Lothar could see blood seeping through his fingers. "Yeah, just got a little cut. I'll be fine, Sergeant."

"Show me."

The soldier peeled his hand away from the wound with Lothar's help, revealing a deep gash.

Lothar stood and faced his medic. "Get a wound dressing—he's lost a good bit of blood." As she rummaged through her pack, Lothar took to searching the cave. A few tawdry beds and animal hides were scattered about the tent, as well as various old scraps of rope and wood. The only item of importance seemed to be a locked storage chest sitting between two cots.

"Sergeant Raiken, are we taking the prisoners back to the palace? They certainly don't seem like master criminals."

Lothar glanced back at the soldier. "Might as well."

His soldiers groaned; they didn't want to haul prisoners all the way back to Pyantir. He didn't want to either, but he hoped the bandits might be useful to the Empire. At least then the mission wouldn't be in vain.

"Check the prisoners for a key," said Lothar, trying in vain to wrench open the lock on the chest. Within minutes, a soldier placed the key in his hand, and he opened the chest. Armor, some gold, and a short stack of papers all lay inside. The money and papers he took, and upon finding nothing else useful in the hideout, made ready to depart. His soldiers gathered the prisoners and headed out of the cave, beginning the long walk back to Pyantir, the capital city of the Shalin Empire.

Oberel's sake. Lothar's aching legs protested as he slowly climbed the stairs of the military headquarters. It had taken the regiment three rigorous days to travel on foot from the cave to Pyantir. Upon his arrival, he had stopped by his quarters only for a change of clothing, then had begun his trek up to the historian's study. He knocked on the door, hoping that Imar wasn't off elsewhere or doing anything important. Immediately, his friend opened the door, face lit with excitement. *Thank Talen.*

"Lothar, you're back! Come in, you must be exhausted!"

Smiling, he entered and sat down on one of the cozy armchairs, feeling the strain on his legs lessen. While Imar made a pot of tea, Lothar looked around the study. So familiar to him, yet he never grew bored of it. He liked to look at the portraits of old faul emperors and empresses, stretching back almost to the creation of the Shalin Empire. The most recent portrait was of Emperor Orwic, who had been sitting on the throne for over fifteen years. To the left of his image was the brave Empress Persec, who died in battle. Next to her hung the image of Empress Ledica, who died from sickness, and so on until they spanned the entirety of one wall. Above and below the emperors, Imar had maps, papers, and truly random things hung as haphazardly as his other trinkets laying on tables and stacked in cabinets. The historian habitually collected artifacts and souvenirs everywhere he went and from every traveler he knew. Lothar loved to pick through them and have Imar regale him with stories about their origins.

Imar sat across from him with a cup of tea in his hands and grinned, leaning forward in anticipation. "How'd the mission go?"

Lothar sighed, looking down. "Alright, I suppose."

Imar's smile vanished in an instant, replaced by concern. "What happened?"

"Don't worry, everyone is alright. They were just a group of petty thieves, though. We brought them back to the castle, but I assume they'll just be imprisoned."

"I see... They certainly are an elusive group." Imar scratched the stubble on his chin and looked at a stack of disheveled scrolls and papers on his desk. "How do you know they aren't who we seek?"

"They were sloppy fighters who wore ragged clothes and had little money. I found these papers though," said Lothar, handing Imar the small pile.

He rifled through the stack, brow furrowed. "Interesting... I'll take a look at these after you finish telling me about your journey."

"Not much more to it." Lothar refused to meet Imar's disappointed gaze as he stood and made to move toward the door. "Well, I guess I should get going."

"Wait! Don't leave now, you just got here!" Imar exclaimed, quickly blocking the exit and putting a hand on Lothar's shoulder.

He fought back a grin; if Imar made him stay, he wouldn't complain. Still, Captain Yulac always had tasks for Lothar. "I know, but I have work to do!"

"You work yourself to death! Look, I'll tell Captain Yulac that I kept you here, alright? Sit down. I have important news for you, anyway." Lothar sat down once more and tried not to fall asleep while Imar poured him a cup of tea. "Now, you first. Tell me exactly what happened."

Lothar recounted the short conflict at the bandit cave, pausing intermittently to let Imar record the entire account on a scroll of parchment. It was both his job and hobby as far Lothar could tell. After finishing the tale, he leaned back, relaxing against the upholstery. "Any more leads on our criminals for me to track down?"

"No... not yet. That cave was my latest find. But that's just how it goes sometimes."

"Have you considered a foreign influence?"

"Of course!" laughed Imar. "That was my first thought, but I can't just walk up to the vault of Valea and dig around in their documents."

"Did Emperor Orwic send them any letters?"

Imar chuckled, leaning back against the chair. "Yes, and they said that they were not involved. What else would they say? 'Sorry about sending criminals to rob your country, we won't do it again?'"

Lothar laughed and shook his head. It did seem like a foolish thing to try. But reasoning with Valea in any way was usually foolish.

"Unfortunately, it most likely *is* foreign interference. We've searched throughout the country, looking for all the stolen gold and silver from the city treasuries, and we've found nothing. It's not so easy to hide something like that from our government, unless the money isn't in the Shalin Empire at all. There's just nothing we can do about it . . ." Imar's grin vanished, and his eyes became unfocused.

Lothar regretted bringing up Valea with his friend and changed the topic. "When does the Akistaria league depart again? It should be soon, right?"

"Ah, yes! That's the news I wanted to mention," said Imar, a devious smile now on his face. "Yulac has ordered that you join him on the journey."

"Me? Wait—why are *you* the one telling me this?"

"Well, he wrote you a letter, but told me you might forget to check your mail," explained Imar. Lothar felt guilt twist in his gut, but he nodded. It was true.

"He has an Akistaria league already put together though," Lothar complained. "Yulac uses the same one every year."

"Indeed, but Valea is only bringing twenty soldiers this time, so we must match their numbers."

"Why would Valea cut their soldier count?"

Imar smirked. "Remember those bombings I told you about? Unfortunately, they're having a bit of trouble with them . . . Poor things. They need to devote some of their soldiers to cleaning up the mess."

Lothar chuckled along with Imar, but shame rose for doing so. He coughed. "What's the latest event there?"

"One of their precious new castles got blown up. They still have no idea who did it!"

"How—An entire castle?" cried Lothar. "How could they *not* know?"

"The humans are special creatures," Imar said, the corners of his mouth turning up in an amused expression. "Anyway, Yulac can only bring nineteen others to the Akarist, and he chose you to be one of them. Even though you're not in the typical regiment, he wants the best."

"You're joking. I can barely wield daggers!"

"But he finds you quite good with magic, so you're going along. Captain's orders."

"I'm not *that* good at magic, you know," said Lothar, taking a tiny sip of his boiling hot tea to avoid Imar's gaze.

"Stop fooling yourself! You're better than Yulac himself." Imar almost looked offended, as if Lothar's statement were a direct insult.

Lothar sighed. "I guess I have no other choice."

"Hey, it'll be good to get away for a while. Again. Oh, how I wish I could journey into the wilderness like you," mused Imar.

Lothar rolled his eyes, grinning. "Imar, you're only thirty-five. I think you'd be fine."

"To be your age again . . . Why, I'd do anything!" He threw his hands up, splashing hot tea on his robes. Amidst mild swearing from Imar, the two laughed emphatically for several minutes afterward. While Imar poured himself another cup of tea, Lothar wished he could lounge here for the rest of the day—nay, the rest of the year. An amused gleam was in Imar's eyes when he sat down again across from Lothar.

"The party leaves in two days."

"Two days!" *What ever happened to breaks? Or sleep?* "I suppose it is getting to that time . . ."

"Indeed. Captain Yulac was only recently informed about the soldier limit. Don't worry, all you have to do is arrive here, at the courtyard, on the twenty-first. Yulac has organized everything."

"What will my regiment do while I'm away?"

"Probably starve to death," said Imar, keeping a stoic face for only a moment before he broke into a smile. "They'll be fine, Lothar. Yulac said they can take the time off."

"*They* get time off, but not me? And anyway, how do you always know everything?" asked Lothar, shaking his head in wonder. "None of this is part of your job."

"This job never had very clear duties. Investigate documents for any evidence of domestic threats, document all my findings, and then send the information to the palace. Plus, instead of visiting the palace themselves, which the captains find tedious, they give me letters and reports that I deliver with everything else."

"How nice of them."

He shrugged. "I enjoy knowing everything. Oh, and I took care of some of your paperwork for you."

"Thanks! You know, I couldn't do this job without you."

"You don't have to thank me, Lothar," replied Imar. "Do you need anything for the Akistaria?"

"No, I'll just bring my daggers and gambeson." Lothar stood up to leave, glad that he could at least rest for a couple of days before departure.

"Safe travels!" called Imar as Lothar exited the study and quickly descended the stairs toward the barracks. He grinned, already imagining the reaction of his regiment upon hearing the news of time off.

5

Melkin

The beaming sun shone through the white fabric of Melkin's tent, casting a warm glow over him. *What time is it?* The three others that slept in the same tent were gone—surely it was far past sunrise. He crawled out of the tent, shielding his eyes from the blinding rays of the sun and gazing around at the bustling campsite. How could he have slept for so long? How could he have slept through all the noise? Moving frantically, he wrestled his boots on, fumbled with the laces for a second, then stooped to re-enter his tent and tear the center pole from the dirt. The fabric fell to the ground as he exited, and he quickly ripped out the small stakes that stretched the canvas to keep it from blowing around as he slept. How soon were they to depart? What had become of the prisoners? In his frustration, he stored the rolled-up tent in a less-than-perfect bundle and tossed it into the appropriate cart, glimpsing the two attackers still tied to their trees.

"Glad to see you're awake!" called a cheerful voice from behind.

Melkin spun around—Vallec was grinning at him. "Who let me sleep till mid-day?" he growled, scowling at him.

Vallec took a defensive step back. The cordial smile vanished, soon replaced by a look of shock. "I'm sorry? You're *insane*. Any other soldier or servant here would have pledged their firstborn to Taleek in return for a couple extra hours of sleep! And by the way, it's an hour and a half after sunrise, not noon."

"Well unlike you, I have a little something called discipline!" argued Melkin, keeping his voice low and glancing around. He started to walk past Vallec—he'd attracted too much attention already. Deftly, the man grabbed his shoulders and slammed him against the side of the cart. He attempted to throw Vallec's hands off himself but found the retaliation useless. Instead, he met Vallec's gaze, only to see his own seething anger reflected back at him.

"Right. And us soldiers have a little something called manners! Wherever in Ryne's name you come from clearly didn't teach you those. All we've done is pack up camp, so watch your next words."

Melkin gritted his teeth, staring into Vallec's eyes. "I told the commander I was to be awakened before sunrise. He agreed."

"Yeah? I once asked to sleep till noon and how do you think that went for me? I don't know who you are, and I don't care anymore—that's between you and Commander Taleek. But everyone in this company is under his leadership now, including you, so you'd better take it seriously. He's a wiser and fairer commander than most, and he owes you nothing more than the respect he has already given you."

Vallec released Melkin. The two glared at each other for a few moments before Melkin shoved past him. The idea that he should gather with his ambassador and fellow servants hardly crossed his mind as he searched the campsite for Taleek. Who did the commander think he was? To double-cross Queen Gladia's personal spy was a ludicrous thing to do indeed. Then, the commander was in front of him, a joyous look on his face.

"Ah, Evarith! We'll depart soon, but we haven't questioned our prisoners yet. Care to join us?"

Melkin was about to start haranguing Taleek but caught himself. There was a glint of threat in the commander's otherwise kind face; he must have seen the argument. Melkin pressed his lips together, keeping eye contact with him. Did he really want to spend the rest of the trip as an enemy to all the soldiers? He *was* quite interested in witnessing the interrogation of the prisoners. It would only be another few weeks with this traveling party—he could endure it.

"Sure." His tone was less than pleasant, but the commander didn't seem to care.

"That's what I thought! Let's see what they have to say."

Taleek invited the other servants and ambassadors to witness the questioning, but most kept their distance. Meanwhile, Melkin and the twenty soldiers gathered around the two prisoners. Their hands and feet were bound against the slim trees, and gags had been stuffed in their mouths, preventing them from causing a racket in the night. The man on the left was wire thin and stood only slightly above five feet. The soaked-through bandage on his shoulder confirmed he was the man who Melkin had injured. His skin and hair seemed unnaturally pale. To Melkin's right, a taller, bulkier man was tied up; he had sustained no injuries from the attack. Soldiers tore the gags from the prisoners' mouths and Commander Taleek stepped forward.

"Who is your leader?"

"Him," sneered the taller one, pointing to a random soldier. The soldier's face turned red as he earnestly denied the accusation. Taleek rolled his eyes.

The two bound prisoners laughed maniacally at their joke. The injured Valean soldier from the night before stepped forward, spear at the ready, but others restrained her. Taleek's eyes were unforgiving as he gripped his spear and stepped forward, pointing it at the neck of the tall man. He laughed and spat in Taleek's face before slipping a stealthy glance to his companion.

"Argh! Ryne's sake!" shouted Taleek, dropping his spear for no apparent reason and rubbing his hands. "Son of a—OW!"

Melkin heard the short one chanting something and rushed forward, clasping a hand over the muttering mouth. The commander immediately seemed relieved of his ailment and looked up in wonder.

"A faul!" exclaimed Melkin as the soldiers stood in shock. "What'd you do with the gag? I don't want him spitting on my hand all day!"

A soldier rushed to stuff the gag back in the faul's mouth. Melkin rubbed the slime off his hand with the faul's jerkin, then stepped back. He kept a watchful eye upon him though, worried he might somehow be able to conjure magic without speaking.

Taleek stood up to his full height. "So, what's a human doing traveling with a faul, huh?" The palms of his hands were raw and red.

"We're getting married," laughed the human prisoner.

"Your honeymoon is about to be cut rather short then, unless you tell us your motive," remarked Taleek. "Then we'll set you free. Even your little husband here who so rudely burned my hands."

Shouldn't they be killed? He supposed Taleek could have been bluffing, but the prisoners only had two choices: take the offer and find out, or deny it and rot in the forest. Still, the man did not speak.

Taleek sighed and turned away. "We're leaving." He began walking through the crowd; the whole company had gathered when they heard their commander scream and were now watching him with stunned expressions, their bodies unmoving. Taleek glanced around and signaled toward the carts. "Let's move!"

Melkin caught up with Taleek, pushing through the horde to appear beside the tall commander. "You want to leave them alive? Their companions are going to rescue them!"

"We'll be long gone by then, and the nearest town is many miles away. Two extra members of their group won't make a difference, especially since one is injured."

Melkin said nothing in response; he was less than satisfied with Taleek's decision. Still, he rejoined his ambassador and fellow servants as the party assumed their formation. He knew who to blame if the prisoners caused more harm.

As the party continued their journey, Melkin noticed that Cirel was staring at him with a strange look on his face. *Awe, perhaps?*

He turned his head, watching the servant's gaze crumble under his own. "Looking at something?" Derision poured forth from his voice.

The servant looked away and muttered a quick apology.

Melkin's thoughts were now filled with questions about the attacking group. What could their motivations be? Last night he'd been sure they were just thieves, but why would a faul be working with a human on Valean land? Maybe he was a mercenary, but the faul seemed too committed, ready to die instead of giving up his motive. Would a hired thief do that? It was unnerving how stubborn the two were. What could compel a faul to be so loyal to a human?

"Who are you?" asked Cirel a few hours later, breaking his mental focus. *Had Cirel never been told to keep to himself?*

"My name? Evarith."

"I was referring to what you do and why you're here. You're not a servant."

Melkin had suspected the question would come up at some point. He hadn't been very careful about his demeanor or speaking with the soldiers and ambassadors as an equal. The soldiers had also probably spread the word of Melkin's actions last night. He really needed some advice from Leina—she could blend in with crowds and unfamiliar company so easily. "What makes you say that? Just because I happen to have many useful skills?"

"I assure you, Evarith has my permission to be here," said the ambassador, interrupting. "Now please, do not insinuate that he is some sort of enemy."

"Forgive me, Sir. All I'm saying is he's not a servant. Not that he doesn't have the right to be here."

"If you won't see reason, why ask? What does it matter, anyway?" asked Melkin, agitation slipping into his voice.

The servant stared ahead. "I suppose it doesn't. I was simply curious."

Melkin nodded and tried to repress his annoyance over the pace of the journey. They were only halfway to the Akarist after a full five days of traveling, a depressing pace. Still, a part of him dreaded their arrival at the Akarist, for it could easily spell his death if he wasn't more careful. The immense pressure of a thousand stones weighed on him, daring him to slip up, to make one mistake. He huffed quietly, letting some of his restlessness flow out of him. At least he felt a bit better physically than he had the previous five days. *Ryne's sake*, was that because of the sleep? Though he did not renounce his earlier anger, the truth resonated deep within him. He had certainly needed the rest.

6

MELKIN

Four days later, Taleek estimated the company was less than ten miles from Lypeth, a border town where they would stop and leave behind any unnecessary supplies. From there, it would only be another ten miles before they reached the castle itself. Melkin glanced around; a majority of the servants and ambassadors were still rubbing their eyes and stumbling along. Hoping they might reach the Akarist by the end of the day, Taleek had woken the campsite two hours earlier than usual. Melkin certainly supported the endeavor; ten days was already far too long for the 150-mile journey on well-trodden roads. It was mildly depressing to think that, alone, he could have accomplished it in five days, maybe six if he were feeling lazy.

Unlike the other grumbling servants, Melkin thought Taleek's plan of twenty miles to be quite attainable. They had started early and could walk well into sunset, since the Akarist would provide shelter if they could reach it in time.

Only a few hours into the walk, he noticed a strange creaking noise from the cart beside him. Odd . . . In the nine days of traveling by the same cart, such a noise had never occurred. Melkin focused on the cart—the back axle looked different, but he couldn't discern exactly why. He turned his eyes up to the ambassador, riding undisturbed atop the horse. "Sir, do you—"

The axle gave way and the back of the cart hit the ground. Those nearby shouted in alarm, but soon calmed down when they realized they were not in any danger. Though no one was hurt, the broken cart presented a problem—what were they to do now? Most of the company gathered around, eyes fixed on Taleek as he stroked his beard in thought. "We can't just leave a cart here unattended. A few of us can walk to town and bring supplies to repair the cart. What does it need?"

Half a dozen soldiers gripped the underside of the cart and lifted the back a foot off the ground. The back axle had given way, but no other parts of the cart were damaged.

"Simple enough. Vallec, Haern, and I will go into town and purchase a new axle."

"Can't we just leave a few people here to guard it and come back later?" asked a soldier.

"The town is not the best place to rest. There's not enough shelter for forty people, and we'll need the cart for the way back. A small group can get to the town and back faster than the entire party can."

The ambassadors and servants nodded, content to rest while the soldiers did the heavy lifting. Melkin leaned back against a tree, closing his eyes in frustration. What would he do for hours on end? Chat with the other servants? That might be the death of him. Though the path to the town seemed easily traversable, he doubted Taleek and the others could repair the cart too long before dusk.

His eyes snapped open as he heard footsteps approaching. Taleek stood in front of him, leaning in before speaking with a furtive tone. "Come with us, we might need your help."

Melkin raised an eyebrow. "Alright."

Taleek then turned to one of his soldiers. "If we're not back an hour before sundown, make your way to the town and leave the cart behind."

Why would Commander Taleek want to bring him along? It must have been important since more suspicions and accusations from servants and soldiers alike would surely follow this strange move. Hundreds of reasons entered and left Melkin's mind before Taleek pulled him aside, less than a mile into the walk.

"Avert your ears," he ordered, pointing at Vallec and Haern. Once they were well out of earshot, Commander Taleek turned back toward Melkin. "I want you to listen in on any conversation the locals are having. At this distance from the border, we may find some key information about skirmishes, rivalries, and such. At any rate, I don't think it could hurt, do you?"

Melkin felt the corners of his mouth turn upward at the thought but suppressed his excitement. "I was planning on doing something similar once the whole party got to the town."

Taleek sighed. "I suppose you could, but the townspeople really don't like our presence. It's quite the small town, and even with only twenty soldiers, I imagine they'll be quite hesitant to aid us."

"You understand that pulling me from the group has only made me stick out more, right?"

"I do. But this town is very near the border. There's an abundance of gossip the people won't disclose to a military commander, if you can believe it. The queen is already taking a risk sending you into the Akarist; I think she would approve of this. *I* consider this to be an extension of your job."

Melkin shrugged. "If they have a tavern or an inn, I'll sit down and listen."

"Great." Taleek called the other two back, and they continued their walk toward the distant town. The three soldiers left Melkin to his own devices whilst they chatted with one another. Once, he noticed Vallec was glaring at him, tightly gripping his spear. Vallec's animosity surprised him—Taleek didn't seem too bothered about his tirade four days prior. Melkin simply looked away with a shrug, ignoring the harsh glare he felt was quite undeserved. Whilst Vallec's hostility did nothing to frighten him, it *did* remind him how defenseless the Valeans would be at the Akarist, how vulnerable they might be if a fight broke out. He stood by his reasoning that the Shalin Empire had nothing to do with the bombings, but the Valean soldiers didn't believe the same. It was a miracle, really, that nothing had ever gone wrong at the Akarist before.

"Evarith, is it?" asked Haern, breaking the prevailing silence.

Melkin jerked his head around to face the soldier. "Yeah."

"According to Vallec, you've survived worse than that spear in the shoulder he gave you last week when you were sparring. Let's hear the story."

He nearly kept silent—he had never told the full thing before. *But why not?* As long as he was careful about his identity it wouldn't be any more suspicious than the antics he'd already pulled.

"A few years ago, I was traveling to Starren Province alone, and a group of bandits attacked my campsite," he started, choosing his words carefully. "At night, I'm unguarded, so I usually sleep lightly. Unfortunately, I did not wake until a man was standing over me with a knife. I rolled in time for him to miss my stomach, and he hit my side instead. I always sleep with a knife in hand, so I stabbed him in the leg before he could finish the job."

Haern and Vallec exchanged looks of disbelief.

Melkin took a slight pleasure in their surprise. "I then ran to my horse and set off toward the nearest town. Surprisingly, I didn't bleed out. The medic who helped me said I should've died, but all I needed were some stitches."

"Do you know who attacked you?" asked Haern.

Melkin shook his head. "I remember his face vividly, but I was . . . a little preoccupied at the time."

"Why were you traveling to Starren Province?" asked Vallec.

Melkin shrugged. "For work."

"Why alone?" Vallec's face was incredulous.

Melkin raised an eyebrow. "Full of questions, aren't you?"

"Full of secrets, aren't *you*," remarked Vallec.

Touché. "You're the one who asked about the story to begin with," said Melkin, keeping a calm voice. He glanced over at Commander Taleek, who was listening from a few yards away, a look of mild amusement on his face.

"A story I'm not sure I believe," said Haern, squinting at Melkin's short and seemingly scrawny figure. Melkin lifted his tunic up a few inches, revealing a scar just below his ribs.

"I stand corrected then," laughed Haern.

"Someday... I'll find out who you are, Evarith. Someday..." grumbled Vallec, shaking his head in disbelief.

Hopefully not. Maybe he shouldn't have told the story; he hadn't even informed Queen Gladia of the details. *Oh well.* There was nothing he could do about it now. Another two weeks with this group, and he would be back to his regular duties.

The town was now in view, about a mile away. Border towns were by nature tiny, constantly threatened by battles, skirmishes, and unrest. They rarely lasted long.

"While we get the axle, I'm sending Evarith to the tavern to buy me a drink," said Taleek, handing Melkin a few coins. "We'll be at the blacksmith."

They reached the feeble wooden fence that surrounded the town. A guard stood at the entrance, eyeing them as they approached.

"Commander Taleek," spoke the woman. "Where is the rest of your party?"

"One of our carts broke down a little under ten miles away. We need an axle from the blacksmith."

The soldier nodded and let them enter. Melkin spotted the tavern near the center of the town and left the other three as they walked toward the blacksmith.

Despite the sun overhead, there were few customers. He supposed he was used to the Hileath inns and taverns, bustling with activity all day and night. Walking up to the counter, Melkin counted the coins in his hand—enough for two drinks.

"I'll have a cup of tea," he said to the rather large tavern keeper.

"No more tea," he grumbled, cleaning a pewter mug.

"Coffee then?" asked Melkin, annoyed. The tavern keeper nodded and stumbled away. It was hard to focus on a single conversation so far from the tables, so he patiently waited for his drink. Once he sat at a table with his scalding hot mug of coffee, he took a painful sip and listened to a table behind him, willing himself to not spit out the agonizing liquid.

"He was supposed to come back yesterday..." lamented a woman.

"He left for that mining job... a month ago?" asked another.

"I told him not to go! Those folk... They were strange, talking about a mining job. It paid too well for me to believe it, but we needed money. Oh, I just—I can't believe I let him go!" cried the first.

"He'll come back soon, don't fret!" comforted the second woman. "Maybe he's just working a little extra. Where was this mining job, anyway?"

The woman sniffled. "East. They said that there was this reserve of metal that needed to be mined."

The discussion continued, but Melkin disengaged. He needed something about the Shalin Empire—anything about the border. Another group was talking from behind him, making him wish he had sat facing the other side of the inn. From the direction of their voices, he discerned they were standing in the corner, rather than sitting and drinking.

"So, what now?"

"I don't know... I suppose we'll just report to him and monitor them."

"What's that going to do?"

"Not sure."

"Didn't Bellant describe someone who looked kind of like him?" asked one of them after a pause.

"Him?"

Though Melkin had deduced that there were three men and a woman, the subject of their conversation remained an enigma.

"Yeah."

"What do you want to do about it?"

"Follow him, I suppose?"

"We could take him hostage. They might give us some money for him."

"For a servant? No."

"Maybe not just a servant, from what Bellant said."

"If we follow him, he'll just lead us back to the rest. If you think we can win a four on forty-five..."

Melkin felt his spine tingle. Why did he sit with his back to the door? *What a stupid idea.*

"We should get Bellant in here... confirm that it's him."

"We're not bringing him into a Valean town. Especially when he's injured." *The faul. The one they'd left alive.*

"Look, he's right there. We take him hostage, at least we'll cause a stir. Plus, they have plenty of money. They'll give us a few gold coins at least."

"Or kill us."

"You know what our jobs are."

He continued to stare at his coffee—they were watching his every move. Discretely as he could, he slipped the knife from his boot and held it out of view from the four. It seemed hopelessly inadequate, but it was all he had. He hoped his path to the door was clear.

The conversation stopped and Melkin heard a pair of footsteps approach him. He could probably take just one of them. Before he resorted to violence, an idea struck him. He took another small sip of boiling-hot coffee, then loudly coughed and sputtered, slamming the mug on the table. A man with a spear stood only a few feet away, taken aback by the outburst.

"I say, this coffee is terrible!" he shouted between coughs. Swiftly, he ran toward the doorway as the other three people in the corner came toward him. Before he could reach the exit, they had blocked it, and he splashed the hot coffee on their faces. Two of them stumbled back into the third, clearing the doorway and giving Melkin enough time to throw the empty mug at the man who'd almost taken him hostage. With his momentary advantage, he ran out the door and into the street. He scanned for the blacksmith, but couldn't see the shop, so he ran in the direction he thought the others had gone.

After minutes weaving through houses and alleyways, he was no longer being directly followed. *That can't be good.* He considered climbing a building to spot his attackers, but the homes looked unstable. He again searched for the blacksmith, but it was nowhere to be seen. From a nearby corner, two of the attackers sprinted toward him while the other two skidded into the path in front of him, the female spinning some kind of ugly cudgel in her hand. Melkin spun on his heel, desperately searching for a nonexistent escape. Locals looked on in shock, attempting to figure out who the villain was.

"Is there a problem?" he asked loudly, eyes darting between the four.

"Let's see . . . you stabbed and tied up two of our companions," said the woman, partly to the gathering crowd.

Two can play that game. "Is that right? Perhaps you should tell them there are consequences for their actions. Attacking helpless servants is generally frowned upon."

"As is leaving two men to die in the forest. Your consequence for that is being taken prisoner."

"Is it now? I took those two down, what makes you think that you're safe?" he asked, waving around his six-inch knife. They outmatched him—he needed to stall for time. The four relaxed their postures and seemed to hold back laughter as they took in his inadequate weapon.

"A scrawny little man like you armed with . . . that thing . . . against four warriors? Please."

"I think that before you take me, there's something you need to know."

"Save your story."

"Fine. I will," said Melkin as he jerked his arm toward the man. When the four tensed up to defend themselves, Melkin sprinted away. Two followed only yards behind, while the others dispersed; they would cut him off, he suspected. The sound of a hammer finally alerted him to the direction of the blacksmith's shop; the opposite direction of where he'd been running. *Of course.* He darted between buildings, evading the danger he could hardly keep track of. The blacksmith was in sight now, but as he got close, two of his pursuers ran in from the side, blocking his route. He whirled around, facing the two that chased him. He'd played into their trap, *again*.

"Alright, alright! I'll give you as much money as you want!"

"You have an army's worth on you?" At least they didn't immediately take him prisoner. Or kill him.

"I'll steal the money!" he shrieked, trying to act submissive and desperate. But he could hear that his inflection wasn't quite right—he really needed to take some lessons from Leina on this kind of stuff. Then, the realization that he may never get the chance struck him.

"Not worth the risk!" shouted one man, advancing.

"Evarith, are these fools giving you any trouble?" asked Taleek from behind him, a dangerous edge in his voice. As Melkin slowly backed up beside Taleek, he saw that Vallec and Haern stood by as well. *Thank Ryne.*

"Now, we can all fight like idiots, or I'll hand you some silver and you all can leave us alone. How does that sound?" asked Taleek, holding out a dozen silver coins.

One man nodded eagerly and held out an enormous hand. After depositing the coins, the four turned away and hurriedly walked toward the blacksmith, leaving the warriors to their own devices. They didn't speak until well out of earshot.

"Who were they?" asked Vallec, a slight quiver in his voice.

"Same group that raided us on night five. They rescued the prisoners, and the faul must have described me. They recognized me at the inn and planned to take me hostage for money."

"So . . . they're just after money?" asked Vallec.

"Why raid the traveling party on their way to the sacred Akarist?" mused Haern.

"I . . . don't know. I'll feel a lot safer once we're in the Akarist," said Vallec. Taleek said nothing, stroking his beard in thought.

"Commander?" said Vallec.

"I don't know."

The four fell silent as they reached the smithy. Haern walked inside the pavilion, examining the new axle that the blacksmith was working on.

Melkin glanced at Taleek's face, looking for any sign of fear or apprehension. He saw none, but perhaps the commander was hiding it. He recalled Taleek's confident statement that leaving their prisoners alive would have no negative consequences. *Without his insistence on sparing the two, the attack wouldn't have happened.* Taleek could have gotten him killed. Melkin returned his knife to his boot sheath and leaned against the wall, letting out a long sigh. He had countless questions and no answers to them.

"Ryne," he swore. "They would have killed me."

"If you'd like to take tonight's watch, consider your debt repaid," said Vallec, keeping a stoic expression as he walked up beside Melkin.

Though he did not feel indebted to Taleek, who had caused this mess in the first place, he supposed Vallec deserved thanks. "I could do that."

Vallec let a smile break through. "Figured you'd come around to your senses."

Melkin nodded, watching as Haern attempted to leave the blacksmith carrying the five-foot pole of solid metal. Stifled laughter came from Vallec and Taleek as the axle repeatedly hit the support posts of the pavilion.

"Can I have a hand here?" he grunted, straining to maneuver the pole out of the smithy. The blacksmith himself was already working on another job, offering no help to Haern. The axle then got stuck between a post and the roof.

Vallec covered his mouth, eyes alight with laughter. "You're doing fantastic on your own, actually."

Melkin sighed and took the other end of the pole, pulling it free and out of the pavilion.

"See, someone's helpful!" complained Haern, failing to stifle his own laughter.

In haste, the four departed from Lypeth, Melkin and Haern carrying the seventy-five-pound iron axle. With the added weight, Melkin estimated each mile took them half an hour. The excitement and fear from the attack having worn off, Melkin felt exhaustion manifest itself in him. He yawned, knowing that sleep would come well after midnight and end before sunrise.

"How's that axle?" asked Vallec.

"It's a wonderful experience. Would you like to try?" asked Haern with a grimace.

Though Vallec initially declined, he and Taleek offered to take it after another four miles into the journey. Melkin and Haern agreed, sweating profusely despite the cool air.

By the time they reached the campsite again, dusk was only a few hours away. Taleek and Vallec were exhausted and fetched some water from their packs while Melkin and Haern lifted the cart a few inches to test its weight. Haern assigned three soldiers to either side of the cart to hold it while he and Melkin removed the broken axle.

"Don't drop it, Ragnar," muttered Haern as he reached under the cart.

"Thanks for stating the obvious."

After Melkin and Haern extracted the old axle, the two of them removed the securing pin and wheels. Vallec and Taleek returned and helped insert the new axle onto the old wooden supports with the help of the six soldiers holding the cart. Thoroughly exhausted now, they finally fit the old wheels onto the new axle and secured them.

"Can't we just rest here for the night, Commander?" asked a soldier. Many others nodded in agreement.

"That's a hefty demand coming from someone who sat around all day," said Taleek with a smirk.

"Well, what about me?" complained Haern.

"You'll live. Let's go!" shouted Taleek, beckoning the traveling party forward.

7

Melkin

A few hours after sunrise, the company reached Lypeth. Taleek had let everyone sleep until their normal waking time instead of forcing them to travel through sunrise, since he was now unconcerned about reaching the Akarist by the end of the day. With forty-four others by Melkin's side, the town felt far safer. Still, as they walked toward their assigned storehouse, his gaze darted between streets and houses, searching for the warriors. For better or worse, he did not see them.

The soldiers tied up the horses in the stables and brought all the supplies inside their assigned building. It was quite dirty and run down, but there were tables and chairs, as well as a dozen cots. Taleek announced they would depart in an hour's time, so the servants and ambassadors left to get drinks at the tavern and relax for a bit. Melkin turned to join them, figuring he would make a last-ditch effort to blend in, but Taleek beckoned him back.

"You can stay, you'll want to watch the choosing ceremony."

Melkin raised an eyebrow in question, but Taleek only grinned at him and turned toward the awaiting soldiers.

"We usually leave behind a dozen, but obviously we're not doing that this year," announced Taleek. The soldiers were rapt, more so than they were on night watch. "Two will do."

Taleek retrieved a quill pen and ink from his bag, then passed out slips of paper for each soldier to write his or her name on. The soldiers folded their slips and placed them in a pile on a wooden table. Taleek shuffled the slips around while the soldiers waited, anticipation plastered on their faces.

"Alright, let's see who stays behind this time," said Taleek. "Any objections to Evarith picking the slips?" No one said anything, so Taleek nodded at him. Feeling quite out of place, he closed his eyes and moved his hand across the table, eventually grasping a slip of paper.

"Atlia."

A woman stepped forward amidst some claps and cheers that might have been sarcastic. The soldiers looked to be enjoying the ceremony, but Melkin couldn't tell if staying behind was a punishment or a privilege.

Again, he searched for a slip of paper and read its contents aloud. "Vallec." Strangely, he felt a twinge of disappointment within.

Vallec looked at Taleek and stepped forward with a grin. "What will you do without your right-hand man?"

"Probably get more work done," joked Taleek. The soldiers dispersed then, leaving behind their plate armor in a pile. Their gambeson suits were allowed inside the Akarist; unlike plate armor, it was quite difficult to hide any significant weapon under gambeson.

"Why don't you just assign the same soldiers to stay behind each year?" asked Melkin, walking up to Taleek.

"It's far more fun this way," he laughed.

Half an hour later, all the soldiers, servants, and advisors gathered in the center of the town. The Akarist was abandoned for most of the year, so all the food had to be brought from elsewhere. It had no stables for horses either, so each person was required to carry a small pack of food on their back. They set off around three hours before noon, now moving considerably faster. They no longer had to deal with the horses, and they walked a pleasant path from Lypeth to the Akarist, through plains rather than forest.

Hours after departing from Lypeth, the Akarist was in sight. Melkin had seen drawings in the library books he'd pored over, but the real thing was quite a marvel to look upon. Two towers were joined by a grand hall, the entire thing constructed out of black stone that seemed to radiate power. The rooftops of the hall and both towers were flat with battlements lining their edges. From its vantage point atop the hill, it overlooked the war-torn border between Valea and the Shalin Empire. For a place of peace and tranquility, Melkin thought it looked quite menacing.

They entered the castle through the large double doors that stood in the center of the great hall. It was the only entrance to the castle, besides the windows. Upon opening the doors, they found it to be dark and deserted.

"Well, it's no surprise that the Shalin Empire is late," remarked Taleek, slipping an amused look to the ambassadors. "Those who think themselves better than others are often late." Melkin smirked at the underhanded comment as the ambassadors all expressed great interest in their boots.

Soon enough, the company had lit the candles in the great hall and in the Valean tower, leaving the Shalin tower untouched. The great hall took up a sizable portion of the first floor, but a kitchen and a lounge were easily located behind it. A trapdoor lay in the corner of the hall, probably the entrance to a dungeon of sorts.

Melkin examined each floor of the Valean tower whilst the others settled into their respective places. Each story was massive, designed to house the many soldiers and servants that would typically be in residence for the event. A spiral staircase jutted through the center of each floor, leading up to the rooftop. The first floor was another lounge area, with chairs and tables for dozens of people. Each soldier deposited their spear and any auxiliary weapons into a holder by the exit of the first floor leading into the great hall. Over a hundred beds for the guards were arranged in a concentric pattern on the second floor, only eighteen of which would be used. On the third floor, there were separate rooms with larger beds for the ambassadors, and little antechambers with smaller beds for the servants. Melkin hadn't considered it before, but figured there were usually only twenty servants, since the rooms didn't accommodate many more. The fourth floor was dimly lit, with many storage crates containing a multitude of things such as ropes, papers, and books. Taleek ordered the food packs to be stored in there as well; it was mostly rice, grain, and dried proteins so the kitchen larder wasn't necessary. The last floor served as a meeting room for the ambassadors; before the Akistaria they would convene there to negotiate their course of action. Melkin walked up the spiral staircase and pushed on the trapdoor to the roof, but it was locked. He sighed and made his way down to the servant quarters, pondering what to do before a commotion sounded from the hall. The Shalin Empire had arrived. Though Melkin was sure that the Valean party wished to rest, all of them gathered to welcome the faul.

"Greetings, honored guests," said Taleek, his voice dripping with forced kindness.

The sight of almost fifty faul surprised him in myriad ways. He had seen faul before on his missions and the one who attacked their camp had been intriguing but seeing them up close and in such large numbers was different. Melkin shifted from behind Cirel to get a better view. They looked frail and short; a majority stood around five feet tall. Like the prisoner and the faul he'd seen a few years ago, they all had very pale skin and hair. The Shalin soldiers wore gambeson like the Valean soldiers, yet it was clear they had a fraction of the muscle mass.

"Thank you, Commander... Takel, is it? I am pleased to not find this place in ruins already, but I suppose the day is still young," said a faul, the leader of the group.

"Indeed it is Captain Yulac, and I'll once again remind you that my name is Taleek. I'm sure that the *ninth* year of my command will be the one where you finally remember it."

"Well—"

"In any case," Taleek said, cutting off Yulac's retort. "My company and I will be glad to join you all for dinner tonight. I'm afraid it is already past lunchtime, else we would have shared that meal as well. Regrettably, your hour of arrival deprives us of that lovely opportunity."

"How unfortunate, alas we were held up for a few hours due to unforeseen injuries, but I suppose you and your army wouldn't know anything of the sort," said Yulac.

"No? Does our strength and size nullify the darkness and danger of the frigid night? Ah but I forget, such things are unfamiliar to you," retorted Taleek with a smirk. Both faul and human were rapt, watching the squabble with reactions ranging anywhere from horror to amusement. Melkin, suspecting that the two held little ill-will against one another, found great enjoyment in the spectacle, barely managing to suppress the grin threatening his stoic face.

"Oh, I love your sense of humor, Takeel! I look forward to joining your company for dinner!" exclaimed Yulac, voice dripping with sarcasm. He turned back toward his group. "Let's settle into our tower now, you all must be exhausted!"

Taleek led them back inside the Valean tower where Melkin made his way up to the third floor with the other servants. He confirmed with his ambassador that he had no duties before heading down the stairs to a door he hadn't explored yet on the second floor. It led to a hallway that stretched the length of the main hall, connecting the two towers together. He found a door about a quarter of the way down and entered, finding himself in the sacred meeting chamber. Though the room was massive, there were only ten seats in total, five for each side.

On the fifth of the month, this is where the two sides would meet and negotiate until both parties agreed to whatever new terms they would set. Assuming he wasn't supposed to be here, Melkin re-entered the Valean tower and took the staircase up to the third floor again. He would hold off his spying on the faul until the next day; best to wait and allow them to get settled in and relax their guard a bit.

He thought about what he would do in the few hours before dinner and stumbled upon a brilliant idea as he passed one of the tower windows. He found Taleek on the second floor and pulled him aside.

"I'll be back in a few hours, before dinner. I'm going to scale the castle."

"Why?" asked Taleek, taken aback. He looked horrified at the notion.

Melkin shrugged. "I'll be out of view from the faul if that's what you're afraid of."

"Sure... Don't do anything stupid." Taleek shook his head, either in disappointment or incredulity. Possibly both. *At least he didn't interfere.*

Melkin shot him a quick glare before descending the stairs down to the first floor. Each of the floors had three windows, covered by animal hide. Upon closer inspection, Melkin found he could unhook the hide at the bottom of the window. It was quite the serious safety flaw, Melkin thought, but he was happy to take advantage of it.

As he always did before climbing, he removed his boots and clipped them to his trousers. Carefully, he opened the window and gripped the rough stone walls of the castle. After pulling himself out of the window and onto the thin windowsill, he closed the window again. He found handholds and footholds in the old, cracked stone and started scaling the wall. The cool, dry, afternoon air was perfect for climbing, and soon he found himself on the second-floor windowsill. Keeping his hands and feet clear of any gaps in the animal hide, he kept climbing, knowing that the soonest he could re-enter would be on the fourth floor, unless he wanted to invite a multitude of questions.

Though he had often wished to, he had never found the time to climb the royal castle itself, or to even ask Queen Gladia if he could. With the endless mystery of the bombings and current strife with the Shalin Empire consuming all his time, he doubted he ever would.

As he climbed, memories from his latest major mission flooded back to him. Queen Gladia had suspected the baron of a major city in Farak Province was keeping more collected taxes than he should have, thus she sent in Melkin to investigate. To listen in on the conversation, he climbed from an easily accessible balcony to the private conference room window and sat on the windowsill for an hour or two. Then he climbed to the office containing the ledgers and entered through the window. The baron was indeed hoarding money, but that hadn't been Melkin's problem to deal with.

Melkin brought himself back to reality and climbed onto the third-floor ledge. He was now about twelve yards off the ground and felt the thrill of heights fill him. He fought back a grin as he imagined what the shocked faces of the servants would look like if he entered. During his ascent to the fourth floor, his left foot slipped while he was placing his hand. As quickly as the mistake occurred and the usual pang of fear hit, he regained composure and steadied himself, swiftly pulling himself up to the fourth-floor windowsill.

He crouched on the windowsill and turned around to gaze out at the Valean landscape. Only some sparse trees populated the otherwise dull plains, but the view from fifteen yards in the air was nothing to be scoffed at. Out of the corner of his eye, he thought he saw a flash of gray near the base of the castle. Momentarily forgetting how high he was, he jerked his head downward and almost lost his balance. More cautiously this time, he gripped the wall and leaned out from his perch on the windowsill but saw nothing. Though he trusted his eyes, he had no choice but to shrug it off—there was nothing he could do about whatever it was. With one hand holding the wall above him, he unhooked the animal hide and dropped inside the fourth floor.

He breathed a sigh of relief at seeing the room deserted. Intent on informing Taleek of his sighting, he descended the spiral staircase.

"Hey!" cried a servant as he passed by the third floor.

"What?" he asked, annoyed.

"How'd you get up there? I just saw you go down the stairs."

"I . . . went back up?" said Melkin.

"I didn't see you," she said indignantly. "I've been sitting right here." Melkin avoided rolling his eyes at the stubborn lady.

"Maybe you need better vision then," he said, continuing his descent. Before he could feel too guilty about the accusation, he found Taleek and once again pulled him aside.

"Hey, I saw some movement from something—or someone—while I was out there. Might want to keep an eye out for anything strange," said Melkin.

"Could it have just been an animal?" asked Taleek.

"Of course. It could warrant a bit of caution, though."

"I appreciate your concern, but right now the diplomatic air is... tense. I have more sensitive matters to focus on, but if you see anything else, tell me."

"Yes, Commander," he said, walking down to the first floor. Better to linger there than with the other servants.

An hour later, Melkin filed into the great hall with the soldiers, servants, and ambassadors. While not mandated by customs of the Akarist, the countries sat separately. Melkin almost sat with the faul, but such an act would have made him stick out even more, so he took a seat with the rest of the Valean servants. They dined upon freshly cooked rice and the dried meat that both sides had brought. Melkin thought it was quite good, but the ambassadors still seemed unsatisfied with the quality of the meal. Melkin supposed this was the harshest time of year for them. After everyone was given their rations, the two servants who had cooked the meal returned to their seats to eat their own portions.

"Would someone go watch the fire?" one asked as he sat.

"Sure," said a soldier sitting nearby.

"You don't have to do that, it's for the servants to manage the fires," said the servant.

"It's fine. I'm finished with my meal anyway," said the soldier with a shrug.

Within minutes, the hall was filled with laughter and conversation—some people were even mingling with the opposing nation a bit. While listening to a discussion between Shalin and Valean servants about customs, Melkin heard a small noise from the kitchen. It sounded like a grunt or a gasp. Melkin turned toward the kitchen and wondered if he should inspect—could he have imagined it? He looked around the room; no one else seemed to have heard it. Then, a Shalin soldier stood up and walked into the kitchen. No, he had not imagined it. Melkin stood, a sort of dread building in him, and entered the kitchen.

The Shalin guard stood holding a bloody knife over the dead body of the Valean soldier who had entered the kitchen only ten minutes prior. As shock passed, rage took its place. Reflexively, he pulled the knife from his boot and pointed it at the soldier, who raised his hands in defense.

"No, it's not—" started the Shalin soldier. He got no further before Melkin charged at him.

He was a few feet away from tackling the faul before he felt a searing pain in his leg. He collapsed to the ground, sprawled out in front of the soldier. The soldier retreated, but Melkin grabbed hold of his ankle and tripped him to the ground. Ignoring the pain in his leg, he crawled on top of the soldier, forgetting that his opponent also had a knife. The blade grazed his arm, but he grabbed the soldier's hand and wrestled the knife from his grasp. After placing it against the faul's throat, the burning in his thigh stopped. Panting, Melkin slipped his own knife back inside of his boot.

"You bastard..." muttered Melkin, his enraged face barely a foot away from his opponent's terrified one.

The soldier opened his mouth, but Melkin quickly pressed the knife to the faul's throat. "Don't even think about it." The agonizing pain of the burn was slowly subsiding. He picked up the soldier and dragged him toward the kitchen door, knife pressed to neck the entire time. "You make one sound and I slit your throat," whispered Melkin.

All eyes turned upon him as he kicked open the kitchen door. For a moment, the room was completely and utterly silent.

"This traitor killed a Valean guard! I saw him standing over his dead body with this knife!"

Screams and shouts filled the great hall. Taleek and some soldiers rushed into the kitchen.

"No!" shouted a guard from the kitchen. Numb as Melkin was, the despair in the soldier's voice made him shudder.

Melkin threw the Shalin soldier to the ground and he slowly stood, face full of sorrow and fear. Captain Yulac grabbed hold of him and pinned his hands behind his back. The soldier did not resist. "Sergeant Lothar Raiken, did you do this?" he yelled into Lothar's ear.

"No!" Lothar looked fearfully at Melkin. "He was already dead when I came in—that knife was in his chest! I only pulled it out to see if the blade engravings could tell who the culprit was."

Taleek and his soldiers emerged from the kitchen. Melkin stood there with his head swimming, his vision unfocused, and blood running down his arm.

"I've accounted for all my soldiers, servants, and ambassadors! Your soldier was the only one who could have done it!" shouted Taleek, face red.

Yulac paused for a moment. "Yes... you are correct. The deceased guard and Lothar were the only ones in the kitchen before this servant of yours entered. Lothar, did the servant kill him?"

"No! I swear he was dead already," lamented Lothar, voice quavering.

"You dare accuse my servant of kin-killing?" Taleek stepped forward, his face inches above Yulac's. Shalin guards rushed up beside Yulac, their faces enraged.

Yulac stepped backward, motioning for his guards to stand down. "I had to check. Lothar Raiken, you are suspected of murder and will spend the rest of your time here in the dungeon. Once over, you will be transported to the national prison for further investigation and sentencing." Yulac pointed at one of his soldiers. "Get some rope and tie him up." The soldier nodded obediently and retreated back to the Shalin tower.

It was strange that Lothar didn't resist during capture, wasn't it? Melkin tried to envision the encounter in his head again, but it was getting blurry, growing faint. Lothar must have used his heat powers to defeat the soldier. But in such a short amount of time? Maybe it was longer than he remembered—he'd watched Lothar enter and then had to walk fifty feet to the kitchen door. It seemed improbable, but maybe...

"Heathe, get a bandage for Evarith," Taleek ordered.

Melkin looked around and took a deep breath. He was used to death, but something felt horribly wrong. For one, these things weren't supposed to happen in the Akarist. *Why now?*

"Are you alright, Evarith?" asked a soldier.

He nodded, "Yeah, I'll be fine," he said. The cut on his arm would heal in days—it wasn't too bad. He turned and saw Haern sitting in the corner with his head in his hands, a few soldiers comforting him. The deceased's name... *it was Ragnar, wasn't it?*

Melkin remembered the jovial soldier who bantered with everyone while changing the axle on the cart only yesterday. A soldier handed a bandage to Melkin, and he wrapped it tightly around his arm, stopping the blood flow.

The faul soldier returned with rope, and Lothar was bound and gagged. Two Shalin soldiers led him downstairs beneath the trapdoor in the great hall.

"I will commit one soldier to standing guard over him at all times and I suggest you do the same," said Taleek, his face still bright red and his breathing labored.

"Indeed. I also think we should allow them weapons outside of their towers," said Yulac, despair and sorrow in his voice.

Taleek nodded in agreement. Melkin noticed the commander was steadying his breathing, trying to appear in control.

"There is no undoing such an act," Yulac continued, "but as the captain of this party, I sincerely apologize. Lothar's actions do not represent the interests of our kind or our country. As . . . strained as we both know relations are, I do not wish death upon any of your men. I assure you; Lothar will face trial and punishment for this evil act committed today."

Taleek nodded at Yulac's statement and turned back toward the frightened crowd. "I invite any member of the party who wishes to take part in the funeral to join us outside. Haern, you may carry Ragnar to his final resting place if you wish."

Haern nodded, his face stained with tears.

"As for the rest of the soldiers, I ask that you ensure the security of our tower. Servants, please clean up tonight's dinner; you'll be glad for something to do."

The Valeans nodded and went to work. As the Shalin party followed suit, Melkin noticed that animosity was now reignited between the two sides. The Valean servants never came within ten feet of the faul and had angry or frightened expressions on their faces. Taleek walked outside along with most of the soldiers and a couple of servants, including Melkin. In dead silence, they walked down the hill. At the bottom, Haern laid Ragnar's body on the ground, for they had no shovels with which to dig a hole. While they stood in silence, five Shalin soldiers came down the hill, ignoring numerous glares from the Valean company. Upon reaching the Valean soldiers, one whispered something to Taleek. Taleek nodded, and the Shalin soldiers started muttering, like the faul Melkin captured a week ago had done. A few Valeans started backing away, but a look of reassurance from Taleek stopped them.

The faul continued their magic, and soon wind currents tore at the loosely packed dirt, creating a shallow hole. Sniffing back his tears, Haern placed Ragnar into the grave and a long silence prevailed. With a nod from Haern, the faul soldiers covered him with the dirt they'd moved and walked back toward the castle without another word.

"Ragnar was an honorable soldier," started Taleek, bowing his head down. "To fall to such a petty act is a tragedy. May Ryne see him through to the afterlife."

"A loyal friend. I would have placed my life in his hands without a second thought," said Haern. "He wished . . . almost more than anything . . . for peace between the nations. I think we should see his wishes honored."

Taleek nodded, and soon many of the others followed in the gesture. "We shall. To the best of our abilities."

Drops of rain fell as the evening night grew darker. Soldiers turned and left to re-enter the castle one by one. Melkin didn't mind the cold, nor the rain, nor the darkness, so he stayed. He wished not to have a barrage of questions thrown his way upon re-entering the castle. The silence of the evening was pleasant enough, despite the circumstances.

Finally, Taleek turned to go. "Come soon, Haern. It's not worth risking your life in the night's darkness," he whispered.

Melkin made out a small nod from Haern, who didn't turn to face the commander. He saw Haern shiver in the frigid night air, despite his thick gambeson. His apathy toward secrecy growing, Melkin retrieved a length of rope, his flint, and his knife from his boots. He picked up a stick that wasn't too wet yet and wrapped the rope around it. It was an oiled rope, made specifically for this purpose. He struck the knife against the flint; the sound caused Haern to flinch and jerk his head toward Melkin. The first attempt failed, but on the second, the rope ignited and soon burned brightly with flame. He handed the torch to Haern, who took it with a nod of his head. Melkin quickly stored away his knife and flint.

"Thanks, Evarith," murmured Haern, "You don't have to stay out here."

"No, I rather enjoy the weather," replied Melkin. He really had nothing else to do.

The barest hint of a smile appeared on Haern's face. The two stood for a while longer until the long torch had nearly burned out. Then, Haern turned and walked back to the castle with Melkin following. He snuffed out the remaining flames of the torch and tossed it aside. Melkin climbed up the staircase to the now dimly lit third floor.

All eyes turned upon him as he entered, and conversation halted. He ignored them, refusing to entertain the questions that were surely on everyone's minds. Taking off his boots, he lay down in one of the hard beds, staring at the ceiling. As much as he might try to purge his thoughts of the tragedy, he could not stop his own questions from occupying his mind. Why didn't Lothar try to blame him? He insisted Ragnar was already dead. It would have been madness to claim that Melkin killed Ragnar in front of him, but it would have been better than the alternative. Only when sleep took over did Melkin's worries cease.

8

MELKIN

After waking, Melkin immediately left the confines of the third floor and descended the stairs to the first floor, careful not to wake anyone else along the way. He sat in a chair in the meagerly adorned lounge and rested his head in his hands, thinking about everything that had transpired. For an hour, he did nothing but let his thoughts consume him. He sorted through confusion, dread, and anxiety, wishing he could be back in his study and away from these people. While bleak thoughts ran amok in his head, others began to wake. Conspicuous stomping echoed throughout the tower, interrupting the peace he so relished. *It could be worse.* Unlike the day before, he heard no laughter or boisterous chatter.

"Oh, there you are," said a voice from the staircase. He jerked his head up and met the eyes of a servant. The same one who had questioned him on the stairs yesterday.

"What do you want?" he asked.

"We... just didn't see you. Wanted to make sure you were alright after yesterday and everything," she said, meeting his glare.

"Oh. Thanks. Yeah, I'm fine." He softened his gaze and willed himself to relax.

"Good. Well, if you need anything..."

"Yeah. I'll let you know."

"I'm Klea, by the way. Thank you for asking."

"Ah, right. Sorry... Klea." He had almost forgotten her name within seconds of hearing it.

"No worries." With that, the servant climbed the steps, leaving Melkin alone once more. From his position, he glimpsed a Shalin servant enter the kitchen with a sack of grain in her hand. He sighed, resigning himself to the once again busy castle.

Another hour later, Melkin filed into the great hall with the others. Again, he sat with the servants while they chatted, waiting for the porridge to be ready. He was quite hungry but wasn't particularly interested in conversing. For now, it seemed he could listen as Klea ranted about her experiences living in Braake province.

"What about you, Evarith?" asked another servant. "Tell us something about Annister."

He had suspected the conversation might turn to him. They didn't really want to become familiar with him, he suspected. He knew his reputation among them; they wanted to catch him in a lie, wait for him to slip up. "Well, I'm sure you've heard plenty of rumors about Lord Thalen over the years."

"Yes?" Klea, Cirel, and others leaned in expectantly. Perhaps they'd never met anyone brave enough to speak ill of Lord Thalen.

Melkin glanced around, as though Thalen might be in the dining hall. "I'll have you know, they're all true."

"His mother had an affair? He's not the lord by birthright?"

"No," laughed Melkin, despite himself. "I didn't know that was a rumor. He's just cruel and narcissistic."

"Oh," said a servant, looking down at the table.

Melkin gave a slight grin. "Lots of executions. The law says that he can't arrest people without cause, but it doesn't specify a level of punishment that they might receive. So, Lord Thalen makes his judgements on a whim."

"What did I say about not insulting Lord Thalen?" asked their ambassador.

"Oh, right," said Cirel.

Suddenly, the servant in the kitchen flung open the door. In that instant, Melkin saw a repeat of the previous night—he recalled the shock that had filled him. No, it couldn't be, could it? Dread hit him as the Shalin servant stumbled out of the kitchen, clutching her head.

"Poison!" she yelled. The word was long and drawn out—almost unrecognizable if not for the context.

Those closest to her rushed forward whilst Melkin searched the depths of his memory for poison recognition. Delirium and dizziness were common symptoms, and unless Melkin had a sample, there was no way he could identify it. Not that it was likely he could find a cure with the limited materials available in the castle. The poisoned servant collapsed to the floor. A soldier of the Shalin empire knelt beside her, but he could do nothing as the servant convulsed on the ground, the entire hall watching in horror. Then she fell silent and still. Time stopped for a few moments—anticipation and shock filled the air. Wracking coughs echoed throughout the room from the poisoned faul, breaking the intense silence.

"Thank Talen, she's alive!" exclaimed the soldier kneeling beside her.

"Don't ... eat ... the porridge," she said weakly.

Relieved murmuring filled the room as Taleek and Yulac entered the kitchen. Melkin kept his gaze focused on them, watching them glance back and forth between each other and the noisy hall. Then they left the kitchen and exchanged a few words with the poisoned servant before addressing the waiting crowd.

"We've accounted for all soldiers, servants, and ambassadors. No one was in the kitchen with the poisoned servant, nor could they have slipped in while she wasn't looking," Taleek declared.

"Thus, we assume that someone must have poisoned the pot or the grain before she cooked the porridge. It could have been early this morning, or perhaps last night," said Yulac. "We will not yet blame anyone, so we ask for everyone here to report any suspicious behavior."

"Commander ... what do we eat now?" asked a servant, glancing around.

Taleek and Yulac turned to each other and began what looked like a stifled yet heated conversation. At last, Taleek stepped forward.

"As much as I resent asking this, one of us Valean folk will have to sample the food. As humans, we have a far greater chance of surviving any poison. Now, since it is our joint responsibility to keep everyone safe, we both feel partially responsible for this mishap," explained Taleek, gesturing to Yulac and himself. "I am prepared to risk it if no others will volunteer."

Immediately, the hands of several servants and soldiers shot up from the Valean side of the great hall.

"Alright, settle down," said Taleek, raising his hand in a gesture of silence.

"If . . . it's any comfort . . . I had a whole spoon . . . ful . . . and I didn't . . . die," murmured the poisoned faul.

Taleek reluctantly picked a servant whose hand was raised rather emphatically and directed everyone back inside the Valean tower to wait. Yulac did the same with his company, ordering that the sick faul be carried back and made to rest. Melkin, instead of going back to the tower, elected to sit in the shared lounge, which he noticed no one wanted to occupy. It was comfortable enough, and not as noisy as his tower. Left alone with his thoughts again, he considered the real possibility that he may not make it out of this delicate and dangerous ordeal alive. And yet there was nothing he could do besides keep an eye out. He still believed there to be an equal possibility of a Shalin traitor as there was of a Valean traitor. Both parties had been wronged, and neither side was amiable toward the other.

He weighed the pros and cons in his mind; perhaps spying on the Shalin Empire would reveal something, but they would be on edge right now. It wasn't a good idea to spy while on edge himself, either. He shifted his foot, feeling the handle of his knife against his leg. At least he had that, but it would do no good against poison or magic. *Why would anyone do this?* The Akistaria was sacred to both countries—the only reason to attack it would be to upset the other country. That was certainly working; there was no shortage of Valean soldiers who looked upon the faul with disgust now. If he could only return to the royal castle, he could investigate. The Akistaria would be held tomorrow, and then there would be another long journey to reach home again. He wondered if Taleek would permit him to travel ahead of the company this time. *Why wouldn't he?* The thought of being home in a week lightened his heart, if only slightly.

An hour later, both companies tentatively ate breakfast after the test servant had shown no ill effects. Afterward, Melkin headed up to the fourth floor, hoping that amongst the clutter from years of Akistarias, he might find something interesting. As he walked by the third floor, he noticed the servants were quietly chatting between activities that served the ambassadors' needs. Why did they bring so many servants? Queen Gladia certainly was right to only send twenty soldiers—he assumed that most people just sat around during the entire stay.

Vallec and Atlia were probably having a great time, wandering around town all day and allowed to go anywhere they wished. Maybe this gathering was a sort of social event as well; a chance for Valean and Shalin soldiers to meet without crossing weapons. If so, it wasn't going too well. He rummaged through the storage crates, eventually finding one that contained some old books. Shuffling through them, he found three that looked interesting and started with *Ships and Trade of Valea*. Few people ventured to the fourth floor, so he settled in, wiped the dust from the book, and began to read.

Many hours later, Melkin stopped reading in favor of taking a walk. An idea had begun to form in his mind about how to spy on the Shalin Empire. If he went down to the lounge, he could crawl out the window and scale the Shalin tower to listen in on any conversations. It was quite safe, even. With new excitement burning in him, he walked down the stairs and across the castle to the lounge. To his surprise though, a faul servant occupied the usually empty lounge. Hunched over in the corner, the servant turned around upon hearing Melkin enter.

"Mind helping me with something real quick?" he asked, flashing a carefree grin.

"Sure . . . what's wrong?" said Melkin, feeling unease twist within him. He swallowed and tried to calm himself.

"Come here, I'll show you. There's a problem with the floor here."

Melkin walked over and examined the edge of the floor. There was a small hole in the corner, with some bluish gray powder around the edges.

"What is—"

Suddenly, air left his lungs—he couldn't breathe. A knife flashed in front of him as he stumbled backwards and slipped his weapon from his boot. The pale face before him contorted in shock, buying Melkin enough time to move in and attack. The faul wielded a knife in his left hand, disorienting Melkin. Growing desperate, Melkin lunged in, stabbing the faul in the foot and disrupting the magic that was depriving him of precious oxygen. Gasping for breath, Melkin moved in with a flurry of attacks, swiping, stabbing, and feinting until he eventually caught the faul off guard and stabbed him in the chest. The faul let out a long, bloodcurdling scream and collapsed backwards. Melkin turned from left to right, panting for breath and watching for any other attackers. He stared at the knife in his hand, dripping with the blood of a dead faul. A moment later, a Shalin soldier ran into the room, brandishing a long dagger. Melkin made the decision in a split second—he had no other option. He turned toward the soldier and pinned their arms against the wall, pointing the bloody knife at his throat.

"Drop it!" he yelled, as the weapon clattered to the floor. "Try one thing! Blind me, choke me, burn me—and I kill you!"

The guard's wild eyes darted around the room. Melkin followed the gaze—Taleek, Yulac, and plenty of soldiers from both nations stood in the doorway, watching the event.

"He—your servant! He tried to kill me!" shouted Melkin to Yulac. The captain's eyes were wide as he glanced between the dead body and Melkin.

"I did not!" cried the soldier he held at knifepoint.

"No, not you! Him!" cried Melkin, pointing to the dead faul on the ground.

"Release my soldier." Yulac had regained his composure and now spoke in a dangerous voice. Melkin let his arm down and stood back in horrific realization. He had no evidence. The soldier he just disarmed was likely innocent. His hands were stained with blood.

Yulac kneeled by the dead servant and examined his face, turning it from side to side.

"I've never seen this faul before in my life."

"He tried to kill me," said Melkin again. He hadn't yet registered Yulac's words.

"Why did you threaten my soldier?"

"I—I thought he might be about to attack me," pleaded Melkin as he backed up toward Taleek and the Valean soldiers.

"I've obviously never seen him before either," said Taleek to Yulac. "You're not hurt, are you?" he asked Melkin. He shook his head. Why was he attacked? How could there be a faul Yulac had never seen in the Akarist? Was he safe from the executioner's blade?

"Everyone is alright then," said Yulac cautiously. "Is that the dead faul's knife?" he asked Melkin, pointing to the bloody knife.

"Yes," lied Melkin.

"We'll deposit the knife in our tower," assured Taleek, taking the knife from Melkin.

"What do we do with the body?" asked Yulac, breaking a few moments of silence.

Taleek ran a hand down his beard in thought. "Do you want to take it for investigation in case someone in the Shalin Empire recognizes him?"

"And, what? Parade him around the city before the body decays? I suppose we could get a sketch made . . ." Yulac searched the pockets and clothing of the dead faul but found nothing. "We'll put him outside and retrieve him when we leave this place. I'm not keeping a dead body in the Shalin tower."

Three Shalin soldiers picked the body up and walked toward the castle entrance.

"Everyone, back in the tower. We leave only to eat," said Taleek to the Valeans, closing his eyes in sorrow.

Melkin started walking back to his quarters, finding himself in his bed after a journey that he hardly remembered. He felt defenseless without his knife. If he could just know what was going on, who was doing all this, then he wouldn't have to die in this horrible castle. The exit was so near, so inviting. He could walk out the front door in under a minute. *Gladia, though.* She trusted him.

Maybe that was it—maybe it was just that one faul who orchestrated the whole thing. The attacks would stop and the Akistaria would continue as planned.

"Evarith? Are you okay?" asked a voice to his left.

"Of course not..." muttered Melkin; he refused to make eye contact with anyone.

"It's going to be alright," said Klea.

"Sure. Unless anything else goes wrong."

"We're out of here in a day," reassured a tall man.

"There's no way that the Shalin Empire wants to stay here longer than we do," said Cirel.

"Unless they're behind it," commented the tall one.

"And do you *really* think that they are?" questioned Klea.

"*I* don't," said Melkin. "But that doesn't change what's happened. I was almost murdered twice, and if that had been an actual Shalin servant, I would most likely be down in those dungeons."

"But you weren't, and you're not. Dwelling upon it will do no good," said Klea firmly.

"We know you've been through an ordeal. We're just trying to help."

Melkin sighed. "Thanks." He meant it.

By the time morning came around, Melkin silently rejoiced that he was alive, and that today was the Akistaria. He was pretty sure that servants weren't allowed to listen in, yet he wondered what the ambassadors would say and if anything good would come from this year's Akistaria. It was still early in the morning, but the ambassadors and servants were waking up; some looked as though they might not have slept last night at all. Melkin was astonished he'd been able to. Footsteps coming up the stairs from below startled Melkin, but it was only Commander Taleek with a few soldiers.

"Ambassadors! We are having a preliminary meeting now on the fifth floor to discuss today's Akistaria. Join me in five minutes," he said. Then he approached Melkin. "I want you there as well."

The joyous mood in the room died down; no one really wanted to attend a meeting right now. Melkin was tired of being singled out—his cover was almost nonexistent now.

"It's usually later than this," grumbled an ambassador.

"Are you complaining about getting out of here earlier than usual?" asked a servant.

"Fair enough," said the ambassador with a sigh. Melkin finished lacing his boots and headed upstairs, wondering why Taleek needed him. The commander was sitting at the stone meeting table, a grave expression on his face. Five soldiers accompanied him, weapons in hand.

"What's wrong?" asked Melkin. He felt his pulse speed up—now everything seemed to spark dread within him.

"Nothing as of now," said Taleek. "I have my soldiers here, but I want you to monitor things. If you see anything, let me know. This meeting is of the utmost importance, considering what's been happening."

"I understand." Melkin stood against the wall to get a clear view of the room and to distance himself from the others.

The exhausted ambassadors filed into the room and sat on the simple stone seats around the table. Though some shot curious or apprehensive glances his way, Melkin ignored them.

"Alright. To business," said Taleek. "The Akistaria will begin in an hour. I know that you all have the people's best interests in mind, but I believe we must have peace between Valea and the Shalin Empire. It seems like madness, I know, but it will have to happen at some point. We cannot fight for eternity, so there will come a time when we come to an agreement. Why not today? It's not my place to advise you all, I know, but considering recent events, I deem it proper. Please, fight to preserve the lives of our soldiers."

"And what if we come to an agreement, but the bombings do not stop? What if they continue to wage a secret war but with greater force? I'm not saying that peace is impossible, but peace for peace's sake may be a blunder," said an ambassador.

"Remember history, Commander Taleek," said another. "We cannot let past atrocities go unpunished."

"Both Valea and the Shalin Empire have paid tenfold for the atrocities. It is futile to continue fighting," said Taleek, raising his voice. "You'll let your *pride* kill more of our people?"

"How dare you accuse us!" gasped the first ambassador, shooting up from her seat and pointing a finger at Taleek. She opened her mouth to continue her tirade before sitting back down and holding her head in her hands. "I'm sorry, it's just—"

"I understand. And to be honest, you ambassadors know more than me about Valean and Shalin history. I ask only that you take an objective stance. Try to see the bigger picture and think about the people our actions directly affect," said Taleek.

The ambassadors nodded, and the six said no more while they pondered what to do. Melkin's eyes flitted toward the window—was there something there? The animal hide blew in the wind, allowing cracks of daylight to stream in and dance around. He thought back to a few days ago when he thought he saw movement on the plains below. Was it that? Then, something appeared behind the window, blocking the light from the rising sun. Melkin's heart skipped a beat.

"Taleek! Do you have the key to the roof?" All eyes turned upon him.

"The—Evarith, what's wrong?" asked Taleek, alarm plastered across his face.

"Do you have it?"

"N-No it's downstairs! Go get the key!" exclaimed Taleek, pointing at the nearest soldier in the room.

"No time!" cried Melkin.

He unhooked the window to see a Shalin servant making their way over the edge of the rooftop, looking down at him with wide eyes. Without stopping to remove his boots, he climbed onto the windowsill and leapt up, catching the edge of the roof. As he pulled himself up, the faul backed up against the furthest battlements. Melkin was unarmed, but the faul brandished a tiny knife. Yet the faul remained on the other side of the rooftop, making no sign he would move toward Melkin.

"What's going on? I didn't think you all were behind all this!" shouted Melkin over the howling wind.

"We're not! Are you?"

"Of course not! Who are you?" shouted Melkin.

"I'm—I'm the spy sent with the Shalin Empire. And you?" asked the faul, approaching Melkin.

Not a very good spy, it seemed. "Stay away! If you played no part, and neither did we . . ." He trailed off.

"A third party . . ." said the other faul. "But who? And why?"

"And if they wanted to disrupt the Akistaria, why only a few murder attempts? Why not just—" he glanced around, searching for the idea that evaded him. "Why not just blow up the . . . Oh my God!" shouted Melkin. He leapt over the side of the roof and landed on the windowsill. Then he placed his hands on the ledge and dropped once more. Fourth floor, third floor, second floor, first floor. Unhooking the animal hide, he dropped inside and sprinted toward the dungeon. Cries of alarm echoed around him, but Melkin only vaguely registered them. He knew what he saw in the lounge, but he needed to make sure. After wrestling open the trapdoor, Melkin flew down the stairs toward the dungeon. Guards barred the way, separating him from the answers he so desperately sought.

"If you two value your lives you will let me in to question him!" exclaimed Melkin, stumbling over his words.

"Are you threatening us?" asked the Shalin guard, placing a hand on his dagger.

"No!" he cried desperately. "Please, I beg of you!"

"Alright," said the Valean guard.

"Wait! I'm coming with you," said the Shalin guard.

"I don't care!" cried Melkin, running in through the open doorway.

Lothar's wide eyes followed him as Melkin approached, grasping the bars.

"Cut his gag!" yelled Melkin at the Shalin guard, who obediently did so. "You didn't kill him, did you?" asked Melkin.

"Of course I didn't!"

Melkin didn't feel he was as good at reading people as perhaps he should be, but he saw neither lie nor malice in the faul's eyes.

"On the night of the murder, did you see anything else in the kitchen that looked out of place?" asked Melkin quickly.

"Uh—well, no . . . I don't think so?" said Lothar nervously.

"Did you see any gray powder at all? On anything?"

"No, I—I don't think so? It's really a blur to me," said Lothar.

Melkin paced around the room, panting. *What to do?* He could evacuate the building, but he had no evidence. Maybe Lothar *did* see something—should he keep questioning him? Or could he show the powder in the lounge to the others? What did it matter, though? Calling for evacuation would be safer, and he wasn't about to sacrifice the lives of so many people for the sake of his dignity. He should have said something earlier while rushing down here—why didn't he? It didn't even matter if this faul couldn't remember—he knew what he had seen.

"The castle is going to explode!" cried Melkin at the guards after over a minute of furiously debating with himself. The two guards sprinted out of the dungeon, Melkin following.

"Wait! Help me!"

Melkin hesitated for a moment, then turned back. Dire as the situation might be, he couldn't leave Lothar to die.

"The key! On the wall!" shouted Lothar, pointing to a hanging key. Melkin retrieved it and grabbed hold of the lock, fumbling with it for a second before inserting the key and turning. The lock clicked open, and Lothar burst out of his cell, running with Melkin toward the exit. Five feet from the door, they paused as a great rumbling shook them. Rocks tumbled down the stairs.

"Get back!" screamed Melkin. He grabbed Lothar and dove to the side of the room, away from the flow of stones. The walls shook and crumbled—the two torches that illuminated the room fell to the ground and were snuffed out, enveloping the room in a sea of black.

9

LOTHAR

Lothar found himself in a strange dream; Captain Yulac was standing over him, arms crossed, while he was in the Akarist dungeon.

"Look what you've done!" he shouted, gesturing to the pile of rubble in the dungeon. Before this Akarist ordeal, Yulac had never looked upon Lothar with such reproach.

"I'm sorry! I didn't do it!" cried Lothar. Then Yulac morphed into the dead Valean soldier, who stood without sound, blood pouring from his chest. Lothar waited with bated breath—would he shout more accusations, or would he defend Lothar's innocence?

Lothar gasped and opened his eyes, the image already fading from his mind. But was this another dream? He couldn't see anything at all, but he could feel something digging into his side—this was no dream. Was he blind? He began panicking as he felt around, taking in his surroundings. Around him, he felt stacks of stone and jagged pieces of rock, but he couldn't see them.

"You're awake," said a voice only a few feet away from him.

He almost jumped out of his skin—that voice, he recognized that voice. The memory of the explosion hit him—the rumbling, falling rocks, and then nothing. It was that servant, the one who'd attacked him in the kitchen and had just been frantically questioning him. The two of them were in the pitch-black dungeon.

"And you're . . .?" His voice shook a bit.

"Evarith."

"So, we're stuck down here," commented Lothar. "How long?"

"Only a few hours. I never fell unconscious."

"So, we still have three days before we're definitely dead from no water."

"Well done." Evarith spoke his words with a mixture of apathy and annoyance.

"Alright then, what do *you* want to do?" The air was thick with heat and dust—it must have been over a hundred degrees. *Three days is generous.*

"I would have started earlier if I wasn't worried about crushing you. We'll start prying some of these rocks from the mass."

He heard Evarith stand up and did the same, catching himself on the wall as he lost balance. His head swam from a combination of sweltering heat and blindness.

"Here's one of the prison bars. Do you have anything to burn?" asked Evarith.

"No, sorry. Only some thin prison clothes."

Evarith grunted and Lothar heard the sharp sound of flint against iron as a spark flashed a few yards from him. A minute later, after many more sparks, a thin coil of rope caught fire. It barely gave any light, but Evarith brought it around the room, fully revealing the size of the task before them. A layer of rocks covered most of the room, and an immense mound of rubble poured out from the doorway.

"Is there any wood around here?" asked Lothar, digging through some rubble.

"I don't see any. Just stone."

"Then we should get to work before it burns out."

"There's some space here, so we can discard the rocks to the emptier parts of the room and see if we can clear the doorway."

Some of the stone chunks were heavier than Lothar himself. Lothar felt a deep despair fill him—they could easily die in here. "Talen, help us."

"Your fake god will not be clearing these rocks," said Evarith.

"You—"

"Want to get out of here or not?"

Lothar glared in his direction but knew Evarith could not see it. He was almost sure the jest was supposed to anger him, maybe make him work with more vigor. Moving closer to the doorway, Lothar gripped a rock and tossed it to the back of the dungeon.

"You're not a servant, are you?" he grunted, heaving another stone from the pile.

"Well done once again."

"No need to be snarky, it's a compliment. Who are you?"

"The Valean spy."

He had suspected something like that; it certainly explained the disposition. "I should have known that your country would be petty enough to send a spy."

"Yours did too."

They had? Lothar recalled one servant acting strange during the journey but had never suspected that they were a spy.

"And if you tell anyone about me, you can be certain I'll reveal that the Shalin Empire sent a spy as well."

"There's no need to threaten me. But do you know what happened? All of this? I heard some rumors from the guards down here, but..."

"All I have are my own suspicions, but I believe them to be true."

"Perhaps you could explain?"

"Well... I suppose we have time for the full tale. Just keep working, alright?"

Lothar was growing tired of the constant frustration, maybe of Evarith as a person. He threw another rock into the pile at the back of the dungeon. "What do you think I'm doing?" he asked, annoyance slipping into his voice.

"In Valea we have dealt with bombings for the past few years," started Evarith, ignoring Lothar's sarcasm. "We don't know who plants them, and we've always suspected it was the Shalin Empire.

But we had no evidence. So, our queen, Queen Gladia, sent me to find the truth. Not to kill or to hurt anyone, just to listen in on some conversations and ensure that we wouldn't draft a peace treaty with a country bombing us behind our backs. If it's any comfort though, I never really thought that the Shalin Empire was behind it."

"And now? What about *this* bombing and the murder?" Lothar gestured around the room in vain, briefly forgetting that Evarith could not see him.

"I'm getting to both questions. I'm not sure if you were told, but a faul disguised as one of Yulac's soldiers tried to kill me in the lounge last night. He told me that something was wrong with the wall and had me look. Then when he attempted to choke me and stab me, I mostly forgot the sight of a small hole with bluish explosive powder around it. And yet, this morning, it made sense. Your spy tried to listen in on our meeting, but I saw him and chased him up to the rooftop. There, it became clear that both sides were confused. He confirmed the Shalin Empire had nothing to do with these events, but that didn't answer my question. '*Why?*' If someone wanted to disrupt the meeting itself, they would have to do it that day, *today*. And, if these people were the same as the ones who were causing havoc in Valea, then they would most likely blow up the Akarist."

"By Talen, the knife. I . . . I think it might have had some gray powder on the handle . . . if I remember correctly," said Lothar hesitantly. "So—"

"Why didn't you say so earlier?" interrupted Evarith, with unnecessary disdain in his voice.

"Well, I didn't remember then! Sorry, but when a strange man runs into your jail cell and starts ranting about 'something being off', it's kind of hard to think!" Lothar was almost fed up with Evarith's antics.

"Ugh, fine. Just—what were you about to say?"

"So . . . the knife . . . if the person who killed that soldier was working on a bomb, and that soldier spotted them, they may have had residue on their hands. Hence the gray powder."

"I see."

Lothar started feeling faint—sweat dripped from his face onto the ground in the sweltering heat. "But... why come to me? Why not investigate the kitchens or the lounge again?"

"I know the style of these people; somehow, they conceal these bombs and light them with no trace. I wasn't sure you would remember details of the murder, but you're a sergeant, whatever that means in your country. So, I took a gamble. I bet on your memory rather than any incompetence by these bombers. It clearly didn't pay off."

"You're the one who hesitated. If your memory is so good, why didn't you evacuate the castle earlier?" asked Lothar.

"Do you really think I want to hear that right now?"

"Well, you're pointing out *my* mistakes, so I figure you do!"

"Fine. Just drop it." Evarith sighed dramatically. "Anyway, it's rather suspicious that this attack aligns with the ones in Valea."

"So now you think that the Shalin Empire did this—"

"Have you had any bombings in the Shalin Empire?" asked Evarith before Lothar finished his question.

"No. But we also haven't *caused* any."

Evarith grunted. "That's what I wanted to know. Don't you think that's suspicious?"

"Why would we blow up the entire Akarist?" exclaimed Lothar in frustration.

"The entire Akarist might not have been blown up, and even so, what's a little slip up? A little too much explosive powder, or whatever they use, and the entire thing goes down."

"H—"

"Or, perhaps your emperor deems the sacrifice to be worthy."

How dare he! "You can speculate all you want. All I can do is tell you what I know!" cried Lothar. "And I *know* we haven't been setting these bombs."

"And you're sure you'd be privy to such knowledge? Who even are you, Lothar?"

"The sergeant of a regiment."

"How many soldiers do you command?"

Lothar swallowed. "Twenty."

Evarith laughed softly. "Alright, so how do you know that your government isn't operating behind your back? Behind everyone at the Akarist's back?"

"How do you know yours isn't?"

"I'm a high-ranking official. I answer directly to the queen."

"And what would be the point of either government operating behind the peoples' backs?"

"To weaken us before a war starts. Not these skirmishes, but a formal declaration of war." Lothar got a distinct impression from his intonation that Evarith was opposed to war as well. The two were silent for a few moments.

"Ryne! It's hot in here!" Evarith said, breaking the brief civil air between the two.

"I feel . . . weak," complained Lothar, taking a break from the arduous labor. He started muttering and felt the air grow wonderfully cool around him.

"What are you doing?"

"Lowering the temperature."

"If you keep doing that, I'll get these rocks out of the way."

Lothar breathed a sigh of relief, cooling the room down significantly. "So, in your hypothetical situation, you people would blame us, and we would become angry at the accusations, not knowing that our own government actually set these bombs."

"Yes. And since you all have had no bombings, it's only natural that your country or a group of extremists from your country would be behind it."

"Well, if it's extremists, then you have no reason to be mad at us."

Evarith grunted. "It doesn't matter. Whoever is doing this is a threat to Valea."

"Well, if you want to find these people, you may want to know that we have had . . . other events, rather than bombings. Lootings of our forts and treasuries in the night with no witnesses. My regiment is one of a few that acts upon the leads that we get, trying to catch these criminals. They've stolen a very considerable amount of money; even our Emperor is getting anxious about them. Now, maybe these were the same people who have been bombing your country, or maybe it's *your* country who orders these criminals."

"The queen did not order those attacks, but it could very well be the doings of Valean soldiers at the border; stealing is a far smaller ordeal than bombings."

"Explosive powder is not hard to come by—"

"Don't you understand? These bombs, they're of no scale ever seen before! That powder I saw in the lounge—it had a blue tinge to it. This is a new, insanely dangerous material. Have you ever seen explosive powder rip apart a stone castle?"

"No . . ." Annoying as he might be, the spy had a point.

"Look. I don't know if it's your government, or your country, or what. But something's happening here; the Akarist was thought untouchable, sacred to both countries. Whoever is doing this wants something, and they won't stop until they have it. I must report this to Queen Gladia, which means getting out of this dungeon. So, let's get moving."

"Indeed," said Lothar, channeling his magic throughout the room. He wasn't sure quite what to think of the situation. Yet if he made it out of here, he could report to Imar and his country could handle it from there. No further need to speculate on Evarith's motives or on his own government's role in all of this. He walked over to the pile and pulled some of the smaller rocks out. The work was long and exhausting, yet they slowly cleared around half of the rocks from the doorway.

"Do you think they survived up there?" asked Lothar, the words breaking a long silence. As he said them, the likely truth hit him.

"I hope so. I never really enjoyed traveling with them, but I don't want them to die."

"Talen will save them," muttered Lothar. He hoped it was true.

"Who's this Talen you speak of?" grumbled Evarith. Indeed, the man *had* just been trying to annoy him earlier. He suspected it was nothing personal, simply this man's pastime.

"One of our five deities. The god of life," explained Lothar, ignoring the annoyance in Evarith's voice. "Guiding the Talwreks, he and the other four deities unified the Shalin Empire . . ." Of course, Evarith didn't care, but he enjoyed recounting the old tale anyway.

Evarith gave a disinterested grunt before throwing another rock from the pile. "There's a sizable piece of rock wedged in the doorway—I'll need your help to get it free."

Lothar walked up next to Evarith and gripped the jagged rock, stuck firmly in the doorway. "I don't know if we can..."

"We *have* to. Three, two, one, pull!"

The rock moved ever so slightly, sending a shower of pebbles down on the two. "I think..." Lothar felt around the top of the boulder up to the collapsed doorway. "I think the ceiling might be resting on this. If we remove it... we might get more than a few pebbles coming down."

"We have no choice—it blocks the exit. Now, pull!"

The stone scraped against the side of the doorway, groaning as it came free after a few seconds of their full effort. Lothar leapt to the side as rocks and debris came tumbling down—chunks of stone from the roof fell not just from around the doorway but the entire room. He crouched down and covered his head. Then, something sharp fell on his arm, causing him to cry out in pain. Still, he cowered for several moments longer as the roof of the dungeon cracked and fell. Finally, the rain of rocks ceased.

"Let's keep going."

Lothar slowly opened his eyes and felt his arm, his fingers coming away wet. "No... My arm, I'm bleeding."

"Can you do magic?"

"Wh—yeah, we don't use our hands for magic."

"Good. I'll look around, just keep the room cool."

Lothar realized that the room was once again sweltering and returned it back to a comfortable temperature, ignoring the pain in his left forearm. "What's ahead?" he asked, hearing Evarith walk toward the ruined doorway.

"Be a little patient, yeah?"

Lothar sighed as he heard rocks rolling around the stone floor. A thought flashed through his mind that perhaps Evarith would just leave him here. Ascend to the surface and let him, the enemy faul, die in this crumbling dungeon.

Then Evarith's voice came closer again. "The staircase is all but collapsed and there's plenty of rubble in the way of our path to the surface, but if we're careful, we should be able to make it."

Lothar started shuffling forward, tripping over unseen rocks and uneven ground. He rested his good hand on what remained of the staircase walls to keep himself upright.

He noticed that he could see blurry shapes in the darkness. "By Talen!" he exclaimed, blinking to make out the vague shape of his hand.

"What is it?"

"There's some light here..." Lothar said. They were around halfway up the staircase, he thought.

"You're right. Keep going."

Soon enough, they reached a solid stone wall signaling the end of the staircase. He could see more now; the outline of rocks on the ground, the piles of rubble that lay around them, and the barest speck of daylight that shone through the debris above him.

"We have to climb up," asserted Evarith, reaching up and pulling himself onto an exposed ledge of stone. Lothar gripped the ledge but stayed firmly rooted to the ground—he had nowhere near Evarith's strength, and his injured arm wasn't up to much.

"Here." Evarith extended a hand down to him. In disbelief, Lothar took it with one hand and used the other to assist as Evarith hoisted him onto the ledge. Lothar stared at the stony expression on Evarith's face, then back down at the staircase's end. *At least the human has some honor.*

"I'm not going to leave you down here," Evarith said, as though it should be obvious. Gingerly, the two crawled through a crack between the giant slabs of stone that were piled above them. Lothar could fit through smaller gaps between the stones than the human could, and thus did not need Evarith's help every step of the way.

"It's there, the light!" cried Lothar, staring at a sizable patch of sky coming through a crack above. It brought tears to his eyes, both from the shock to his senses and from the nearness of freedom. He coughed a few times, expelling the dust and dirt that he had breathed in from the debris. Evarith inched his way up beside Lothar; his cold eyes and hard face finally showed a hint of relief. Lothar turned to his left and jerked back in shock. Only a few feet from him lay a faul servant.

"Molaib's sake!" he cried, inching toward the servant. Lothar strained his arm, reaching for the wrist of the servant and eventually taking hold. He searched for a pulse, adjusting his grip several times, but there was none to be found. He racked his mind for the name of the servant—he vaguely recognized the face. "She's dead . . ." he said, fighting back tears.

"We have to go," said Evarith.

This time, his usual monotonous voice ignited a flame in Lothar. "Do you feel nothing at all, human?" cried Lothar, facing Evarith whose expression settled into anger once more.

"If we don't go, we'll be amongst them!" Evarith gestured around at the surrounding stone. "This thing could collapse, crush us both!"

Wishing to escape the terrifying reality of their situation, Lothar bit his tongue. Still, the man's lack of emotion was disturbing, to say the least. He grabbed the next ledge created by the collapsed stones and continued to scale the debris with Evarith. As they gradually climbed closer toward the surface of the debris, Lothar felt his seething anger and fear turn to hope. Then, when Evarith began to help him up onto yet another ledge, they felt the stone shift. Evarith's concentrated face turned to one of horror as the ledge slid down, yanking their hands apart and crashing into the slab of stone Lothar stood upon. Lothar leaped to the side and braced himself on another piece of stone, but that too shifted and fell, wedging Lothar between the giant slabs.

"Evarith!" he shouted, surprised his chest had not caved in from the pressure. He got lucky—the full weight of the stone slab was not on him. It must have caught on something else, lessening the load.

"I'm fine!" Evarith shouted in return, sounding as annoyed as usual. The voice came from beside him, but he could not turn to look. "Just trapped. So close to the surface."

"What now?" gasped Lothar.

"I don't know."

Lothar tried to move an arm or a leg, but the stone did not relent. Though he could not turn to look, he thought he might have heard voices from above. No, he must have been imagining it, hoping in vain for rescue.

"Did you hear that?" gasped Evarith.

Maybe it wasn't his imagination. "Rescuers?" he asked hopefully.

The two began yelling, hoping the voices they heard would come to save them. His throat grew raw, but he felt the weight on top of him lessen marginally. A few minutes later, he could breathe again. He was still trapped, but the load was easier to bear. The voices grew louder, and sunlight poured into the crevice in which he was caught.

"Hold on a little longer down there!" he heard a female voice shout. After the rescuers lifted the last piece of stone from him, Lothar was free. Exhausted and panting, he stood up, shielding his eyes from the blinding sun. He turned to see a man pulling Evarith from the rubble, too. They made it, they were alive.

"Thank you . . . I have no words for your kindness . . ." he said to the pair, in awe of his rescue.

"It's nothing," stated an older female faul. The man was tall and fit, with graying hair. Beside him, Evarith stood up and briefly thanked their rescuers.

"I'm Elvine," declared the faul, "and this is Gillan."

"How did you find us? Why are you here, I mean," asked Evarith, shaking his head. "I don't recognize either of you from the Akarist."

"We and a few others heard the explosion from miles away in the small border towns. We came to investigate and are now rescuing any survivors," explained Gillan with a grimace.

"*Are* there any others?" asked Lothar, relief washed away by dread.

Elvine's face fell. "No. Not so far."

The words rang in Lothar's ears as he and Evarith stood there for what felt like an eternity.

"I'm so sorry," said Elvine. She and Gillan left them staring at the rubble of the Akarist and walked away to search for more survivors that didn't exist. He wanted to believe that Elvine was wrong, that there could exist others beneath the rubble. But each stone wall had crumbled into oblivion and each pillar had been shattered into pieces. The entire castle had been razed to the ground. Lothar's breath shortened—he felt the world spin beneath him. He—He had to leave, to go home, right?

He lifted his head, his eyes stinging as he watched Evarith walk away. *Does he not care at all?* Refusing to stand any longer upon the decimated Akarist, the ruins that served as graves for Captain Yulac and Lothar's lifelong friends, he began walking as well. Why did *he* survive while the noble ambassadors and brave soldiers died? Was it some glorious plan of Talen's, or a cruel joke of luck? Tears ran down his cheeks, blurring his vision as he walked alone on the deserted plains. He would have to go back—have to report all of this. And then what? Go on with his life? Would Emperor Orwic declare war against Valea?

No, he didn't want to go home; he wanted to run away from the utter nightmare in which he stood. But he had sworn an oath to the empire; his duty to tell the tale was the only thing that kept him from falling to the ground in misery and giving up. Lothar began channeling magic, wishing to warm the frozen abyss growing within him, but succeeding only in keeping out the autumn chill.

10

Lothar

While hours faded from one to the next, the scenery surrounding Lothar remained bland and full of dead trees scattered on dull, lifeless plains. At some point the town he sought came into view, perched atop its barren knoll. Two days prior, the Akistaria league had passed through, but their brief stay felt like a lifetime ago.

Upon seeing no one outside the tall stone wall that wrapped around the town, he feared it had been deserted; usually messengers or traders could be seen going to and from the little border towns. Then, as he approached the solid wooden gate, a guard opened a window and gazed at Lothar, upper lip curled in disgust. Lothar looked down—he was covered in dirt and blood, clad in ragged prison clothes.

"No one is permitted to enter Harolin at this time."

"Why?"

"Don't play dumb, the Akarist is destroyed! No survivors have been found. We don't need that happening here."

News of the fruitless search must have spread before his rescue. He had seen no travelers on their way to Harolin, but he had not taken the main road. Someone wanted everyone in the Akarist dead, and he wasn't going to make their job easier.

"I'm Sergeant Raiken, the sole faul survivor from the Akarist." His tone was devoid of emotion—he couldn't conjure the energy for conviction.

"I don't think so," said the guard, pursing his lips and glancing left and right. "Why do you look like an escaped prisoner?"

"I just crawled my way through a mountain of rubble!" Perhaps he did have the energy. He would die if no one believed him—there was nowhere else to go.

"Sergeant Raiken, you're alive!" shouted another guard, running up to the wall and opening the gate. "That's no prisoner!"

"I—I'm sorry—the search parties haven't reported any survivors. Are there any others?" asked the first guard, looking back at Lothar.

He shook his head, fighting the incoming tears. "I need a place to sleep and some food. I must go back to the capital. I must report what I've seen."

"Yes, come in, Seargent," said the second guard. Lothar remembered him now; the two had shared a drink before the Akistaria league set out from Harolin.

"Thank you, Deleok." Lothar walked into the small town, unwilling to let relief replace the deep sorrow that filled him.

"Get some food and water. I'll find clothes and supplies for you," said Deleok, handing Lothar some coins.

Lothar took a seat at the inn, holding a glass of mead in one hand and a glass of water in the other. He set them down and rested his head in his hands, obscuring his tear-stained face from the inn guests. After a few deep breaths, he took a sip of water and found he was parched beyond belief. He gulped down the rest of the water and set the cup down; his head felt marginally clearer, and he began to ponder his situation. The people of Harolin would shelter him for now, but he needed to plan his next steps.

He took stock of his physical well-being now that he was safe. The pain in his arm had faded to the background of his mind, but he would still have to wash and bandage it later. At least it wasn't broken, and physically, he wasn't injured anywhere else. *What did it matter anyway?* As he started on the mead, Deleok walked into the inn and chatted with the innkeeper for a few minutes before walking up to Lothar.

"There's a room for you here. I left some supplies in it."

"Thank you, Deleok. You didn't pay for it, did you?"

"Well, I would have, but no, the Earl of Harolin did. I told him about you. He'll probably get compensated by the emperor in turn, since you *are* part of the Akistaria league."

"I'm glad." At the mention of the league, Lothar found himself imagining his friends sitting next to him, sharing drinks and laughter as they used to.

"I'll leave you now, Seargent. If you need anything, you can talk to me or the earl."

Lothar nodded and continued to drink the mead. If he had known he was spending the empire's money rather than Deleok's, he would have ordered something stronger. He shook his head, collecting his thoughts again; he would have to leave tomorrow, and on foot, at that. The nearest city offering carriage rides was dozens of miles away.

He walked upstairs and into his designated room, the wooden floors creaking beneath his steps. Appreciation filled him, bringing tears to his eyes as he saw what Deleok had provided. He washed up with a bucket and rag, wincing as the gash on his arm stung, then changed into new clothes—a soldier's outfit, complete with a coat of gambeson armor. Sitting on the cot-like bed, he examined the pile of supplies left for him. Two weapons, a twenty-inch majoril dagger and a ten-inch auxlar dagger each with their own leather sheaths, lay on the floor. Basic medical supplies sat beside them, and Lothar wrapped up his arm in the clean bandage provided. He lay on the bed and closed his eyes, exhausted, and not just physically. Perhaps, upon opening his eyes, he might wake up in the Akarist, and everything from the moment he stepped into the kitchen until now would just be a terrible nightmare.

Disappointment filled Lothar upon waking—his hopes were in vain. Still, he forced himself out of bed and prepared for the next leg of the journey.

He would have to leave today, there was no time to waste. Emperor Orwic would believe him, right? The thought flashed through his mind, and he swallowed, imagining himself in the throne room, a sneer on Orwic's face as he dismissed Lothar's claims. He tried to clear his head of the image, though his lack of evidence could not be denied. Seemingly, Valea hadn't done it, but he couldn't prove it. Orwic and the people of the Shalin Empire would want to hear that Valea had, without a doubt, committed the crime. They would want to blame their pain and anger on the humans.

He left the inn and headed toward the general store to buy some camping supplies with the funds that Deleok gave him. Lothar sighed, loath to begin another arduous journey. His feet still ached from the long walk to the Akarist, and they already protested his walk around Harolin, where he purchased dried food, a compact tent, and an extensive map showing the entirety of Anzelon. With his leftover coins, he walked back to the inn, intent on buying another glass of water before his journey. He could drink from streams on his walk, but he'd have to plan his route carefully; the nearest water source was close to a common battleground where skirmishes between humans and faul often took place.

As he reached for the doorknob, a shout from within the inn startled him, and he put his ear to the door, listening to the commotion. With dread sinking into his gut, he drew his new majoril dagger and threw open the door. His eyes went wide; Deleok and another guard restrained a hooded, struggling figure by his arms. The figure looked up and met Lothar's gaze; in the eyes that he remembered as so cold and hard, there shone true fear. Evarith.

"Calm down! We have weapons!" shouted Deleok. The other guard pulled their dagger and held it a few inches from Evarith's throat. He went still, eyes darting between Lothar, Deleok, and the dagger.

"Those two were planting a bomb!" cried Evarith, gesturing toward two frightened faul standing to the side.

"How insensitive of you!" shrieked an inn guest.

"We already checked back there. There is no bomb," said Deleok.

"Then it must have been moved. It was there! I swear on Ryne—"

Lothar winced at the mistake—the inn fell silent for an instant.

"I mean—not—"

Deleok pulled the hood back from Evarith's head, revealing jet black hair and olive skin.

"Humans! You make a mockery of the tragedy with your lies!" exclaimed an inn guest, standing and pointing at Evarith.

"This *man* was trying to pickpocket me!" cried one of the frightened faul that Evarith had indicated before.

"I saw it!" exclaimed the other.

"So . . . do you have clearance to be here?" asked the other guard.

Evarith glanced around. "Yes."

"Show us the papers."

"No." Evarith sighed, looking more annoyed than fearful now.

"Alright, let's take him to jail. The earl will decide his fate," said Deleok.

As the guards led Evarith out of the inn, he stared at Lothar with a pleading expression. The inn returned to its regular activity as Lothar furiously contemplated the dilemma. The idea of walking home now was far more enticing than getting caught up in Evarith's antics again. Did he owe it to Evarith? The man had saved him, but anyone with a shred of morality would have done the same. Could he let himself walk away without at least hearing what Evarith had to say? No, he couldn't. Plus, he was a sergeant and thereby permitted to interrogate Evarith—it might even give him more evidence to bring back to the emperor. *What's the worst that could happen?* Lothar left the inn and followed from a distance, watching as Deleok led Evarith into an unmarked building.

Lothar took a seat in the town center, figuring it was a good idea to wait before entering. He watched as Deleok and the other soldier left the jail and made their way toward the earl's home. Could Lothar trust anything that Evarith said? Would this questioning only lead to Evarith spouting lies and half-truths?

Once the guards had disappeared, Lothar stood up and walked over to the jail. It was a building made of rotting wood and rusted nails that looked like it might topple over any minute. He pushed open the front door and breathed a sigh of relief; Evarith was the only prisoner there. The man had stuck his hands outside the metal bars of the cell and was fiddling with the lock, trying to pry it open, it seemed. Upon seeing Lothar, Evarith's eyes grew wild, and he rushed forward, grasping the bars of his cell in desperation.

"Lothar, you have to let me out of here! There *was* a bomb!" cried Evarith.

The memory of a similar cry flashed through Lothar's mind. He was the one locked up then, pleading for Evarith to let him out before the castle exploded. How likely was it that Evarith was correct again?

"Lower your voice! Where's the bomb planted? I can't just evacuate the whole town."

"It *was* at the inn, but I suppose they moved it. Maybe to an important building? Or maybe it's just in a different part of the inn," guessed Evarith, a pained expression on his face. "If you don't let me out, I could be sentenced to life in prison! For a crime I didn't commit."

"But you *are* here illegally!" argued Lothar.

"Yes, yes, but—listen, I know things now that I didn't before, and I *need* to be let out of here! If anyone gets injured by the bomb, I can help them! You know my strength!"

To Lothar's knowledge, Evarith hadn't explicitly lied to him before. Did that mean he could be trusted? *If it would save lives...* He found the key on the wall and unlocked the cell quickly. After Evarith retrieved his belongings, the two rushed to the inn, Lothar's heart beating unnaturally fast.

"Everyone, this inn may explode! Please evacuate!" shouted Lothar, feeling that the words coming from his mouth were someone else's.

"What's that man doing with you?" cried an inn guest.

"Do you want to live? Get out!" screamed Lothar back. "Head for open ground, it could be in any building!"

As most of the inn guests rushed out of the building, Lothar and Evarith headed back into the street. Suddenly, they found their path blocked by six town guards, likely the entire force of Harolin.

"Lothar, what in the name of Talen are you doing?" cried Deleok, brandishing his daggers. "You're causing mayhem and consorting with the enemy!"

"I trust that there is a bomb—"

Lothar covered his ears and cowered with everyone else in the street as a deafening boom broke through the air, screams following soon after. The explosion came not from the inn, nor any other building along the street, but from the town center. The place where many Harolin citizens congregated after evacuating their homes.

"Oh, that's not good," gasped Evarith.

"By the deities!" Deleok cried, running off with the other guards toward the destroyed area. He shot Lothar one last glare, leaving him standing with Evarith, his feet rooted to the ground.

"We have to get out of here!"

"Yeah? And why should I leave with you?" Lothar backed up and faced Evarith.

"You want to stay here? Why? To be taken prisoner and sentenced to death for treason? You broke me out of jail!"

"I'm sorry for doing that then!" Lothar turned toward the town center and began running, intent on fixing whatever damage he'd caused with his reckless trust.

"Be sorry all you want! It's prison or freedom."

Lothar paused and turned toward Evarith. "We need to help people!"

"Look! Hardly anyone's hurt!" yelled Evarith, his voice barely audible over the shouting. He gestured back toward the town center, where dozens of faul paced around in a panicked state. Only a few guards were tending to injured civilians—the rest were trying to calm the crowd. Evarith approached Lothar, coming within a yard. "Come with me. Say you were tracking me down—I don't care. They won't find me. But, if you care even a little bit about those who died at the Akarist, you'll come with me!"

Lothar glanced around; the crowd was no longer focused upon the human in a faul town. "Fine."

As Evarith started sprinting toward the walls of the town, Lothar struggled to keep pace. At the end of their path was a stone wall; the town exits were in the opposite direction.

"That's the wrong way! The gate's over there!" Lothar gestured behind himself, but Evarith did not glance back.

"We're not taking the gate! They'll be blocking it!"

Lothar had no idea what Evarith was talking about but continued to run—he had no other choice. How could he be running from the law? He was supposed to be a soldier of the crown, uphold the law, and arrest criminals like himself. *Traitor*. The word echoed in his mind. He was a traitor. The thought caused him to stumble and almost fall. If he took Evarith in as a prisoner, would anyone believe his story? Could Lothar still get out of this?

Evarith ran toward a lower section of the wall, about ten feet high, and leapt, grabbing the top and pulling himself up. Lothar stopped short in horror.

"I can't do that!"

"Yeah, I know!" Evarith pulled out a length of rope and dropped one end down. "Tie it to you somehow!"

"Where?" He heard footsteps from behind—the guards must have seen them running.

"To your ankle, for all I care!"

Lothar gripped it tight in his right hand, wrapped it around his wrist, and prayed to Talen it wouldn't come free. When Evarith yanked the rope, Lothar felt as though his arm would be torn out of socket. He gripped the rope with his other hand, supporting himself as best he could. As he neared the top, Evarith grabbed his torso and pulled him up. Crouching on the narrow wall, he unwrapped the rope from his bruised wrist and turned his gaze to the ground below.

"I have to jump down?"

"Unless you want to stay up here forever . . ." said Evarith, jumping down and rolling as he hit the ground.

Lothar swallowed as he gripped the ledge and kicked his legs over the wall, holding on to the top for a second before letting go.

"Ow!" His legs buckled beneath him, and he fell to the grass.

"You're fine," said Evarith. "Now run, the guards will be after us!"

"Where are we going?" asked Lothar, shaking off the pain in his legs.

"To Valea."

"To Va—What?"

"Just follow!"

LOTHAR

"Stop!" said Lothar, stumbling to a halt. "I deserve answers, now!" After jogging for the better part of an hour, Lothar suspected they were quite close to the border. He would *not* enter Valea.

"Fine." Evarith turned around and glared at Lothar. He didn't even seem remotely out of breath.

"I broke you out of jail, show some gratitude," panted Lothar, bracing himself on his knees.

"I suppose you want to know why I was there in the first place?"

Lothar nodded, wishing the world would stop moving beneath his feet.

"I didn't trust you. What was I going to bring back to the queen? Almost nothing besides the descriptions of a few attacks, and the word of a random faul that the Shalin Empire was not involved. That's poor, very poor evidence. Then what? Everyone would disregard your word and we'd all blame the Shalin Empire and possibly go to war. I was already at the border, so why not go deeper into the Shalin Empire and spy on you, maybe some government officials, perhaps the emperor himself. I could gain *actual* evidence, uncover the mystery."

"You dare—"

"But I was wrong. You spoke the truth."

The dizziness passed and Lothar stood, staring at Evarith in shock. *Is he actually displaying . . . humility?*

"You see, when I was scouting out that town, I realized staying at the inn could be a fantastic way to gain information. My short stature allowed me to blend in quite well this morning, and I had no issue listening in. Then I heard a commotion and stood to investigate. Behind the inn, in a concealed little nook, a human and two faul were pouring bluish-looking explosive powder into a wooden box. The same that I saw in the Akarist. I couldn't react before the faul alerted the guards, and the human hid with the box. I don't know where he went, but I recognized who it was. Gillan."

Lothar's stomach dropped. "The one who rescued us . . . You mean—"

"He's part of some third-party bombing group blowing up all these buildings for some reason. To cause chaos, to rebel against the government, I don't know. This group consists of both faul and humans. On our way to the Akarist, our campsite was attacked by a group of bandits. I captured two of them, one human, and one faul. But they refused to tell us a word about their plan or their leader."

"If they were able to delay your arrival to the Akarist... even make you miss the meeting day entirely... by Talen... It would look terrible. More bickering or even all-out war. But why?"

"I already said, I don't know."

"Why would a human risk being seen in Harolin?"

"The town? Well, maybe if he was seen running from the inn as it exploded, they could blame it on a human. More chaos. The people are angry, Lothar, and both countries will blame the other for these explosions. If war isn't declared, uprisings or revolutions may occur. If it is, that won't go so well either."

"So, I'll just go back home and tell the emperor?"

Evarith laughed without humor. "No, not going to work. We don't have evidence, and while Queen Gladia might believe me, I doubt you could say the same about your emperor. Everyone in that town thinks we caused the explosion."

"Talen's sake... I suppose these bombers must have thought the inn would clear out once you accused them, so they moved the bomb to the open."

Evarith nodded. "They only had one bomb though, and it was too small for the town center. An inn will collapse and crush everyone inside if a beam is destroyed, which doesn't take that much force. When they blew up the bomb in the open, the only thing it did was throw some shrapnel."

"Why do you think Gillan and Elvine rescued us from the rubble?"

"Maybe Elvine wasn't part of the bombers. Maybe they wanted a couple servants to spread the word of the tragedy and incite more anger." Evarith threw his hands in the air and let out a long sigh. "I can only theorize."

"Alright so you implicated me to explain your little theory, for what?"

Evarith sighed and began pacing, an angry demeanor about him. "I don't know. I would have passed out in the heat of the dungeon without you, and you broke me out of jail, branding yourself as a traitor. You were going to let yourself be caught and sentenced if I didn't convince you."

Lothar crossed his arms "What'll you do now?" A part of him suspected an ulterior motive. Or did Evarith really just want to save him? The man didn't seem like the type, but Evarith's actions had surprised him before.

"Go home. Await further instruction from the Queen. Or..." said Evarith, eyes lighting up. "I could investigate."

"Wait—you still want to spy on us?"

Evarith stopped his pacing and faced Lothar. "No, not on the Shalin Empire. On these bombers, raiders, whatever you want to call them. Find them, eliminate them. If they're not stopped, they won't relent, I suspect. I like my job, Lothar, I don't want a war or rebellion or whatever comes of this."

"You'll stop this alone?"

"No... I was getting to that. I'll need more insight, more knowledge, and more access. I'll need a faul."

Lothar stood, mouth agape, figuring he had misheard the proposal. He stared at the ground and ran through the words in his mind again. "You would *want* to work with me? Why?"

"Want is a strong word." Evarith grimaced. "But I suppose so."

Lothar said nothing. By doing this, he would really be a traitor. If seen working with Evarith, there was no way out. He would be throwing out his long-held loyalty to his beloved country, the one he had served faithfully since he was eighteen.

Lothar eyed Evarith, sizing him up. His own daggers hung by his waist, and he could use magic on a whim, while the human only had a small knife. He could defeat him and take his job back, his life. But could he live with himself? Evarith hadn't actually committed any crime besides being in the Shalin Empire... besides concerning himself with the safety of Anzelon. He could have run away as soon as Lothar let him out of jail, but he was genuinely concerned about the bomb and the people it might hurt, even if they *were* faul. Evarith wanted to avenge those who died at the Akarist. He and Lothar were the only two with the knowledge they had. How could he let chaos and mistrust reign when he had the power to fight against it? Lothar looked into the cold eyes of the man who he not only resented, but who had also saved his life.

"I have a condition: we each gather a few friends. An informant, or soldier, or something like that. We don't know how extensive or powerful this group is. We'll need as much power and knowledge as we can get," asserted Lothar.

Evarith glared at Lothar for a long moment; the man's jaw was clenched, and his eyes narrowed. "*Fine.* If you insist. A maximum of three others—I want to travel light and fast. Only people you would trust with your life."

Lothar nodded. "Agreed. Where should we meet up again?"

Evarith thought for a second. "There's a town in Valea close to the border—"

"I'm not going into a Valean town."

"Just to the more rural area by it. No one will see you."

Lothar pursed his lips in frustration and let out a breath. "Where is it?"

Evarith pulled out a map from his pocket, showing the immediate area around the Akarist. Lothar leaned in to see; just to the left of the now-destroyed castle was the town of Lypeth. Evarith drew his dagger and Lothar jumped back, drawing his majoril dagger in response. Evarith rolled his eyes and stabbed a hole through the map, marking the spot where they would meet, and held the map out to Lothar. "Here. Make sure you have camping supplies for as many people as you bring. We're not staying at inns."

Lothar sheathed his dagger and took the map, meeting Evarith's set, determined gaze.

"I'm trusting you, Evarith," he warned.

"I know."

11

Melkin

After an eternity of walking, Lypeth was finally in sight. Melkin had started to doubt his knowledge of the area and had given his only map to Lothar. The main roads were clear enough though, and he no longer bothered to hike through the tall grass plains. He kept his identity concealed by pulling his hood over his head. Only three people from the ruins knew his face, and odds were good that he wouldn't run into them. And if he did, they might not want him dead, considering they'd helped rescue him. Still, he kept a hand near his dagger beneath the folds of his cloak. He wondered if the 'rescuer' who had given him the weapon took part in the murder of almost a hundred people.

From what he had heard along the main roads, no more survivors had been found. Messengers jogged along the paths, carrying bundles of parchment and envelopes, alerting the nearest towns and cities. But that was it. A rather small reaction for the enormity of the event. He recalled the explosion of Thalen's castle in Annister, where soldiers and medics rushed in from the city and beyond to tend to those who were injured. Now, there was nothing to be done.

Taleek was dead. Haern was dead. The servants who were concerned for him—a cold man who evaded conversation and didn't belong in their ranks . . . they were gone as well. He felt sick remembering their last moments and how he could've told them to run. He hadn't. And they were gone. Melkin purged the melancholy from his mind; ruminating over the past wasn't going to get him to Lypeth, or the capital, any quicker. He knew what to do now. Or at least, he had an idea.

Lothar's condition that he be able to recruit more faul was a steep ask. So much so that Melkin had almost denied it, almost sought out a different faul to get information from. But he didn't think anyone else would have agreed to help him, at least not without some form of persuasion. Either way, he was committed now. The only people he would trust were back at the castle in Hileath. It would take him five days at least to get there and another six or seven back with them. Maybe he would just stay at Lypeth until Lothar returned and not gather anyone else. But would three or four faul want to follow the lead of a human? Melkin shook his head. No, he would need to recruit a few others, if only to make sure he led the investigation.

When he reached the northern gate of Lypeth, he was famished and parched, but knew he had to keep his guard up. For the time being, he planned to keep both the news of his presence at the Akarist and his survival from the public. For a while longer, he would keep his disguise up.

"Don't you know what's going on out there? No travelers at this time," said a guard, barring the entrance with his spear.

"My name is Evarith, and I come from the Akarist. You can confirm it with the two soldiers who remained in town, if you wish. Their names are Vallec and Atlia."

Melkin leaned on the fence as the alarmed guard retreated from the gate. Despair filled him; he might not get a moment of rest for a long time. A while later, the guard came back with a red-eyed, disheveled Vallec. Upon seeing Melkin, his jaw slackened, and his eyes went wide.

"I can't believe it... Yes sir, that's him." Vallec and the guard rushed to the gate and let Melkin in. "How—By Ryne... are you alright?" asked Vallec, putting a hand on Melkin's shoulder.

"I'm alive." He brushed the hand off. "I could do with some water."

"Yes, of course. You'll tell us both what happened?" The gleam of hope in Vallec's eyes made Melkin feel sick; he would only be tearing the man's hope into tatters

Melkin nodded as he entered the storage building; it looked quite similar to how the party had left it three days ago. Atlia was standing by the doorway and gasped at the sight of him—she dropped her satchel and clasped both hands over her mouth.

"Get some water," ordered Vallec softly, and Atlia dashed into a back room as the men sat on the hard, wooden chairs. Melkin put his elbows on the table and rested his forehead in his hands.

"Are there any others?" asked Atlia, flashing a look of concern at Vallec as she set down a jug of water and took a seat. Melkin hesitated for a second before raising and shaking his head. Vallec and Atlia shared a look of deep sorrow; tears welled up in the woman's eyes and Vallec stared at the table, his face out of view from Melkin.

"Except for a faul," he amended. His throat felt like sandpaper—each word was painful in more than one way. He was exhausted in body and mind from everything that had happened over the past few days. *Was it only days?* It felt like weeks.

"Please, tell us the everything." Atlia's voice was somber, but calm.

"I'm not a servant," he sighed, "as you two probably know. I was sent by Queen Gladia to investigate the Shalin Empire's dealings with the bombings."

"A spy."

"Yes." For some reason, he felt guilty speaking the words. He took a large sip of water, preparing himself to recount his experience. Describing each detail in full, he told the story beginning with the departure from Lypeth and ending with his escape from the ruins with Lothar. Vallec and Atlia remained silent during the entire story, rapt.

"By Ryne... So, you came back after that?" asked Vallec, incredulous.

"No. I need you two to swear that you won't reveal what I'm about to tell you."

"Evarith . . . we can't do that. We're going to have to report to our general once we get back," said Atlia, not meeting Melkin's eyes. She balled her hands into tight fists, then loosened them with a swallow. "It's our duty."

"Fine." He might as well leave now anyways. There was no time to waste. He drank the remainder of his water and stood to make for the door.

"Wait," said Vallec. "You tell us, and if we agree that secrecy is merited, we won't tell anyone."

Melkin turned back. He didn't need to tell them, but a part of him wanted to. With a deep breath, he leaned back against the wall and told them of Harolin, his jailing, and his partnership with Lothar—including their plan. Again, the two listened intently, only speaking after he finished the story.

"What if it *is* the Shalin Empire though," mused Vallec.

"No. Attacks in both countries, the Akarist explosion, the humans and faul together, it can't be a government thing. I'm going to stop it," Melkin asserted. He began to pace, stopping as he realized his mission may still be in jeopardy. "What are you two going to do?"

"Not tell anyone," Vallec replied after a moment of hesitation.

Melkin breathed a sigh of relief and resumed his pacing—he needed to clear his mind and focus on the mission at hand.

Vallec shook his head in incredulity. "I—I can't believe . . . An— and you're sure you want to bring a faul into our country?"

"Yes. Do you have any money lying around?"

Vallec pointed him in the direction of a small coin purse, which Melkin promptly grabbed and then left the building without another word. Melkin noticed the townspeople spoke in whispers, shuffling around with haste and fear. His own fear was borne from a different cause. Again, he walked around the town while keeping an eye out for the warriors who'd jumped him four days ago. Taleek and Haern were there to save him then. He took a breath, clearing the gloom from his mind and entered the small general store. It was filled to the brim; all manner of things were stacked in every open space Melkin could see. Dried food, traveling supplies, and even alchemy materials filled the shelves; and that was just what he could identify on his way to the shopkeeper he'd spotted upon entering. Still gripping his dagger beneath his cloak, he approached the woman.

"Do you have any tents?" he asked.

The lady seemed to cower in fear—Melkin realized with a start that he had been glaring. He took a breath and relaxed a bit, easing his brow.

"Yes . . . over here." She hastily gestured at a bin just behind her. "You can pick out whichever ones you'd like."

Melkin walked over to the pile of tents as the shopkeeper stood to the side and started rummaging through them. They were all too bulky to carry on one's back.

"Any linens?" he asked.

She pointed him in the direction of some oiled linen cloth, which would do fine. It was getting cold this time of year, so he'd use it as a mattress and blanket of sorts. With his remaining money he also bought a map, a spear, and some dried food. He would have no time to cook a hot dinner—he had to move as quickly as possible, especially since the journey back to Lypeth would be considerably slower. It was a meager supply, but he would buy better tents, food, and camping supplies in Valea's capital city, Hileath.

He returned to the storage building, where Vallec was pacing with his spear in hand. As Melkin closed the door behind him and set down the empty coin purse, the soldier's head snapped up.

"I want to help you." Vallec planted the butt of his spear against the wooden floor, his face set.

"I'm leaving for the royal castle right now."

Vallec glanced around. "So? I'm ready to leave."

Melkin paused—he'd known Vallec for two weeks. And yet, he'd saved Melkin's life once already. Could he trust Vallec simply for that?

"Please." Vallec's shoulders dropped, and his hard expression softened into one of sadness and desperation. "I—I'll go mad if I just sit around instead of avenging my friends' deaths."

Melkin pursed his lips, considering the offer. Vallec *had* shown an unwavering loyalty toward Taleek. He hadn't forgotten the tall man's fighting abilities either. "Join me when I return. I must get to the capital, and I'll be faster alone."

Vallec looked a little hurt, but pursed his lips and nodded, nonetheless. "I'll be here, I swear. Do you want to take any of the horses?"

Melkin had forgotten about the horses they had left at Lypeth, but having one would certainly make the journey quicker. "Yes, thanks."

"Good luck," said Atlia, staring at Melkin with solemn eyes. Nodding his thanks, he approached the door and grasped the handle.

"Evarith," said Vallec, catching Melkin's eye as he looked back. "Be safe."

He kept a walking pace with the horse until out of sight of Lypeth, then urged the mare into a canter. The forest was only a day and a half away, so he wasn't too worried about tiring the horse out in the few hours that remained until nighttime. Traversing the dense underbrush of the forest would be slower on a horse than on his own feet, so he'd have to turn her loose at the entrance anyway. Melkin decided he would avoid the main roads that the Akistaria party had traveled. Now, more than ever, they would be bustling with messengers, which meant bandits galore.

What would the capital be like when he returned? He was quite sure that news of the Akarist would reach by then, so the city would likely be in an uproar. Gathering troops for war took forever, but such an egregious act as blowing up the Akarist might spark some haste. He prayed he could get an audience with the queen, but without any evidence, she might be persuaded to think the Shalin Empire was behind it. On the other hand, if she believed him . . . he might not have to enact this scheme. The thought lifted his spirits as he rode on past dusk. Only once the sky became as dark as the Akarist dungeon, did he stop for rest.

As he laid out his linen near a stream where the horse could drink her fill and graze the fresh grass, Melkin's thoughts turned to the dungeon for the thousandth time. Guilt ate at him as he once again remembered the precious minute in which he had paced back and forth in front of Lothar's cell, not saying a word. He had been too afraid to cause mass panic where no danger lurked. How in Anzelon did that cowardly action warrant *his* survival and the deaths of everyone else? He was sure that Vallec and Atlia wished for their commander to walk up to the Lypeth gates instead of himself, and he couldn't blame them. Melkin closed his eyes and imagined a dozen tents, scattered around little cook fires, and forty-five humans chatting cheerfully to break the ubiquitous night silence. He swallowed his guilt and sadness; only three of the forty-five voices would ever be heard again.

Four and a half days later, Melkin blinked, bleary eyed from his long days of travel, to make sure the city in the distance was not some mirage brought about by desperation or exhaustion. *Thank Ryne.* The city of Hileath had never beckoned to Melkin as it did now. For a moment, he wondered if he would make it before he collapsed from exhaustion. He took a deep breath and began to gather all the remaining strength he had. Failure was not an option. He had to make it to Hileath, then back to Lypeth. Then to wherever in Ryne's name their mission brought them. The thought of so much travel when he was already so tired brought on a wave of depression that he couldn't give in to. Instead, Melkin focused on the city in the distance once more and continued to put one foot in front of the other.

Hileath was a city of stone; great towers loomed over the stout buildings that sat beside wide stone walkways. So deep in the heart of Valea, there were no walls around the city, though it bustled with soldiers keeping guard. The city sat in the center of a triangle formed by the largest military academy in Valea, the royal castle, and the Palzar river trading port. Thus, it was never empty, never quiet. It was not the wealthiest city in the nation, but as Melkin set foot on the stone walkway, he was comforted by its familiarity and warmth. A similar size to Annister but infinitely more inviting to Melkin than that horrible place. He had lived here in the city for a while before moving into the royal castle. Glancing to his right, he saw the silhouette of the intelligence academy against the setting sun, its stone battlements and pillars all too familiar to him.

He searched the depths of his memories for directions to an inn he used to visit late at night while enrolled in the academy. It had good food, a needed contrast to the free academy meals, and an open, inviting air.

Once again, a memory of Taleek flooded back into his mind, from when he'd forced Melkin to rest after the campsite was attacked. He hated wasting more time, but it was as necessary now as it had been then. A short walk later, he opened the door to the small, cozy inn and paid for a room and some water. He collapsed in the bed and fell asleep.

Thankfully, the bustling inn woke him before the harsh glare of the sun could. He left within minutes of waking up and took the main path from the city toward the royal castle. With all the soldiers and travelers along the roads, he could relax his vigilance a bit and not worry about pickpockets or getting robbed. Though the royal castle was visible from the city, the path leading to it was over five miles long. At least he *could* see it. A slight fear that had begun to build within him eased at the sight. It was still standing, it wasn't destroyed.

As the familiar granite towers and halls came into focus, relief filled him at finally being home, but it was quickly replaced by fresh guilt that no one else stood there with him. So many would never return, never see this castle or their homes, again. Melkin walked with his hood pulled over his head in secrecy—he would not reveal his return until he could speak with the queen. And if she would not acquiesce to his plan, if she could not believe that there was some mystery organization out there, he would need to approach the others in secret. He knew they would listen to him, but would they believe him? As far as he knew, neither were Shalin sympathizers. The Valean people as a whole despised the Shalin Empire—would *anyone* believe him?

The guards traversing the roads near the castle wore grave expressions, and those at the entrance let him in wordlessly when he pulled down his hood to reveal his identity. Only those in the meeting room that day had known that he went to the Akarist, so he was relatively unconcerned. For all anyone knew, he had been on some other mission of Queen Gladia's and had just returned. He walked through the open portcullis, listening intently to the conversations as he passed, but hearing nothing of importance. Unnoticed, he made his way toward the east wing staircase and took it up to the second floor, where he entered his room and closed the door.

Melkin sat on his bed for a few moments, head in his hands. He wasn't quite sure what to feel. Sorrow, dread, anxiety, longing? Journeying to the Akarist, he had yearned to be back here, back to his job. It felt like years since he'd last been sitting at his desk. He rubbed his face with his hands and got up off the bed. All he needed to do was complete this mission, not wallow in grief.

He changed out of the filthy servant clothes and into his lighter outfit he typically used on his missions. It was getting cold out, yet the high-quality fabric would keep him warm better than the stiff wool he'd had to wear as a servant. Instead of putting back on the cloak given to him at the ruins of the Akarist, he donned one from his stash instead and left for the throne room. The castle seemed emptier than usual, and those who walked the corridors did so with bowed heads. Melkin registered all the grimaces and solemn expressions of those he passed on his way; the news of the Akarist must have weighed heavily on everyone in the castle.

"Melkin. You're back, I see," said one of the grim-faced guards outside the open throne room doors. Melkin peered inside, but the queen was nowhere to be seen.

"I must speak with Queen Gladia. It is urgent."

"She's not seeing anyone right now," said the guard. His voice was quiet, and he refused to make eye contact. The same fear he'd had about finding the royal castle destroyed started to grip Melkin again—his instinct told him something was very wrong. The guard, Melkin could see, was attempting to hide pain and wariness behind a stony expression, but the façade was weak.

"Go on."

"Queen Gladia . . . is deathly ill. She may not make it."

Melkin opened his mouth, but no words came out. Nausea built inside—was this a coincidence, or something more? He turned and fled down the stairs. Fareod . . . no . . . the words that he'd said in that meeting replayed themselves in Melkin's mind. She had to hold out. Queen Gladia . . . she was made of iron—she would not give up.

He arrived at the door he had sought but couldn't remember finding his way through the corridors—his mind was filled with grief and confusion. After knocking, Melkin stared at the ceiling for a few moments, which felt like eons, before the door opened and

Leina raised an eyebrow at the sight of him. He was sure he still looked terrible, even after the change of clothes. However, a small grin appeared on her face.

"You know, I did find it hard to believe that you had died. It just didn't seem right."

"It was quite a close thing, Leina."

"Well then how *are* you alive?"

"It's a long story, but I need your help," he said, walking into the room. Leina shut the door behind him as he sat down on a chair.

"Sure, what do you want me to do? Who am I sweet-talking this time?" she asked with a grin.

Melkin felt a twinge of annoyance; he hadn't traveled half the length of Valea to recruit this bubbly, carefree version of Leina. Everything was at stake—how could she not know that? "I assume you know the state of the Queen?"

Leina's smile vanished in an instant. "Sorry."

"You don't even know why I'm here."

"That's why I asked."

"The short version is that there's an organization that wants to cause chaos in both Valea and the Shalin Empire. They're behind lootings in the Shalin Empire, the bombings in Valea, and the destruction of the Akarist, the casualties of which I assume you are already familiar with. If you come with me now, we can stop them as well as whatever plan they have. With the Queen ill, things are even more volatile than I thought them to be. I have no tangible evidence, but if this group isn't stopped, chaos will reign. It seems they want to make Valea and the Shalin Empire angry at each other for atrocities that neither were responsible for."

Leina scoffed. "So... you want me to believe that the Shalin Empire *didn't* assassinate the queen's advisors and twenty specialized soldiers?"

"They lost theirs as well."

"They could have miscalculated the range of the bomb."

"Yes, I know."

"Alright, I believe you, of course, but you still haven't told me exactly what you want me to do. Do they have a headquarters you need me to infiltrate?" asked Leina. Melkin could tell she was suppressing a grin.

"No, I—I don't know anything about them. I just want you to come along. Your skills will be needed at some point."

"At some point?"

"Yes. Leina... I trust you, alright? There's no one else I trust more." It was true, but admittedly, not saying much.

"What did you do with Melkin?" laughed Leina. "I've never known you to seek help by choice."

"Maybe this is something I can't do alone." He wasn't sure she would agree if she knew the full reason.

"Alright then, I suppose I'll come with you. It really is quite boring here, you know? Just going over those papers again and again, and with the queen out of—"

"Leina, you could die."

She shrugged. "Yeah, I know. Are you trying to talk me out of it now?"

"No, I—alright, come with me," said Melkin with a sigh. The two of them left her quarters and started toward the stairs. "I have someone else I want to recruit."

"Well, I'm flattered to be your first choice."

Melkin rolled his eyes. "Get serious, Leina."

"What, am I not allowed to make light of the situation?"

"It's not really the appropriate time."

"Says who? And who is this... other person?" asked Leina, miming air-quotes.

"Galdur."

She raised her eyebrows in shock. "Why do you want *him*?"

"I trust him... somewhat. Don't you trust me, Leina?"

"Of course."

"All will be explained shortly, then. I know what I'm doing." He ignored Leina's eye roll as the two reached the royal quarters—giant suites, almost like palaces in and of themselves that housed the members of the royal family. He approached the double doors to one of them, silently cursing the absence of door labels to indicate whose room it was.

He hesitated for a second, fist inches from the door. He didn't technically need Galdur; he already had two people. But the prince, while very likely a burden, could also be quite useful. And with the recent assassinations and Fareod's play for power.... No, he *had* to convince Galdur to join him.

"Don't you dare enter Fareod's room," muttered Leina.

"Wouldn't dream of it." He knocked on the door and held his breath. It was opened by a red-eyed Galdur, who stared at him in shock.

"Hey Galdur..." started Melkin. "I need your—"

Leina stepped in front of him, cutting him off. "We're so sorry to bother you right now, Galdur, but do you think we could come in for a minute to discuss something with you?" She spoke at a relaxed pace, each word laced with sympathy. Melkin had to resist rolling his eyes at the change of character.

"Ye—yeah, you two can come in," stuttered Galdur, wiping his eyes and closing the door after the two had entered. He barely glanced at Melkin as he dropped into his chair and held his head in his hands. Melkin remained by the door as Leina sat down in one of the ornate chairs near Galdur.

"I can't imagine how you feel right now, and I'm here if you want to talk about it."

"Thanks Leina. I'm—I'm alright for now, I think." Galdur blinked and turned to Leina, focusing on her words. "I hope she'll recover just as fast as she fell ill. May—maybe I'll wake up tomorrow to her beaming smile and warm hug. Ryne, I hope so."

The two sat in silence for an infuriating amount of time. Maybe he shouldn't have let Leina take the reins on this conversation. "I know these past few days have been extremely hard for you, Galdur," she said. "Not only one, but two pieces of devastating news. Unfortunately, we also need to talk to you about the other."

Melkin pursed his lips, fighting the impatience that was building up inside of him and consciously worked to keep himself from pacing. He started tapping his foot—with each passing minute, war edged closer.

"Melkin requests your help with a mission he has now. An extension of your mother's orders, you could say." That wasn't quite true, but Melkin suspected that Gladia would approve, nonetheless.

"What could you need me for?" asked Galdur, looking at Melkin seriously; all the lightheartedness in Galdur seemed to have gone. The young man he'd known a couple of weeks ago was already so changed. What would happen to him on this journey? Melkin swallowed, guilt welling up inside of him at the request he was making of the prince. He cleared his throat and stopped tapping his foot.

"I want you to come with me, to wherever our mission leads us." He told Galdur everything he had told Leina.

"Why not tell my brother or the guards?" asked Galdur.

Melkin looked him in the eye—he needed to get the gravity of his next words across to Galdur. "You know the answer to the former." He watched Galdur process his words, then swallow and dip his head just slightly. "To the latter, I don't want this to become public knowledge. This is an extremely covert mission and may be best for your own safety as well. As I said—assassinations. You may be *second* in line to the throne, but you're still in line."

"So... you want to protect me by bringing me into this life-threatening scheme?" There *was* a hint of humor still alive inside of the grieving prince.

Melkin shrugged. "You have some skills we could use as well. Are you coming or not?"

"...I'm not sure about the skills part, but yes, of course. If you think I'll be of use and that my mother would approve of it, that it will help avoid war, then I'll follow you." Galdur stood up and leaned against the wall, closing his eyes with a sigh. "But... by Ryne... why does everything fall apart at once?"

"I know what you mean, Galdur," muttered Melkin. "Gather anything you might need."

"Just my spear... Do you want me to bring some money?"

Melkin had a few spare coins in his room, but not nearly as large a collection as Galdur. He nodded. "That would be great." A few minutes later, the three of them left the royal quarters and headed down the stairs. Odd looks were thrown their way from soldiers and servants—the young prince with his spear and two renowned spies were quite a sight. Melkin elected not to tell Galdur that his disappearance would look suspicious in more ways than one.

"I don't like the idea of the castle guards seeing us three leave together," Leina said after the three had entered her quarters so she could grab her own things.

"Can you order them to not question us?" asked Melkin, looking at Galdur.

"I'm not sure... I don't think so, because of my age and the circumstances here. They would need a reason."

"Can we make something up?" Melkin asked, glancing between Leina and Galdur. Galdur just shrugged and turned toward Leina, who looked deep in thought.

"I can't think of a good reason for the prince to leave so suddenly... especially in these circumstances," Leina admitted, packing her bag of supplies.

"Don't worry then, I have another way. We're going to *my* room."

A short while later, the three entered Melkin's study.

"I can't believe you're not taking your spear," grumbled Melkin, glancing at the dagger that now hung at Leina's side. It looked like a similar length to Lothar's larger dagger.

"Why do you care? I can fight better with a dagger anyway."

That wasn't saying much, but Melkin figured he'd be better off keeping that to himself. He rummaged through his storage chest and pulled out throwing knives, an assortment of cloaks, and a large coil of rope.

"Make yourself unrecognizable," he ordered to Galdur. Luckily, the prince was already wearing ordinary clothes, as he usually was, but the Hileath people knew his face well.

"Put your hair up," suggested Leina, handing Galdur a short black ribbon. He did so and donned one of Melkin's finer cloaks.

"Good enough," said Leina.

Melkin tied the rope against the bedframe, the heaviest thing in his room.

Understanding lit Leina's face as she approached the window to look below. "I see."

"No..." whispered Galdur.

"Yes," said Melkin with a grin.

"Wow, Melkin is *smiling*!" Leina bounced on her toes and grinned mischievously. "He must really enjoy your fear."

"You can't climb too well, can you, Leina?" asked Melkin. He had to expedite this process before Galdur could back out. There was no time for jokes.

"I'll be fine with a rope."

"Obviously. I meant the wall."

"Then no, I would prefer not to climb that."

Melkin drew a throwing knife and peered at the edge of the window where it met the stone frame. He pressed his knife against the sealant, but it was too hard to cut through.

"Stand back," he ordered, picking up his spear and driving the blunt end into the window with all his might. It cracked but did not shatter. *Well-made windows, the enemy to every intruder, or escapee.* Again, he hit the window, and the center broke away, falling to the grass two stories below.

"Are you sure this is a good idea?" asked Galdur. Melkin glared at him. "Right, dumb question."

After a few minutes, he had cleared most of the glass, taking extra care at the bottom of the window where the rope would lie.

"Let's hope no one heard or saw that. Leina, you're first," he said, throwing the coil of rope out the window. "Watch out for the shards of glass on the ground. I'm climbing down without boots, so see if you can clear away some of the pieces as well."

"Won't I be recognized once we leave?" asked Galdur.

"Just act natural. Keep your gaze averted and your hood up. The guards only care about those exiting from the main doors. We'll just walk into the city and beyond," said Leina, crawling out the window. "We're at the back of the castle, so no one will care."

Melkin kept his hands on the rope just in case the bed frame was too light. The rope pulled tight and jerked a couple of times, but soon the weight lessened—Leina had reached the bottom. "Your turn," prompted Melkin, giving a slight nod to Galdur.

Glancing back at Melkin with a nervous look in his eyes, Galdur placed his hands on the windowsill and put one leg over.

"Just make sure to grab the rope once you get your other leg over."

"Really? I had no idea," retorted Galdur, kicking his left leg out. Melkin smirked at the sarcasm, glad the prince could summon more of his typical humor, if only to distract himself.

A moment of fear struck Melkin as he watched Galdur hold on to the windowsill with only his fingertips. Then, he felt weight shift to the rope and heaved a sigh of relief. Killing the prince would not be good. Melkin wondered if Galdur really *did* have a better survival chance on this mission than he would have in the castle. Certainly, climbing a rope would not be the most dangerous obstacle encountered on their journey.

Once Galdur was down, Melkin untied the rope, gathered it back up through the window, and re-coiled it, putting it neatly back in his storage chest alongside his other possessions. Donning his throwing knife sheaths, he made sure his room looked like it had before he arrived. If anyone came into the room, the broken window would be the only thing out of place. He clipped his boots to his belt and grabbed his spear, throwing it to the open ground before vaulting over the windowsill. The stone here was much smoother than that of the Akarist, much harder to climb. At the Akarist, he'd wanted to come home and scale this castle, to reach the top and see what it was like on the roof of the tallest tower in all the lands. Unfortunately, that would still have to wait. Once he was back on solid ground, he slipped his boots back on and grabbed his spear.

"Let's go."

12

GALDUR

"Hey!"

"What?" he grumbled. He'd been staring at the ground, reliving recent memories of his flight from the royal castle and the reasons he'd done so. His mother lay dying, yet he'd abandoned her.

"I asked if we could have some of that money you brought," said Melkin, waving a hand in front of him. Galdur wasn't surprised to hear annoyance in the man's voice. He must've had to repeat himself.

"Sure," he said, taking a shaky breath. He pulled out a handful of gold coins from a purse around his waist. He had been leaning against the inside wall of a Hileath general store while Melkin and Leina shopped for camping supplies. Melkin took a few of the coins from his outstretched hand, and Galdur put the rest back. He shivered in the cold of mid-autumn; there was a lit fireplace in the stone-walled shop, yet the chill breeze came in strong through the open doorway. A minute later, Melkin and Leina returned with a few satchels of camping supplies, and four compact tents.

"That's it?" asked Galdur, regretting the words as they left his mouth.

"Yes, let's go."

A sense of dread filled him; the journey ahead would be far from comfortable. He missed his carriages and bed already. It seemed like a torturous trick, Melkin bringing him along. What could *he* do? Nothing that neither Melkin nor Leina could do, that was for sure. If they just wanted money, he would have gladly given Melkin as much as requested. So, why was he recruited—taken away from his mother when she needed him the most?

For the first time, he truly thought about the danger that he might face and felt foolish for accepting Melkin's offer. There was only one thought that comforted him. When Melkin had that steel in his eyes, he was scarcely wrong. There was only one other person who he trusted in the same way, and she was lying on her deathbed. Galdur tried to block the memory that rushed into him, but he was carried away as if by the tenacious flow of a river.

Galdur was sitting on one of the chairs in the family room of the castle. He fidgeted with a loose thread on his shirt while he waited for the medic to return. Fareod sat beside him, yet neither looked at the another. His heart was beating rapidly. It had not slowed a beat since he'd heard of his mother's sickness, since he'd glanced upon her frail, weak figure—so at odds with her usual appearance. It felt like years before the medic entered with his verdict, but Galdur suspected it was only a half-hour. The door to his mother's room closed with a sinister creak as the man approached.

"Your mother is alive for now, but she has been stricken with a strange malady. I can hardly find similar records in my books. My best guess is that she contracted something when Annisik Castle exploded. Perhaps her wounds became infected, though they looked normal to me—"

"Can you do anything about it?" asked Galdur, cutting off the speculation.

"I'm not sure. I'll tend to her, but I can make no guarantee that she'll live," said the doctor, standing up. "I cannot say that it is even probable." With that, the man left.

Galdur put his head in his hands and stared at the floor. He heard Fareod stand up and slam the door on his way out as Galdur continued to sit and stare at their mother's door for another million years.

Galdur shivered as the memory moved through him, but at least it didn't seem like Melkin or Leina had noticed he'd spaced out. Melkin picked up a discarded newspaper before they left the shop, but news of the Akarist had not been printed yet. Oral versions of the explosion had spread throughout the city as if it were a disease, though. Most conversations that Galdur overheard as the trio made their way through Hileath led to the same conclusion: The Shalin Empire. From what he could hear, the news of his mother's condition had not left the castle. The three hardly said a word to one another as they neared the outskirts of the city. Melkin seemed content to let him and Leina speculate over where they were going. For now, they traveled along one of the many pathways that extended out in a dozen directions from the city to the various important sites and buildings.

"Shouldn't we get horses?" asked Leina as they walked away from Hileath.

"No, we're going through the Halarain Forest, and not by the main paths."

"And you don't want to ride around it?"

"We'll get through it faster if we walk; there might be a city or town that sells them near our destination."

"Most likely not, but I can't ride anyway," said Galdur. Melkin turned toward him with a raised eyebrow but said nothing. "Where are we going, anyway? What *is* our 'destination?'"

"Wait until we're further away," said Leina softly. Melkin nodded in agreement, continuing to lead the trio at a quick pace. Though Galdur, tall as he was, could keep this pace for now, he dreaded a day's worth of walking so fast. Especially through the dense Halarain forest, which they were sure to reach by tomorrow.

An hour later, they were out of earshot of any farmers or laborers around the city and had begun walking through a small grove. Galdur appreciated the silence and calm of the almost deserted forest they were traveling through. It felt good to be surrounded by nature, away from the city that seemed to be simultaneously solemn, angry, suppressed, and hectic.

Melkin sighed before he spoke, breaking the silence. "We're meeting the others in Lypeth."

"Where's that?" asked Leina.

"North," said Melkin dryly.

"So I had gathered."

"On the border. Valea's side," said Galdur, without thinking.

"Yes, that's correct," Melkin said with a moment of pause. Like there was something else he wasn't saying.

"What others?" asked Leina after a pause.

"Well, Lypeth—Lypeth was the town that we all stopped at. Before going on to the Akarist," said Melkin slowly, this time without his former dry tone. "We left behind two soldiers, one of whom agreed to help me upon my return with you two."

"Just the soldier, then?" asked Leina.

"No. There was another survivor. He and I investigated a bit after the explosion to confirm what I told you two earlier." Melkin paused for a moment and pursed his lips as he looked around at the forest. Galdur wasn't sure he would like where this was going. "He's a faul. Of the Shalin Empire. We . . . decided that it would be beneficial to both our countries if we worked together."

Galdur tripped over his feet and had to steady himself on a tree. *What?*

Leina stopped in her tracks and Melkin turned around to face the two of them. "With a *faul*?" she exclaimed.

"You . . . trusted him with our affairs?" asked Galdur, caught between his respect for Melkin and concern for his country.

Melkin rolled his eyes, crossing his arms over his chest. "They don't want chaos either. They don't want whatever this group of bombers wants. He knows things about the Shalin Empire that might be useful in the hunt for these terrorists. He seems quite good at magic, and he knows people."

"He knows people? You mean you're having him recruit his friends too?" Leina was nearly shouting now.

Melkin just raised an eyebrow at her, his voice irritatingly calm. "Are you afraid of them? Just don your normal disguise, Leina—like always. You've consorted with more dangerous folk."

"Why didn't you tell me before?"

"Would you have refused?"

"Maybe."

"You said you trusted me."

Leina paused for a moment. "I don't think having them around Galdur is a good idea."

Galdur had to agree with Leina. He didn't like to villainize the faul, but they could easily assassinate him, especially if Lothar was as powerful as Melkin claimed.

"We won't tell them. I have no qualms about Lothar, though— the one who survived with me. I may not read people as well as you do, Leina, but I'm sure that he is honest. I ordered him to only recruit people he absolutely trusts, so if he follows through, then you will have nothing to worry about. In any case," Melkin turned to look Galdur in the eye, "you may refer to yourself as Galdur, no need for a different first name. Even Ravinyk is probably a foreign name to the general faul population."

"Alright then," said Leina. Melkin began walking again. Galdur and Leina looked at each other with wary glances and followed. "So, we're picking up this soldier and then what?"

"The rest will arrive near Lypeth. The soldier's name is Vallec, by the way. He and Atlia—"

Galdur barely heard what Melkin was saying, for he was just beginning to realize what consorting with faul meant regarding his status. "Hold on—you're asking me to illegally harbor faul in Valea? Me, the *prince*?" He was shocked by this more than anything else.

"What did you expect, to chat across the border line? If you go into the Shalin Empire, you're also a criminal."

Galdur gritted his teeth. He had *expected* not to work with faul in the first place. But he couldn't turn back now, and he found that he didn't want to. Still, the idea of being a traitor did not sit well with Galdur, especially if Fareod—No, he couldn't think about that right now. Galdur took a deep breath. The faul could very well turn out to be helpful on this mission—perhaps Melkin's judgement was right. Plus, if any of them threatened Galdur, Melkin and Leina were sure to defend him.

"Let me ask you this, Melkin," said Leina. "You say you trust Lothar and Vallec?"

"Mostly. At least not to betray me."

"What did you tell them your name was?"

Melkin sighed. "Evarith."

"Ah . . . I see how it is."

At last, Galdur finished setting up the compact tent. Thank Ryne he'd finished before the orange sun finally dipped below the horizon. The tents were rather intuitive to pitch but required precision to keep the lattice structure from folding over on itself before all stakes were in place. Though Melkin and Leina had pitched theirs within minutes, it took Galdur nearly an hour. He wrapped himself in one of the thick woolen cloaks they had bought, noticing that neither Melkin nor Leina seemed to need theirs. Without the pleasant warmth of the sun, Galdur felt significantly colder and even more miserable than he was before. He was about to crawl inside his tent for some warmth before Melkin approached him.

"Come here, you're going to learn how to make a fire."

Galdur followed Melkin a few yards away and crouched down beside him. Though he was freezing cold, the chance to learn a useful skill was exciting. In his hands, Melkin held a stick and a twelve-inch hunting knife.

"You take the knife and run it down the stick, making these curls," explained Melkin. "Then, you find various sizes of sticks to build the fire. I've already done so, but next time you'll do the entire process."

Galdur looked at the intriguing stick with dozens of thin curls running down the side. "What do I start it with?"

Melkin pulled out a piece of black rock and struck it against his knife once, twice, three times before the curled pieces of wood caught flame.

"Now we just gradually add larger sticks until a nice sized fire is burning. Not too big though, because we don't want to attract attention or burn the forest down. It's more of a safety precaution in case any of us get dangerously cold," explained Melkin, beginning to add twigs to the small flame.

"Nice to know it's not for a hot meal . . ."

"Get used to it. You can take first watch tonight. Wake me up when the moon is about there," said Melkin, pointing to a spot in the sky, "and not a minute earlier, understand?"

"Loud and clear," said Galdur, instantly forgetting where Melkin had pointed. He sat down on the ground, his weary feet glad for a respite he was sure Melkin and Leina did not need. He added small sticks to the fire, wincing as the flame licked his hand. A short while later, he had built the fire to a size he assumed Melkin would deem suitable. He felt Melkin could have been a little more specific in his instructions, but perhaps that was the point; he wanted Galdur to figure it out himself.

He looked around, watching to see if Melkin had retreated into the shadows and was watching Galdur from afar. He saw no one but hardly trusted his own eyes against Melkin's shadowy figure. What had he been ordered to do? *Oh, right—take watch.* Pulling his hands away from the warmth of the fire, he stood up and leaned against a tree. He squinted, attempting to peer into the powerful darkness of the forest, but the light from the fire had blinded his night vision. There was absolutely no way that he would see an intruder, especially before they saw him. He sighed; he had to stay awake either way. Melkin had ordered it.

13

Lothar

Lothar glanced at the soaked, grimy wanted paper before tossing it back onto the street where he found it. The words he read, however, stuck in his mind.

"... faul by the name of Lothar Raiken wanted for the bombing of a small border town ..."

He pulled his hood further down over his head, staring at the ground as he traversed the city paths. If he turned himself in now, could he convince his superiors of his innocence? Could he reverse the damage that had been done? To himself maybe, but to the Shalin Empire? He purged the thought from his head once more, for the thousandth time. The poster was a stab in his chest. It wasn't in the newspapers yet, but it would be soon. There was a sketch of him at the castle and it would soon be retrieved, replicated, and shown to soldiers all over the country. It wasn't even much of a stretch to think the faul who had blown up the town square had blown up the Akarist as well. He shivered in the cold and summoned heat, careful not to draw any attention to himself in this crowded city. At least Emperor Orwic didn't seem to be completely blaming Valea yet, or it would be plastered on the covers of every newspaper in the Shalin Empire.

The wanted poster also visually described a human who had apparently helped Lothar set the bomb—Evarith had never revealed his name to the guards. Lothar suspected that even with a perfect sketch they would not find him in any corner of the lands. As for himself, he didn't exactly blend in with the common folk, clad in gambeson and armed with daggers as he was. In fact, he looked quite like a guard, meaning civilians wouldn't question him, but other guards might wonder what an unfamiliar face was doing in their midst. He walked at a brisk pace, trying his best to not draw attention to himself with any suspicious behavior. At least he had already bought food for the walk ahead of him, a two-day trek to Pyantir, where the military school was. He had taken a carriage from a city near Harolin, to the city he was in now, Elepic, cutting the journey down by a significant number of days. The accounts of his crimes had spread slower than he'd walked, but during the journey, fear of recognition never abandoned him. As he left the thick of the city, he summoned more heat to surround him, hoping the incessant rain would stop soon.

An hour later, he was walking through the plains of the Shalin Empire. Though he worried less about being captured here, he was increasingly despondent by the absence of companions. He yearned for the company of the powerful faul he loved and respected. Especially Captain Yulac, whom he had looked up to for the past eight years. Everyone had died thinking he was a traitor. Lothar felt nauseous—he *was* a traitor.

Walking the narrow alleyways of Pyantir, Lothar found that he barely remembered which house he was looking for. He felt confined in the close quarters between the tall wooden buildings, especially after crawling out of the collapsed dungeon only days ago. But he had to admit that it was easy to get lost and stay hidden from any searching guards. The crime-ridden, dirty alleyways of Pyantir were extensive, making up most of the sprawling city. Though it was the Empire's capital, it was certainly not the richest or largest city in the country.

He listened intently for any shuffling feet, but the city was quiet, consumed by darkness. *Why is everything so intimidating at night?* He saw the place he was looking for across the street and breathed deeply, letting his fear out in a slow breath. Just as his nerves lessened, a fresh pang of fear hit him—hopefully she hadn't been called to service, or worse, ordered to hunt him down. Keeping as silent as he could despite his shaky limbs, he crossed the street and climbed the outside stairs to the second floor of a two-story housing complex. He hesitated for a moment before conjuring up the courage to knock on the door. The shriek of metal sounded from inside as a blade was drawn from its sheath. *At least she's home.* The door opened, revealing a short faul whose eyes widened at the sight of him before narrowing in anger.

"As—" He was pulled inside the house and slammed against the wall, cutting off his next words. She had an auxlar dagger pointed at his throat before he could even think about retaliating.

"Come to turn yourself in?" she shouted, pressing the dagger to his throat.

"Astrid!" he gasped, flattening himself against the wall to avoid the sharp blade. "I need your help!"

"Why would I help a criminal?" she spat, leaning in closer to him.

"Please, just listen to me, Astrid! You'd really believe a poster over your friend?"

She hesitated for a moment, keeping a firm grip on Lothar but making no move. "Fine." She took his daggers one at a time from their sheaths and tossed them on the floor before removing her dagger from his throat. He doubled over, panting as the fear dissipated, but the shakes remained. Astrid stood with her arms crossed. "Speak."

Lothar slid down the wall to the floor and began. He told her of his appointment to the Akistaria league, the murder, his imprisonment in the Akarist, his escape with a human, and finished with his arrival in Pyantir. It took almost half of a precious hour, but he wanted Astrid's help and he couldn't hope to win her over if he withheld anything. During his story, Astrid had loosened her grip on her dagger and sat in a chair near the door. Lothar hoped this meant she believed him.

"I see." The scowl she had worn throughout the conversation had disappeared by the time he'd finished. "I—we were to arrest you if we saw—"

"I know. But the reason I came here, Astrid, is because I trust you."

"You do?"

"Yes. I want you to come with me on this mission." He told her of Evarith and his plan.

"You want me to join you on a suicide mission?" asked Astrid with a raised eyebrow. "This plan . . . it's insane. Evarith has no idea where to go, who to look for. Nobody does."

"I understand. You don't have to come along," said Lothar, reaching down to pick up his daggers. He wasn't sure if Evarith would want a random soldier knowing all that she did now, but he couldn't force her to join him.

Astrid turned and paced for a few moments. "I . . . don't know, Lothar," she said, clenching her fists.

Lothar nodded. "I don't blame you." He wasn't going to force Astrid to join him—she'd experienced enough hardship in her few years as a soldier. Still, a deep pang of disappointment rang within him. He could have gone to any soldier from his regiment, but all held extreme hatred for Valea. Though Astrid had fought against humans at the border, the letters she'd written to him over the years proved her hate for the war. "Do you think—Can I sleep here for the night?"

"Sure. You don't mind the floor, do you?"

"That's fine."

Astrid gathered some blankets for him, and he laid down in the corner while she retreated to her room. Sleep came easily to him; the wooden floor was a nice improvement from the cold, rocky earth.

A little after dawn, Astrid woke Lothar and suggested that he leave. "I assume you have somewhere to be, but if you want to stay here longer, I don't mind."

"No, you're right," said Lothar, standing up. "Thank you for everything."

"So, you *are* leaving now?"

"Afraid so. I *do* have to get moving," said Lothar solemnly as he stretched his aching muscles. His legs were just as sore as they'd been a week ago—the constant walking ensured that. Luckily, the pain in his ribs from nearly being crushed between stone slabs had lessened a bit, and his bruises no longer pained him with each movement. Still, he didn't feel that his body was quite ready for the miles upon miles of traveling ahead. He laced his boots, picked up his satchel, and started walking toward the door.

"Do you think that if you and Evarith stop this . . . group . . . could there be peace?"

Lothar turned around and sighed. "Peace? I don't know. But maybe we could avoid an all-out war if that's what this is coming to."

"Well, I've thought about it a bit . . . and I really have nothing to do here. I'll join you."

"Are you sure?" Astrid's fear was well-founded. They might not succeed and there was a very real possibility of death.

"Yes. Where are we going?" She donned her gambeson and strapped her daggers around her waist.

"The military headquarters. I'm recruiting Imar as well."

"Who's he? And should I resign, or leave a letter, or what?"

"Imar is the historian and investigator on domestic threats. And . . ." Lothar thought for a moment; Evarith didn't tell him what those he gathered should do. "No, we have to leave immediately, unnoticed. Resigning will only draw attention to your absence. Thank you, Astrid. I—I'm really glad to have your help." Lothar felt tears well up within him again; he was overjoyed to have someone by his side after days of loneliness.

She shrugged. "How do we get into the military headquarters? You're wanted."

"*You're* not."

Two hours later, Lothar leaned against a tree in the small, dense forest that was next to the military headquarters of the Shalin Empire, praying to Talen that he blended in with the trees and foliage. Even without the added weight of his criminal status, anyone who spotted him would regard a strange faul hiding in the trees as suspicious. He peered through the brush, awaiting Astrid's return with Imar.

The forest wasn't often occupied, but any minute a soldier might wander through, see him, and arrest him.

Talen's sake, was he actually longing to be in Valea? Where he didn't have to fear his own people, but the enemy instead? He took a deep breath, clearing his head of the grim thoughts. He trusted Imar, and he wasn't sure if he could do this without the older, wiser faul. Indeed, Imar deserved to know the truth, or at least the beginnings of it, about the group he had pursued for so long. He blew the air out of his lungs slowly, trying to ease his pulse. Lothar had nothing but admiration for Imar's persistent efforts; what would he say upon hearing the story? He glanced to his left and started—Astrid was walking with Imar toward the forest. He breathed a sigh of relief; she had convinced him to meet out here, to hear him out. They approached Lothar's hiding spot, and he stepped into view. As Imar's eyes fell upon him, the faul stopped in his tracks, a wide smile growing on his lips.

"Lothar!" he whispered loudly.

"I told you he was here," said Astrid with a dismissive wave.

"Yes . . . I had hoped it was true but even so . . . I'm so glad to see you alive, Lothar. I knew the things they said about you couldn't be true. But why are you here?" Imar came up to Lothar and wrapped him in a tight embrace. When he stepped back, Lothar drew Imar and Astrid deeper into the forest and once again recounted his story.

Imar listened eagerly from his seat on the forest floor. Though the faul was almost a decade older than Lothar, he lit up with the kind of curiosity that usually vanished in adulthood. His facial expressions were open and obvious—the faul had likely never told a lie. After he'd finished, Lothar watched as Imar shook his head, the faul's keen mind processing the shocking information.

"By Helinka . . . So it's not been Valea all along . . . I can't believe it."

"Will you help us?" asked Lothar.

"Will I help you? Of course I will! After years and years, this is my chance to understand . . . . But where will we be going?"

Lothar paused for a moment. "It will be dangerous . . ."

"All the more reason to not let you do it alone."

Lothar grinned. "Get everything you want from your quarters; you're not coming back soon. Tell someone you found a lead and are leaving on an expedition to find evidence of Valea's involvement in the Akarist tragedy. That should put the government off for the time being."

"I'll do just that," said Imar, turning away and leaving Astrid and Lothar alone in the forest.

Lothar stood for a long while, his body unmoving while his mind worked to figure out if there was a faster way to return to the border than the way he'd come. Astrid leaned against a tree a few yards from him, silently watching him think through their next step.

"Once we leave here... we'll be safe," he muttered absentmindedly.

Astrid responded with a dramatic eyeroll. "Yeah, *right*."

Lothar turned toward her, letting a small smirk creep onto his lips. "One can hope."

"Sure. You know, you asked Imar and I if we're prepared to go on this dangerous mission and whatnot, but are *you*?"

"Of course," said Lothar, again without thinking. He was, wasn't he?

"Okay." She nodded, her tone genuine. "I just wanted to be sure."

Another half an hour later, Imar returned with an auxlar dagger and pack of supplies.

"Where's the other dagger?" asked Astrid, glancing at the short blade in Imar's hand.

"I only have an auxlar dagger. Perhaps we could buy a majoril on our way?"

Lothar nodded. "We'll have to buy camping supplies anyway. But let's get moving, we can't afford to waste any time. Evarith may have traveled a great distance for his companions, or maybe not. I suspect he won't want to wait for us."

"Didn't *he* request *your* help?" asked Imar.

"Yes, well... I had to convince him to let me gather companions. If you knew the man, you'd understand my haste."

"Indeed?" asked Imar, grinning. "And why is that?"

Lothar sighed. How to describe the enigma that was Evarith? "I would say he's annoyingly selfless and frustratingly arrogant." He thought back to Evarith's scowls, sarcasm, and calculated actions. The human was surprisingly intelligent and had gone to great lengths to save Lothar—for the simple reason that he was a person who needed help. Or was it because he wanted Lothar to help him on this grand mission?

"You mean for the wrong reasons?" asked Astrid.

"Sometimes. And sometimes . . ." he trailed off.

Imar chuckled, watching the expression on Lothar's face. "I see. I am eager to meet him."

"Tell me if you're disappointed or not." He imagined Imar's grinning face next to Evarith's cold one.

"Oh, I will. But you never answered me earlier." Imar grinned and raised an eyebrow at Lothar. "Where *is* this meeting place?"

Lothar sighed and pulled out the map Evarith had given him. He unfolded it and pointed at the hole made by Evarith's dagger. "Right there."

Astrid furrowed her brow. "I'm not too keen on going into Valea. Again."

"Neither am I, but that's where we're going," said Lothar, sighing again. "Ever been there, Imar?"

"Nope. But hey, it'll be a new experience!"

Lothar shook his head in wonder at Imar's joyous expression. "That's one way to look at it."

They trudged on through the small forest before emerging in view of Pyantir once more, this time from afar.

"I suppose we're not taking any of the main paths," mumbled Imar as the three of them began walking through the knee-high grass.

"Just be glad we're not going north," said Astrid, nodding her head toward the eternally icy region.

"Indeed, I am," said Imar. "You've been?"

"Oh yes, a few times."

"Why?"

She shrugged, looking down at the grass. "Born there."

"So, you said that you transferred from the active military to the passive guard," said Imar after a few moments of silence. "How's that going?"

"Eh, it's pretty boring. But better than the alternative."

"The military?"

Astrid nodded slowly. Suddenly, her eyes lit up. "Do you two know how to ride horses?"

Lothar and Imar shook their heads. "No, do you?"

"Yeah . . . I hoped for a minute that we could get there sooner if we rode horses. They're sold in Pyantir."

"They don't teach it in training since it takes too long to learn," said Lothar.

"Where did you learn?" asked Imar.

"Just . . . as a child," said Astrid softly. "I remember now—they took that part of the training out. I think they wanted more soldiers for the border," she said, gritting her teeth.

"How do you two know each other?" asked Imar, breaking another few moments of silence.

"Yulac . . ." said Lothar, a pang of sadness hitting him. "He had me scout out any people that I thought would be a good fit for his battalion. Must have been about . . . three years ago? Well, I asked Astrid if she would join, but she declined since Yulac's battalion is mostly peaceful and doesn't often interact with humans. We stayed in touch, though."

"Except for when I was at the border. Which was most of that time."

"About half of the time. And I did write you letters."

"Yeah. That was nice, but it didn't make up for everything that happened there."

Lothar nodded, tremendously glad that he had never ended up there. He had heard stories, mostly from Astrid, and had no desire to take part in the destruction.

14

LEINA

Leina squinted, trying to see past the early morning haze. Behind her, Melkin, Galdur, and Vallec were starting a fire in a shallow cave, setting up a sort of meeting ground for the faul's arrival. Melkin had ordered that she watch for Lothar and the others, so she paced back and forth, bouncing on her feet in anticipation of seeing a faul for the first time. Then, a spot in the distance piqued her attention; the silhouettes of three figures, walking toward them.

"I see them," she said, turning back. Melkin squinted from his spot by the campfire, then walked up beside her. "I don't. Are you sure?"

"Yes."

Not a minute later, Melkin caught sight of them, too. He nodded at her and waited for their approach. Leina unhooked her crossbow from her belt and loaded it.

"What are you doing with that?" asked Melkin.

"Preparing to defend Galdur if needed. Or myself."

"They don't know what he looks like. You're being paranoid."

"And you've never been paranoid about anything, *Evarith*?"

"Speaking of which, I intend to keep that as my name for now," reminded Melkin for the hundredth time. He had already told them that Vallec didn't know his name and that he wanted it to remain that way. Leina followed suit; she had given Vallec her last name and intended on doing the same with these faul.

In another minute, Lothar and the others were fully visible, and Leina studied the blond-haired, light-skinned faul. One of them was older and taller than Melkin, towering over the other two faul. *Unusual.* The middle one looked to be over five feet tall with a mass of shaggy hair on his head. Last, a short female faul walked beside the two, her long hair pulled back in a braid. While the two males appeared wiry and frail, she looked quite strong—and angry. Leina bit back a laugh; her fears *were* unfounded. How could these creatures pose any sort of threat?

The three faul approached, and Melkin walked in front of Leina, face-to-face with the middle faul.

"So, who are these that you've brought?" Melkin glanced at the other two faul, a disapproving glare on his face. A strange reaction, seeing as he was the one to organize all this. Leina frowned. Melkin was also more lenient, more forgiving of the Shalin Empire than most people in Valea were. Perhaps Lothar, who must be the middle faul, had refused to help unless he could bring along companions? Yes, that would make sense. Satisfaction and disappointment filled her at the realization, but she shoved them aside; the full story would be revealed soon, one way or another. She stood back and waited in anticipation to see what the faul would do.

Vallec stepped up beside Melkin. Leina suspected he would intervene before Melkin could ruin the meeting too quickly; he seemed to be more diplomatic.

"I was about to ask the same." Lothar eyed her and Vallec, but with a look of genuine interest rather than reproach.

The older faul's gaze flitted between the four humans, then to their makeshift campsite in the distance. "Could we warm up by your fire, perhaps?" he asked, spreading his hands in a gesture of peace.

"Yes, come." Vallec beckoned toward the campfire. Leina leaned against the stone wall of the cave while the faul entered without a word, glancing at each other nervously. Galdur was sitting in a sort of concealed little corner of the cave, looking like he was trying to melt into the walls. Lothar stood beside Melkin while the other two faul sat by the fire.

"So, assuming that Lothar briefed you two on why you're here, do either of you have any questions before we get started?" asked Melkin, breaking the silence.

"You're Evarith?" asked the tall faul, a slight grin on his face.

"Yes."

"Perhaps we ought to start with everyone's names, just for future reference?" suggested Vallec, sharing a smile with the tall faul. "I'm Vallec, soldier of the late Commander Taleek's brigade."

"Imar, historian of domestic threats."

"Lothar."

"Galdur."

A silence emerged, and eyes fell upon her. "Kierth."

"Astrid."

"Well, that was extremely informative," said Melkin, his usual sarcasm seemingly amplified by their new company. "Now, on to business—"

"Wait. You never told Galdur and I the full story."

"Yes, I'm aware. We shall recount it again. Once more."

Lothar must have already told the two other faul since neither seemed too interested in the details. Of course, Melkin had kept the story a secret from her and Galdur. Pushing aside her frustration, she listened intently to the story, considering the details she had been so keen to hear for the past week. No, since she had been assigned these never-ending cases on bombings in Valea. This might be her chance to hunt down the people who had been the bane of her existence for the past few months. As the story was revealed, her mind worked to connect the dots. *Blue gunpowder?* She had to figure out what they used in their bombs. *Faul and human working together?* It opened up a whole new avenue of questions but made a great deal of sense. Oh, this was far more exciting than her work back at the castle.

" . . . If nothing is done, chaos will reign over both our countries. Our queen is ill, and I suspect more assassinations. Your country, so I hear, has lost a great deal of funds. So in short, we may carry the fate of Anzelon."

Imar chuckled, looking at Melkin. "No pressure."

Melkin only stared back with furrowed eyebrows, dampening the moment of lightheartedness. "Now that we all know everything, our priority is to locate these people. These bombers. Any ideas?"

"We could go back to the ruins. Maybe they're still there," said Lothar.

Leina scoffed. "If they saw you and Evarith back there, they would know something is happening. The longer we can go with them still thinking they rescued two docile servants, the better."

Lothar sighed. "I agree, but it's better than nothing."

"*Nothing* might not be our only other option," said Melkin.

Imar leaned back against the cave wall. "You have a better idea?"

"That's why we're *here*, isn't it? Where might they be?" Melkin studied everyone in the room; he really needed to soften that glare of his.

"Anywhere, right?" said Astrid in a low voice. Though she wore a scowl similar to Melkin, Leina was taken aback by her soft tone. Or perhaps it was apathy.

"Well, how big do we think the group is?" asked Leina.

"They must have immense funds and resources, considering how spread out they are and how many bombs they've created. But we don't know how many people," said Melkin.

"Well, if they were in the Shalin Empire and Valea at the same time, probably a lot," said Imar who sat staring into the flame.

"Couldn't the robberies and bombings be unrelated?" asked Astrid.

"Yes, but what they're doing costs a lot of money," said Melkin. "That's the genius of it all. The operation is so large-scale that only a government could *reasonably* pull it off."

Leina walked forward a few steps. "These bombs are on a scale never seen before. A newly built stone castle was ripped to shreds. An ancient castle thought to be indestructible was next. That's not just explosive powder, and it must cost a fortune, whatever developments they're making. Unless they're using magic, in which case—"

"They're not. Magic can't do that," said Lothar.

"Not even a team using their magic simultaneously?"

"No," said Imar and Lothar together.

"Not even someone extraordinarily powerful?"

"Please, Kierth, enlighten us on our own magic," said Astrid, crossing her arms.

Leina naturally kept her expression flat but was taken aback at the faul's sarcasm. "Hmm... Well, forgive *me* for trying to get anywhere with this conversation."

Imar turned to Astrid. "It's not worth it."

Astrid just shrugged, averting her gaze from the group.

"But anyway, the bombings and robberies aren't the only crimes I think they're guilty of," said Imar, facing the rest of the group. His now serious face was a stark contrast from his previously jovial one.

"Indeed?" Lothar raised an eyebrow, turning toward Imar.

Imar hesitated, then nodded. "Children have been kidnapped from orphanages, about thirty so far. No witnesses. No traces. We're dealing with masters in their crafts here."

"Right. I almost forgot," said Lothar, looking at the ground.

"But we have no reason to believe those criminals are part of this bombing group," said Astrid.

"In any case, if we assume that they're in both the Shalin Empire and Valea, where would the leader be?" asked Lothar.

"They may not have a permanent location," said Melkin.

"And so..." Lothar stood and stretched. "Going back to the ruins seems like the only option after all."

Leina began to pace back and forth. "They may not even be there."

"But they may," said Imar with an encouraging smile.

Astrid looked toward the humans. "Why are you afraid of going there?"

Melkin kept his tone cool, but Leina spotted the frustrated foot-tap he often did. "Afraid of wasting time. I don't have to explain why this chaos is bad, do I?"

"Alright, alright. There are plenty of rural areas in both nations where they could have settled down," said Vallec.

"Well, since these mass attacks have only been occurring recently, we could assume that they bought a plot of land not too long ago to set up a headquarters." Lothar looked far too excited for a rather trivial revelation, Leina thought.

"We can't trace every piece of recently purchased land," Imar pointed out. "We don't have the records, and it'd be a pain to track them down." Lothar's face fell.

"Fine. We'll go back to the ruins," said a very irritated Melkin.

As the seven walked to the ruins, Leina noticed how the faul were struggling against Melkin's unrelenting pace through the tall grass, constantly stumbling or tripping. She found the heavy panting from Lothar and Imar to be rather irritating to listen to, especially since it was almost the only noise between the seven. After an hour of walking with very little conversation, Leina could just see the outline of the Akarist in the distance, though the others were yet to spot it. Great stone pillars and walls jutted out from the ground, supporting nothing and surrounded by massive piles of black rubble. She suppressed her shock at the sight of the destroyed sacred building. She never believed the legends of Ryne's blessing upon the construction, but even so . . .

"By Oberel . . ." muttered Astrid.

"Evarith. You and I should stay back here," said Lothar. Melkin looked as though he were about to protest, but he gave in without argument and remained behind with Lothar.

"I'm staying back as well," said Galdur, joining Melkin and Lothar. Astrid raised an eyebrow at the declaration, yet she made no comment. Leina, however, suspected the prince was afraid of what he might see ahead. Without another word, Leina and the others continued on. As they neared the ruins, they saw that it was crawling with soldiers—faul and human alike—who paced about, their intent a mystery. Civilians, as well, crowded around the ruins; it was impossible to tell who might be a bomber. While Leina kept the pace that Melkin had previously set, the others began to drift behind.

"Come on. We have to go in further," said Leina, waving them forward. There was a decent chance that someone at the ruins could be useful to talk with, a lead in this impossible-seeming investigation.

Imar shook his head, glancing at Astrid. "No, we should wait here. Watch for people leaving the scene."

Leina grunted. "We won't be able to tell who they are."

"We don't know what they look like anyways. It's no use making ourselves more visible," said Imar. A fierce shout from the ruins stopped the bickering and brought their attention to the commotion. Spears and daggers were thrust into the air as soldiers, standing on top of the ruined castle, faced off against each other.

"No..." muttered Astrid, her breathing sporadic, a look of horror on her face, almost as if she knew what was coming.

"Faul scum!" The dozens of voices carried the sound to their ears. Leina wanted to look away, but she couldn't bring herself to. Scanning the landscape, she watched the civilians cower and run away from the ruins that were about to become battlegrounds.

"Valean bastards!"

"Abominations!"

"Talen's mistakes!"

"We have to leave!" cried Astrid.

"Who's afraid now?" asked Leina. Astrid whirled around, glaring at Leina with a deep look of hatred and placing a hand on her dagger.

"Stop." Vallec put himself between the two, brow furrowed in concern. Leina scowled—now was not the time for diplomacy. If they wanted to succeed in their mission, they couldn't afford to placate Astrid.

Astrid edged around the tall man. "You have *no clue*, Kierth. No clue at all. What are you, some delicate government official? Ever seen people die?"

Leina raised an eyebrow, not sure if she should be amused or offended at the insinuation. She wondered what Astrid would say to her should she recount the numerous deaths she'd witnessed, that she'd played a part in. Despite never seeing the fabled battles that ensued here on the border, she thought herself quite versed in the subject of death.

"Astrid, please," said Vallec.

"No, Kierth is going to get us killed if we stick around," said Imar, raising his voice. Now Leina was really caught off guard; the faul had seemed reasonable. *Why is everyone so daft?*

"We have a job to do. My commander didn't die for us to give up."

"We're not giving up, we're just making a different plan."

"We already talked about different—"

"There." Leina pointed in the distance, where around a dozen people were leaving the scene, camping supplies on their backs.

"They could be anyone," suggested Imar, squinting.

"Who would be out here, traveling at a time like this?" Leina clenched her fists in frustration.

"Why would they still be here, so long after it happened?" asked Astrid.

"Let's just follow them—why not?" asked Vallec. Imar nodded and left to get the other three while Leina kept her eyes trained on the group. As they walked parallel to the travelers, they stayed a good distance from them, hoping their presence would go unnoticed. Melkin and Lothar kept an even greater distance; they had no way of knowing if Elvine or Gillan were part of the group, but none of the travelers seemed to match the description she'd been given. Galdur left Melkin and Lothar and rejoined the other four, probably tired of whatever arguments Lothar and Melkin were having. The two would likely kill each other within the coming week, Leina thought. That was a problem for later, however.

"They'll notice us at some point," muttered Vallec, around a mile into the walk.

"Do you have a better idea?" asked Imar. *What an enigma!* A minute ago, he was protesting Leina's actions, now he supported them. Well, at least he had some sense in him. She supposed he was an anomaly in the faul world for his likeability. Perhaps she could bring him closer to her side...

Leina shrugged. "I mean... we could ask them where they're going."

"That's a terrible idea," spat Astrid.

"They outnumber us. If they were to attack, I wouldn't like our odds," Imar mused. Leina rolled her eyes; it seemed he would continue to tread the middle-ground.

"Kierth, be reasonable. Following is our best option," said Vallec.

"Not if they're irrelevant to our mission," argued Leina.

"We need you, Kierth. Please don't do anything rash." Galdur had a scared look in his eyes; he had kept almost completely silent the entire day. *Does he seriously still think these weak faul could harm him?*

"I'm not so sure about that first part." Astrid made no effort to keep the statement from Leina.

"Indeed?" Leina started walking toward the traveling group and felt a hand clasp around her wrist. She whirled around to see Astrid had a firm grip on her. The faul drew her smaller dagger as Leina tried to break free, to no avail.

The faul's grip was like iron. "You're not ruining this. We're against the odds as it is."

She leaned in closer to Astrid, trying not to show the fear that gripped her. Now, the faul were no longer a nuisance; they were a real threat. One that she'd overlooked earlier. "Let. Me. Go."

"Will you stay here?" asked Vallec.

Leina forced a deep breath, unclenching her muscles. "Yes," she lied. Astrid released her and she continued to walk with the group for another few hundred feet, all the while drifting to the back. Then, she slipped away.

"Talen's sake," Imar said, over a hundred feet from her already.

"Alert Evarith and Lothar in case something happens. We don't want to draw attention by restraining her again. It just made her angry." Leina clenched her jaw in frustration at Vallec's words. She wasn't being oppositional; she was doing what was right.

How could the others not see that they needed to do this? If they kept following, they could waste precious time on a false lead *and* anger this group of travelers. Then of course they would blame her for suggesting they follow them. She had no choice. Soon, the other four caught up to her, only a hundred feet from the traveling party.

"Come to insult me?"

"I wish," said Astrid.

"To prevent you from dooming us all." Vallec's words were laced with disappointment.

"Perhaps you've come to witness our salvation instead." Leina trusted her instincts; they steered her right far more often than wrong. She could plan all she wanted on her missions, but nothing was ever certain. As she'd learned long ago, what one did in those uncertain scenarios determined their skill as a spy. The five approached the group of faul—and was that a human at the back?

"Do you need something?" asked one of the male faul in the group. He put a hand on his long dagger, glancing between the members of the group. Leina paused for a moment—she hadn't thought this far ahead.

"Sorry to bother you, but have any of you seen any suspicious activity around here?" she asked, flashing a warm smile.

"Suspicious? No . . . What are you all doing out here?"

Leina kept a pleasant expression. "I could ask you the same."

The faul shrugged. "Sure. We're hiring people who might be interested in a mining operation in the far east. And you?"

"Trying to help those at the border who may be injured or hurt from recent skirmishes and events. Some semblance of order amidst all this chaos."

"How noble of you all . . ." said the faul, his eyes once again scanning the group. "Say, if any of you, particularly the tall man there"—he gestured at Vallec—"would like to come mine for us, we'd appreciate the help."

"Where specifically?"

"We can only reveal its location to those who agree to mine for us. It's a very . . . unique mine. Very high rewards for working there as well."

"We'll pass . . . but thank you for the offer. I wish you the best of luck in finding workers."

"And you all in restoring order," said the faul, grinning.

Leina turned away and began walking, the other four following. They met up with Melkin and Lothar who had been following a few hundred feet back, hoods pulled over their heads in disguise. Only once the miners were out of earshot did Melkin speak.

"You better have learned something invaluable from them."

Leina recounted the conversation despite glares from Imar, Vallec, and Astrid.

Melkin stared at her for a few seconds, his expression unreadable. "Now they know our faces. They were going east anyway, so nice job at revealing us."

Leina bit back her surprise and glared at him. "None of us had any way of knowing if they were bombers or not. And they could have stopped at towns on the way, slowing us down. You're welcome."

"We still don't know that. They could just be miners," said Lothar, shaking his head. Leina refused to feel embarrassed or be conciliatory. She had helped the group by gathering information—her *job*.

Melkin sighed. "No, they're the bombers." At everyone's looks of shock, he explained how he heard two women in Lypeth talk about how one of their husbands went missing in the east after accepting a mining job for some mysterious people. "So yes, they are most likely the people we are seeking."

"*And*," said Leina, glaring at the others, "there were a few humans in that group."

"You didn't know any of this when you walked up to them, though," said Lothar.

"It's done. What do you want from me?" Leina stepped a few paces in front of the group and turned to face the six, gesturing her arms at herself then opening them wide in a shrug.

"Maybe an apology? To admit you did the wrong thing?" said Astrid. *How could anyone be friends with her?*

"Well, you're not getting that. I've just saved the very core of this mission. I deserve thanks!"

"Thanks for disobeying the group and giving them faces to work off of!"

"Alright, enough. You're not children, it's done, lay off her." Vallec motioned for the seven to continue walking, and Leina fell back in step.

A long silence followed Vallec's interruption. She was surprised that Melkin disapproved of her actions; he knew she could talk her way out of it. Was he expecting a risk-free journey? Were *any* of them? She played the conversation back in her mind, recalling how he didn't sound too angry. Maybe he was glad Leina had disobeyed orders without having to approve of the 'reckless action' himself. Yes... to maintain his credibility—it made sense. Still, hadn't known him to be so adept at manipulation; that was always her specialty.

Of course, the three faul hated her now. *As if they didn't before.* From how Gladia and Melkin spoke of the faul, Leina had decided she would come in with an open mind; maybe what she'd been taught all her life was wrong. But no, of course it wasn't.

"But where exactly are we going? Just east?" asked Imar.

Astrid sighed. "There was . . . I remember hearing about a dispute over a plot of land bought a couple of months ago. A real rural area near the coast of some rocky region in the east."

Galdur's head snapped up. "The Dalyuben Hills?"

"Yes . . ." Astrid furrowed her brow.

"Out of curiosity, why do you know that?" asked Imar, a grin touching his face.

"I study maps a lot . . ." Galdur quickly stared at the ground, but not before Leina saw a tinge of red on his cheeks.

"Anyway," Astrid continued, "This . . . group wanted to buy the land, including a square mile or two of inhabitable coastline region to the north, but the few people who lived there protested the sale. The buyers had more money though, so the inhabitants were kicked out. One of my friends wrote to me about it."

"How far away are the Dalyuben Hills?" asked Melkin.

"Fifty miles, give or take," said Galdur. "But if you say the coast . . . that's a bit further. It's strange, though . . . I've never heard of any precious metals or resources to be found there. I mean, that's why most of it's not inhabited."

"We'll go there anyway," said Melkin. "We don't have a better lead."

"Yes, and we've endangered ourselves far too much already," said Lothar with a sidelong glance at Leina. She glared right back at him but said nothing. She'd already said everything.

15

ASTRID

After the fiasco with Kierth's insubordination, the group was mostly quiet for the rest of the day. That didn't matter; she was glad to have some quiet, to be spared from the incessant ramblings of humans. Astrid dropped her pack of supplies on the ground and fished out the tents they had bought on their way to Lypeth. It was a specially shaped piece of fabric with some stakes, an ingenious design. She started setting it up, often glancing around the campsite in spite of herself.

Each time her eyes fell upon the Valean soldier, she shuddered. The warrior look, the armor, it all brought her back to the border. They *were* at the border, she thought, the realization striking her for the hundredth time. Was there a chance the two of them had crossed paths before? Could he have had a hand in all the horrors she'd witnessed? His enormous traveling pack as well, seemed sinister. Did it hold poisons? Explosives? Weapons for the killing of faul?

Again, she tried to shake off the image of the soldiers at the ruins of the Akarist. Surely after they had left, people had died. There was no doubt in her mind about that—she had seen it happen before, endless times. Taking a deep breath, she finished setting up her tent, slamming a hefty rock into the tree-stake until it was firmly embedded in the wood. She tried to look at the positives: they were back in the Shalin Empire, she had Lothar and Imar... the list stopped there.

She marveled how this seemingly reasonable man, Vallec, could scare her more than the insane woman who had almost gotten them all killed earlier. Her eyes flicked to the girl. She was slight in build, energetic, and had needlessly long hair—definitely not a warrior. An entitled baroness, perhaps, or a government official. Someone who hadn't worked a day in their life and had never faced consequences for their actions. That girl wouldn't last a day in the military if she thought she could get away with going behind the group's back and taking matters into her own naïve hands. Yet here she was, a saboteur in their midst. *What a strange reality.*

"Galdur, start a small fire," ordered Evarith, his deep, harsh voice cutting through the silence of the campsite.

Turning her attention back to her present situation, her eyes fell upon the Valean tents. Larger, and made of sticks sewn into fabric that sort of collapsed into a bundle when the stakes were taken out. Set up, however, it formed an interesting lattice structure. She found them strangely intriguing; a small part of her wanted to walk over to one of them and take a closer look, figure out how it worked. *Ah well.* Instead, she turned back to her own tent and dug through her pack for some spare cloth to use as a mattress.

After the sun disappeared below the short treeline, Astrid suspected Evarith would probably set up a night watch shortly. He didn't seem like one to linger around a campfire at dusk; he would want the group to get rest and get moving in the morning. As Astrid sat in her tent eating her dried dinner rations, she glanced over at Galdur who was making a somewhat feeble attempt to start the fire. She had to stifle a laugh at the incompetent man's attempts to scrape a knife down the length of a stick. *Who is he?*

"Listen up! We're taking night watch in three shifts each night," announced Evarith.

Astrid looked up, meeting his eyes. Was he always so grumpy? How could Lothar have relinquished all power to him?

"You will have complete focus on your surroundings. Bandits, bombers, and two governments might all be after us at this very moment. I'll take the first watch, Astrid you're next, and Vallec you're last. Now get some sleep!"

Astrid crawled into her tent, eager to make the most of her meager sleeping time. She hoped Evarith didn't expect her to wake up at the proper time on her own, but what did she know about the strange man's expectations? She laid her head on the rough ground, plastered with jagged rocks and sticks. It felt like no time had passed since she was last here at the border. Except then, she was in a camp of people she trusted, people whom she could talk to. But that had only made it so much more painful. She felt a pang of sorrow in her chest at the friends who had died here. Before memories could once again overwhelm her, sleep stole her away.

Astrid felt a hand on her shoulder and jolted awake, reaching for her dagger before remembering where she was. She heard footsteps as Evarith scurried away from her tent. With a sigh, Astrid rubbed her eyes and crawled out of her tent into the cold night, shivering as the frigid air struck her skin. Evarith was nowhere to be seen; he had probably gone back to sleep by now. Astrid had no idea when she was supposed to wake Vallec, but figured she would make herself comfortable in the meantime. Grabbing the lowest branch of a nearby tree, she tested her weight and determined it was sturdy enough. With great effort, she pulled herself onto it, cursing her short stature. The fork of the tree was now within reach, so she climbed up to it and stood, grasping the trunk for balance. Now, ten feet off the ground, she had an almost clear view of the entire campsite. The fork in which she stood obstructed her view a little bit, but the fact that she could now see into the distance more than made up for it. A fair amount of moonlight illuminated the camp, showing the dim silhouettes of tents, trees, and a few small animals that strode about the forest.

"Clever, but you really should seat yourself up here," remarked a voice from above. Air left her lungs, and she almost fell out of the tree. Catching herself just in time, she looked up to see Evarith perched on the highest steady branch, overlooking the entire camp site.

"You—Are you trying to kill me?" She worked to steady her breathing and calm the rampant pounding of her heart.

"Quiet now, you'll wake the others. No . . . I am simply watching," he said, his voice calm and smooth.

"If you're so keen to be out here, how about I go back to sleep?" she asked. Who was he to spy on her?

"That won't do . . . How about you come up here instead? It really is a better view."

Astrid was wary but began climbing. This might be the worst time to fall and break a bone, but at least she could blame Evarith if she fell. She edged her way up the thinning branches until she reached him. His cloak blended him in with the shadows of the tree branches and leaves, making him almost invisible. Under Evarith's watchful glower, Astrid sat on a sturdy branch near his and gazed out at her surroundings.

"When do I wake Vallec?"

Evarith pointed to an arbitrary spot in the sky. "When the moon is over there."

"I can't see what you're pointing at, for Oberel's sake."

"When the moon is about halfway between overhead and the horizon. Haven't you done this before? You *are* a soldier, right?"

"We usually have four shifts. And how do you know that?"

"It's not hard to tell."

"Great. Now aren't you going to leave?"

She could almost hear Evarith roll his eyes as he descended the tree without noise. She breathed a sigh of relief, unwilling to admit that the shadowy man made her uneasy.

For a few hours, she sat up in the tree, watching her tranquil surroundings with keen eyes and ears. Once her muscles grew stiff, she descended to the ground and stretched her legs. Her military experiences were beginning to come back to her again, invading her thoughts like nothing else ever could. The peaceful nights, chaotic days, and small moments in between filled with the kind of comradery one only builds in war.

After the moon had reached the approximate location Evarith had indicated, Astrid walked over to Vallec's tent and nudged him awake. She then retreated back to her own tent, averse to any more socializing, and fell asleep within moments.

Her eyes fluttered open in the early hours of the morning to the sound of birds. After lacing up her boots, she collapsed her tent, folded it, and packed it in her bag. Vallec, the only other one awake, was stirring something in a pot over the small, rekindled fire.

Though the tranquil sounds of nature should have calmed her, they did the opposite, as if the current serenity foreshadowed something ominous. Astrid sighed audibly. She missed home. Pyantir was so far away. So far away.

"Wake the others," ordered a voice from behind her.

She whirled her head around—of course it was Evarith. He really needed to stop doing that to her or she might *accidentally* thrust her dagger in his direction.

"Why don't *you*?" She turned to meet his eyes as the man walked past her. Leaders were supposed to at least do something in the camp. It felt strange to argue with a superior, but she had never pledged herself to his command; she had no obligation to follow his orders.

"Just do it."

Astrid sighed and decided that now wasn't the time to fight; she did as he ordered and roughly woke the four others.

Without a word, but with a few exchanged glares for good measure, the seven gathered around the fire. Vallec had brought small bowls with him and doled out stew to each of them. Astrid took her bowl with apprehension, but soon realized how eager she was for a hot meal.

"Vallec, didn't I say to only take what you need?" said Evarith, eyeing his bowl of stew with suspicion.

"No, you didn't." Vallec had a smile creeping onto his face despite Evarith's glare.

"Then it was *implied*."

"Should have been more specific. And what do you care? I lug it around."

That's what his giant satchel is for! She fought back a laugh at the realization; perhaps Vallec wasn't so bad. At least, not compared to the other humans. While they were eating, Evarith explained the moon locations that signaled the end of watch shifts to the group. Galdur seemed very interested, but Astrid nearly rolled her eyes; she was positive the lecture only happened because she had pointed out Evarith's lack of forethought.

"—and again, I expect full attention on the surrounding area."

"Didn't seem to be your highest priority when you were chatting with me last night." It felt good to be allowed to say whatever she wanted. He wasn't a captain or sergeant that demanded her respect.

"Wouldn't have had to if you'd known how to do your job."

"If only you could have informed us beforehand."

"If only I didn't have to."

Astrid turned to the side, rolling her eyes out of Evarith's view. There was no use in retorting again. The man would refuse to admit he could have organized the watch shifts better. She was beginning to understand that Evarith rarely admitted to being wrong.

"Let's get moving," ordered Evarith as soon as everyone had finished eating. Vallec smothered the fire and stored his pot and bowls away while the rest cleared up camp, eliminating most traces of their stay.

For a while, they walked in silence, similar to the day before. Lothar was first to break the tranquil air and began to chat quietly with Imar, away from the humans. Astrid, growing tired of the solitude, joined them after a while.

"I wasn't really supposed to be there, you see? So, I plunged the room into darkness—they just thought the candles had gone out!" laughed Imar.

"You're lucky you weren't fired," said Lothar, smiling.

"I know, I know. But hey, I had to be there." Imar turned his attention to Astrid after finishing his story.

"How was night watch?" asked Lothar, welcoming her to the conversation.

"Could have been worse. But obviously a longer shift than what we're used to. Plus . . ." She glanced toward Evarith.

"Ah, I see." Lothar sighed and shook his head.

"What type of magic do you have, Astrid? I feel like you told me at some point along the way, but I have a terrible memory—"

Lothar glared at Imar, cutting him off.

"What?" Imar's smile faded as he looked between the two of them.

"It's alright, Imar. I don't do much magic. Technically I'm an air wielder, but all I can do is summon a light breeze."

"Oh . . . I'm sorry for asking." Imar seemed to find his fingernails quite interesting all of a sudden.

"It's . . . it's fine." She wanted to cut off that conversation.

In the moment or two when the three went silent, Astrid noticed that Vallec, Kierth, and Galdur were talking separately from Evarith, who stared ahead with a scowl.

"So . . . I'm sorry if this is sensitive, but I really don't know much about the border fights. How are they different from a . . . war?" asked Imar, cringing at his own words.

"It's okay, you can ask. A lot of non-military folk from around the border regions fight with whatever weapons they can find—it's not pretty. Neither our Emperor nor Valea's queen have drafted people, obviously, so everyone there fights of their own accord. We soldiers are supposed to negotiate as many conflicts as we can, but . . ." Astrid took a deep breath and her eyes drifted south, toward the border. "The people at the border . . . they just don't relent. A lot of their friends and family die and they avenge them, and the cycle continues. But a real war . . . it would be so much worse. You know how the people in Pyantir are. Their families and their jobs keep them from enlisting in the military. But if they were forced to, by law or because they had to protect their land . . . Talen knows."

"The rest you've taken . . . it's certainly well deserved," said Imar. "Though I'm not sure I would call being a city guard, 'rest.'"

Astrid grinned. "Pyantir is a big city, and there's plenty of crime, but at least I know I'm fighting people who chose to wrong others."

"And I'm sure not having to deal with humans has been good as well, right?" Imar chuckled, glancing over to the humans.

"That was one huge benefit to the job." Her smile faded slightly. "Until *Lothar* brought me here," she teased.

Imar shook his head, feigning disapproval. "Can't believe he would do such a thing."

Lothar grinned. "You know me, always wanting to make you two suffer."

Astrid and Imar laughed. The three continued to talk for the next few hours until Evarith called for a midday break. The sun was shining down on them, lightening her mood in spite of the chilly air. Astrid watched Lothar retreat into the forest and emerge a few minutes later with four sticks that were roughly the sizes of the majoril and auxlar daggers.

Lothar beamed as he held them out. "Hey, let's get in some sparring practice."

Astrid grinned, taking two of the sticks and backing up. Imar watched from the side as the two hunted for openings in each other's stances. Astrid's attention narrowed until her full concentration centered on Lothar. She lunged forward, evading a poorly timed swing of Lothar's stick. He struggled to defend himself from Astrid's strike, and she pressed on, leveraging her advantage with strike after strike. He parried and got in a few of his own thrusts, but he never connected with her. She darted in and out of Lothar's range until she caught him in the chest with the fake auxlar dagger.

"Ow! By Talen, Astrid!" he exclaimed, laughing and massaging the spot.

"Sorry..." she said, cringing. She *had* hit him pretty hard with it. Lothar looked to the side and his smile faded. She followed his gaze; Evarith, with a nasty glare on his face, walked up to them.

"Stop this incessant noise. You'll draw the attention of everyone in Anzelon!"

Lothar stepped forward, coming within a foot of Evarith. "This isn't just *your* mission, Evarith. I say we could all use some practice here."

"I don't need your opinions, Lothar. I have plans, and you can feel free to take over if they don't work. But they will."

His rough voice made Astrid shrink back a bit; it was quiet and dangerous. As Evarith and Lothar stood unmoving for several tense moments, Kierth, Galdur, and Vallec approached the scene with apprehensive looks.

Lothar blinked, taking a step back. "Right, well I'm glad your 'plans' led to our discovery by these bombers. As you said, they know our faces now."

Evarith stepped forward again, leaning in to bring his face inches from Lothar's. His eyes narrowed, and he gripped his spear with the anger of a man going into battle. "That was not my plan. It was Kierth's, and I disapproved of it. If only I hadn't brought her... oh wait. It was you who forced me to bring companions, wasn't it, Lothar?"

Kierth, Galdur, and Vallec's jaws slackened as they stared at Evarith in disbelief. Astrid watched with mild horror, hand on the dagger at her side. If Evarith made even one move with that spear of his...

"Your lack of judgment led to that fiasco, not my reasonable ask." Lothar started pacing, gesticulating as he spoke. "You know, I thought maybe your friends could help keep your arrogance in check. But now I see that *all* of you humans are arrogant!"

A silence reigned over the seven of them. Astrid had never heard Lothar yell in such a manner—at all, actually. She didn't think the kind, soft-spoken faul was capable of it. The two glared at each other for what felt like an eternity.

At last, Evarith strode past Lothar, not pausing to glance at any of the six. "Break's over."

Lothar wiped droplets of spit from his color-drained face with shaking hands. As the humans followed their seething leader, Astrid leaned in closer to Lothar. "Do you still want to follow?"

She and Imar watched as Lothar sighed and turned toward the humans, dozens of yards away. "I suppose so."

16

VALLEC

Vallec tossed and turned inside his tent, thinking back to when Evarith had returned to Lypeth a couple weeks ago. It had taken Vallec minutes at most to come to terms with the external threats he might face on this mission. Now, the internal threats scared him infinitely more. The argument between Evarith and Lothar still rang in his ears, spurring on the unsavory tensions that marked the passing day. He racked his mind for the dates. On the morning of the eighteenth, the company had gathered in Lypeth together. It was now the night of the twentieth. Three days into their journey, it seemed that the group would tear each other apart and Evarith wouldn't do anything to stop it. Taleek had been all too right about the man and so was Lothar. Arrogant and brilliant, a dangerous combination. How had he not seen that Evarith was a spy beforehand?

The thought of his former commander made Vallec yearn for his leadership. Who amongst the seven of them had led a group before? Lothar certainly, Imar maybe. However much he appreciated that Lothar was not weak-willed, Vallec had heard the words, *"you humans"* loud and clear. While Vallec resented Evarith's incompetence in leadership, he couldn't overlook the man's lack of prejudice against the faul. *He just hates everyone.*

Since his thoughts were too heavy to allow him to drift off, Vallec crawled out of his tent into the crisp night air. Perhaps he could have a conversation with Imar, who was on first shift of the night watch. He seemed amiable and open-minded, from what Vallec had gathered so far. He searched the camp but saw no one in the dim moonlight. Vallec didn't think Imar had been in the military, but perhaps the faul knew a thing or two about staying hidden while on watch. As Vallec circled further and further away from the heart of the campsite, he found Imar walking away ... *How strange.* Vallec jogged to catch up with the faul, eager to ask what the matter was.

"Imar, is everything alright?" he asked, coming within talking distance. Imar had a folded square of parchment in his hand, held at his side.

"Oh!" Imar whirled around, his wide eyes turning soft once more as he recognized Vallec. The piece of parchment vanished beneath Imar's cloak. "You gave me a fright."

"Sorry ... What are you doing? And what was that?" He pointed at Imar's cloak.

"I'm just ... thinking." Imar's expression was soft, yet the usual humor was missing. "Writing down my thoughts. Everything seems so complicated, you know?"

Strangely, the faul looked agitated and calm at the same time, but his words rang with an undeniable truth. Vallec stepped closer. "Yeah, I do."

Imar nodded, closing his eyes for a moment. "I've ... I've been researching domestic threats for fifteen years now ... since I was twenty. Collecting information, searching, following clues ... all to no avail. And now, to at last know ... in such a sudden manner ... It's strange. Especially since this is the first time I've worked with humans."

"You know ... my commander, my friend for over a decade, died in that explosion. And to now be on this almost impossible mission ... I don't think I've really comprehended it yet." Vallec started pacing. "And with what's been happening these past few days, I just feel so shaken up. I used to supervise an organized group of professionals led by one of the greatest men I ever knew. This—it's laughable compared to that. I don't know what to do about it."

Imar smiled and inclined his head. "I wish I had some piece of wisdom to help. I wish I could save this mission from its inevitable failure. None of the other five, maybe not even us, have the right idea about each other. Lothar seems to think that Evarith represents all humans . . . but I disagree. Leina seems to think she's a savior of sorts, and Astrid thinks she's a lunatic. Neither are correct. Nobody is either wholly good or bad, don't you think?"

He paused to mull it over. "I've never thought about it before. Yes . . . I agree. I suppose what you faul lack in strength, you make up for in intelligence." Vallec found he was able to smile for the first time that day.

Imar chuckled softly. "No, I would not say that. I mean, your friends seem quite intelligent. Kierth and Evarith."

"In some ways . . ." Vallec moved next to Imar, who had shifted to gaze at the stars. It was a very clear night, and the autumn chill refreshed his mind.

"I see . . . Whenever I find myself in a troubled mindset, I look at the stars. Aren't they beautiful?"

Vallec smiled. "Indeed."

Interrupting his peaceful state of mind, his earlier concern resurfaced. Imar . . . he'd never answered the question, had he? "But why *were* you so far out from the camp?" he asked, still staring at the sky. The stars danced across the night sky . . . until they didn't. *Where did they go?* It was like all the lights in the sky blinked out. Vallec looked around, but he couldn't see anything—the world was completely black. Panic rose in him and the cool, tranquil air in his lungs suddenly became stifling.

"Imar?" He couldn't even see his own hands. "Imar!" He reached out, feeling in vain for anything around him. Hearing a shuffling from behind, Vallec spun around. "Imar what's g—" A hand clamped over his mouth. *What in Anzelon?* A searing pain pierced through his side. He screamed and fell to the ground, pressing his hands over the excruciating wound.

This was it. This was how he would die. Blind, in the middle of nowhere, in agonizing pain.

He heard a sharp, short scream from behind him. What was happening? Were they under attack? How had both he and Imar missed the attackers? They had failed... and now everyone else, asleep in their tents... He looked up to the sky again. At least the stars were back. He turned his head and could see blades of grass take shape in front of him. *Wonderful.* Just as his sight returned, he was going to die.

"... ec! Vallec... Vallec!" Was someone calling his name? Someone grabbed him and turned his head. A face took shape in front of him—Evarith.

"Vallec! Vallec!" Evarith's voice was so distant. His vision was going dark again. That probably wasn't a good sign.

"Imar! By Talen!" shouted another voice.

At least he couldn't feel anything anymore.

Vallec woke up to a sharp pain in his side, almost as if he'd been stabbed. *Oh, right.* He wished to go to sleep again. It had been quite nice.

"Vallec, you're awake!" exclaimed Evarith, leaning over him. For once, his expression was full of relief rather than scorn.

"It seems so..." said Vallec, struggling to keep his eyes open. "By Ryne... what happened?"

Evarith grimaced. "You were stabbed..."

"Obviously. By whom? Did you catch them?"

"By Imar."

Vallec blinked. It couldn't be true, could it? As he stared at Evarith, he waited for the ever-stoic face to break, to show some hint of a lie. But of course, it didn't. At last, Vallec nodded, a pit settling to the bottom of his stomach. "But—Why?"

"All we can assume is that he was a member of the bombers. I was hoping you could tell me what happened and shed some light on why he tried to kill you."

"Can't you ask him? Where is he now?"

"Dead. I—He was going to finish you off. I tried to aim for his arm, but I missed."

Vallec swallowed; why did he feel like mourning the person who'd tried to kill him? "How did you get to us so quickly?"

"I was out there, too, watching for threats." Evarith averted his gaze; a sheepish look came over him. "I *may* have fallen asleep, but your scream woke me. Then, I saw a dark cloud in the distance, and when it vanished, Imar stood over you, knife in hand. The others woke a few seconds after."

"Where are they?"

"Leina and Galdur are outside—"

"Leina?"

"Kierth."

"Ah, I see . . ." His head was pounding, but at least it was clear that Kierth, no—Leina, had lied to him about her identity. She and Evarith really *were* quite similar.

"Anyway, we rushed you to the nearest town; luckily it was in Valea, about five miles away from where we were. I don't know if they would have accepted you, even injured, in a Shalin town."

Vallec furrowed his brow. "I thought we were in the Shalin Empire."

"We were. But right on the border, the rural border, and the closest town was in Valea. Why were you outside? And why were you two so far from the camp?"

Vallec described his conversation with Imar and the attack. "My vision went dark somehow, then I spun around as he stabbed me, I suppose."

"So, if you hadn't spun around . . ."

"Yes . . . like that story that you told to Haern, Taleek, and I," said Vallec with a sad smile. The two fell silent. He just wanted to go to sleep, but he also had something to say to Evarith.

"How could Lothar have been so stupid!" exclaimed Evarith, startling Vallec.

"You were fooled as well . . . I do wonder why he was leaving the camp, though." Vallec kept his voice calm; he needed Evarith to cool down.

"Probably to tell the bombers our location. He didn't expect you to be awake, I suppose," said Evarith. "I wish we could have followed him!"

Vallec nodded and looked around the room, taking in his surroundings. He furrowed his brow. It didn't really look like a medic's room.

"You're in an inn. There was no doctor here," said Evarith, following Vallec's gaze.

"How am I alive then?" asked Vallec. He lifted his shirt a few inches; the wound was stitched up, though the job seemed rough.

"Leina and I did it. We both have some amount of medical knowledge."

Vallec nodded. He was glad Evarith had washed the blood off his hands; that wasn't a sight he wanted to see. "Thank you for that. How big is this town anyway?"

"Just big enough to have a one-room inn apparently. But quite small."

Neither Vallec nor Evarith spoke for a while.

When the moment seemed right, Vallec took a breath and asked what was most important. "What will you do now?"

"We'll just keep going... Leave you with some money so you can get back home when you're well, and we'll be on our way."

"Good plan. Tell me, *how* do you suppose you'll accomplish this?"

"What do you mean?" Vallec said nothing, letting Evarith think. He wanted him to figure it out for himself. "*I'm* supposed to be the cryptic one," said Evarith, with a hint of a smile.

"Evarith, do you really think that you can lead these people to the Dalyuben Hills and beyond?"

"If they listen to what I say, obey my command."

"They will if you properly lead them."

"I am!"

"No, you're not."

"Not you, too..." Evarith rolled his eyes and sighed.

"Lothar was correct. You're not infallible; none of you are. Though you may lead them, they are not your sworn soldiers. Lothar and Astrid think all humans are self-centered, so make them see otherwise! They need your respect, just as you need theirs."

"None of them have earned it, Vallec! Besides you, I suppose. And Leina to an extent."

"That doesn't matter right now. I don't need your respect anymore, but these people... They left their homes and whatever families they have to fight with you. For the sake of Anzelon."

"What do you know? You've never led."

Vallec winced at the abrasive comment. "Yes, but I was Taleek's right-hand man, as you know. I learned a thing or two. Taleek didn't know half of his soldiers' names, but he knew that they had signed up to protect their country and to endure a long journey. Because of that, Taleek respected them. He respected you, even though he didn't really know you."

"I—I just can't, Vallec. These people... I didn't want this many people. It's Lothar's fault. I just wanted one faul for information."

"First of all, that was a stupid thing to say in front of the others. But setting that aside, they may be useful."

"But they may be a hindrance."

Vallec shrugged. "It doesn't matter. You have no idea what you're up against. You may have a plan now, but if you think it won't change, you're insane. Evarith, don't be stupid like you were before. I thought you had changed."

Evarith stood there, avoiding Vallec's gaze.

"You must be strong! All six—five of you are doing this to save thousands of lives! It's going to be hard, and there are going to be disagreements, but you can do this! I could have gone back home, but I didn't because I truly don't think this is hopeless." He was praying that he could get through to Evarith, he had to. "And not to inflate your ego, but Lothar is not fit to lead this thing. So whether or not you want to, you are the only one who can."

"No, I wouldn't want him to, anyways."

"I know that."

"What should I do then?" Evarith looked defeated. Probably a good thing at this point.

"Talk to the others. Sparring is good, it works great in the military. Just don't let them fight each other if you think they'll try to hurt their opponent. Listen to them as well; hear their opinions and their ideas."

"Leina and Galdur will be suspicious of Lothar and Astrid..." said Evarith thoughtfully.

"You'll have to work through that."

"What if Lothar purposefully betrayed me using Imar? Can I trust that Astrid isn't also a traitor?"

"Think about it. Were there any hints that Imar was a traitor? I can't find any, but maybe you can."

Evarith was silent for many moments. "Maybe."

"Astrid is making no efforts to seem neutral, like Imar did. And you said you trusted Lothar; he seems righteous enough to me. You have to trust someone sooner or later, Evarith."

"Your advice is far easier said than done. I've been betrayed by others. More than you know."

"And there more that won't betray you. Listen, I repeat only what Taleek taught me. I should hope that you held him in high regard."

"I did."

"So then, the way forward may be difficult, but it's also obvious."

Evarith was quiet for a moment. "Thank you, Vallec. I wish you could come with us."

"I'm not the only helpful one."

"Hmph. Well, anyway, you'll be missed."

"I'll return. I swear it. When I can move again, I'll find you all, somehow. If I can't, I'll be in my house in Hileath. Three streets down from the intelligence academy, fourth house on the left."

Evarith nodded and turned around, leaving the room.

"What about my money? Trying to keep me here forever, Evarith?" called Vallec back.

Evarith grinned and turned around, pulling out a handful of coins and giving them to Vallec.

Vallec set the coins on a table beside his bed. "May Ryne guide you."

As Evarith left, a pit of dread formed in his stomach. Would he be able to make good on his promise? Even staying awake was a laborious task now. He gritted his teeth and tried to sit up, wincing as a searing pain made its way through his side. Nearly crying out in agony, Vallec collapsed back against the pillow, beads of sweat forming on his brow. He, one of Taleek's best soldiers, reduced to this from a simple stab wound? No, it would not do. He muttered a prayer to Ryne. He would make it back. He *had* to make it back. Ryne would see him through.

17

Lothar

Lothar paced, staring at the ground, waiting for the return of the humans. Ten hours after the attack—he still couldn't bring himself to think of it as a betrayal—and he had done nothing but sit or pace. He might have spent those hours clearing his mind, organizing his thoughts, pondering the nature of the attack and what it meant for the mission. But he couldn't seem to think. To process. To understand. He didn't remember much of the past ten hours. Astrid sat, perched on a tree above him, waiting too. She had gone hunting a couple of times, made meals, and watched their surroundings.

It was around midday when Astrid pointed out three figures in the distance. A spark of something roused in him. He didn't even care if they were the rest of the bombers coming to avenge Imar. Lothar needed something to bring him out of the everlasting numbness.

As they approached, their figures were unmistakable. The humans. He was glad they were safe, and yet he also felt disappointment at the sight. He didn't want to talk to them. Certainly not to Evarith or Kierth. Galdur was always so quiet and frightened looking, Lothar hadn't yet formed much of an opinion.

"Vallec is alive and well," said Evarith as the three finally made their way over to him and Astrid. Relief filled him upon the realization that Imar had not killed a man in cold blood. At least, as far as he knew.

Lothar nodded as Astrid hopped down from the tree. He didn't want the humans to come any closer and was glad for Astrid's proximity. He wanted Imar back. Melancholy welled within him before he could stop it. Guilt and loathing replaced it in an instant, though he couldn't help but be drawn to the memory of the faul he thought he had known.

"We're going to walk for a while longer, then stop for some sparring and rest. Someone can cook dinner if they wish to," said Evarith with his usual dry and calm tone. Annoyingly calm. "Any objections?"

"How far are we from the plains?" asked Kierth.

Galdur answered, "Fifteen miles. If we stop in a few hours, we should arrive tomorrow while still well rested, and not be camped too close tonight."

Evarith nodded. "Good plan."

Lothar stayed near Astrid as they traveled, yet while the humans conversed with one another, the two faul remained silent. He had plenty of things to say, plenty of thoughts bouncing around in his head, but he didn't feel like voicing any of them. Astrid had not known Imar as he had. As they walked on for hours, he noted the occasional glance thrown his way by Kierth and Galdur. The depressing revelation struck him; he looked like a fool and a traitor. He forced the thought down—he didn't want to think about it.

"What's that?" asked Kierth a while later. She pointed at some sort of stone structure south of them, along the border, it looked like.

Evarith squinted and shielded his eyes. "I'm not sure."

"Wait, I think I know," said Galdur. "I think it's the old Akarist."

Lothar turned toward Galdur. "There was an old Akarist?"

Galdur nodded. "Before the war even began, before the intense rivalry between our countries, there was a meeting ground set up for the two states to discuss disputes. That's it."

"What's special about it?" asked Astrid.

"Nothing really. The soldiers all swore oaths that they would never attack anyone unless their king or any of his advisors were threatened, or if the soldiers themselves were threatened. It was a neat system, but once the new Akarist was set up, it became obsolete."

Lothar hadn't heard Galdur speak so much since the two had met. *The man must be some sort of cartographer.*

"I thought that 'Akarist' referred to the building itself," said Kierth.

"No," said Lothar, before he could stop himself. "It's an ancient faul word." Kierth's face flashed with annoyance, but Lothar continued. "Akistaria means 'sacred meeting'. Akarist refers to the place where that happens," said Lothar, trying his best to translate the complex faul language that even he barely knew. Imar might've known it. Sadness threatened Lothar again, but he couldn't let it settle. The topic of discussion turned from the Akarist, and Lothar was once again left to his own thoughts.

Hours later, the group stopped. Lothar sat down on a tree stump while the others set up their tents and began practicing with their spears. Struggling to keep his eyelids open, he gazed out at the sunset; wondrous layers of pink and orange banded across the vast sky. The cool breeze of late afternoon blew his hair back from his eyes, and the cloud coverage kept the sun from blinding him. It had been warmer than typical for a late autumn day. He wondered if such beautiful weather would come again before winter was over—probably not.

Glancing to his side, he saw Evarith coaching Kierth and Galdur's sparring. The gentle thuds of the shafts hitting each other were interrupted by short comments and suggestions from Evarith.

Kierth dropped the spear to the ground and stretched her arms. "It's too heavy!"

Evarith picked it up and handed it back. "You can't use that dagger of yours. If you hate the faul so much, why do you want their weapons?"

The words piqued his attention. He turned to watch the interaction out of the corner of his eye.

"It's a piece of metal! It has no meaning. It doesn't belong to anyone."

Evarith just stood, arms crossed. "Some would disagree with you."

"Who cares? Plus, I can use my crossbow. I don't like fighting in close quarters anyway."

"Fine. Galdur, you seem to have remembered everything I taught you."

Galdur grinned. "Can you teach me how to throw knives? You never got around to that in our lessons."

"If there's time." Evarith walked over to Lothar. "Care to join us?" The words sounded forced. He suspected Evarith's instinct was to phrase it as a command, but he seemed to be trying not to.

"Not really."

"Why not? Everything's alright! Vallec is alive!"

"Why not?" echoed Lothar, now looking up and into Evarith's cold eyes. "Why not? My friend just died!"

"Your friend? He stabbed Vallec!"

Astrid hurried over from where she leaned against a tree. After Kierth and Galdur approached as well, Lothar felt all eyes upon him as he stood up to face Evarith.

"I'm aware. Yet he was my friend for over a decade!"

"Well, what do you want *me* to do? Hold a funeral for him? Ask Ryne to see him through to the afterlife?" shouted Evarith, his rage-filled face only a foot away from Lothar's. "You're the one who brought that traitor into our camp in the first place!"

Kierth was stoic beside Evarith, but Galdur cowered back. Astrid and Lothar stood their ground. He would not back up. Not for this.

"Don't go there, Evarith!" shouted Astrid. "None of you saw who he was, either!"

"Yes, I mourn the loss of him! I mourn the loss of the faul I thought I knew, not the one that he was! Can't you understand that?" asked Lothar, trying to assume a diplomatic tone.

"I can't understand being friends with someone for ten years and not seeing past the façade!"

"If I could go back, I would change things, but I can't! Are you going to order me to forget my friend?" Lothar stepped forward, his face now just inches from Evarith's. "Are you going to do that? Because I swear on Talen that if you do, you will continue alone, you arrogant bastard. Go on, I know you want to."

Evarith flinched at the last words. It felt like an eternity passed before he turned away. "Set up camp. Lothar, Astrid, Kierth, you three are taking night watch."

Lothar and Galdur breathed sighs of relief. His anger turned once more to apathy as he resigned himself to his night shift. He wanted to sleep but figured nothing good would come of arguing at the moment.

"Why do you care?" asked Astrid.

"What?" he asked, turning to face her.

"If you want to leave, I'll follow you. The mission is probably doomed anyway. Maybe more so if we stick with them."

Lothar sighed. "Not all humans are like him. Vallec wasn't."

"Vallec isn't here anymore."

"I know. I don't think we can do this alone, though."

"If you say so. I follow *you*, just so you know."

"Thanks, Astrid." She began walking away but turned back.

"You can wake me a bit early, by the way."

"I won't do that to you."

She shrugged. "The offer is open."

He nodded and sat back down on the same tree stump as before. The sky grew dark as he sat, simply admiring his surroundings. Then, he remembered that he too had to set up a tent. Lothar stood up, closing his eyes for a few moments to gather his energy. He couldn't help but think that if only he had found someone else, he could have left Imar back at his study by Pyantir. Yes, that would have been optimal. Then Imar never would have died. Lothar shook his head—no, he could not think this way. Imar had endangered the mission, and that was the real reason why Lothar never should have brought him, right? Yet he could not erase the nearly infinite supply of memories with the faul; lounging in his study, listening to his sage advice, voicing his troubles to the one person who would listen. The faul had been more of a father to him than his own—that was undeniable. He and the five deities, they had been there.

So why then would he deceive Lothar for a decade? Lothar sat down on the tree stump after everyone had gone to sleep. He couldn't care less that he was supposed to be keeping a proper watch for intruders; he had to think now. It was the only way out.

The scene replayed in his mind. Evarith threw that knife and missed, hitting Imar squarely in the chest instead of the arm as he had intended. Lothar had screamed, but Vallec's safety had been of more importance than Imar's. Before leaving, Evarith had ordered that his body be hidden in case they were being tracked. The grass had already been stained with blood, though. Astrid did it when Lothar outright refused to. He couldn't look as she walked into the forest alone, carrying Imar's body.

Lothar took a deep, shaky breath trying to focus on what was most important. Imar had to have been a member of this bombing organization. Perhaps his duty for them took place mostly in his study so he could do his government job at the same time. This plot with bombings and lootings had only surfaced recently, after all. What a fortunate position, though—domestic threats historian. He could cover the tracks of his fellow bombers easily. By Talen, how important had Imar been to this group? Anger welled up inside of him, directed not at Evarith or the humans or the gods, but at Imar. At the faul who sold out his country, the faul who nearly killed a man, the faul who had betrayed Lothar. He was sure that he had meant something to Imar. If the bombers ended up finding their campsite from Imar's information, perhaps Lothar would have been spared in the following massacre. But that was not Talen's will; he could not forgive Imar for such selfish reasons.

The tears that fell down Lothar's face washed away his guilt. They fell not for Imar anymore, but for the bond that the two had shared. Talen would understand his sadness. By the will of Talen, he had survived the Akarist to be here, to aid Evarith, and to stop the bombers. He could endure this. He would have to.

"By the Gods," he whispered, the flame of purpose burning inside of him.

Lothar woke in the morning with that flame still burning fiercely. The sadness was by no means absent, but he also felt driven. With an eagerness that he could only have dreamt of yesterday, he packed up his tent and gathered his things, all without Evarith needing to pester him about it. Galdur was last to rise and Lothar noticed the young man's frantic behavior as he packed up his tent. Though

Lothar knew hardly anything about human aging, he suspected the man was younger than twenty.

Despite Lothar feeling substantially better, the atmosphere was still stiff with tension, and he wondered how much longer it would last. It couldn't go on forever, could it? His mission now was to ease the stress, to work with the humans as best he could without placating them.

Evarith summoned the group. "Let's go. I hope you all will agree that we must remain silent around these parts now. The hills are close, and they could be anywhere."

Lothar nodded, relieved that he and Evarith could agree on something.

Around an hour later, Galdur spoke up. "The hills will appear soon. Unlike other hilly regions, these are almost entirely rock."

Soon, Lothar felt the ground become rougher and harder. The grass then gave way entirely to rocks and dirt. Boulders and rock formations plastered the land.

"We should look for caves. If they've dug tunnels into the land, they'll be hard to spot," said Evarith.

Galdur studied the map in his hands. "We're about ten miles from the coast now. If anyone is nearby—"

A deep rumbling shook the earth beneath their feet. Lothar lost his balance and stumbled on the jagged rock.

"You know," whispered Kierth with a hint of humor, "I think when we find these mines, we'll know it."

"Yes . . . probably," whispered Evarith. They continued walking for another half-mile before Kierth stopped and stared into the distance, frowning.

"What is it?" asked Galdur.

"I think—it might be a mirage, but it looks like the ground drops off in two miles . . . Yes. There's land on either side but what looks to be a gap in the middle."

"Drops off? Like a cliff?" asked Lothar.

"Yes. Galdur . . . are there any cliffs in this region?"

Galdur swallowed and squinted at the map. "Can you see anything past the drop off?"

"No. Nothing. It looks like the world's end."

"No, there are no such cliffs here." Galdur's voice shook, and his fingers were trembling as he traced a path along the map. Lothar wasn't quite sure they could trust the man about every minute geographical detail, but he had to admit the formation Kierth described sounded strange. Within another few minutes of walking, the rest of them could see the strange cliff as well.

"Now I see land on the other side. It looks like a hole..." said Kierth.

The land sloped upwards before dropping down, obscuring what lay below. They hid behind a craggy rock that blocked their view of the vast hole and kept them from seeing the bottom. Each was silent; no one wanted to leave their cover.

Evarith took a breath, grasping the handle of a throwing knife. "I'll go first." He edged himself out from behind the rock, dropping to hands and knees and crawling toward the cliff edge. After a cautious glance, he seemed to gain more resolve and moved himself further over the edge. Turning back, he beckoned the group closer with a wave of his hand. Galdur shook his head and refused to move out from cover even as the rest followed Evarith's orders. Lothar peered into the depths below and his mouth dropped open. A chunk of land fifteen yards high and spanning a mile in length and width had been completely removed. Faul and humans alike crowded the area below.

"What are they doing, Kierth?" whispered Evarith.

"They have pickaxes..."

Two ladders led up from the pit to the natural land. Luckily, the tops were distant from the five of them. Lothar whispered a prayer to Talen that no one would see them.

"Astrid... you said this land was bought two months ago?" asked Evarith. Despite his contempt for Evarith, the quiver in his voice scared Lothar. Even lying beneath the Akarist ruins, Lothar had never heard Evarith's voice shake.

"Uh... yes... That's right," she said. Her horrified face was also one that Lothar scarcely saw, and he was gripped by terror. A booming voice sounded from the pit.

"Ready! Stand clear all!" The figures below backed away from an area in the mine. "Three, two, one!"

A deafening boom pierced Lothar's ears as an explosion beyond anything he'd seen before burst out from the cleared area. It seemed to ignite smaller explosions closer to the figures, who jumped back and screamed in terror. His ears rang and he glanced around, the looks of shock on his companions' faces reflecting his own. Once the smoke cleared, they saw a giant chunk of rock had been blown away. Evarith motioned for them to retreat, and Lothar found he was eager to oblige. Galdur was still curled up in a ball, cowering.

"That's the kind of bomb used to blow up the Akarist," declared Evarith. "It has to be."

Lothar tried to speak, but his throat was dry. He took a drink of water from his pack. "What could they be mining for? And why such a hurry for it?"

"I don't know, but it can't be good," said Kierth.

Lothar half expected Astrid to make some sort of remark about the obvious nature of the statement, but Astrid too, looked as terrified as the others.

Kierth shook her head. "Sorry, that wasn't helpful. I meant that we should either find out what it is, or why they need it."

"Let's watch again," suggested Evarith. Galdur still refused to comply but was now sitting up straight and looked marginally less terrified. Lothar peered over the edge again and saw the workers pick up pieces of something and put them in boxes. Then the boxes were hauled up the left edge of the cliff by rope and another worker unloaded the pieces into crates on a wooden cart. Other workers used their pickaxes to rip chunks of material from the newly formed crater and put those pieces in the boxes as well. Again, the five retreated behind the boulder to discuss.

"That cart, it may lead us back to the bombers," suggested Lothar. "The material has to go somewhere."

Evarith's eyes lit up. "We should follow it once it departs."

"I want some of it . . ." said Kierth, to no one in particular. *Is she insane?*

Galdur stood, walking closer to Kierth. "L—Kierth, *no*. There are guards by the cart. You'll never get past them."

"But what if I went into the pit and stole a chunk of rock? I could test it! You know I can, Evarith, so why not?" A devious smile was on her face; her terror seemed to have vanished.

"Kierth! You can't go down there!" exclaimed Lothar, trying to keep his voice to a whisper.

Evarith sighed. "He's right."

"Oh, you would!" cried Kierth. "I've seen you do more dangerous things."

Evarith stood in front of her; for once the glare had disappeared. "Kierth, please. I think you can do it, but it's just too risky."

Kierth stared into the distance and stayed silent.

18

Leina

She needed a sample of that material. This could be the key to the bombers' method of destruction; the very thing she had agonized over for months.

"We'll just wait until the cart leaves, most likely at dusk. I'll watch over the pit first and we can switch every couple of hours," said Melkin. Lothar and Galdur sat down by themselves and stared off into the distance, minds elsewhere. Leina distanced herself from the others and waited to see if anyone came or went from the gargantuan mine. She hoped more miners arrived often; if not, then her plan wouldn't work.

An hour later, figures appeared in the distance. She squinted, trying to make out the details. Humans and faul, unbound, led by two spear-wielding humans. *They must still be under the impression that they can leave.* The clothes of the new laborers were neat enough, similar to her own. She almost left immediately to blend in with the arriving miners but held herself back; she would need some help. Melkin wouldn't let her go and neither would Lothar. Galdur might help if she insisted, but what could he do for her?

Leina thought for a moment and decided to risk it, walking over to Astrid and sitting beside her.

"What do you want?" Astrid stared ahead, not meeting Leina's gaze.

"The material they're mining down there." She kept her tone factual, waiting for Astrid to react.

Astrid scoffed. "So? What do you want me to do about it?"

Leina pointed to the cluster of arriving people. "See that group in the distance?"

"Yeah?"

"I'm going to join them. Getting into the pit unharmed won't be a problem. They need workers and from what Evarith said, I can only assume they take their workers and keep them prisoner in the mine."

"If you want go on a suicide mission that's your decis—"

"I don't. But will you help me get out once I get the sample?"

"You want me to help you in another one of your reckless, endangering missions?"

Leina swallowed her pride, fighting back a grin at the opportunity to persuade an enemy—her specialty. That's what Melkin had brought her along to do, after all. Even Astrid could be convinced, she was sure. "You think this mission is doomed, don't you?"

Astrid clenched her jaw and looked Leina in the eye. "Yes . . ."

Leina waited for the faul to ask how she knew, but Astrid didn't seem to care. "This is our chance. Maybe my plan last time was a bit rash, but I've thought this over. We need to understand this group, and the secret might lie fifteen yards below us. This mission is *almost* madness, but I can tip the scales in our favor. Get an edge up. With no risk, we *are* doomed. Plus, if I get captured, you all can leave, and no harm will have been done."

Astrid sighed in annoyance, but Leina could see her features soften. "What do you want me to do?"

"Once I've collected the sample, I'll make a run for it toward this cliff edge. Guards will follow me, so I need you to blow rock dust in their eyes, their mouths, their noses, whatever."

"I can barely do magic, Kierth." She rolled her eyes. "Forget it."

"You said you could summon a light breeze."

"How do you know that?"

"I'm a spy, Astrid, I hear conversations. Look, the group of miners are coming so I need to leave. Will you help me?" Leina removed her dagger sheath and quiver of crossbow arrows and set them on the ground. She recalled how nervous this used to make her, going unarmed into dangerous territory. By now, she'd done it dozens of times.

"Yeah, sure. How will you get back up?"

"Tie a rope for me. Evarith will have one." Leina glanced at her companions. Galdur and Lothar were still off in their own worlds while Melkin had his gaze fixed on the mines. She silently cursed herself; the group of miners were too close to the ladders for her to join up with them now, but Leina already had a second plan brewing. She covered herself as best she could with her gray cloak and kept low to the ground, the folds of her cloak camouflaging her into the dull, monotonous surroundings. Her heart pumped rapidly; this was Melkin's expertise, not her own. At last, she could almost reach the first ladder but hid behind a sizable boulder to wait for the right moment. She breathed a sigh of relief—she hadn't been seen. Leina unclasped her cloak and let it drop behind her; everything would fall into place now. At the top of the ladder, the guards were letting in the miners. She emerged from the rock and stumbled her way to the guards, panting as though she had been running for hours.

"Please . . . I fell behind . . . I need this job . . . I . . . must feed . . . my family!"

"You fell behind?" asked the guard closest to her, pursing his lips.

"I'm sorry!"

"Hey Efti! This one in your group?" called the other guard down into the pit. No one responded.

The nearest guard shrugged. "Eh, just throw her in there. She's not gonna do any harm." He turned toward her, his look of apathy replaced by derision. "Get down there and get to work."

She turned and descended the ladder, coughing as she neared the bottom. With alarm, she realized just how much the rock dust obscured her vision and hampered her breathing. At the bottom, an enormous man thrust a pickaxe into her arms.

"Mine the blue-speckled rock from the crater and put them in the crates." Leina gagged as he leaned in, and his foul breath engulfed her nostrils. "Don't hit the blue specks with the pickaxe head-on, alright? Go!"

She obliged, walking in the direction of the other miners, matching their sluggish pace. The man's words nearly confirmed her suspicions about the nature of this mine. If the pickaxe caused a spark against the blue flecks . . .

Her foot caught in a rock crevice, and she slammed into the hard stone below. Her shoulder hit a particularly jagged piece of rock, sending a sharp pain through her arm. She gritted her teeth and stood back up, glancing at the cliff edge above before continuing toward the newly formed crater. She touched the stinging wound on her shoulder; blood was already beginning to soak through her tunic. Leina forced down all fear and glanced around at the mine; chunks of rock had been stripped from the ground, leaving it pockmarked and with hardly any specks of blue to be seen. Leina hoped she would go unnoticed, but the other miners were mostly men and muscular women, while the weaker faul and humans transported the crates of rock across the large mine. The patrolling guards seemed to have already taken an interest in her, watching her every move as she languidly made her way across the mine.

At last, she arrived at the deep crater where others were mining. She swallowed, dropped a few feet down into the pit, and scanned for any bits of blue among the gray. Though she spotted many veins, Leina approached the one furthest from any guards, hoping they would lose interest in her presence. With great effort, she lifted the pickaxe and swung it toward the wall of the crater, knowing for certain her technique was poor. Her heart sank when she realized the stone was unchanged—she would have to put all her effort into this. She dragged the pickaxe back into position, braced her legs like some of the other miners were doing, and swung.

Leina estimated half an hour of this at most before her arms gave out; each time the pick clattered against the solid rock, the vibrations threatened to pull the tool from her grasp. Only her fear of accidentally causing a spark against the blue specks kept her arms steady enough to hit the same spot over and over. After an eternity, a crack formed near a blue-speckled vein and some chips fell from the spot she was working on. She aimed for the crack, using every ounce of strength to keep her arms steady enough to hit the thin fracture. Her eyes began to water, both from the thick air and the exertion she felt throughout her body. The stinging wound on her shoulder paled in comparison to the deep burning and aching in her arms, but she couldn't leave now; she would never hear the end of it if she endangered Melkin's mission without anything to show for it.

In a last-ditch effort, Leina wedged the pick into the crack and pulled with her entire bodyweight. The crack widened. Leina steadied herself and took a deep breath before again heaving her full weight behind the pickaxe. The fist-sized piece of speckled rock came free, causing Leina to stumble backwards. Quickly, she regained her bearings and caught her breath.

Without glancing around, she pocketed the piece as discreetly as possible and continued to mine at the vein with light swings, using only enough strength to keep up the act. Her arms were lead, but she had to stay for a bit longer; it would look too suspicious otherwise. *Another five minutes.* Sweat was dripping into her eyes, and she tried to convince herself that eventually she would blend in with everyone else and be free to escape. She swung again, but the impact wrenched the pickaxe from her weakened grip, and it clattered to the ground. A guard whipped his head around and strode toward her, weapon drawn and at the ready. She braced herself on her knees, catching her breath and blinking the stinging sweat from her eyes.

"Pick it up!" he roared. She obliged, wishing she had given up earlier and made a run for it. She would have had a head start then. Now this guard was upon her and looked ready to kill. She bent down and clutched the heavy tool, beginning to swing it against the sloped surface once more. She couldn't keep it up—the point was falling well below the mark she aimed for, dangerously close to the blue specks.

"Higher!"

She winced—he had yelled straight into her ear. Before she could make another effort to hit the wall higher, the pickaxe once again slipped from her grasp and fell to the rock beneath her feet. In the split second before his face contorted into an even angrier expression, time slowed. Would she die down here after all? She glanced at the cliff again and saw a face peering down at her helpless self in front of the guards.

Tearing her eyes away from the figure, she failed to register the hand before it connected with her face. The impact of his palm spun her around and she landed on all fours. She barely kept herself from crying out in pain while the man demanded once again that she pick up the tool. She did so, grasping its wooden, sweaty handle and standing up amidst the pain she felt throughout her body. Only a minute; that was all she needed to reach the wall. Pickaxe firmly in her grasp, she took a breath before spinning around and planting the end of the tool squarely in the guard's chest. He roared in pain as she climbed out of the crater, thankfully not falling on her face. Guards tried to close in on her, but they were slowed by fits of coughing and wheezing, while the air before her felt slightly cleaner. *Thank you, Astrid.* She accelerated, reaching the wall just as a length of rope fell.

Leina gripped the rope with both hands before reality hit her. She could not climb this, not as tired as her arms were. Guards were roughly thirty yards behind her. She tied the end of the rope around her torso despite the tremors in her hands. Twenty yards. She tried climbing the rope and using her legs to bear most of her weight, but she could only scale a couple of yards before her muscles gave out. It was all she could do to hang on the rope and keep her toes wedged onto their holds.

She glanced back at the pursuing guards who had drawn their spears and daggers; they would easily be able to reach her if she stayed there. Ten yards... five—there was nothing she could do. Then the rope jerked and pulled her from her perch, both saving her and nearly giving her whiplash. She held onto the rope shakily as she was lifted upwards, out of reach of the thrusting spears and swinging daggers below. At the top, she got her arms over the edge but couldn't pull her body over. Melkin hastily grabbed her and shoved her behind him onto solid ground before cutting the rope without saying a word.

"Kierth, you idiot!" exclaimed Lothar.

"Shut up, we have to go!" commanded Melkin. Astrid thrust Leina's dagger and quiver into her arms, and she strapped them on with trembling fingers. She grabbed her pack and crossbow, which had already been loaded for her.

They sprinted, following Melkin's lead and chased by half a dozen guards who spilled over the wall from their ladders. Leina turned and shot at the closest guard, not watching long enough to see whether she hit her mark or not. Lothar whirled around to face their attackers, and three of them fell in an instant. Melkin threw two knives, stopping the final two guards. She panted—how long could she sustain this speed?

Melkin jerked to the side, pointing at a rock formation. "Here!"

The five crowded down a narrow passageway leading into a tiny cave and sat, careful not to bash their heads on the low ceiling. She leaned back to catch her breath and let the fear leave her body.

"Are you okay, Kierth?" asked Galdur, his voice quavering. She nodded, unlacing her jerkin and pulling her arm out of her tunic sleeve.

She reached for the waterskin in her own pack, but it was bone-dry. "Water," she ordered.

Lothar was quick to retrieve his waterskin and hand it to her. She winced as she washed the wound, soaking part of her clothing in the process. She sighed; that was more annoying than the pain of the wound itself. Rummaging around in her pack, she found bandages and wrapped up her shoulder.

"Did you at least get whatever they're mining?" asked Melkin. She pulled out the chunk of blue-speckled rock from her pocket and held it up for him to see.

"Well thank Ryne for that . . ."

Leina rolled her eyes. "Thank *me* for that."

"Ryne!" swore Galdur, resting his head in his hands, "You could have died, Kierth . . ."

"Oh really?" she asked, snapping her head up to face Galdur. He said nothing, only stared back with pain in his eyes. She sighed again and laced up her jerkin, her shoulder feeling significantly better now. She regretted lashing out at Galdur; he was genuinely concerned about her. "Sorry . . . And thank you, Astrid."

"Yes . . . The others were quite surprised I agreed to help you. I figured you'd do it either way, though."

"Why did you? You seemed to want me dead the other day." She kept a flat voice, daring the others to react.

Lothar threw his hands up in frustration. "Because however stupid and irrational your plans are . . . well, they both worked. And you need to stop going behind our backs because it's really pissing us off, but none of us want you dead, Kierth." Lothar rested his head in his hands.

Leina rolled her eyes. "Please, even if I had shared my motives with Evarith, he would have overruled me."

"And what would those motives be?" asked Melkin, raising an eyebrow.

"I want to test it. I think our mystery bombers are using the rock to enhance their bombs."

Lothar leaned forward. "Why do you think that?"

"The smaller explosions around that large one we watched in the mine. The veins of the blue stone, they must have ignited," she said, repeatedly tossing the rock up and catching it as she spoke.

"I might have said yes," said Melkin, after a pause.

"But you might not have."

Melkin nodded. "Yes, I might not have. Because I don't want you to die."

"Why are you scared of me taking a risk if I'm prepared to take it? You're no less rash than I. The number of times I've seen you scale walls with only shallow cracks in the stone keeping you from falling to your death . . ." Leina shook her head in disbelief and gazed into Melkin's eyes. "I've never stopped *you* from doing stupid things."

Melkin was silent for a moment. She knew what he was thinking—that she never had such power over him. But for Melkin to voice that thought would make him look controlling and hypocritical, which he sometimes was. Leina hoped he was tactful enough to keep his mouth shut.

"It doesn't matter right now," said Galdur. "We need to agree before we act next time."

Leina glanced at him, surprised he had weighed in on the discussion at all.

Lothar nodded, leaning back against the wall with a sigh. "Agreed. And I'm sure that was quite an unpleasant and painful experience for you, Kierth, but it could have been far worse."

"It's Leina. Leina Kierth," she said, her quiet admittance penetrating the silence of the cave. No one spoke for a while. They sat in the dim light, listening to shuffling feet come and go near the cave opening.

"Clever hiding spot," Lothar whispered, peering at the narrow opening.

"Yes... I noticed it earlier when we were walking here," said Melkin. "Even if the guards were to find us, they would have to enter single file, putting them in quite the nasty spot."

"Are we still following the cart?" asked Astrid after another long silence.

"Of course. We'll just have to be extra careful. Wherever it leads... we might find answers there," said Melkin.

When the footsteps from outside had stopped, Melkin crawled out of the cave and surveyed the area before motioning for them to join him. Leina gazed at the cart, now attached to a horse and flanked by guards. A few minutes later, a rider mounted the horse and the soldiers strapped down crates of rock with thick leather bands.

Lothar turned toward Melkin. "Should we start moving now? Get closer before we can't see them anymore?"

"No. I would, but it will be safer if we follow them once it's darker," said Melkin. "Leina will be able to see them."

At last, a whip cracked, and the horse began a slow walk forward. The darkening sky was both a help and a hindrance, shielding them from watching guards and concealing the cart they had to follow.

"Gods, you sure you can see that, Kierth?" muttered Astrid, squinting.

Leina watched the black speck in the distance. "Of course."

They followed, always staying at least a mile to the side and back the cart. In the cold night air, Leina retrieved a spare cloak from her pack and donned it, having discarded her other one on the cliff above the mine. The horse moved languidly, encumbered by the hundreds of pounds of stones it dragged. Melkin watched the rear of the group, his spear at the ready, while Leina walked ahead, empty-handed. The others were glad to have their weapons drawn at all times, but she left hers in their sheaths. Her arms couldn't take much more, and she felt that even holding her dagger for so many hours would tire her out. She wanted to be as rested as possible for whatever dangers might lurk at the end of this mysterious journey. As the night grew darker, Leina found it harder to see but could still make out the vague shape of the horses in the distance. The hills continued, but the rocky ground gave way to grass and trees once more, further veiling the horse and cart from their view.

"Evarith, I can take your place," whispered Lothar.

"It's fine."

"You need to rest your eyes."

Melkin sighed and let Lothar take over, though the few times Leina glanced back, she saw he was still attentive to their surroundings.

Galdur walked beside her. "Sorry, Leina. I would offer to take over for you, but..."

"I understand, it's alright." During the next hour of travel the trees became denser, but Leina never lost sight of the transport group—her eyes and focus stayed razor sharp despite her exhaustion. Still, her heart skipped a beat each time a stick snapped, or the dead leaves of autumn crunched under their feet. With a jolt of fear, she imagined one of the distant guards turning back and spotting the pursing group.

"They can't hear us from here," assured Melkin. Leina chose to believe him, though she wasn't sure how he would know such a fact. "Just step lightly."

"Galdur, where are we?" whispered Lothar.

Galdur was silent for a moment. "We've traveled up the coast of the Shalin Empire, some miles inland. No one lives in this region. There are very few water sources besides the ocean."

As they crested a hill, Leina could make out a bright, powerful light. "A fire in the distance... That must be where the carts are heading. We need to stay out of sight if we're going to spy on them."

Melkin squinted, stepping forward. "Let's get there first, then we'll figure out where to hide. The trees look dense anyway."

Soon, details of the site came into view. In the center of a clearing on a hill, there sat a massive bonfire. Dozens of single-person tents littered the campsite, all of different designs. Some looked identical to ones she'd seen in Hileath, while others were more like those that Lothar and Astrid carried. The campsite was teeming with both faul and human, chatting and laughing with one another. Some could be told apart by height or skin color, but others with heights similar to her own were indistinguishable as either race. She looked back at Melkin, waiting for instructions.

"It's loud there. We'll be fine if we get closer," he said, waving them on toward the hill. Leina took a shaky breath and swallowed; she hated hiding in the shadows. If only she knew more about these people, she could try mingling with the crowd, asking questions, and gaining more information. But that required planning at the very least, and these people might know each other quite well. The five began climbing the hill; they were only a few hundred feet away now.

"I—I—By Ryne..." Galdur was breathing shallowly, and Leina could see panic written all over the young prince's face. He was standing twenty feet behind the other four with wide eyes, unmoving. Leina and Melkin turned back and approached him.

"What's the worst that could happen?" whispered Melkin as if he was confused.

Galdur looked at him for a few moments. "We... could *die*?"

Melkin shrugged. "Well, either you join us and we die together, or you don't, and you're left out in the cold night alone if the rest of us die."

Leina glared at Melkin. "But that's not going to happen. It'd be good to have another pair of ears listening to this crowd. If we have to run, we don't want to lose sight of each other either. Please, come." She reached out and offered him her hand.

Galdur took one more deep, trembling breath and looked between Melkin and Leina. He nodded and let Leina pull him back into the group.

19

Galdur

Galdur stared at his shaking hands. He was further from danger than his four companions, yet he must have been more terrified than any of them, considering that they stood still, eyes focused on the campsite in front of them, while he struggled to bring himself to even glance at it. He stood over twenty yards from the tree line, but the laughter and noisy conversations carried even to his ears. He wondered what the lively and boisterous crowd would do to any innocent travelers who stumbled upon them. Galdur shook his head, clearing the thought, and directed his attention to the cart. The rider had dismounted and was now engaged in conversation with a person from the camp. The guards that had flanked the cart were unloading the contents and carrying the crates full of blue rock into the camp. All involved were smiling and chatting with one another; he couldn't imagine them harming anyone.

Then he remembered watching from above, petrified, as Leina collapsed to the ground at the mine. His friend had been in danger, and he had been paralyzed by fear. When he had finally broken his trance and alerted Melkin, the four had rushed to stop the guards and tie the rope around a sturdy rock. Lothar had even tried to burn her pursuers, but he was too far away from the fast-moving guards. They had known what to do immediately.

Right, the campsite—the bombers. Galdur blinked and reminded himself that these people might appear docile, but their true nature had already been revealed by the murder and enslavement of hundreds.

Why did he have to be here? The others would hear everything—he could have stayed at the bottom of the hill. Why hadn't he?

"You were right, there's much more as you go deeper!" laughed the horse rider. "Look at all this!"

Galdur brought his attention to the cart again, listening to the conversation.

The faul beside the rider had a broad smile on his face. "We knew there would be! Come, join us for dinner and tell of your success!"

"Thank you! The day has been long, and . . . well, I wouldn't really call it daytime anymore," said the rider, looking to the stars. As the two dispersed into the crowd, their conversation blended into many others. A few minutes later, the cart had been unloaded and people were taking dinner from a large pot over the fire. Everyone seemed to be settling down, waiting for something. One of the guards mounted the horse and began heading back in the direction of the mines.

"Listen up!" commanded a female voice over the chatter. Instantly, the commotion died down. Galdur risked a peek from behind his tree and saw a faul standing atop a rock, addressing the rest of the party. Around forty people in total.

"Welcome back. It's been a few weeks since we could get most of the officials together, so don't expect another one of these for a while. Obviously, some faces are new and some are missing. We can't get everyone from Yane to the Northern Mountains, but we do have plenty of news to discuss."

Her tone was friendly, yet powerful. He wished he had the power to command like she did—he'd never had much practice with the whole thing. Strange for a prince, but Fareod always got the coaching.

"First, some unfortunate news. This morning, informant Imar was found dead in the woods."

Galdur's heart skipped a beat and gasps resonated from all around the campsite. He felt a mixture of relief and terror fill him—they were in the right place. In front of him, Melkin kept Lothar from falling and started whispering something in his ear.

"Fortunately," the voice continued, "we are far enough along that Imar's position is no longer central to the plan. Still, his information is invaluable to the success of our operation. Imar was tracking a group that may very well prove dangerous in the future. From a letter he sent before joining them, we know three of the group's members. Astrid Inaria, a short, very muscular faul with long hair—"

"Muscular? A faul?" interrupted someone.

"Indeed so. And Lothar Raiken, a faul sergeant, average height, short-ish hair. Lothar was one of the two Akarist survivors and he believes it to be his duty to stop this war. Imar also mentioned Lothar was working with the other survivor, a Valean spy by the name of Evarith. We're working on sourcing official sketches of the two faul to show our rangers and scouts." Galdur glanced at his companions, watching their eyes turn wide and jaws slacken. Melkin looked ready to catch Lothar again.

Another voice jumped in, "Have you seen the newspapers around Harolin? They report that a faul named Lothar Raiken broke a human out of jail who was found in an inn, trying to steal from a customer."

"Ha! No, the human found some of us trying to set a bomb in that inn; we ended up blowing the central square instead," said another.

"But we still don't know his identity?" asked the leader.

"We searched the files in the royal castle. No one by the name of Evarith, but we heard rumors that a spy named Melkin Edaireth had been sent by Gladia for some sort of mission. Other spies are of course out on missions for the military and whatnot, but this one was quite esteemed, from what we know. He hasn't returned yet."

"Same person?"

"We can't tell. I . . . don't think so. There's no record of this man being sent to the Akarist. Gladia . . . I don't think she would send a spy to the Akarist. We think that she might have sent him to investigate the Annister bombing instead, which would make more sense. We can only speculate, though."

"I see... Have we looked into the surname, 'Evarith'?" asked the leader.

"Briefly. We haven't had a lot of time, but we found something in Annister as well as in Starren Province. We're looking into it, but don't have any useful information yet. It's of course possible that Imar misheard the name Edaireth as Evarith, but the two are just as likely different people. Why would a spy use such similar names?"

The leader was silent for a moment. "Hmm... I'll think about that. Keep investigating and report back to me. In other news, the amount of teleium brought to us today is remarkable, but we also have to process it quickly. Of course, most of this rock is impure, but we may be able to abandon the mines soon. I want to move this gathering site to a new location for which you'll get the details soon. Once your assignments are complete, meet there for more instructions. Understood?"

Variations of "yes" echoed throughout the campsite.

Though the walk here had been grueling, Galdur was now rapt. His eyelids no longer drooped—instead, his body was filled with energy as he listened to the commanding, confident voice.

"Good. Any recent news on the Shalin infiltration?" asked the leader.

"Not much. Truly a tragedy, the death of Imar. He was the closest we got to the emperor himself. Fortunately, Orwic is prepared to go to war since he's always hated Valea. If Fareod is crowned, we shouldn't have any trouble."

"What's the situation with the queen?"

"I am happy to report that her condition is deteriorating. The poison was a success."

Galdur's stomach dropped. *Poison? No... who could have? One of these bastards here?*

"Wonderful, have our Valean guards expedite Fareod's inauguration as soon as she dies. Then we can really get moving!"

Was he—no—please don't say he was—Galdur didn't want to know anymore. He stood frozen and wide eyed, wishing he could somehow close his ears.

"Will do!"

"I'm surprised the fool actually followed orders. And succeeded at that!"

Galdur's breath became labored; he felt weak and dizzy. He barely caught himself on the tree as he stumbled, unable to keep his knees from giving out. Leaves crumpled beneath him, and four pairs of eyes fell upon him. He willed himself to remember how to use his legs and took a breath. *Focus.* He prayed no one in the camp had heard him stumble.

"Keep him under strict guard. I don't want to use our backup if we don't have to," said the leader.

Backup, what backup? Backup for the throne? Galdur was next in line, and then he racked his brain, but the name was out of reach.

"Yes, well, about that . . ." said a sheepish voice. "Fareod's brother has gone missing, along with another castle spy, Leina Kierth. We don't know where the two went, but if Fareod dies, we won't know where to find him."

"What happens then?" asked another. "If the king is dead and the heir is gone, who rules? Does it go to the next in line?"

"We don't know, but it's not a position we want to be in."

"Correct," said the leader. "For now, let's just make sure that Fareod lives."

"Of course."

"And until these Valean spies show up somewhere else, we have greater priorities. Keep an eye out but don't compromise your assignments. What news from Paeline?"

"Not much more, the training is going well. No intruders so far, and the children seem to be happy. The site has been kept stocked with food, water, clothing—everything. According to her reports, the eldest should be ready within a week."

"Excellent. Any other questions I have I'll ask individually. Good work. I know it's been a long journey, but soon everything will fall beautifully into place. A new day will dawn, my friends! Long live the Talwreks!"

Cheers sounded about the campsite as the bombers split into their separate groups. Galdur had only just been able to make out that last word—it sounded made up to him. Melkin, closest to the tree line, turned around and signaled for the group to leave. The five rushed down the hill, hoping the reborn chatter in the campsite masked the crunching leaves.

"Stay low, keep moving," said Melkin in a hoarse whisper.

"That faul—that was Elvine!" whispered Lothar. "By the Gods..."

"The one from the Akarist? Your rescuer?" asked Leina.

Melkin nodded, glancing back at the four of them. "Yes."

A million questions and emotions raced through Galdur's mind, but none so powerful as his wish for sleep. Still, Melkin forced them to walk for another hour or so in hopes of getting as far away from the campsite as possible. The other four occasionally whispered a word or two to one another, but no one voiced any of their thoughts on what they'd all just heard at the campsite. Perhaps they were all too tired. At last, Melkin signaled for them to stop in a valley, hidden from any onlookers.

"I think we ought to get to sleep tonight... I'll try and take the whole night watch so you all can get some rest. Not that there's much night left, and I'm afraid we do have to get moving in the morning," said Melkin. None of them argued with that.

Though morning came far too soon, Galdur was glad he'd been able to sleep through the few hours of night. He had earned some meager hours of rest, despite his mind being wrought with unfriendly emotions.

"Let's get moving, we can talk and eat breakfast while we walk," said Melkin.

"Where are we going?" asked Lothar, yawning.

"Southwest, I suppose. It seems we're sort of on a peninsula right now, and that's the way off."

"Good plan," said Leina.

Galdur thought it strange that neither Astrid nor Lothar objected to the order even though they would be traveling toward Valea.

"We got the information that we wanted," said Melkin. "And hopefully they never noticed that we were there."

"I'm not so sure I wanted to know half of what we heard," muttered Galdur. He was surprised again to see nods of agreement from Leina, Astrid, and Lothar.

Melkin just shrugged. "I think we were all shaken up by what we learned, but that's exactly what we aimed to do. Learn and gather information. Now we must find a path forward."

Astrid glared at Melkin. "You don't seem too shaken up."

"I've had some time to think about it. Staying awake even during a short night makes it quite long indeed."

Astrid mumbled her apologies, staring at the ground.

"War," muttered Lothar. "By Talen..."

"Yes, war seems to be their motive. That's probably one of the best pieces of information we gleaned from that. The other was how deep the operation goes. There's no possibility of eliminating this group through brute force—"

"Brute force?" asked Astrid.

Leina smirked. "Assassinations."

Melkin nodded. "Yes, that. No, there are too many people, too deep in the government, who are too good at disguising themselves—like Imar."

"Alright, so what do we do?" asked Lothar.

"I suppose we have to stop their plans in other ways. If their goal is to start a war then we must find some way to prevent that from happening."

"Why do they want it? We still haven't figured that out," said Leina.

"It doesn't matter. Well, to some extent it does, but we can't waste any more time finding that out. They want war and we must stop it," said Melkin.

"Before we explore how, tell me, *are* you this 'Melkin Edaireth' character?" asked Lothar, glaring at Melkin. A pit of dread formed in Galdur's stomach. He had seen this coming.

Melkin sighed, a fatigued expression on his face. "Yes."

Lothar softened his glare; he must have been surprised Melkin did not respond in anger.

Astrid's face remained scornful. "So you both lied to us?"

"We didn't lie," said Melkin. "We gave you our surnames. That's not lying."

"I gave *my* surname, you didn't. In fact, which is real? Evarith or Edaireth?" asked Leina.

Melkin pressed his lips. "Why does it matter?"

"Trust," said Lothar. He turned to Melkin. "Maybe you don't think that matters, but I do. So, if you think we should trust you and follow your orders, tell us."

"Evarith *is* my real surname, and Edaireth is the name I told the castle. On my missions, I use Evarith—without my first name, of course. If anyone were to look into the name, they would find the records of a poor Annister citizen. No need for a fake backstory or forged documents. As spies, we're known mostly by our first names so that we can't be tracked as easily. It's far simpler to find records of a surname than a first name. So, if I tell people my name is Evarith, and they perhaps suspect I'm a spy, I have a backup. They would check the castle records and wouldn't find me. If they look for 'Evarith,' they would find a genuine record, just not that of a spy. Oh, and if they *do* put two and two together, the names sound similar enough that it wouldn't necessarily look like I had lied. The bombers have done *exactly* as I predicted others would do, so what's the problem?"

Leina shut her eyes in frustration; how could he not get it? "You never told me! I thought you trusted me."

"I do. I told you my *real* last name, just not the one on record at the castle. I didn't think it was important."

"Hmph."

"I'm sorry, alright? I didn't mean to hurt any of you."

"We still need a plan. Right now, we're walking aimlessly," said Astrid.

Galdur sighed. "If Fareod is crowned, he'll declare war,"

"And if Orwic remains emperor, he won't object," said Lothar, shaking his head. He perked up and turned toward Leina and Melkin. "What about that brother of Fareod? Do you know where he went?"

Melkin turned to Galdur. "I do."

Galdur took an enormous breath, summoning the courage to speak. Everyone had their eyes on him now. "Right here..." He waved stupidly. "Galdur Ravinyk."

"You. You're the prince of Valea?" asked Astrid, an incredulous smile appearing on her lips, as if she didn't think a man like Galdur could be the prince. He wasn't surprised. Galdur nodded, refusing to meet the eyes of either faul. Guilt wracked him; he had genuinely come to think well of them. And now they had been lied to, *again*.

Lothar's hands were balled into fists as he stared at Galdur's. "Why didn't you tell us earlier?"

Galdur's eyes darted between the two faces. "I—I was afraid!"

"Afraid? Why?" asked Lothar, as if he couldn't imagine what might cause Galdur's apprehension.

"You're faul! I mean—any of you three could have assassinated me, and if Imar had known, he might have!" cried Galdur.

"Okay, it's alright. You don't have to yell," said Lothar, his tone calm and posture relaxed. His demeanor reminded him of Gladia, in a way.

"Yeah," said Astrid. "I mean, it's not like you could have known that Imar was a bomber... But it doesn't matter now."

"I'm sorry," said Galdur, fighting back tears. "I just—it's a lot. Everything." The bombers had talked about poisoning his mother only a few yards from him. He thought that sleep had calmed him down, and it had, but it hadn't healed the gaping hole inside.

"It won't be long until they use what they saw at the ruins to connect the five of us together," said Melkin. "We must act now."

"What do we do?" asked Lothar.

"Well, we could try to find where they're meeting next," said Leina.

Melkin stared into the distance, his eyes unfocused. "No. We may not even gain any information from that, and it could take far too long. I think... Well, what started the rivalry between Valea and the Shalin Empire?"

Lothar stroked his chin. "That's a question for Imar. I mean, I've heard plenty of more recent stories from the border, but as for the very start of the animosity? I've heard about an old Valean king sending soldiers into the Shalin empire to capture a group of very powerful faul and take them prisoner. Then, all of the faul were killed. Something about being afraid of their magic and wanting it gone."

Astrid nodded. "That story is told everywhere in the Shalin Empire."

"Not in Valea. I've never heard that before," said Galdur, raising an eyebrow. He was glad for a distraction—anything to occupy his thoughts. "Fareod told me stories of a group of powerful faul coming into Valea and raiding towns, cities, and villages before finally being stopped by soldiers."

"Do you trust Fareod's stories?" asked Melkin.

"I've seen the story in books as well. And it was ten years ago that Fareod told me for the first time. I doubt a nine-year-old Fareod was trying to deceive me."

Astrid whirled around. "Wait—Fareod is nineteen?"

"And he's the crown prince? How old are you, then?" asked Lothar.

"Seventeen."

"By Talen!" exclaimed Lothar. "Out of curiosity . . . how old is everyone else?"

"Twenty-one," said Leina.

Astrid nodded. "Same."

"Twenty-three," said Melkin.

"Gods . . . I'm twenty-six!" cried Lothar. "Almost a decade older than you, Galdur!"

"Ahh, you're not that old Lothar," said Melkin with a wry smile. "I'm sure you've got a couple more years left in you . . ." At Lothar's glare, Melkin coughed and continued, "Anyway, back to the matter at hand; we don't have a clear story to go off of?"

"Well, at the border there seemed to be this culture of families losing their loved ones, becoming enraged, and fighting to avenge them. Over and over. When statues of the Five Deities or temples of prayer were destroyed by the humans, it would get worse. Not to mention when land was gained . . . it was *horrible*."

"And statues or temples of Ryne were never destroyed by you faul?" asked Galdur, immediately regretting the words as they left his mouth. Four heads immediately turned to him, and he averted his gaze.

To Galdur's immense surprise, Astrid grinned slightly. "Of course they were."

"I didn't know you were religious, Galdur," said Lothar. "These two aren't," he said, pointing at Leina and Melkin. That was true.

"You four get distracted quite easily, don't you?" commented Melkin. "Shouldn't someone know this history? I expected that you would, Galdur..."

Galdur tried to ignore the evident disappointment in Melkin's voice. Throughout the past week and a half, he had asked himself why he was brought here. What could he do for this group? This was it, and he had failed. "It's been overshadowed. After all, it must have happened around a century ago," said Galdur.

"Why are you so curious, Melkin? Maybe we don't need to know the history," suggested Lothar.

"I think this is the most direct route. I assume the bombers want to exploit history to cause this war. So, if we know why the two countries are so angry at one another, we might discover ways to hinder their plans," asserted Melkin.

Lothar grinned. "About that name, by the way, did anyone hear what Elvine called them?"

20

MELKIN

"Before you delve into faul mythology, let's figure out where we're going," suggested Astrid.

Lothar looked crestfallen. "It's not mythology, it's—"

"Galdur, where are we?" asked Melkin, cutting off Lothar.

"Still in the Shalin Empire, about seven miles from Valea. If you want to go to a shop—"

"Leina, Galdur, and I are too well known now to walk into a Valean store and buy a history book after being gone for over a week. It would most likely be fine, but I don't want to risk it if we don't have to. Lothar and I are wanted here in the Shalin Empire. Astrid, does anyone know that you're gone, besides the bombers?" asked Melkin, his mind brimming with possibilities despite the absurdity of having to buy a book on their mission.

"I don't think so . . . I'm just a city guard, so probably not."

"If we're going into a Shalin town, I could blend in," said Leina, a grin spreading across her face.

Lothar furrowed his brow. "Why would you need to? Astrid will be fine."

"Well, in case there are any bombers who recognize her. I can talk my way out of a great deal of things. I'm a little tall, yes, but it's not that bad. Plus, I have a feeling that this information may not be in any old history book. Else we might know the truth by now."

"Fine," said Melkin with a shrug. "Unless you want to go, Galdur, then that's settled."

"I'll stay behind.

"You're sending *Kierth* with me to buy a *book*?" asked Astrid, a look of disgust on her face. Leina glared at Astrid in turn.

Melkin fought the urge to roll his eyes. "Yes. Where's the closest Shalin Village?"

"About fifteen miles west and a little north, I think. A town called Nuwelke. Still have that map?" asked Galdur. Melkin fished out the map from his bag and handed it over. "Twenty miles west," he amended after a good look.

"We're going there, then. Let's hope they have history books," said Melkin. "Unless anyone has any other ideas?" No one responded.

"Back to my point about Elvine," said Lothar, "She called this group of hers the Talwreks."

"Some made-up name?" guessed Melkin.

"Not at all. See, around a thousand years ago the Shalin Empire was far from its current glory. There was mass fighting and unrest. Local warriors would band their villages or towns into small states to fight the dozens of surrounding enemy states. A few larger states sprung up now and again, but they were unstable and torn apart quite quickly. Leaders of these towns would rule with an iron fist to keep their states intact and to get enough supplies for the constant war."

"We get it," said Leina.

Astrid chuckled softly. "Hey, let him have this."

Lothar scowled. "While this was happening, Valea was already a stable kingdom. I don't think it changed much over the years. Well, Valea didn't conquer any of these faul-inhabited states, but the faul were afraid of being kicked out of their land, slaughtered, overtaken, or forced into slavery by the humans. After all, Valea already didn't permit faul to live within their borders, so if they wanted to increase their land, the process was obvious.

So, a faul named Eiphen Prezanos pleaded with his town on the border of one of these states to start trading with the neighboring states, claiming it would strengthen the faul race. This was quite the revolutionary idea and caused him to be exiled from his town, along with any faul who dared agree with him. Then, he heard a voice speaking to him. The god Talen told him to continue this pursuit. He and his followers called themselves the Talwreks, which translates to 'Talen's guided'. Though Talen started it, all five deities encouraged the Talwreks in their own ways. Talen granted them extended life and health. Helinka helped them create cunning plans to convince people to join them and whispered words of wisdom in their ears. Molaib threatened their enemies and gave the Talwreks a good afterlife. Kaima blessed them with incredible magical abilities, and of course, Oberel gave them the strength to continue and defeat their enemies. With the deities on their side, the Talwreks miraculously united the entire faul race into the Shalin Empire."

Melkin could almost hear everyone processing the story in the few moments of following silence.

"Why would they call themselves that?" asked Leina.

Lothar put a hand to his chin. "Well, if they're trying to say that they have Talen's blessing—"

"But they have both humans and faul in their group," said Astrid.

"They could have converted," said Galdur.

Astrid sighed. "I suppose. Still seems like a strange name."

"War would break the continent apart, right? So maybe it's the reverse. The Talwreks united the Shalin Empire, this new group destroys it," suggested Melkin. He considered this conversation to be a waste of time, but they had nothing else to do on the way to Nuwelke.

Lothar's face lit up. "Or maybe they want the Shalin Empire to conquer Valea as an extension of the Talwreks' mission."

"You think they could?" asked Melkin with a raised eyebrow.

Lothar shrugged. "I don't know."

"Why would humans support that?" asked Leina.

"I . . . don't know," said Lothar, throwing his hands up in defeat.

"Well, perhaps it'll reveal itself later," said Melkin.

Lothar nodded, a pained expression on his face. "Perhaps. You know, something else struck me as odd about Elvine. Something looked familiar about her..."

"Something else besides her being at the Akarist?" asked Melkin, doubtful.

"I didn't see it when we were at the Akarist since I had... other things on my mind. But something..."

Melkin shrugged, leaving Lothar staring into the distance with unfocused eyes. Silence reigned for a good while, giving him some time to sort through his thoughts. He wished to think upon the conversation and about how to stop these Talwreks, but only one concern came to the front of his mind: the upcoming hunt for a history book. It was just a town, he reminded himself, a small part of their mission, really. Surely Leina *did* have his trust, right? He trusted her to not betray him, that he was certain of. But did he trust her not to fail him? Yes, he told himself, but was it true? Maybe. He hadn't seen enough of Astrid's skills to know if she might fail. How could he trust Leina and her with the fate of so many people? Night watch was one thing, and he was still wary about that—especially after Imar. But this was a whole other dilemma. The worst that could happen, he supposed, was that Leina and Astrid would be captured. Not a good outcome but better than all five of them being discovered and killed.

"Are you alright Galdur?" asked Lothar, breaking the silence. There was no response as Galdur continued walking, seemingly having not heard the question. "Galdur?"

Galdur jerked his head up. "Hmm?"

"I asked if you were okay."

"Oh. Yeah, I'm alright."

Leina shook her head. "I don't believe you. It's your mother, right?"

"Her being on her deathbed was bad enough... I can't believe she was poisoned. I can't believe my bastard of a brother did it!"

"Fareod won't stay king," said Lothar. "If we want to stop the coming war, he can't be."

"What can *we* do about it?" asked Galdur, throwing up his hands in a hopeless gesture.

"Probably kill him," said Melkin, not missing a beat. It seemed like the obvious course of action to him. No one responded, yet four pairs of eyes turned on him. "What?" For once, Melkin found silence to be unnerving.

"He *is* Galdur's brother..." said Lothar sheepishly.

"No, it's okay. For what he's done, he deserves it. I wouldn't do it, but he deserves it," said Galdur. "I just don't know how we'd do it. I mean, if he even becomes king, he'd be heavily guarded."

"We'll figure that out once we do some research," said Melkin. Astrid rolled her eyes. "A riveting task."

"Better than being chased by a vicious group of extremists?" asked Leina.

"No. Not as interesting."

"Well, I certainly wish I wasn't wanted by the government," said Lothar dryly. "But alas, Melkin had to go and get himself *captured*."

"Yes, I apologize deeply for stopping people from getting hurt," said Melkin, frustrated by yet another tangent.

"Which you didn't accomplish," muttered Lothar.

"Yes, I did. I spotted the inn bomb, which would have *killed* people. Anyway, I have to ask you, Galdur," he said. "Elvine mentioned a backup plan after Fareod. So, who's in line to the throne after you?"

"Melkin!" cried Lothar, throwing his hands up in exasperation.

"What?" Why did they keep looking at him like he was crazy for asking the obvious questions?

"I've been thinking about that, and I remember now. I have a cousin, Esadora Ravinyk. Her father was Gladia's youngest brother, and he died in battle just after she was born. Her mother then succumbed to disease and she was made an orphan."

"I suppose the ah... Talwreks could have found her," said Melkin. "That would be why they were upset about your disappearance. If Fareod dies, they would kill you and Esadora would become queen."

"Melkin, do you really think that Galdur wants to hear this?" cried Lothar.

"It's the truth! I'm not going to lie."

"Can we not pretend that my mother is already dead? She's strong; she can overcome this. She *will* overcome this. The guards will find the poison and she'll be treated."

Lothar glared at Melkin, cutting off the retort on the tip of his tongue about the unlikelihood of that.

Another hour or so later, he stopped the group for lunch and some sparring.

"Can't we take a nap?" asked Leina, rubbing her eyes.

Melkin set down his pack. "No." It was imperative that they practice while sleep deprived; the same state in which they'd fight true enemies.

"It's alright. Kierth, come train with me," said Astrid, a sly smile on her face. Leina flashed a look of annoyance at Melkin before joining her.

"Galdur, Lothar, come here," said Melkin, pulling out the spare knives he kept in his pack. They'd had an enormous amount of money to spend in Hileath, so he had bought extra throwing knives just in case. Melkin rolled his eyes at Lothar and Galdur's hesitant gaits as they walked over. Melkin rolled his eyes. "Relax. I want to show you two how to throw knives."

"Oh!" said Galdur, relaxing his stance. Lothar stood, waiting with a flat expression. Melkin handed each of them a throwing knife, and Lothar turned it around in his hands, looking at each angle.

"Lothar, this is your tree, so stand about two yards from it," he said, pointing. He directed Galdur to a tree beside it, hoping that their aim wasn't so bad as to injure one another. "Grip the knife by the handle, put your right foot in front..." He waited for them to comply, noticing Lothar held his knife in the wrong hand. "Lothar, hold the knife in your right hand."

Lothar switched hands. "You sure...?"

"Don't you hold your dagger in your right hand?"

"Yeah, my auxlar dagger."

"Which one is that?"

"The shorter one." The two stood there for a few seconds, eying each other with confused looks.

He thought back to fighting the fake Shalin servant in the Akarist. It dawned on him—he was an idiot of a spy. "You all are left-handed."

"Oh . . . yeah."

Melkin stroked his chin. "I suppose you would just put your left foot forward then and hold the knife in your left hand." Lothar obliged. "Now bring your arm back and release the knife." Lothar's hit the tree but didn't stick, while Galdur's stuck for a second, then fell. "Not bad, not bad." He tried to recall first learning to throw knives, but couldn't remember if he had any experience before the academy. "Lothar, don't bring your arm so far back. Galdur, give it a little more power. It has to rotate a half spin for it to stick in the tree." They tried again and both got their knives to stick. "Nice job. Keep practicing at that distance for now, and we'll go further a little later." Melkin turned away and walked over to Astrid and Leina, eager to ask the faul a question.

"One more! Come on, push!" exclaimed Astrid, standing over Leina who was on the ground doing push-ups. Slowly, Leina completed the last push-up and collapsed to the ground. "Alright, good job!" Astrid was grinning; he couldn't remember if he had ever seen her *happy*.

"My arms are *so* sore, Astrid! Was my torture in that mine not bad enough?" asked Leina, still sprawled out on the ground.

Astrid laughed. "Won't happen again if you keep training like this. Perhaps praying to Oberel wouldn't hurt either!"

"Who's he?" asked Leina, sitting up. "Hey look, I'm almost your height!"

"The God of strength, something you'll need if you go around insulting people like that."

"Mmm, yeah, or I could just use my crossbow . . . Can't really overpower that."

"Having fun?" asked Melkin, a smirk creeping onto his lips.

"Oh, lots," said Leina. "Astrid's just trying to kill me is all."

He raised an eyebrow. "Mind if I interrupt?"

"Please do," said Leina.

"Astrid, you fight with your ah . . . majoril dagger in your left hand, correct?" asked Melkin, directing his attention toward her.

"Of course."

"We humans would use our right hand for the main weapon. Have you ever fought a human who was wielding a dagger like that?"

"Only once."

"What happened?"

"Well, we were both caught off guard by it. I'd practiced it a few times in my military training, but not often since the Valeans typically use spears, and we use daggers. It's something that we soldiers are aware of, but it's never at the front of our minds."

Melkin nodded. "I only just learned. Did you know, Leina?"

"Yes, I think so. Somewhere in the back of my mind. What does it matter though?"

"Nothing, I was just thinking... How did the fight end?"

She shrugged. "Like any dagger fight. I injured him and he ran away."

"Thanks, Astrid. We're going to leave in a few minutes, alright?" Away from his companions, he drew a throwing knife from his sheath—far too short to fight with in close quarters—and held it in his left hand. He frowned slightly at the feeling. By no means was he an excellent dagger fighter, and he didn't use two like the faul did, but Melkin wondered nonetheless if he could become accustomed to the feeling. Maybe he didn't have to.

Melkin put the knife away and walked over to Lothar and Galdur, watching them for a few seconds before interrupting. "I have something for you two." He pulled out two throwing knife sheaths from his pack, bought for this purpose. "It goes around your leg. Neither of you brought too many weapons, so I figure you could use a few extra." Galdur and Lothar took the sheathes, which each held three throwing knives.

"Thanks, Melkin," said Galdur, grinning as he wrapped the strap around his leg. Lothar nodded his thanks and did the same.

"Let's go. We have to reach that village soon," said Melkin, strapping up his bag. He looked over to where Astrid and Leina were chatting—at least they weren't at each other's throats anymore. "Let's move!" he shouted. "How much further, Galdur?"

"Ten miles west."

"When there's... two miles to go, the rest of us will hide while you two go on to the town," said Melkin. "Do you have any sort of plan?"

"Find a store, or a library, or a town hall I suppose. The earl of the town might have some history books lying around," said Leina.

"Just... be careful," said Melkin.

Leina stared at him in disbelief. "As if I don't know."

Five miles from the town, they rested for the night. If the two had to run away, Melkin wanted them to have energy, and Leina thought it best to not explore the town at night. Once morning came, they traveled another three miles, at which point the town that Galdur had brought them to became visible. It was larger than Melkin had expected; he saw some stone buildings amongst the wood and straw ones. They searched around for some form of cover and came across a small ditch. "You two go on ahead," said Melkin, motioning for the rest of the group to join him in the ditch.

"If anything happens, we'll be right here," said Lothar. Melkin watched as the two of them began to walk toward the village. He told himself that they were competent. He told himself that at least Leina would do this job *better* than he could, even if he wasn't a criminal. Deep down, he knew he was right. Still, he failed to believe it.

21

ASTRID

Astrid's hand gravitated toward her majoril dagger, gripping it in fear of attack. Not that she was a criminal—well, she sort of was—but every single aspect of this excursion made her feel on edge. She hated the secrecy, the uncertainty of what might happen. Her eyes darted about as she and Leina walked paths through the farms on the outskirts of town. Farmers gave them strange looks as they passed by, pausing in their labor to glance at the two.

"Stop. You look like you're about to attack someone," said Leina.

Astrid let go of the dagger and tried to relax. "You really don't look like a faul, Leina. Too tall, and your black hair stands out."

"That's why you're here, in case I get into trouble. There's more risk with both of us but a better chance that we'll survive if anything happens. Look, this is my specialty. Disguising, acting, that kind of thing. So if all goes well, you can just stand beside me and wait while I do the talking. I'll have a cloak on, so the only visible part of me will be my face." Astrid nodded, feeling marginally better. "Oh, and if we're asked for names, yours is Porela Leith. I don't want to risk it if your disappearance has been discovered by now."

Astrid nodded. "I wish you'd have brought your crossbow along. I've seen what you can do with it."

"We couldn't risk drawing more attention. It's an expensive, bulky weapon."

It was logical, but she still felt exposed. Astrid had her daggers, of course, but they felt insufficient. The thought of the bombers being here somehow, and capturing them, didn't settle well with her. As much as she hated her time at the border, a simple life or death fight was far more appealing than this. And though she was quite sure that the girl walking next to her would be flattened in any close-quarters fight, she admired her cool, calm demeanor. Perhaps Astrid could appear carefree to any onlookers, but no matter how much reassurance Leina gave her, she could not hide her inner fear.

They approached a feeble fence surrounding the town. A Shalin guard stood at the gate, eyeing them as they walked forward. Leina stepped forward, putting herself slightly in front of Astrid. The woman had her black hair tied up and slicked back beneath her hood, concealing its obvious color. Astrid wasn't sure if it was coincidence or if Leina had planned to arrive at this time, but the sun had ended up behind them, making it hard to judge the color of Leina's skin. It really wasn't that obvious anyway, just a shade or two darker.

"What business do you have here?" asked the guard, scrutinizing the two.

"Good day, we are simply travelers in need of food and rest," said Leina. Astrid tried to slow her breathing as the soldier squinted, looking the two of them up and down.

"Names?"

"Sarthia Haufe," said Leina, not missing a beat.

The soldier's eyes turned upon her. "P—Porela Leith."

"Welcome to Nuwelke. Times are strange—don't stay for long."

"Thank you, sir," said Leina. They walked into town, down the various streets to nowhere in particular. "Excuse me, do you know where we could purchase books?" asked Leina of a passerby, flashing a gentle smile.

"Books? There's a shop that way," he said, pointing down a street to his right. They took the path indicated and soon came across a small building with a sign reading "Nuwelke Bookstore."

"Good place to start," muttered Leina. Walking into the store, Astrid gazed around at the papers, scrolls, and books that lined the shelves.

The shopkeeper leaned on the counter, a bored expression on her face. "What can I do for you?"

"Do you have any history books here?" asked Leina.

"History books, eh? They're over there, two silver coins apiece." The two shuffled over, finding five shelves that held a couple dozen books each, as well as a few piles of stacked books on the floor. Astrid rushed forward and began grabbing volumes from the shelves, checking the spines, and shoving them back.

Leina put a hand on her arm. "Calm down. We have plenty of time."

Astrid nodded and took a breath. She leisurely pulled a title from the shelf, found it to be useless, and placed it back in its proper spot. Perhaps if she organized the shelves, she could forget about this nightmare of a mission.

"Here," said Leina, holding up *A History of the Shalin Empire*. Astrid felt her anxiety unwind a bit and relaxed. She brought it back to the shopkeeper and paid two silver coins for the title.

As the two left the shop, Astrid glanced down the streets, watching for bombers. "Can't we leave now?"

"No. And stop looking around like that. You wouldn't be able to recognize a Talwrek anyway."

That did nothing to calm Astrid, but she followed Leina nonetheless to the town tavern; she had no choice but to trust her. Leina beckoned Astrid inside to a table and sat.

Astrid leaned in, glancing around the inn. "Why are we here?" she whispered.

"Let's take a look," said Leina, her voice at a normal speaking volume.

"Why are you being so loud?"

Leina kicked her under the table, and Astrid figured she'd better follow along. For some reason.

Leina pulled out the book and riffled through the chapters. "Here we go, chapter eleven, 'The Valean and Shalin Controversy.'"

"What does it say?" asked Astrid.

Leina glared at her from above the edge of the book. "I'm getting there." She skimmed over a few pages. "Ah! No... this is no good!" she exclaimed. "It's the story that Lothar talked about. More in depth but the same ideas."

"Maybe that's the true story."

"It's not. It wouldn't make any sense. I'd bet that if we went into a Valean town we would see the same story that Galdur told us."

"Hmph. Then what should we do?"

Leina closed the book. "We're going to talk to the earl. Normally I would say we should go to another town, but we *are* under time pressure."

"Why did we come to a tavern?"

"Didn't want to read in the middle of a shop. Travelers always stop at taverns, but they don't buy books. What do you want to drink?"

"To drink—What?" exclaimed Astrid.

She rolled her eyes and stood up. "If you don't tell me, I'll get you something random. Play the part."

"Uh—fine. Coffee.".

Leina smiled sweetly. "Wonderful." She walked up to the counter and began chatting with the innkeeper. Astrid shook her head in wonder. Leina was trying to be discreet, yet was talking with everyone? This was a strange way of staying inconspicuous. A minute later, Leina sat down, a cup of coffee in one hand and tea in the other.

"You got me black coffee?" asked Astrid, looking inside the cup.

"You didn't specify anything else. Now drink it."

"Fine." She usually had milk in her coffee but choked down the bitter liquid anyway. "Can we go now?"

"Yes." After returning the mugs, the two left the tavern and went back into the frigid air. Leina thrust the tome into Astrid's arms. "Hold this."

Astrid stored it in her pack as they approached the town hall, the most magnificent building in Nuwelke. That wasn't saying much since every other building was stocky and plain, but it did stand three stories high with some basic designs carved into the stone around its entryway. A narrow, decorative ledge wrapped around the entire third floor. Soldiers stood at the entrance, barring their way in.

"What business do you travelers have with the earl?" asked one soldier. Astrid shifted from foot to foot, unnerved by the fact that the guards seemed to know of them already.

"May we not simply speak to him?" asked Leina.

"You may, but our earl does not wish to engage in idle chatter, so we must hear your purpose."

Leina looked nervously at Astrid, then back at the soldier. "We bring . . . grave news. My friend and I, we keep track of where future border conflicts may appear, and we have seen signs that this town may soon be attacked."

Astrid had no idea where Leina was going with this, but figured all she would need to do was play along. She hoped that Leina would explain it to her later, but given past tendencies, found it improbable.

The soldier's eyes went wide, and he lost his commanding demeanor. "I—I see. Right this way, second floor. You may have to wait," he said, gesturing toward the main doors leading into the town hall. Leina gave him a solemn nod of thanks before passing through with Astrid. Leina led the way up the stairs to the second floor, where benches sat outside an ornate closed door.

"I assume the earl is seeing someone else right now," said Leina. "We'll just have to wait." Astrid sighed, taking a seat on the benches. Leina sat beside her and leaned in close. "We have to act as inconspicuous as possible. Yes, it is strange to buy a book and get some drinks before talking with the earl about this kind of news, but once we get the information, we can leave."

"How will you get said information?"

"I'm working on that . . ."

"You're—what? You don't have a plan?"

"Well don't shout it to all of Nuwelke. I said I'm working on it, so if you'd please leave me to think, that would be great."

Astrid opened her mouth, but thought better of it, electing to stare at the floor instead.

"Do you think you could take the guards in this town?" asked Leina, many minutes into her scheming.

"Hmm? Yeah, of course. They look like they haven't seen combat a day in their lives."

"Good."

Another twenty minutes later, the door opened and a sullen looking faul walked out. He glanced at them on his way down the stairs, a strange look upon his face. Leina stood up and began walking into the earl's chambers, Astrid following. The earl, an average looking faul in height and build, was flanked by two guards with daggers hanging at their sides.

The earl pressed his hands together. "And who might you two be?"

"My lord, we are simply travelers. We wondered if you held any of the old history books."

"The old history books? I'm afraid I don't know what you mean."

"My apologies, I am referring to the story of how the skirmishes began between Valea and the Shalin Empire. You see, my companion and I have been trying to keep some order around these lands—a difficult job in such trying times, as you must know."

"I do indeed. Nuwelke thanks you two for your efforts in preserving these vulnerable towns."

"Of course." Leina nodded at the earl's diplomatic statement. "But to prevent conflict, one must know how it started, wouldn't you agree?"

"My dear, you must know the story, yes?" He recited the same story that Lothar and the book had told without waiting for their reply.

"Ah yes, a classic story, but isn't there another part, something else?" Astrid was rapt, mesmerized by the change in formality, in tone, of Leina's voice. The cordiality that seemed so effortless, and that she knew was just a front.

"Something else?" asked the earl.

"Yes . . . That's not the whole story, is it?"

The earl pinched his brows in thought and shrugged. "I don't know any other details, but you're free to go up to the third floor and look around for a book on the subject."

Leina bowed her head, "Thank you, my lord."

Astrid followed Leina out and they headed up the stairs to the third floor. At the top, Astrid paused for a second. It was dim, lit only by a few candles and the light pouring in from the large windows that led to the ledge they had seen from the street. The room contained everything from trinkets, to furniture, to books. Dust and cobwebs coated many of the artifacts.

"I'll look for it," said Leina.

"What do you want me to do?"

"Watch the stairs. I . . . have a suspicion. Just keep watch."

Astrid shrugged and stood by the stairs, out of sight of anyone who would come up them. She drew her dagger and stayed attentive while Leina searched for the book.

". . .Earl . . . urgent news . . ." said a voice from the second floor, a quarter of an hour into Leina's search. Astrid whirled around and put a finger to her lips, trying to listen to the conversation below. Leina paused in the middle of putting a book back, her brow furrowed.

"They seemed friendly to me. Are you sure?" It was the voice of the earl.

"We've received a tip. Supposedly, they were seen a few days ago . . . enemies of the state," said a guard.

"That shorter one, she seemed suspicious as well, a bit tense," said another guard.

"They're onto us," whispered Astrid.

"Are they coming?" asked Leina.

She listened once more. "Take three other guards, but don't kill them. Bring them in for questioning."

"Yes, my lord."

Astrid heard footsteps approaching the bottom of the stairs. "They're coming!" She cursed herself for crying out and blowing their chance at surprising the guards.

"Do what you have to!" responded Leina. She had found a large pile of books buried underneath some furniture and was sorting through them.

Astrid glanced at the razor-sharp edge of her dagger and winced; she didn't want to kill these people. An old table lay nearby, and she slammed it against the ground, breaking the legs away from the tabletop. As the footsteps approached, she grasped a table leg and braced herself.

The first guard reached the top of the stairs, and she swung the leg, hitting her square in the chest and sending her back down the stairs.

"Hurry up, Kierth!" she shouted as the guards recovered and began to scale the stairs again. Suddenly, the room went dark, throwing her off just as the second guard reached the top of the stairs. The guard gripped Astrid's wrist before she knew it, but she twisted her arm and swept her foot under his leg, sending him to the ground and bringing back the light. The third guard arrived, and Astrid hit him with the table leg as she felt the air sucked from her lungs. When he fell backwards down the stairs and his focus on the magic was broken, Astrid could breathe again.

"Here!" shouted Leina, waving a tome in the air.

"Let's go!" She ran toward the window, a crazy idea forming in her mind.

Leina laughed. "I like your thinking!"

How is she laughing right now? Astrid struck the window with the table leg, shattering it into a million sharp, deadly shards. She leapt out the window and onto the narrow ledge. Her heart skipped a beat—she had never climbed this high. Quickly, she took a breath and glanced to her side, where Leina's face showed fear for the first time that day.

"Put the book in the bag!"

Leina undid the strap and dropped the heavy book inside. Astrid dropped her feet over the ledge and began her descent, Leina following. Astrid wasn't the greatest climber, but Leina didn't seem to be much better. At about three yards from the ground, Leina dropped down.

"Let go! They're coming!" shouted Leina. Astrid released her sweaty grip on the rough stone and dropped to the ground, stumbling a bit as the shock of her landing reverberated through her legs. "Are you alright?" asked Leina.

"Yeah, let's go!" She wiped the sweat from her eyes and took off sprinting with Leina. They ran in no particular direction, just away from the pursuing soldiers.

"There!" shouted Leina, pointing toward the gate from which they entered the town. A moment of hope flared in Astrid; the small town didn't have that many guards. Then she saw the civilians. They crowded in from the sides of the streets, not yet blocking their exit, but perhaps . . .

Leina's foot caught on a stone, sending her flying to the ground. Astrid turned on a dime, reaching her hand out to assist Leina. Only then did she notice that the hood of her cloak had been flung back, revealing her jet-black hair and darker skin. Gasps filled the streets; the townspeople's faces turned from confused to angry. Astrid pulled Leina to her feet, but the way to the gate was now blocked by the crowd.

"Get back!" shouted Astrid, but the townspeople ignored her. She was with the enemy.

"A human!" spat a female.

"Kill her!" shouted another. The words were repeated by many around the circle, turning into a mad chant within a few seconds. Leina suddenly winced in pain and gripped her arm; Astrid looked around to figure out what was wrong and saw a few of the civilians muttering. Suddenly, Leina clasped her hands around her own neck and whirled around, her eyes wide in desperation. Anger boiled up inside Astrid; she hated that trick.

"Get out of the way for Talen's sake, you miserable bastards!" she shouted, brandishing her dagger to clear the way out the town. She jabbed it forward and slashed over and over as she pulled Leina behind her through the crowd. Astrid's blade grazed a few of the muttering faul and Leina began to breathe again in short, sputtering breaths. Leina drew her own dagger and waved it around, ready to defend herself from the civilians who wished nothing more than to kill her.

A rough shove into Astrid's side sent her reeling into Leina, but the slight woman was able to regain balance and keep Astrid from falling. Self-preservation kicked in, and Astrid's vision tunneled like it had during border skirmishes. She stabbed the stomach of a particularly stubborn faul, who collapsed to the ground in pain. Either this would anger the townsfolk or scare them. Thankfully, the latter occurred, and some of the angry crowd backed up. Her gambeson armor defended her from most of the small knives that were thrust at her by the townsfolk, but some still managed to break through the less-protective sleeves and graze her arms. After Astrid sliced the shoulder of another faul who attempted to stab Leina, more of the crowd backed up, resorting to creative insults and swears rather than violence. Astrid kept shoving through the crowd with Leina on her heels, until eventually, the throng parted just enough for the two of them to slip through the last few people and make a run for the gates.

The gate guard ran toward them upon seeing them, but Astrid slipped to the side and delivered a solid kick to his back. As he went down, she ran along the dirt path out of the town.

"Stay on the paths!" shouted Leina. The farmers they passed looked vaguely interested in the commotion but continued with their labor instead of getting involved. If she and Leina didn't trample the farmland, she supposed the farmers wouldn't try to stop them from escaping.

Leina pointed to the ditch where their other three companions were hiding. "There!" Astrid could see Melkin and the others running to meet them; they must have been watching for their return.

A mile and a half further, Melkin reached them and stood with his spear in his hands, gazing out at their pursuers. Astrid stopped and rested her hands on her knees for a moment before turning back to face the guards, taking her place beside the humans. Three guards—they could be defeated if necessary. Lothar and Galdur soon caught up, brandishing weapons of their own. Melkin stepped forward as the guards approached.

"Leave. Now. And we won't hurt you," he said in a threatening voice to the closest guard, about ten yards from him.

"Those two are enemies of the state!" a guard shouted.

"Why?" asked Leina. Her wide-eyed expression made her seem afraid and innocent.

The bewildered guard turned to his companions, then back to the five. "Well . . . what do you have in your pack there?"

Leina unstrapped the pack on Astrid's back and held the book in the air. "A book?"

"There! You've stolen a prized possession of the Earl!" The closest guard stepped forward, brandishing his two daggers. Then, his face turned from determination to pain as he stumbled backwards, dropping both daggers and clasping his hands together.

Astrid whipped her head around to see Lothar softly muttering behind Melkin.

"Argh!" cried the guard as he fell against one of the other soldiers.

"Stop this!" shouted another guard.

"Leave us!" Melkin stepped forward with his spear pointed at the guards.

The three unhurt guards looked between one another, then back at the five. "Fine!"

Lothar ceased his muttering, and the injured guard began running back to the town, probably on the hunt for cool water. With a glance backward, the other three guards followed.

Astrid let out a sigh of relief. The tension within her finally dissipated as the sweat from her face dripped onto the grass, and blood from the small cuts on her arms soaked through the fabric of her gambeson.

22

LOTHAR

"I'm going to assume buying that book was not an option," commented Melkin, arms crossed.

Lothar shouldn't have been surprised that Melkin didn't first ask if the two were okay.

"We *did* buy a book," said Leina, pulling a large, leather-bound tome from her satchel.

"Yeah, it gave us Lothar's story," said Astrid, rolling up the sleeves of her gambeson. "Oberel's sake," she grumbled.

"What in Talen's name happened to you?" asked Lothar when her wounds were exposed. "Are you alright?"

"Yeah, I'm fine," said Astrid as she wiped her arms with a clean cloth from her pack. Lothar looked closer—the cuts were very shallow, and he let out a sigh of relief.

"The guards came after us," said Leina. Astrid pulled out two bandages from her bag and Lothar helped her wrap them around her arms.

"Well, what's that book?" asked Melkin, pointing at the much slimmer, older-looking book that Leina had pulled out of the pack.

"*This* is the true history book. Hopefully."

Melkin raised an eyebrow. "Hopefully?"

"I don't know if you noticed, but we didn't really have a lot of time to go looking through it," said Leina, rolling her eyes.

"Start from the beginning," suggested Lothar. Leina nodded and recounted the events at Nuwelke while the five of them walked further from the town, into a forest for shade and cover from any onlookers.

"The Talwreks must have reported you as enemies and described your faces to the papers after you talked with them at the border," said Lothar. "You must be criminals in all of the Shalin Empire."

"Perhaps so. But we're alright," said Leina.

"You don't seem to be the injured one," pointed out Melkin.

Leina scowled and stuck her arm out, showing the several charred bits of her sleeve. "As I said, those faul *did* burn me."

"Anyway, the guards weren't after you because of the books, right? Just because you were reported as criminals?" asked Lothar.

"Correct."

"Well, why did the earl not want to tell you the history?" asked Lothar.

"I would assume that he doesn't know, since it was lost in a pile of dusty books," Galdur answered for Leina. "His mansion is probably quite old, and that history book made its way there a while ago," said Galdur. "We should read it, though."

Leina handed Galdur the book. "You can, I need to relax for a bit."

As Leina, Astrid, and Melkin walked away, Lothar sat down beside Galdur who was already poring over the weathered pages.

"Some of this is just background information, not that it's a long book anyway," said Galdur. "The text is really faded—I can hardly read it."

"There," said Lothar, pointing to a chapter heading. "The True War"

"Right. I'll try to summarize instead of reading every bit of it. Okay, so . . . about a hundred years ago, there was this big fire in the Shalin Empire. Heard of it?"

"The fire of 1145? Yeah, it burned down a great border city, Ozen. Killed thousands . . ."

"That's the one. No one could find the cause of the fire, but some government officials thought that perhaps Valea had committed the atrocity, since the city was so close to the border."

"I've never heard that. Were there any other preexisting tensions between the Shalin Empire and Valea?"

Galdur skimmed through the page. "No, I don't think so. I mean, the Valean folk have always been afraid of faul magic and the Shalin folk have felt the same way about the humans' physical strength. Plus, religion and such. Anyway..." he trailed off as his eyes skimmed the page. "These government officials got together and decided they would spy on Valea. Oh, and a letter was sent to Valea, but they denied the incident."

"Naturally," said Lothar without thinking. Galdur glared at him. "Sorry, I didn't mean it that way. I don't think Valea was behind the fire since I was never taught that."

Galdur nodded. "The Shalin Empire didn't just send one spy though. They sent a team of ten very powerful faul who volunteered for the mission. Oh... This is a bit like the stories that you and I know. These faul weren't children, yet they had very pronounced abilities. They were all from Ozen." Galdur tapped his finger on the page. "This says that one of them could control people, another one could talk to animals—"

"That's incredible," mused Lothar.

"Yes... I remember reading a bit about similar abilities. They're extremely rare, right?" asked Galdur.

"Yes. I'm sure the book talks about who was sent, their lineage and such. These kinds of faul, they are rumored to be descendants of the first Talwreks, carrying the original blessing of Kaima."

"Wow..." Galdur seemed lost in thought for a moment, and Lothar felt a deep sense of satisfaction fill him. He recalled when back in the Akarist ruins, he began to explain his religion to Melkin and was met with scoffs and eye rolls.

Galdur blinked and refocused on the book in front of them. "Anyway, the faul didn't hurt anyone as they were traveling toward the capital of Valea. Back then, faul and humans were allowed within each other's country if they were checked in at the border, so these faul were in Valea legally. However, once they had set up a camp near the royal palace, one of them parted from the group, went to steal some documents, and was captured. He was tortured until he revealed the locations of his companions."

"The king of Valea ordered this?"

"Looks like it. Apparently, it took three days for the faul to crack and spill his secrets. They had him gagged for most of it so that he couldn't do magic. Why is that?"

"Why can't we do magic while gagged? Every time we channel magic, we ask the goddess of magic, Kaima, for help through a special chant in the ancient faul language. We ask her to give us her magic and she obliges if the faul can channel it correctly. It takes a good bit of training."

"So, she gives you magic whether it's for a good cause or bad cause?"

"Yeah." He shrugged. "As long as we can channel the power as our own, she doesn't discriminate."

Galdur nodded and turned his attention back to the book. "There's a long chase here..." he said, skimming through the pages, "but eventually, all nine other faul were captured when their food was poisoned by their pursuers in the dead of night. They were already fleeing the country, halfway to the Shalin Empire. Lothar...I think you should read the next part."

Lothar took the book from Galdur's arms. "Why?"

"I don't know some of these faul words. Just... I think you should read it."

Lothar scanned the small, messy letters scrawled across the pages. "All ten faul were then held in the dungeons of the capital city of Valea for a week and tortured to find out if there were other spies and what their motives were. Anytime one of the gags were removed, guards would surround the prisoner and point spears at them to make sure they didn't use magic. Then..." Lothar sucked in a horrified breath as he saw the words that were written next. "By the deities... The king finally determined that the faul were telling the truth, but he wouldn't let them go as they were. Not even with payment offered from the Shalin Empire. He sourced information from around the kingdom and through his own spies in the Shalin Empire, and stumbled upon a process that extracts a faul's magic."

"What's that word?" asked Galdur, pointing to a word scrawled angrily on the page.

"Elentac. That's what we call the process..." Lothar took a shaky breath before continuing. "He forced each of the faul to channel all their power into a single piece of rock by torturing other faul prisoners that were already in their dungeons, being held for petty theft and crime. One of the ten continued to refuse despite the torture and they were killed. Nine of them channeled their power into the stone, not knowing of the full consequences that performing elentac holds. They became husks of their former selves and died a month after being sent back to the Shalin Empire." Lothar took a shaky breath, fuming at the injustice, the pure brutality done to some of the most powerful faul in history. "Why... Why would he do this? How could your country have done this...?"

"Lothar, look at me," said Galdur in a low voice. Lothar glared at him, as if he could see Galdur's ancestry in his eyes, as if he could catch a glimpse at the man who had committed this crime.

"I did not do this. I never met my great-grandfather. I barely know his name and he's dead now. No one alive today took part in this. Haven't we fought enough?"

Lothar took a deep breath. Yes, they had. And he knew it. He nodded and closed his eyes for a moment. "Why... is this story not told?"

"Let's continue. We have to finish this," said Galdur. He took the book out of Lothar's hands. "The stone was dubbed 'Incantir' by the Shalin Empire, which means...?"

Lothar thought for a second. "The fallen."

Galdur nodded solemnly and read more in the book. "Valea apologized and gave the Shalin Empire a thousand gold coins. The empress of the Shalin Empire said that all was forgiven. However, in secret, all the soldiers near the border gathered to attack Valea. The empress funded them and gathered even more soldiers from other parts of the empire.

Three days after the empress 'forgave' Valea, a third of all active soldiers in the Shalin Empire attacked them. They gained a considerable amount of land before Valea mustered their forces and fought back. After a year, it was clear that a stalemate was inevitable at the border, but neither side would give up. The Shalin Empire demanded that Valea return the Incantir, but they claimed it had been lost. The long war continued until twenty years later when Empress Ledica of the Shalin Empire was crowned. She made an agreement with the queen of Valea at the time that they would not draft people to fight at the border, yet neither could agree on a plan to create peace. The skirmishes there have raged on ever since, with volunteers from both sides fueling the fire. The stone containing the magic of the faul has never been found."

Lothar looked down at the ground; tears were falling down his face even though he had never known the people for whom he mourned. Galdur glanced backwards and Lothar followed his gaze, seeing Leina, Melkin and Astrid listening to the story from a dozen yards away.

"How much did you three hear?" asked Lothar. He was loath to repeat the story.

"Everything after the ten faul were sent into Valea," said Leina.

"Why is this story not told in the Shalin Empire?" repeated Lothar, breaking a silence that must have lasted a thousand years.

"Everything that doesn't appear in the modern version puts part of the blame on you," said Leina.

"Yeah? It's also not said that you tortured faul into performing elentac!" cried Astrid.

"Well, you attacked us without warning! You all killed far more innocent civilians than ten!" retorted Leina.

"It's both countries' faults!" exclaimed Galdur, stepping between Astrid and Leina. "By Ryne, haven't our countries fought enough over this? But neither Leina, nor Melkin, nor I tortured those faul! Astrid and Lothar didn't send spies into Valea, nor did they launch a surprise invasion! Are we here to argue over history or to prevent a war?"

The five were silent for a minute. "Sorry," said Leina. "But I think I did have a point. Obviously, parts of the story were removed in the Shalin Empire to make the country look better, and the same occurred in Valea."

"So why is the elentac taking place not included in our version of the story?" asked Astrid.

"I would guess it's because the government would rather the people not know that their magic can be stolen, that some of the best faul in history, their idols, were made to perform elentac. It's far more heroic for them to have been ruthlessly killed in prison. Maybe the threat of losing their magic would have demoralized the soldiers as well," said Lothar, his voice growing steadier as he began to understand.

"Why wouldn't the king just kill them? If he knew that it caused death anyway..." mused Melkin.

Lothar sighed, taking the book back and flipping through the pages. He really didn't want to read the words again, but they needed answers. "It says here that he wanted to ensure their magic did not live on. In other words, if they were killed before the elentac was performed, their extraordinary magic would be reborn in another faul. Whereas, if their magic was stored in an object through elentac before their death, it wouldn't be passed on—thus ending the threat of their magic to the humans."

"Did he have any basis for such reasoning?" asked Leina.

Lothar shook his head. "Not as far as I can tell... But there's not a lot of research on this subject. I don't know who discovered the process, but it was long, long ago; probably before the Talwreks united the Shalin Empire."

"So... elentac is worse than the death it causes, I assume?" asked Melkin.

Lothar met Melkin's cold eyes. "Yes. I suppose the nine thought that because their power was so strong, the process wouldn't kill them. Obviously, they were wrong." Lothar looked down. Thinking about elentac made his stomach churn and his eyes sting. "Call me selfish, but I wouldn't do it if I were in their place. Not for anything."

"So, what do we do now?" asked Galdur.

"Well, if the Incantir hasn't been found yet... perhaps returning it to your emperor would please him and the faul at the border, if not the rest of the empire. If it was willingly handed over by a human..." Melkin's words trailed off and Lothar could see him thinking through all possibilities.

"How? If Valea has been searching for over a century and obviously never found it... What chance do we have?" asked Astrid, a discernible note of hopelessness in her voice.

"Well, Valea hasn't exactly been searching for that long," said Galdur. "I'm the prince, and I never knew of this. Surely the vast majority of people in the kingdom don't know of it, though each baron and lord presumably has this book. The Incantir must have been searched for in secret and for a limited amount of time, if at all."

"How would it have left the castle?" asked Leina.

"Once the faul gave up their magic, I'm sure the king didn't really care what happened to the stone," said Melkin.

"Does the book say anything about that?" asked Astrid.

Galdur flipped through some pages. "Yes. The king tried to take the power from the Incantir... somehow... but it didn't work."

"That's not really how magic works," said Lothar. The idea of a grown man staring at a chunk of stone, willing the power into himself was mildly humorous, if not morbid due to the circumstances.

"So once the king failed to absorb the power, he most likely discarded the Incantir, or had someone hide it," said Galdur.

"Why would he do that?" asked Leina.

"Well, just to anger the Shalin Empire, perhaps. Yes, maybe after the surprise invasion was launched, he had it hidden in retaliation. He could locate it if he found some sort of use for it, but otherwise... it was lost to history," said Lothar.

"So, we have to find this... thing, *and* make sure that Fareod isn't crowned king?" said Astrid.

"It would seem so," said Melkin.

"Where do we start?" asked Leina. "Is there anyone we know that could help?"

At this, Lothar felt a pang of sadness—Imar might have known about the Incantir. As a member of the Talwreks, he almost certainly did.

"Not that I can think of," said Melkin. "I doubt Vallec would know anything about this."

"Where is he?" asked Galdur.

"He said he would make his way back to his home in Hileath when he was well enough. Three streets down from the spy academy, the fourth house on the left."

Leina nodded. "No point in bothering him."

"Hmm, maybe . . ." said Galdur, trailing off.

Leina raised her eyebrows. "Yes?"

"Well, I doubt that the king went to hide this thing himself. He probably sent a guard or something. There *is* a way to find who the guards were back then."

"How?" asked Lothar.

"We keep records of province guards going back hundreds of years," said Galdur with a grin. "We'll use those."

Lothar glanced to where Leina and Melkin were sharing a knowing look. Melkin faced the rest of the group, grimacing. "Problem is, the records are only kept in the vaults of the capitol buildings."

A long silence followed this statement; fear of being captured by a lord of Valea momentarily replaced the shock he still felt from reading the book.

"Let's move, we'll have to go south anyway. No matter which province we want to go to," said Melkin.

"Each capitol building has these records?" asked Lothar, peeling himself off the ground and onto his weary feet.

"Indeed," said Leina. "The record books track prisoners, guards, and servants in the entire province. That way, spies, traitors, and escaped prisoners can be located easily. Whenever the transfer of servants and prisoners occurs, all provinces have records of them. Most importantly, if any of the documents are destroyed or lost, there are copies in other places. Since all the vaults are quite secure, it's not too much of a risk to have several copies."

"Then we have the choice of provinces, right? We could go to any of them," said Astrid.

"I would advise against Hilean province. The capital will be more heavily guarded," said Galdur. "And before you ask, I have no power there; I can't just ask for them."

Did he truly not? Lothar knew that Galdur wasn't the *crown* prince, but he had still assumed that Melkin had brought the prince for his power. Lothar shook away the thought; Galdur had been plenty useful by now.

"We should probably pick up a newspaper at some point and find out what's going on, what they think happened to you," said Leina.

Melkin nodded. "We'll try to get to a town shortly." He sighed in frustration. "God, I'm not too keen on stealing documents from *any* of the lords or ladies in Valea. They could inflict quite severe punishments."

"Could we not just ask?" suggested Lothar. "Would any of the lords or ladies believe us?"

"We still have no proof. And not enough time to show anyone the massive mine back in the Dalyuben Hills. These are protected, valuable documents," said Leina.

"Surely all the lords and ladies know the old history, right?" asked Astrid.

Galdur shook his head. "Remember, their focus is not the war, it's balancing their province's economy and governing their people. It's very possible they *don't* know. In fact, I doubt they do."

"What are they like?" asked Lothar.

"Most are very patriotic and probably wouldn't believe us," said Galdur. He turned toward Leina and Melkin. "Do either of you have a reputation among them?"

Leina looked toward the skies, deep in thought. "Most of them probably have an inkling that Gladia has sent spies to make sure they were all in line. For a lord, it's not hard to find who Gladia's top spies are. I wouldn't be too surprised if at least our names are known among them."

Lothar sighed, clenching his hands in frustration. "Would any of them *not* want a war between Valea and the Shalin Empire? Surely some of them wouldn't want their land to be torn to shreds." He knew peace was not that simple, yet he hoped there might be a lord or lady who could be reasoned with.

Melkin glanced at Leina, a strange expression on his usually cold face. It put Lothar on edge, seeing the stoic man showing something that looked like apprehension.

"What is it?" she asked, her fearful voice confirming Lothar's suspicion.

Melkin gritted his teeth, grimacing. "Yes. There is one lord who would never want war. Lord Thalen of Annisik Province."

23

LEINA

Melkin spoke the name with such hatred that Leina felt on edge herself.

Galdur sucked in a breath. "Of course." He muttered a short prayer to Ryne.

"Who is he? What did he do?" asked Astrid.

"He's an entitled, cruel, self-centered, whiny bastard of a man," said Melkin, his voice lathered with contempt and loathing. "I lived under his rule until I was sixteen. He—To build his new, grand castle in Annister, he didn't hire stone masons or skilled laborers. He drafted young men between the ages of sixteen and thirty from around the country for ten years. Almost everyone drafted died. Ryne, it was awful . . . And that's only one example." A look of deep sadness shone in his eyes. "But he would never want war. He hates everyone who gets in his way, not just faul. A war would threaten his rule over his province; he might even be killed in the fighting. Especially since Annisik province borders the Shalin Empire."

"So, you think this Thalen character would give you the guard records?" asked Lothar.

Melkin laughed, but Leina knew he didn't think the idea was humorous at all. "Depends on whether his stubbornness or sense of self-preservation wins out. But, if he decides he doesn't want to give up the information, I'd feel no remorse over harming him."

"The bad news is we have to cross a little over half the width of the continent," said Galdur. "We'll go south first, then west until we reach the province. Is twenty miles from the border enough distance? I don't want to get caught in any battles. Or worse."

"That should be fine," said Leina with profound relief. She hoped she'd never have to see the sight of thousands of soldiers walking to their deaths.

So far, no news had reached the group about Gladia. *She must be holding on for the moment.* If she died, Fareod would still have to be crowned and soldiers mustered before war could be declared. There was still time to walk the 140 miles separating them from Annisik Castle.

After over an hour, Galdur finally broke the calm silence. "What's the government in the Shalin Empire like? There aren't any provinces there, right?"

"Just an emperor, his designated officials, and the earls. The earls are largely similar to Valean barons, I think. They can be elected or inherit the position in any town, really," said Lothar.

Galdur nodded, furrowing his brow. "Who are the designated officials? What do they do?"

"They're people who the emperor appoints to watch over sections of the empire and departments of the economy, but there aren't any set borders they oversee. They can make autonomous decisions within reason, but the emperor can always overrule them. Or just remove them," said Lothar.

"I wish that were the case for Valea. Gladia would have gotten rid of Thalen a long time ago. Instead, it's seven different inheritance lines. Thalen's heir will inherit Annisik Province, no exceptions. It's a good system when our monarch is unjust, but it's horrible otherwise," said Melkin.

Leina frowned. "Does Thalen *have* an heir?"

"No. Around five years ago he *somehow* convinced a woman to marry him, but no children yet. Perhaps he's unable," said Melkin with a smirk. Astrid chuckled at the jest.

"Does he know you in particular?" asked Leina, looking at Melkin. She had always been too afraid to talk to him about Thalen, but he seemed quite eager to rant about the man now. In all honesty, she'd never heard such impassioned speech from Melkin.

"I doubt it. I was at the new Annisik Castle when it exploded, but I can't say if he saw me or not. And he definitely didn't know me when I lived there—I was just another one of his thousands of subjects."

"And you left when you were sixteen?" asked Lothar.

Melkin nodded. "I would have left earlier, but it took me some time to get enough money."

"Then what can the queen or king do? Seems like the lords hold most of the power," said Astrid.

"For starters, each province pays a percentage of their income to the monarch. Then he or she can distribute the money amongst the entire nation however they see fit," started Galdur.

"And thank Ryne for that. Gladia used some of that money for relief efforts in Annister. It wasn't enough, but it helped," said Melkin.

"They can also declare war and create laws that apply to the entire country," continued Galdur.

The other four kept discussing politics and the governing bodies of the two countries, but Leina tuned them out eventually.

A little while later, Lothar interrupted her thoughts. "So you're also a spy, Leina?" The early afternoon sun was now bearing down on them, lessening the bitter cold they'd been traveling in for the past few days.

"Yes," she said, realizing that she'd never explicitly told them. It *had* been obvious though, in her opinion. "Melkin and I went to the same academy, two years apart."

Lothar raised an eyebrow. "What was it like?"

"Everyone learns the same basic skills for the first year, and then each student chooses one of three specialties to study for another year. Clearly, we chose different paths," said Leina, pointing at Melkin, then herself.

"What exactly *are* your jobs?" asked Astrid.

"A couple months after I graduated, I was moved to the castle to be one of the queen's personal spies. Before that, I worked for the military," Leina said.

"Only four spies live in the castle—the rest have other jobs. We go on whatever missions the queen or king wants us to. I was moved to the castle after a year and replaced an older spy who retired," said Melkin, joining the conversation.

"Does that mean Leina is better than you?" asked Astrid, a small smile appearing on her face.

Melkin smirked. "Not necessarily. There are more spies of my kind, and she got lucky."

Leina made a hurt face but couldn't conceal her smile. "That's not true!"

"Do all the other spies work for the military?" asked Lothar.

"Some work for lords or ladies. Some work for hire. I mean, the Hileath academy is pretty small and it's the only decent one in Valea. There just aren't *that* many spies."

"You are—were—a sergeant, right? What was that like?" Melkin asked Lothar.

Leina hoped they would stop for the night soon. The orange sun was nearing the horizon, and though the view was beautiful, she would have preferred to admire it sitting down.

"Oh, nothing too special. I had a lot of work to do organizing missions and such. But of course, Imar—" Lothar swallowed and glanced at the ground. He took a breath. "Imar was there to help me with all that. I would also plan my missions based on his information on where domestic threats might be. It was a lot of work, but I really felt like I was doing something good for the nation. Over the years, I captured dozens of bandit groups and criminals. To be honest, I loved it."

Leina wasn't surprised to hear the sadness and regret in his voice. The same regret plagued her when she considered the job that she loved—and might have thrown away by joining this mission. But she would never be a personal spy under Fareod, especially considering what he had done. An idea began to form in her mind, something that she would need to do in the next town they visited.

"He doesn't like to admit it, but he's one of the strongest faul in the country. In terms of magic, at least," Astrid in a low voice, staring ahead.

Lothar made an apologetic face. "That's not true."

"Yes, it is."

"I don't even come from a powerful family. In their constant drunken stupor, my parents could barely do magic."

Astrid shrugged. "That changes nothing about your ability."

"How does magic training work anyway?" asked Galdur. The prince was always so curious to learn. Leina supposed she was interested as well, though not nearly as much.

"Most parents teach their children as much as possible, but if they learned from their own uneducated parents, they might not be the best teachers. We could pay for classes on it, but most don't," said Astrid.

"How did you two learn?" asked Leina.

Lothar grinned. "If you join the military, you get free training. It's a very good incentive. Training can only do so much though; natural ability plays a large part."

Astrid shook her head, a slight smile on her face. "They gave me so many lessons to bring out my ability. To no avail, though... What I did at the mine was the height of my abilities. I suspect that only my fighting skills got me admitted into the military."

"What's the height of *your* abilities, Lothar?" asked Melkin.

"I don't really know... I could definitely kill, if necessary, but I haven't pushed myself to my limits yet," said Lothar, averting his gaze from Melkin's.

"Why not?" asked Melkin.

"Don't push the old man, Melkin," said Leina in a mock-condescending tone. Lothar chuckled at her jest, and the five fell silent for a moment.

"Ugh, why did all of this have to happen in the middle of winter?" complained Galdur, pulling his woolen cloak around himself.

Melkin glanced at him. "It's not winter."

"And we'd better be finished before it is. It's freezing."

"In Pyantir it's far colder," said Lothar.

"And north of that, even colder," said Astrid.

"You're one to talk, Lothar, you can just heat yourself up whenever you want." Galdur rubbed his hands together for warmth.

"Well, I rarely do. Even I can't keep warm in the Shalin cold for an entire day. Or perhaps I could, but doing so would leave me exhausted. I . . . can show you all, though." Lothar began muttering strange words and suddenly, the surrounding air grew warm. In spite of herself, Leina smiled; the cozy temperature was wonderful. But just as quickly as the warmth had come, it then disappeared. The chill returned and the wind bit once more at Leina's face, hood or no hood.

Astrid frowned. "Why'd you stop?"

"Can't keep it up forever. We'll be stopping soon anyway, right?"

"Yes. In fact, this is a nice clearing, so let's stop now," said Melkin. "Now we have some time to spar. Lothar, Galdur, keep practicing with those knives. Astrid, Leina, I want to talk to you two." Leina furrowed her brow, wondering what Melkin had in mind. As Lothar and Galdur went over to a couple of trees, Melkin beckoned Leina and Astrid toward himself. "Astrid, can you get four sticks that mimic the size of your majoril and auxlar daggers?" As she nodded and walked away, Melkin turned toward Leina. "I wanted to apologize."

"What for?" she asked, meeting his eyes.

"I've . . . doubted your abilities on this mission. You're alive right now because of a significant amount of luck, but that wouldn't have had to be the case if I had trusted you."

Leina nodded, letting pent up bitterness dissipate. She unclenched her jaw and took a breath, surprised at her anger. "I'm younger than you, Melkin, but I care just as much about this mission. I'm willing to die for it, as is everyone else. I need your trust."

"And from now on, you'll have it. Everyone here will. I swear by it," said Melkin.

Leina kept her gaze steady as she stared into Melkin's cold eyes. He was always the hardest for her to read—what might his motives be for saying this? Was he lying to her or to himself? She decided that for now, it was best to take him at his word, but continue to keep her own council. "I hope you can hold yourself to that."

Melkin nodded in return. "I trust that you'll also find out something about that rock?"

"I will, but... well, I need some time to work on it."

"Perfect, you can stay up with Lothar on first watch."

Leina rolled her eyes upon seeing a wry smile break out across Melkin's face. Apparently, he didn't want her to get any sleep.

Astrid approached the two of them, carrying two shorter and two longer sticks. "What now?"

Melkin took one of each, examining the fake weapons. He waved around the shorter one, frowning. "You use this one for parrying, right?"

"Typically. But it can be used for offense as well, depending on the situation."

"I see... I want to try fighting you, Astrid," said Melkin, moving into a fighting posture. They held the longer majoril daggers in their respective dominant hands. Leina watched them spar and was surprised when it ended with Astrid catching Melkin in the upper thigh. A pit formed in her stomach at the realization of just how much more skilled these two were than she was.

Melkin winced and massaged the spot where Astrid hit him. "Of course, I fought with my right hand, and you used your left."

Astrid nodded. "What's your point?"

"Well, if I ever face a faul with a dagger, I want to be prepared. I need to be able to fight a left-handed person better than they can fight a right-handed person."

"You use a spear, though."

"Believe it or not, it's quite hard to carry a spear while trying to sneak around. I've had only a dagger during most of my missions."

"I see," said Astrid. "You're already plenty good, though. Most faul aren't as good with a dagger as I am."

Melkin nodded. "I'd rather not risk it, though."

Leina put a hand on her hip. "Sounds great, but why am I here?"

"You also need to learn. Humans don't often fight with daggers, so if you're skilled with them, you may throw off any faul opponents we might have to face."

She raised an eyebrow and felt a smile curve her lips. "You're not going to try and teach me the spear again?" For years he had tried to persuade her to give up the dagger, with which she was mediocre, and pursue the spear instead, with which she was *abhorrent*.

"No. But I *will* teach you," said Melkin, pointing at Astrid.

"What? I'm not using a human weapon," she said, crossing her arms. Melkin raised an eyebrow and held out his spear in front of Astrid. She reluctantly took it, glancing at Melkin. "Well . . . maybe I could try it . . ." said Astrid quietly, hefting the weapon in her hands.

"Excellent." Melkin turned his attention back to Leina. "Now, it's better if you practice against a faul, so I'll spectate as you spar with Astrid."

Astrid gave Melkin his spear back and picked up the faux daggers. Leina took the two daggers from Melkin, twirling them around in her hand as she moved to face Astrid. The lithe faul lunged and struck three times in an instant—Leina's wild swings barely parried them in time. The two circled each other, but while Astrid's eyes were focused and sharp, Leina barely knew what weaknesses to look for in her opponent's stance. The faul had a devious grin on her face as she lunged in once more, launching a flurry of attacks that Leina struggled to see, much less block. She retreated, stepping further and further back until—

"Ow!" cried Leina as Astrid jabbed the auxlar dagger into her midsection.

"Sorry," said Astrid, cringing as Leina staggered back with a hand over her torso.

Melkin stood with his arms crossed, watching her with mild amusement. "You two keep sparring. Astrid, please don't kill Leina, you're only practicing." Leina rolled her eyes and huffed in annoyance.

Astrid nodded as Melkin walked away to check on Galdur and Lothar. The sun had almost reached the horizon, yet Melkin seemed intent on training. Facing danger again must have ignited some urgency.

Leina and Astrid assumed sparring positions again and again. They fought till the light was nearly gone. Astrid went a bit easier on her for the duration, and though she ached all over by the end, Leina was at least no longer freezing. Instead, the two were drenched in sweat, panting, and exhausted from the ordeal. Melkin came over while the two were sitting on the ground, resting their heads against a tree. For a moment, Leina thought they would be reprimanded for not training.

"Set up your tents. We'll continue to practice tomorrow." He walked away, leaving Astrid and Leina alone again. Leina struggled to her feet, her aching legs and feet protesting every movement. Astrid didn't seem to have the same issue.

"You have some real potential, Leina."

"I do?" She raised an eyebrow in disbelief; each round had ended in another jab to her body. On the whole, she felt utterly incompetent.

"Oh yes. You'll hold your own against a decent faul, I'm sure. Against Melkin or I—of course you'll lose. But you aren't terrible. Plus, you two both have to get used to the auxiliary weapon."

"Thanks," grumbled Leina. She looked around for her bag while Astrid began to set up her own tent.

"Better than I thought you might be," continued Astrid.

Leina glanced up to see Astrid smirking. "Why's that?"

"Well, I didn't know you were a spy."

"What did you think I was?"

"I don't know. Some pampered government official, I guess. Where do you come from, though?"

"I could ask you the same."

"You first," said Astrid.

Leina sighed as she lethargically took supplies from her bag and began to set up her tent. "Born in Salerite. It's a city in Starren province, the richest city in Valea."

Astrid's upper lip curled in disapproval. "Oh."

"Relax. Its reputation doesn't mean that everyone there is rich. I come from a line of servants to one of the extremely wealthy families that live there. My family had some sort of old debt to pay off, so we were basically indentured servants. They gave us shelter and food, but hardly any money. I didn't want that life, so I ended up saving money for the academy and a carriage to get there. I left when I was sixteen, like Melkin."

"And how did you obtain this money?" asked Astrid.

"I can be . . . persuasive," said Leina with a slight smile. Astrid's face turned to horror, and Leina rolled her eyes. "No, nothing like that. If one acts helpless on the street, rich people may give them some money. Of course, occasionally they may want to give a little more than that . . . but that's what weapons are for, are they not? Luckily, it didn't happen too often." To her surprise, Astrid grinned at her.

Leina smiled back. "You know, those were some interesting days . . . I look back on them with a sort of fondness. I send my family most of the money that I make, so soon they'll be able to buy a place of their own." Astrid came over to help Leina finish setting up her tent. "And you?"

"A remote spot in the northern Shalin Empire. It's covered in snow and ice for most of the year, but you sort of get used to it. Anyway, I always wanted to join the military, so I did. Not much more to it."

Leina glanced at Astrid. Her instinct told her that Astrid was holding something back.

"And your family?"

"They're still there. They . . . didn't really want me joining the military."

"Worried about you?"

Astrid nodded slowly; her grin had vanished.

"Sorry, I didn't mean to pry."

"Not sure I believe that," Astrid retorted, "but I suppose I don't blame you."

Leina nodded, feeling a bit guilty but still no less curious. After the two finished setting up their tents, Leina fished out the brilliant blue stone from her pack and sat down by the fire that Galdur had been working on while she and Astrid were sparring. She held the ore near the flickering light and gazed at it, turning it over in her hand.

"What are you doing?" asked a voice a few yards away. She flinched and looked up to see Lothar walking toward her. He sat down on the opposite side of the fire and looked at the stone in wonder.

"I'm going to see what I can do with this teleium," she said, examining the blue flecks that ran through the ore. "How do you think they refine it?"

"I don't know. It probably explodes if it gets too hot. Maybe they don't refine it at all."

"I was going to break it apart into some pieces," said Leina. "Then we can experiment on smaller pieces."

Lothar shrugged. "Sure. Just don't cause any sparks." Her pulse quickened at the thought, and she met Lothar's eyes, which were as apprehensive as she felt. The warning given to her by the man at the mine flashed into her mind—he had clearly ordered her to not hit the blue specks directly.

"You have a point. But we have no choice." Leina took a stone the size of her fist and hesitated before bringing it down on the teleium. "Can I have one of your throwing knives?" Lothar handed her one and she positioned it tip down against the chunk of teleium.

"You're going to dent my knife," warned Lothar.

"Do you have a better idea?"

"Good point. I'll just get Melkin to sharpen it for me."

Leina nodded, glancing up at Lothar with mixture of a smirk and grimace. Edging backwards, she hit the throwing knife with the stone in her hand, flinching as the teleium . . . did nothing.

"Well, we're not dead," said Lothar.

"Shouldn't you be watching for intruders?" suggested Leina.

"Maybe."

Leina glanced up at him briefly before staring down at the volatile ore in front of her. Again and again, she struck the rock until it broke in two. After hammering for hours with her makeshift chisel, she had eventually broken the chunk of teleium into several dozen smaller pieces.

"Don't let any of the pieces fall into the fire," said Lothar.

"Do you always state the obvious?" asked Leina, struggling to keep her eyes open despite the bright fire in front of her.

"No, I do it specifically to annoy you," he said. "Not to prevent us from dying or anything."

"Now you're becoming like Melkin. He's a bad influence."

Lothar nodded and grimaced. "That he is." Leina leaned back on her hands, breathing deeply as she admired the work that she had done. "You should get some sleep. It's definitely been a couple of hours."

Leina sighed. "Thanks for sitting here with me."

"Anytime."

24

Melkin

Melkin laced his boots and gazed around the campsite; the dark sky was just barely illuminated by the sun which hadn't yet crested the horizon. This was his favorite time of day. He took a deep breath and let it out slowly as he looked at the dying fire. Astrid sat beside it and stared at him with an odd expression as he approached.

"What's wrong with you?" she asked, shaking her head.

"What?" He felt as though he were about to be accused of something again.

"It's still dark. Why make me take watch when you're up?"

Melkin shrugged, about to retort when he saw the figure of Leina lying on the ground beside the fire. "Ryne's sake!" he cried, kneeling down beside her.

"It's alright. Apparently, she was breaking apart that teleium rock and didn't feel like going back to her tent to sleep."

"Is she okay?" asked Melkin, standing up.

"Yeah. Just tired."

Melkin breathed a sigh of relief and looked around, spotting a heap of small stones collected on a larger, flat stone in front of

Leina. He picked one of them up and stared at it, seeing the blue flecks of teleium scattered throughout the pebble. After retrieving a small drawstring bag from his pack of supplies, he stored away all of the teleium.

Astrid's silent gaze seemed to judge his every action. "You'll let her experiment with it, right?"

Melkin turned to her, a blank stare on his face. "Why wouldn't I?"

"I don't know. Just making sure."

Why was Astrid being so defensive on Leina's behalf? In fact, he'd noticed that everyone was less haughty recently. He stored the small bag away in his pack, pondering the strange nature of their group.

"You can get more sleep if you want, you know," said Astrid.

Melkin stared into the distance, deliberating on what to do before dawn. "I know."

"So why don't you?"

Melkin shrugged and moved to gather firewood. "I can be useful right now. It's only an hour until sunrise. I'll start making breakfast."

"Do you usually relax at all when you're working? Is this any different from your job?"

Melkin thought for a moment. "I usually work alone."

An hour later, Melkin was turning a rabbit on a stick over the fire while Astrid woke up the rest of their companions.

"Sorry, I have to wake you now," said Astrid, kneeling beside Leina. Melkin rolled his eyes at the deflection of blame; Leina was definitely a bad influence on Astrid.

She yawned and sat up, then her eyes went wide. "Where is it?"

"Relax, Melkin put it away."

"Oh."

Melkin deposited the cooked rabbit onto a plate and the five of them ate breakfast, a meal of a couple rabbits and some vegetables he found.

"Thanks, Melkin," said Lothar, a look of genuine appreciation on his face.

"Shouldn't have gotten rid of Vallec's pot though," said Galdur, prompting laughter from Astrid, Leina, and Lothar.

"Well, next time we do one of these missions, you can bring the pot," Melkin said with a smirk.

"Will do."

The five finished eating and broke down the campsite, folding and storing their tents in their packs while Melkin began piling dirt on top of the fire, smothering the flames.

"I want to test something," said Leina, bouncing on the balls of her feet.

"We have to move—will it take long?" asked Melkin, strapping his pack closed.

"No. Lothar, I need you. I want to make sure."

Melkin turned toward Leina, noting she already had the small drawstring bag in her hand. She must have taken it from his pack while he wasn't looking.

Leina bent over and placed a pea-sized piece of teleium rock onto the ground around ten yards away from everyone. She stood back, looking at the four with a cautious glance. "This might be loud. Alright, Lothar, do it."

As Melkin gazed at the tiny stone, Lothar began to mutter. A second later, he flinched as a surprisingly loud snap hit his ears and the rock burst apart, creating a large cloud of smoke and sparks. A few seconds later, a hole a few inches in depth and width had been torn into the ground.

"By Ryne..." said Galdur.

"You were right, Leina," said Melkin softly, eyes still fixed upon the hole in the ground.

"You don't say."

"I suppose it's late enough—we can set up camp," announced Melkin after the group came across a nice clearing in the dense forests of Valea. The company had walked all day; Melkin hadn't given them a lunch break. He felt strangely guilty in denying the group a break, but they had all agreed it was necessary to reach Annisik Province as quickly as possible.

Leaning back against a tree, he watched as the sky turned a brilliant orange and pink where the sun met the ground. Frowning, he realized that the walk today had seemed shorter—the five had talked the entire way. He wanted to sleep—he *really* did—yet now they needed to train. He was sure that he wasn't the only tired one. He looked around to see Leina massaging her legs and Galdur stretching his arms up to the sky. Grief crashed into him as he remembered traveling with the Akistaria company, with Taleek, Haern, and Vallec. He let out a sigh, pulled his tent out, and started setting it up, wondering if Lothar had shared a similar journey. His gaze fell upon the faul, setting up his tent nearby.

"Lothar, what was Yulac like?" he asked, indulging the moment of curiosity and grief.

Lothar was quiet for a moment, either thinking of an answer or pondering why Melkin would ask such a question. "He was strong and understanding. Well, strong in the faul way, you know? I had known him since I'd graduated from the military school, but once I became a sergeant, we grew to be friends. I've only ever served under his command, so he was sort of an idol of mine. I think Taleek intimidated him, yet he never showed it for the sake of all his soldiers. We were all terrified there."

"Terrified? Of us?"

"Oh yes. I mean, we had our magic, but you knew Taleek. Most of us are a foot and a half shorter, with a fraction of the muscle mass."

"Fair enough," chuckled Melkin. "He never meant any harm though. The day of the Akistaria, he begged the ambassadors to sue for peace."

"Really?" Lothar's face showed a new admiration, a new respect for a man he'd never spoken to.

Melkin nodded, closing his eyes for a second. He could picture the tall, strong commander and wished he were still alive. What was the end of the Akistaria like in past years?"

"I wouldn't know. This Akistaria was my first. We had to match your soldier count, so Yulac decided he would take only his most powerful faul."

"Then you admit you're powerful?" he said with a smirk.

Lothar just shrugged. "I suppose."

Melkin couldn't quite read his passive expression but didn't push the matter. "It was a last-minute decision to send me, because of the bombing of Annisik Castle. I only found out I was going a week before departure."

"Imar only told me two days before," said Lothar with a grin.

Melkin shook his head in disbelief, remembering Imar's cheerful demeanor and understanding nature. "Did he give you all your news?"

"Well, I would often forget to check my mailbox, so Imar would usually fill me in on anything important that he heard—" Lothar's voice broke, and he took a breath. "He was one of those people who just knew everything that was going on all the time. But... he's gone now."

Melkin hammered the stakes of his tent into the ground, wondering how to respond. "I'm sorry... The last I saw of Taleek was when I jumped out the window to confront your spy. I wish I had known. I wish I could have thanked him for everything, said goodbye," he said after a few moments had passed. He felt a stinging sensation well up in his eyes and he closed them to fend off the sadness. "I wouldn't have had to if I had just acted sooner."

Lothar shook his head. "You saw the ruins. A minute earlier would not have changed it. You would have just died with everyone else if you'd tried to usher them out."

Melkin blinked away the tears, staring at the ground. "I don't know."

"I do. But I'm sorry you never got to say goodbye. You know what haunts me? I knew Yulac for eight years, and he died thinking I murdered Ragnar. It was such a flawless setup—I knew I was done for the moment you entered the kitchen and I was caught holding the knife. I don't know why I even picked it up... I don't remember what was going through my mind. I can still see the utter disappointment in Yulac's eyes as he came to the only rational conclusion he could."

"You never blamed *me*, though... That might have been your one way out," said Melkin as he finished setting up his tent. He paced over to a tree and leaned against it.

"You didn't do it. I figured if they ever found out that it had been someone else, I would want them to at least know that I had never lied."

"One slip in that kitchen and I would have killed you. I know you're more powerful than the magic you showed there. Why didn't you stop me?"

Lothar laughed without humor. "What, did you want me to kill you? I don't think that would have worked out well. No, I was too shocked at the time to use my magic precisely, and I didn't want to seriously injure you. Again, if the truth had come to light, I wanted no one to be able to think less of me. I like to believe that Yulac never really thought I was a murderer, that he just locked me up to appease you all. I suppose I would have been given a trial back in the Shalin Empire, but who knows how that would have gone?"

"You did nothing wrong, Lothar. Yulac valued honesty, right?"

"Of course."

"So if he had known the truth... he would have been proud of you."

Lothar nodded slowly, staring out into the distance.

"What was the prison like?" asked Melkin after a while.

"Gods, I think I purged the memory from my mind. When the guards changed, they would bring me a ration of food and water. I didn't know the faul soldiers too well, and obviously the Valean ones looked at me with disgust. I was gagged almost the whole time, except for when I was eating, and the guards kept their weapons pointed at me while I ate. Never did I consider that I could be a traitor to my country, to the laws of the Akistaria." Lothar paused for a moment before looking back at Melkin. "Then, when I broke you out of prison, I became a true traitor. I broke the law and that was my decision, not a misunderstanding." Lothar finished his tent and leaned against a tree across from Melkin.

"That's not true and you know it. Of course there was a misunderstanding, that's what the entire plan of the Talwreks is based off of. Do you think your emperor would still be contemplating an all-out war on Valea if he knew the true reason behind the lootings, kidnappings, and the Akarist explosion?"

"I suppose not." Lothar grimaced; his pain and regret were so clear in his expression that Melkin, for the first time, struggled to meet his eyes.

"You're not a traitor, Lothar, no matter what the law says. Besides entering the Shalin Empire in the first place, I never committed any crime that should have gotten me arrested. You broke me out of jail so we could set things right."

"You told me that if I cared at all about those who had died, I would help you. And I did. If we stop the war, their deaths aren't in vain."

"Seems like such a distant goal. I really didn't know how deep this organization ran until the night at their campsite. I thought maybe we could just wipe them out and move on to stopping war from there. With Fareod, though . . . it's far more complicated."

"You don't say," said Lothar. He seemed to deflate a bit at the weight of what their group still had to face in the coming days.

"Melkin!" shouted Astrid from behind. "Come, let's spar!"

Melkin sighed, feeling the fatigue in his joints after so much walking and so little sleep for the last few weeks. Was it too much to want a break? "You can practice throwing knives with Galdur if you want to," he said to Lothar while walking toward Astrid. She handed him two of the sticks, which were carved into shapes that more closely resembled her daggers. Unfortunately, the thinner ends meant that they were likely to hurt more, too. "Leina, the bag of teleium is in my pack for you to experiment with," he called out. She was setting up a workspace by the fire Galdur was lighting.

He squared up against Astrid, the two of them using their dominant hands. Their bouts of practice were occasionally interrupted by the sharp snap of exploding teleium, but he figured it simulated the normal distractions that one would encounter in a fight.

After sparring for several rounds, Melkin sat down against a tree, panting heavily. Astrid had won five times, but he had won twice. "Are you not exhausted?" he asked, massaging a spot on his abdomen where Astrid had hit him especially hard.

"No." Astrid was bouncing lightly on her feet, evidently not tired despite the sweat covering her face. "I was thinking . . . I want to try sparring right-handed against you with your left hand. That way, if I have to fight a faul, I could surprise them."

Melkin stood up and shrugged. "Fine." He switched hands and waved the stick around, grimacing at the feeling. The strange sensation made every movement just a hair slower, more lethargic. After ten rounds, Melkin found himself warming up to his left hand and saw that Astrid was doing the same with her right. Still, Astrid kept the upper hand as the night progressed and their bouts grew more intense.

"We're going to sleep soon!" called Lothar.

"We'll be done in a moment!" Astrid called back. "One more round?" she asked. Melkin nodded and summoned his remaining strength. He struck toward Astrid's forward leg but received a parry and counterattack, which he deftly dodged. Circling for a few more moments, Astrid lunged forward and swung her majoril stick, missing Melkin by a mere inch as he jumped back and parried her next strike with his auxlar stick while striking with his majoril. The bout lasted far longer than any of their previous rounds. Astrid stabbed toward Melkin's midsection and was caught off balance as Melkin stepped to the side while parrying her incoming strike at the same time. Quickly, he stuck his foot out and she tumbled to the ground, her auxlar flying out of her grasp. Before she could attack with her majoril dagger, Melkin had his own pointed at her neck.

He grinned. "I win."

The next morning, Melkin and his companions packed up their tents and ate breakfast hastily. They were now a little over a hundred miles away from the old Annisik castle and they were eager to eat away at the remaining distance.

"I just realized, this is the farthest I've been into Valea," said Lothar. "If anyone saw me here, I'm sure they would attack me in an instant. I feel somewhat calm, though."

"I'd like to think that you're exaggerating about the danger," said Galdur, staring ahead into the distance. "But I don't really know . . ."

Melkin shrugged. "Well, we're no more vulnerable to the Talwreks here than we were in the Shalin Empire. And I'd be concerned if you were afraid of the forests of Valea."

"It's hard to think that way when I've feared this place my whole life. It's unnerving. You didn't feel the same when we were in the Shalin Empire?" asked Astrid.

"Nothing related specifically to the Shalin Empire. I was uneasy because of our task, but that was it." Why *did* he feel less vulnerable here? He truly wasn't afraid of the Shalin Empire, but even so... "What about you two?" asked Melkin, looking at Leina and Galdur.

"Definitely more comfortable here. I'm glad to be back in Valea," said Galdur.

"You don't even have to ask me that," said Leina with something between a smile and a grimace.

Melkin nodded. "The Akarist was far more troubling to me than this mission. The murder, the poisoning, the uncertainty of it... Lothar, for all you suffered in prison, it was torture not knowing what was happening, or if—if we would survive."

Lothar nodded. "I don't doubt it."

"In fact, I feel much better knowing what our opponents are doing," said Melkin.

"Well, I'm glad you're happy," said Galdur with a small laugh.

"They don't know what we're doing. Not yet at least. They don't know where you are," reasoned Melkin, looking at Galdur. "You heard them at the bonfire."

"We'd be lost without you, Galdur," remarked Lothar. "I'm a sergeant, or I was, but I always had a navigator with me. What else did you learn as the prince?"

Galdur sighed, clenching his jaw. "Not much. Mostly studied maps, obviously. No one ever taught my brother or I how to fight. Melkin was the one who taught me how to use a spear during my copious free time."

"When did *you* have time to do that?" asked Leina, looking at Melkin with incredulity.

"I have my ways..." he said, grinning. "I always found it asinine that the royal family wasn't taught to fight. Their guards do a remarkable job, but with all the assassination threats.... Anyway, I told Queen Gladia I was doing paperwork, but went to ask Fareod if he would like to learn. He sneered at me, and his guards ordered me to leave. So then I went to Galdur, who was eager to learn, and I brought him out to the training grounds to teach him."

"My guards told me that I could have lessons from them instead, and I agreed. Our first lesson was nowhere near as good as the ones with Melkin. I think they were afraid to hurt me, afraid to criticize me. So, I resumed the lessons with Melkin and soon the guards told me to stop associating with him. They only relented after much persuasion," explained Galdur.

"Really?" asked Melkin, grinning. "You never told me that."

"Oh yeah . . . well I was afraid that if you knew the guards didn't want you around me, you wouldn't keep teaching me."

"What did they have against me in the first place?"

"They thought you were dangerous, I think. Mind you, I was only fourteen and you were twenty, so maybe it was a little strange."

"How long did this go on for?" asked Lothar.

"Two years, give or take," said Melkin. "I stopped around a year ago when I became busy investigating all of the bombings."

"Did Queen Gladia ever find out her top spy was training the prince?" asked Astrid.

"Maybe, maybe not. No one ever said anything to me."

"Nor to me, but my mother was always quite busy. I don't think my guards asked her when they told me to stop training with you, Melkin. I think they just viewed you as unsafe."

"I wouldn't be surprised if she turned a blind eye to it. She neither wanted to condone me skipping my work, nor to protest your training."

Galdur smiled, yet sadness shone in the young man's eyes. "I hope so."

"Pity I never got around to the whole climbing thing with you, Galdur," Melkin said. "Though I suppose making you climb the castle walls might have gotten me in a little trouble."

"Can you still teach me?" asked Galdur, a smile touching his lips.

Melkin gave a slight grin. "Sure."

"Leina, have you found out anything new with the teleium?" asked Lothar.

"Not much. I'm sure the Talwreks were using their heat wielders to light the bombs, hence why no witnesses ever saw anything in Valea. The faul that lit the bomb must have been concealed, hundreds of feet away."

"Can you do that?" asked Galdur. "From so far away?"

"If you know in your mind's eye exactly where the bomb is, then yes. I'm not surprised they have some talented faul on their side."

"What else, Leina?" asked Melkin.

"I'm working on a way to neutralize the bomb, or to at least make it less powerful than it is now. I've tried a few things with what we have, but I haven't found anything useful yet."

"Try to not exhaust our supply; we might need it for something else," said Melkin.

"Yeah, I know."

"Like what?" asked Lothar.

Melkin looked at him. "Thalen."

"What, you want to blow him up?" asked Galdur.

"Well, what I want and what we need to do are very different things," said Melkin, gritting his teeth.

"You do know that we're supposed to be working *with* him, right?" said Lothar.

"That does seem to be the case," grumbled Melkin. His reasoning for going to Thalen was sound, yet he now found himself wholly regretting the decision.

"No one let him get near Thalen," said Astrid to the other three.

"I'm sure I'll be able to keep my composure." After a moment of silence he looked up to see his four companions staring at him with various looks of apprehension. He sighed—he couldn't blame them.

25

GALDUR

Galdur narrowed his eyes, focusing only on the tree in front of him and the motion of his arm. He no longer felt the cold wind as he brought his arm back and released the thin metal blade. There was a satisfying *thunk* as the knife embedded into the tree, not far from where he'd aimed.

"Ugh!" cried Lothar in frustration.

Galdur jumped, brought out of his trance by the exclamation. All three of Lothar's knives sat at the base of his tree.

"These... barbaric weapons are useless!" exclaimed Lothar, pacing with his fists clenched.

"Lothar! I didn't think you would get so upset over a weapon," said Galdur, taken aback by the sudden fury. He had only seen Lothar like this once before, but he thought Imar's death was more important than his struggle with the daggers.

Lothar took a deep breath. "Look... I just... I could never get used to sparring with daggers back in school, alright? It was years until I even had a shot in battle with them. This... it's useless. I can't learn this stuff as fast as you all. Look at you, you can already hit the tree from five yards."

"I know, but it's not useless, Lothar. If you couldn't speak, you'd have no defense in a fight."

"You think that hasn't been told to me by my superiors before? That I'd be helpless without magic? I'm perfectly aware of my dependency, but I have no other choice. It's my one gift, Galdur. My one gift."

"I think you're wrong," said Galdur. "I truly believe you can do this, and the idea of you giving up scares me. I don't want you to die."

"That's why I'm training, but this practice is doing no good," said Lothar, taking a breath. "Unless my enemy stands still two yards away from me, then I have no chance."

"You have to try. What else are you going to do around here?" asked Galdur.

Lothar stared at the sky for a moment. "I suppose you're right." He walked over to the tree to retrieve his fallen knives.

"Take it slow. Better to consistently hit a close target than to miss all targets. Stand back only two yards like we did the other day."

"Hey Galdur!" called Melkin. Galdur whipped his head around, facing the man. "Come, I'll teach you how to climb." He heard another knife hit the tree behind him and another frustrated grunt from Lothar.

"You've got this," he encouraged Lothar, before joining Melkin by a tall, broad tree.

Galdur suspected that if he ever had to climb anything else, it would be far more challenging than this tree before him. He thought of the rough stone walls that Melkin climbed so effortlessly, how there were no long limbs of timber to hold onto. But before he could attempt the climb, he received a lengthy lecture on how to fall correctly, including different variations for different situations. Although Melkin seemed genuinely worried about his safety, Galdur suspected it was because of his position as heir to the throne, not out of sincere concern for him. Still, if it meant that he wouldn't fall to his death, he wouldn't complain.

"Of course, when you climb as high as I do for my missions, there's not much you can do if you fall, but it's nice to know anyway," said Melkin, finishing the lesson.

"What's the highest you've fallen from?" asked Galdur, not really sure if he wanted to know the answer.

"Nine yards, give or take," said Melkin. "Try not to do that."

"Yeah, I got that much," muttered Galdur, sizing up the tree. It was devoid of leaves so late in the year which somehow made it more daunting. He gripped the lowest branch anyway and found a foothold, as Melkin had shown him.

"Once you get to climbing walls, the hand and footholds are much smaller, but you can still climb most of them," said Melkin.

"That's not helpful right now." Galdur pulled himself up onto the lowest branch, grunting and struggling the whole way. His upper body strength paled in comparison to Melkin's, but he continued to climb, facing away from where he was sure Melkin was watching with a smirk.

"Also, when you climb walls, you'll want to take your boots off. I'm usually able to clip them onto my belt in a couple seconds, so it doesn't waste that much time, really," said Melkin.

"You couldn't have gone over this while I was still on the ground?" asked Galdur, pressing himself up against the tree trunk. There were many places for him to put his hands and feet, yet he felt his forearms giving out. He stood on a large branch and leaned back against the trunk to rest. His feet were now a whole two and a half yards off the ground and he sighed at his lack of accomplishment.

"Not bad. Unfortunately, if I were an enemy, I could easily kill you with a spear," said Melkin, his head a few feet below the branch Galdur was standing on.

"Not at your height." He saw Melkin's face contort into offence at his remark and laughed hysterically, almost falling off the tree.

"You'd better climb. And fast."

Galdur obliged, stifling his own laughter. Now after releasing some of his tension, he wasn't as careful and scaled much faster. At about six yards from the ground, he sat on another branch, feeling a knot of fear begin to form in his stomach. He almost wished that he had asked what the injuries were that Melkin had sustained from his nine-yard fall. He took a breath and mustered enough courage to glance out at the landscape surrounding them, but quickly looked back at the tree trunk, panting in fear. He shut his eyes and swallowed, willing his arms not to shake. Trying again, he opened his eyes and this time was able to keep focus for several seconds, watching Leina and Astrid spar while Lothar threw knives. Galdur watched another one bounce off the tree and felt a pang of disappointment, but the next one stuck. He looked down but couldn't see Melkin anymore; he must have gone to do something other than watch Galdur inch his way up the tree. He faced north toward the Shalin Empire, the place he once thought to be evil, that many in his country still believed to be evil. The air was chilly, but Galdur did not feel cold with the sun warming him from the horizon.

"Wonderful, isn't it?"

Galdur jumped, grabbing a tree limb before he could fall off. As soon as his heart found its way back into his chest, he peered around the tree trunk to see Melkin perched on a branch on the opposite side of the tree, smiling with pleasure. Galdur blew his hair out of his eyes and looked back at the horizon. He was about to point out that Melkin had used the word 'wonderful' without a trace of sarcasm but couldn't bring himself to ruin the moment. "Yes... it is," he replied quietly.

"Let's go up further."

"I don't know..." Galdur peered through the branches above him to the rest of the tree.

"I'll go first, just follow the path I take," said Melkin.

"Fine," said Galdur with a sigh. Melkin sure had a lot of faith in him. A scary amount seeing as his grand plan seemed to hinge on Galdur. He watched Melkin scale the remaining couple yards, avoiding the thin branches and resting in a fork at the top. Gingerly, Galdur grasped the first branch and began to test his weight on it.

"You've got to be more confident."

"Yeah? It's kind of hard to do that right now..." Galdur's voice was shaky and he felt his cheeks flush with embarrassment, which embarrassed him further. At least Melkin probably couldn't see his face turn red from the top of the tree.

"I'm just saying. Or you could stay down there. Just don't fall,"

"*You* brought me here."

"*You* asked for it. This stuff is risky."

He had indeed asked for it. His hands were sweaty, though, and his heart was beating faster and faster. A pang of fear hit him every time he moved an inch and whenever he looked down at the ground.

"I can't." He leaned back against the thick trunk and took a seat on a branch again. Soon after, Melkin descended and sat beside him. "I'm sorry, I just . . . I'm not like you," said Galdur with a sigh.

To his surprise, Melkin just shrugged. "Maybe not such a bad thing."

"Do you enjoy this when you're on your missions?" asked Galdur.

"Oh yes. You see, Leina has to deal with the perceptiveness of others when she tries to falsify papers, gain access to restricted areas, or glean information. All I have to do is listen in from windows and scale buildings. I know my abilities and that's typically all that matters."

"Well, there's the slight downside that if you fall, you die."

Melkin shrugged. "You know what happens if we get caught. What difference does it make?"

Galdur felt a pang of guilt at the thought. "You wouldn't necessarily be sentenced to death if caught, though."

"I suppose not. I don't like any of the alternatives though."

He shook his head, incredulous. "Why did you become a spy then? Why does anyone?"

"I can't speak for everyone else, but I had a few reasons. One, great pay. I'll be able to retire within a decade. Two, you get to work alone in most cases. Three, you answer directly to either the monarch, the lord or lady you operate under, or the commander of the regiment. And even then, you have a great deal of free will."

"And that's why you didn't want to join the military?"

"A few of many reasons, yes."

Galdur nodded. "Well, if the pay is so great, where's all your money? Not that I mind, but I've funded this whole mission."

"I had the queen keep it in a vault so it couldn't be stolen. Gladia will fund anything I need for my actual missions, so I don't usually use it for anything."

"What *do* you plan to do with it?"

"Well, I had originally planned to buy a small house in the countryside, away from anyone else. I could go into town once a month to buy some food and get the rest from hunting. With my current income, I'll have more than enough within ten years."

"You said 'originally.' What about now?"

Melkin hesitated for a second. "Same plan, assuming everything works out and Fareod hasn't spent everything in the vault by the time it does. What did you plan to do with your life?"

Galdur clenched his jaw, wishing that Melkin would stop assuming his mother was already dead and that he would need to take the throne from his brother. "I wish I knew. I've thought about it for a long time, yet never decided on anything. Being a navigator or a soldier would have been great, but as a prince, I just don't think it would have ever worked. Maybe if Fareod produced an heir it would have been alright, but I never knew when—" Galdur swallowed, a wave of sadness coming over him. "I never knew if I would ever become the heir. After all, my mother isn't that old, only forty."

"I think you'll make a great king."

"Don't go there," pleaded Galdur. Dread once again filled him, though this time not from the height. "I don't want to think about it."

Melkin shrugged. "If you insist."

Galdur continued to stare out at the landscape for some more time, taking in the sights of Valea. Trees and grass. Not the most exciting, but from up in the tree, at sunset, it looked enchanting. Strange, he thought, that even though his bedroom window was several times higher than this, it felt far less real.

"Why did you bring me?" The question seemed to escape him before he could stop himself, like a river breaking through its dam.

Melkin looked at him for a few seconds, an almost pitying expression on his face. "You're the prince."

"That's it?"

Melkin shrugged. "I trust you."

"Why? All you had really seen of me was during our training sessions." Maybe his diligence with the lessons had proved something, but was that really it?

"What does it matter?"

Why didn't Melkin didn't want to tell him? What could his reason possibly be? "What, did you plan to use me for ransom? Did you want my money? My nonexistent influence? Leverage against the faul? Against anyone who tried to stop you? The moment you found out about my mother, did you have your plan formulated? Did you already want to protect me from my brother? Just tell me, for Ryne's sake!"

He felt immense satisfaction at seeing Melkin taken aback at his anger. Galdur *was* angry, and he felt as though he was being toyed with by being brought on a mission with four other people who were ten times more powerful than he.

"Some combination of those, yes. I don't know that many people, but I've known you for some time. You're a hard worker and you never expressed much hatred toward the Shalin Empire. I wanted another human along so I could take leadership without being overpowered by the faul. I wanted to protect you in case of another assassination attempt and I knew that Fareod would never be able to remain king if my plan was to work."

Was that all? Did Galdur expect more than that? Some hidden agenda only Melkin knew about? He wished he were home—he was so, so very far away. Maybe if he closed his eyes, he could wake up in his bed.

"I don't understand your anger. You've been very useful! Look, even if you weren't heir, I wouldn't regret bringing you, alright? And if I hadn't brought you, you'd be dead!"

His tone was as compassionless as ever, and yet Galdur felt some sort of closure. He swallowed and nodded slowly, his anger dissipating. Indeed, perhaps it was a good thing that he wasn't like Melkin. But his plan had worked so far, and he was right. If Galdur wasn't with Melkin right now . . . well the company might be lost, and he might be facing assassination. He sighed and leaned back, staring once more at the sunset, as if it could take him away from the future he dreaded would come to pass.

"How about we go down now?"

"That's probably a good idea." He took a deep breath and lowered himself, a moment of panic hitting him before he found a sturdy branch beneath his dangling feet. He made his way down, resting just once along the way before finally reaching the ground.

"I'm not dead," said Galdur with a shaky breath.

"You're stronger than you look," said Melkin. "I'll give you that. Now go make a fire."

Galdur walked over to the center of the campsite and started searching for dead wood to make the fire. He found he'd grown to enjoy the quiet monotony of building the fire, his one small purpose every evening. The ritual washed his mind of confusion and anger as he carefully began to shave tiny curls of wood in a dry stick. With the third strike of his flint and steel, the stick caught flame; Galdur piled on twigs and blew carefully on the fire until the kindling caught. Soon, a bright blaze was burning and Galdur sat back, admiring the ease with which he had done it—a far cry from his first attempt.

"Hey Galdur," said Leina. He turned around to face her; she was carrying the bag of teleium. "Want to experiment with me?"

"Sure. Is Lothar helping?"

"Maybe. I didn't want to distract him."

Galdur walked over to her and glanced at Lothar. "I *really* don't think he'll mind. Lothar! Come over here!"

Looking relieved and excited, Lothar walked over, storing his throwing knives in their sheaths as he walked.

"What are we doing today?"

"I'm not sure. Detonating the teleium underwater was my best guess and it didn't work. And I don't have a lot of chemicals to work with . . . basically none."

"Do you know how it works?" asked Galdur. The three walked away, to an open space where the teleium was unlikely to ignite any foliage.

"It ignites at high temperatures caused by magic or a spark. But nothing besides that. I've had to consult many alchemists for my previous missions, but I know little of the craft myself. Plus, I don't have any good equipment."

Lothar grinned. "You're asking us for ideas, then?"

"Yes. I'm all out. We *need* some way to disarm it, or at least lessen the explosion."

"You could . . . crush it up?" suggested Galdur.

"I don't think that will work."

Galdur shrugged. "Neither do I, but you asked."

"Alright, now stand back," said Leina.

"Now who's being redundant?" asked Lothar with a smirk. He began to mutter, and Galdur hurriedly covered his ears a split second before the coarse teleium powder ignited and exploded with the usual snap and bright sparks that accompanied the detonation.

"That went well." Lothar had definitely been taking after Melkin and Leina with his sarcasm.

"Yeah . . . I'll think a bit more about this later," said Leina. "Ugh! What did I think I would be able to do without a laboratory?"

"You may still find something. And if you don't, there are still uses for the teleium. I don't like the idea of fighting fire with fire, but it might be our only option," said Galdur. "I really don't think it was retrieved in vain."

"Thanks." Leina nodded in understanding.

Galdur nodded back and turned to find Melkin, leaving Leina to chat with Lothar. He saw him sparring with Astrid and approached while they rested between rounds.

"Hey, I was thinking . . . there's a town not far from here—about four miles north. Someone should go and grab a newspaper."

Melkin thought for a moment. "Who?"

"I don't know. Leina?"

"Why not you?"

"Oh, uh, I don't think . . ." he trailed off.

"You should. If you wear a cloak, you're no more likely to be recognized than Leina."

Galdur averted his gaze. "If she doesn't want to, I will, I suppose."

"Fine. Don't be out too late." Melkin turned back to Astrid and held up his spear in a guard position. Galdur went to tell Lothar and Leina his plan.

"Sure, I'll go," said Leina. "But why not you?"

Galdur sighed. "I'll mess it up, I'm sure of it." He didn't want to be questioned about this. He may have contributed to the mission, but he still wasn't confident in his abilities, particularly when it came to Leina's specialty.

"How about you come with me?" suggested Leina. "I don't know where I'm going, and I'm not keen on getting lost at night."

"It's right over there," said Galdur, pointing in the distance. Leina glared at him. "Alright, fine." He grabbed his spear, lamenting that he had to leave the safety of the fire so late at night. However, as the pair left camp, he had to admit that it was comforting to have Leina by his side, as long as she didn't have any rash ideas. Galdur tied his hair up again while she undid her long braid.

"If we could buy food here as well, that would be good. But the newspaper and any posters are our priority. How big is this town?" asked Leina.

"Not too big. I doubt it will have a wall, but it might have some guards."

He was correct. As the town came into view, they could see that there were indeed guards patrolling the border, but no gate. Galdur guessed that, at most, 150 people lived there. They probably got all their supplies from the city forty miles away. He and Leina approached a guard at the border of the town, who gripped his spear loosely and did not point it at them.

"What business?"

"Travelers. We can pay for some food and a newspaper."

"Too late to shop for food, you'll have to wait till morning. You don't have to pay for papers though, they sent us too many. Just came in with the evening runner." The guard pointed at a newspaper stand. "Haven't read it yet, but the man who brought it said it had some bad news." Galdur felt dread build inside of him again, his mind coming to a conclusion that his heart rejected. Plenty of bad things could happen in a kingdom, right?

Leina retrieved a paper from the stand and glanced at it before stowing it under her cloak. Galdur felt drops of rain start to fall as he glanced around at the nearby buildings for posters. If there were any, he couldn't see them in the dim moonlight. He swallowed; the eerie town had him on edge, wishing for the comfort of the campfire, for warmth and light.

"Can I send a letter?" asked Leina. She had to repeat the question to the distracted guard.

"Oh, yeah, sure. Just give it to me, and I'll deal with it in the morning."

Leina handed him an envelope and turned back toward Galdur, a slight smirk discernable on her face.

"Can we leave?" he asked, hating how his voice shook. To Galdur's immense relief, Leina nodded, but she turned back after a few paces.

"Sir, if I may, we saw some strange people on the roads. They made us uneasy, eyeing us from a distance like they did. Do you have any news on criminals or wanted folk?"

"Hmm? Oh, there might be some news about that in the paper, not that I'd know..." The soldier yawned loudly. "If—" Another yawn. "If you see any suspicious activity, you can report it to... another soldier. Not me." Leina nodded and walked away, Galdur following behind.

"It's too dark to read the paper," she whispered.

"What was that envelope?"

Leina glanced back. "Nothing too important. I'll tell you all once we get back to the campsite."

Galdur nodded, dread replacing the matter of the envelope in the forefront of his mind. He tried his best to walk as casually as possible for the whole four miles. Though he knew that it was too dark for anyone over a few dozen yards away to see them, he still felt exposed. By the time they reached the bright blaze of the campfire, the light drizzle had begun to soak through his clothing.

"Did you find anything?" asked Melkin, rushing up to them.

"A newspaper," said Leina, sitting down by the fire. Galdur and the others followed, warming themselves in the enticing heat. As Leina pulled out the newspaper from beneath her cloak, Galdur and his companions leaned in to catch a glimpse of the front page. Before Galdur read the headline, he would have bet his life on what it said in spite of what he desperately wished for. He registered nothing around him as he read the headline, for in that moment, there was nothing else in the world.

Queen Gladia Ravinyk Dies at Age Forty-One.

26

Leina

It would have been impossible for Leina to not take in her companions' reactions to the news in the instant that their eyes fell upon the headline. Lothar closed his eyes and when he opened them again, Leina saw true fear. He knew the consequences of the news as well as anyone. Astrid's face contorted into a scowl that seemed to curse the very existence of a prince she had never met. She almost didn't have to look at Melkin—he'd known this would happen and had probably come to terms with the truth long ago, not that she suspected it was too hard for him to do so. She'd also expected it ... but the shock was only marginally lessened. The scariest reaction of all though was Galdur's blank stare and labored breathing. For a moment, the only sound in their campsite was the sizzle of rain as it hit the blazing campfire.

"Deities, save us all," whispered Lothar. Then, the campsite broke into a mess of anger, sadness, and fear.

The late hour had given them no choice but to sleep so they could continue traveling the next day. After waking, the news rushed back to her in a depressing wave. She stared at the roof of her tent, wishing she could retreat into her dreams, though they hadn't been pleasant either. As Leina crawled out from her blanket, the night before plagued her mind. The distraught cries from Galdur, anger from Astrid, and vain attempts to calm the situation by her and Lothar were rattling to think about. Melkin had not assigned a night watch—he had at least been a little tactful. Almost too tactful for him. In the past, Melkin would never leave them unguarded in such an open space. Perhaps he was realizing his own fallibility.

The campsite felt deathly still. The rain had ceased, thankfully, but the air was chilly, and she shivered, feeling miserable. The waterproof tent had done wonders to keep her dry, but it was little comfort against everything else. As tears rose to her eyes, she tried to block out painful memories, but she didn't succeed. She saw Gladia's warm smile as she congratulated Leina on a job well done and remembered her keen mind for diplomacy and unwavering sense of duty, even when facing impossible challenges. Leina wiped the tears from her eyes and left her tent. The rising sun was obscured by clouds, but it was light enough to see outside. Yawning, she wondered why she had awakened so early. Melkin or the third night watch usually woke her. Was she afraid of intruders, too? Had Melkin's anxieties rubbed off on her?

Her cloak, which she'd taken off before sleeping, was still damp. Frustrated, she left it atop her pack to dry and walked over to the remnants of the fire, hoping to find a warm ember or two. Then, she spotted the iconic figure of Melkin sitting in one of the trees. She rolled her eyes as she met his gaze, which presumably had been focused on her since she crawled outside of her tent.

"How long have you been up?"

"An hour or two."

"I thought you were going to get some rest?"

"I was too anxious about possible attacks. Still, we went around six hours with no guard, I believe."

"And . . . ?"

Melkin sighed. "Yeah, I feel a bit better. Quite a bit, actually."

Leina nodded. "I thought as much."

"Wake up the others. We have to go. Time is of the utmost importance now."

She woke up Lothar and Astrid, her depressive state magnifying upon seeing them remember the events of the night before. Pausing outside of Galdur's tent, she glanced behind; Melkin's eyes were still focused upon her. She glared at him with reproach. They did indeed have to move swiftly now, but she was loath to disturb Galdur. She swallowed and reached gently for the tent-flap, pulling it open to see Galdur awake and sitting with a blank stare.

"Umm... We have to go."

Galdur nodded, still not meeting her gaze. She turned away, willing the tears that came to her eyes to disappear. The four of them gathered by the fire that Melkin had resuscitated and for an awkward moment, said nothing.

Melkin clasped his hands together and leaned forward. "We have to go through the rest of that paper."

"I still have it," said Leina. "Luckily it didn't get soaked."

"We can read it while we walk," said Melkin peering over at Galdur, who was hastily packing his tent away. Leina started walking over to help him, but he finished quickly, doing a sloppy job in the process. "Let's go," she heard Melkin say from behind her. His voice had never sounded so cold and harsh. Why? Was this his twisted way of mourning? He started walking, Leina and the others trailing behind him.

Before the campsite had left their view, Melkin sprang the question. "Right, so what else does the paper say?"

"Umm..." Leina glanced over at Galdur's pained expression and Melkin's cold one. She scanned the first page, which was all about the unknown illness and Fareod's coronation. Flipping to the second page, she found some information about Fareod's plans for the future. "Well... He—Fareod—has publicly announced that he plans to declare war as soon as he ascends the throne..." she paused upon seeing Galdur's face contort into a scowl of pain and anger. "You know, maybe we shouldn't—"

"We need to know this. Reading it is not going to change what has happened," said Melkin, not looking back at her. Against her better judgment, she read on.

"Once he declares war, Orwic will have the opportunity to respond before Valea attacks. He'll either negotiate with Fareod or muster his own forces in return."

"The latter option is far more likely," muttered Astrid.

"Besides, Fareod's not going to settle for peace. That's the whole reason he killed Gladia in the first place," said Melkin. At this, Galdur's head snapped up.

"Can we not talk about this?" His eyes were narrowed in anger, but a hurt and betrayed expression shone through. Melkin faced Galdur, their faces no more than a foot apart.

"I'm sorry, Galdur, I really am. Look, I was friends with Gladia."

Leina was too stunned to intervene; she sucked in a breath as she saw Galdur's face contort into shock. Melkin had to shut his mouth, he had to. Galdur's lower lip trembled. "How could you—"

"We must keep moving forward, though. We don't have time for this!" cried Melkin. "Maybe I judged wrong in bringing you, alright? You can leave, take a carriage back to the castle. You don't have to stay."

He probably didn't mean to hurt Galdur. He probably didn't mean to hurt Lothar during the times that they'd fought either. If Melkin wanted to hurt someone, he would do it without words, she thought with bitter humor. But that didn't matter now. Of course it didn't.

Galdur stared at Melkin for a second, tears in his eyes, before he turned and ran.

"Galdur, wait!" called Leina, but the prince did not stop. "Lothar, go talk to him!" she cried. Lothar took off while she strode up to Melkin, who had the audacity to look surprised.

"Don't make him stay if he doesn't want to. We can kill Fareod on our own. It'll be riskier without Galdur by our side, but if he's a hindrance—"

"You idiot!" Leina yelled. "Do you seriously think that he wants to go back home right now? You think he wants to see the murderer of his mother crowned? He wants revenge, Melkin! But more than that, he needs support! Fareod is his brother, and he killed their mother—not just the queen, Melkin! His mother. I know that you accepted the inevitable, but he held out hope. Hope that is now crushed."

"You think that's never happened to me? You think I've never lost anyone important to me? That I've never been betrayed? You're wrong. But I kept going."

"He's not giving up! But he needs compassion! You two aren't the same. Whether or not you needed sympathy after what happened to you, I don't know. But he does. Would it be that difficult for you to help him out? To show that you are, in fact, a friend? Because right now, I think he doubts that!"

She glanced behind to see Lothar had managed to stop Galdur. She took a breath, softening her scorn.

"For Ryne's sake, you brought a seventeen-year-old into a maze of conspiracy and espionage. Can you even imagine what he is going through? Truly?"

"I didn't steal him from his home! I asked him for his help. You were there."

"You were the only person besides his mother who treated him as something more than a political pawn. How could he refuse?"

"By saying no?"

"He trusted you! If we help him now, all of us, he'll get through this and be more than happy to help us take down his brother." She addressed Melkin, but saw Astrid standing to the side, arms crossed.

"She's right, Melkin. I didn't see it before, but I do now. And do you really want to bet on Galdur staying alive if he's not with us?" asked Astrid, turning to face Melkin.

He stood there, face blank. Eventually he looked down. "Alright."

A wave of relief washed over her, but the battle was not won yet, she knew. Leina glanced back over to Galdur and Lothar as they approached the three. Galdur's face was full of loathing, though she wasn't sure if it was toward Fareod or Melkin. Probably both.

"No need to stand there, let's get moving," said Lothar, starting to walk ahead with Galdur beside him.

The group traveled in silence, without any mention of the newspaper, until a bit after midday, when Melkin asked how far they were from Annister.

"About eighty miles," said Galdur when no one else answered. He took a shaky breath. "You know..."

"What is it?" asked Lothar.

"Mom was the one who encouraged me to study maps," he said, sniffling.

"Did she make you memorize all the regions and everything?" asked Leina.

Galdur gave a short, tearful laugh. "No. We just studied them for political reasons and stuff, you know? But I didn't want to learn all the history and politics that Fareod constantly learned about, so I just kept studying the maps. Sort of stupid of me, right?"

"Not at all. I don't think any of us considered how we would get around when we formed this group." She didn't mention Melkin. The grieving prince hadn't taken one look at him since the morning. His anger was justified.

"I never thought I'd get to see so many of the places I saw on my maps..." he continued. "After all, I was kind of locked up in the castle for most of my life..."

"I doubt this is your idea of a vacation," said Astrid.

Galdur shook his head and wiped his eyes. "I suppose not. I always wanted to leave the castle, to leave the city, though. Fareod—Fareod didn't. He was always poring over his books—I mean, how much history is there to learn, really? He read up on military tactics and on the history of the Shalin Empire, too. He told me about what he read sometimes, though. We would sit and he would talk about what he had learned, sort of giving me a summary, really. I—I feel like I've lost him too."

"Did he change?" asked Leina.

Galdur nodded. "Pretty much. He always hated the faul and the Shalin Empire, like my grandmother, but he was never cruel or derisive toward any humans. Then, I guess when he was my age, the... the Talwreks contacted him or recruited him or something. I don't know how it all started, and I can only guess. But he became more self-centered and more entitled. He started to act like he was already king. For Ryne's sake, I don't know how I didn't see this coming!" cried Galdur in frustration.

"Don't be an idiot—it's not your fault," said Astrid.

Leina put a hand on Galdur's shoulder. "You can't blame yourself for your brother's actions. Your mom would be proud that you're here and that you can carry on her legacy."

Galdur nodded. "Mom was always trying to persuade him to keep an open mind about the Shalin Empire. You know that, Leina."

She nodded. Galdur had once again left Melkin out of the conversation.

"She tried to make peace even when her advisors said that it was useless. They weren't bad people, just more realistic than she. I hope it's not too idealistic to think that her goal is possible now, despite everything . . ." said Galdur. "We have to think it can be done."

"If only she had been in power when Empress Persec ruled the Shalin Empire. We might have had peace," said Lothar. "Or at least, formal peace. I'm not sure if the border fighting would have stopped though. That's the will of the people. But Persec was relentless in vying for peace. Even desperate near the end of her rule."

"Wasn't she the empress before Orwic?" said Galdur.

Lothar nodded. "Yup, she was Emperor Orwic's niece. After she died, the crown went to him, since she was an only child."

"My grandmother was queen while Persec was in power, I believe," said Galdur. "Hence why peace was never possible."

Silence followed. Leina pondered how luck could be so twisted. Gladia and Persec missed each other by a matter of a few years.

They traveled without any more heavy conversation for the rest of the day. Leina was glad for that; she had been able to forget her surroundings and everything that plagued her mind as she walked through the forests of Valea. After they finally settled for the evening, Astrid and Melkin once again sparred while she, Lothar, and Galdur sat by the fire. They comforted the prince while he mourned for Gladia and prayed to Ryne.

Leina took a breath. "This responsibility shouldn't be yours, Galdur, but if you want to carry on, you'll have to forgive Melkin."

"I can't right now. Maybe tomorrow I'll be able to talk to him, but I can't yet. He should know better. How could he not?"

"That he should," said Lothar, nodding. "You two want the same goal, though. We all do."

Galdur swallowed and nodded. "I'll think about it."

As they went to set up camp that night, Leina was extremely thankful for dry tents and cloaks, courtesy of Lothar's magic. The next morning, all were in far better spirits than they had been the previous day and were making good progress toward Annister. Leina found herself greatly calmed by the day of 'rest.' Not physically, since they had walked over a dozen miles, but nothing happened to increase anyone's anger or grief, and she enjoyed talking with the others. Melkin was a bit impatient, of course, but Leina suspected that Galdur would soon be amenable to discussing the future. Still, they walked without mention of either the newspaper or the tragedy for the first few hours.

"Galdur," said Melkin. "Did Gladia ever tell you what she said to Thalen at the new Annisik Castle?"

"No. I—I was told that she humiliated him . . ."

"Well, it was really the only reason I was able to keep my composure there. She brought me for protection and so I could hear what she had to say. Suffice to say, the prospect of Thalen's humiliation was enough for me to readily agree." He then recounted the entire speech that Gladia had given. She couldn't be sure of it, but it sounded like a word-for-word retelling.

Galdur was smiling by the end of it. "She hated Thalen. But there was nothing she could do about him."

Melkin shrugged. "If she had asked, I would have killed him."

"You know, she did mention that once. But she figured the risk was too high, I think."

Melkin sighed. "She was always reasonable that way."

"Yes," said Galdur, his voice shaking.

Astrid smirked. "I must say, I do hope to meet this Thalen character. Not that I'm too good in these kinds of negotiating situations, but he intrigues me. Most of my superiors in the Shalin Empire were . . . kind enough I suppose. And Emperor Orwic was never unjust to his people. At least, as far as I know."

"I heard of one official being quite unpleasant, but I think Orwic just fired him," said Lothar.

Melkin sighed. 'How I wish . . ."

"Leina..." said Galdur after a while, "did you want to check out the wanted section of the newspaper, like that soldier suggested?"

"Sure." She fetched it from her bag and didn't have to flip too far back in the paper before she found it. "Oh dear, we are all here..."

"All of us?" asked Lothar. Leina glared at him. "Right. Stating the obvious."

"I'm assuming that they just stole the descriptions from a mix of the sketches and those Talwreks we talked to near the Akarist ruins," said Leina. "First up is Melkin. It seems you are deemed more important than me here. Melkin Edaireth. Short hair, clean shaven, muscular, strange hazel eyes, five foot and five inches tall; Oh look, they gave you a couple more inches!" Galdur, Lothar, and Astrid burst out laughing.

"That's not true..." muttered Melkin. "Strange hazel eyes? What does that even mean?"

"It does fit," laughed Astrid.

Leina glanced over at Melkin. "I assume that's how the castle guards described you to the writers of this section. When was your sketch drawn?"

"Four years ago."

"That would make sense, then." Leina read past the description and her stomach dropped. "They've found it out. It says that you've kidnapped the prince and are handing him over to the Shalin Empire with the help of Astrid Inaria and Lothar Raiken. You've got a bounty of five-hundred gold on your head."

"That story is wrong," said Astrid. "Obviously."

"Oh, the king knows it's wrong. The bombers know that it's wrong. But it will certainly stir up anger amongst the townsfolk of both nations," said Leina. "The point is, they know that the five of us are together."

Galdur shook his head. "How? You two were out of sight back at the Akarist, and we weren't seen clearly at the Dalyuben mines."

Melkin sighed. "Ryne, I'm an idiot. Fareod was right there! Right there when Gladia assigned me to the Akistaria mission. Once I came back, it only took one guard to recognize me and report back to Fareod. Imar said that Lothar was working with an 'Evarith,' but

I'm sure the Talwreks were able to see through that disguise with the information from Fareod."

"Well, that's just wonderful. Let's read the rest of the descriptions so that we can disguise ourselves if necessary." With a sigh, Leina started on Galdur's entry. "Shoulder length black hair, six feet tall, thin lips—"

"Hey!" cried Galdur. "It does not say that!"

Leina stifled a laugh. "It does! The list goes on and on . . ."

"I'm not surprised. You are the prince after all," said Lothar.

Galdur nodded, peering over Leina's shoulder. "Yeah, they did make a lot of sketches of me. And every guard and servant in the castle knows what I look like."

"You're not wanted for any crime, just missing because, you know—Melkin kidnapped you and all."

"Right, of course," said Melkin. "Sorry about that."

Leina scanned the page, running her finger down the rows of text. "I'm next."

All of a sudden, Melkin snatched the papers from her grasp. "Let's see here. Long black hair, pronounced cheekbones, five foot and five inches tall, clear skin—alright, these writers are clearly biased." He thrust the paper back into Leina's hands but looked more amused than angry.

Leina smirked. "Unfortunately, I'm not special enough to be accused of a crime. My role in this is unknown, but it does say I disappeared around the same time as Melkin and Galdur. I'm wanted for questioning."

"I . . . don't think that's a lie. There's nothing explicitly connecting you to Melkin, right? Perhaps they really don't know what you're up to," mused Lothar. "Your appearance in Nuwelke might soon point them in the right direction, though."

"It also looks better for them if the faul are responsible for Galdur's disappearance," said Melkin. "They probably do want to question you."

"Last night, I sent a letter to the royal castle from that town. It probably hasn't even left yet, but it was addressed to Fareod."

At this, Melkin, Lothar, and Astrid all stopped and turned toward her, their eyes narrowed in suspicion.

"Relax, I didn't do anything stupid. I told Fareod that I'm tracking you, Melkin."

"Why?" asked Astrid.

"Well, I intend to clear my name. That could be useful for a number of things."

Melkin pressed his lips together. "I'm not sure that will work."

Leina shrugged. "Neither am I, but it's better than nothing. But I thought I should let you all know."

Lothar nodded. "Thank you. Hopefully we'll see a change in the newspaper about you in the next week or so. Who's next?"

"The faul. Lothar, you're first. You're accused of plotting to deliver Galdur to your emperor—oh! And apparently you also took part in the bombing of the Akarist. Might as well just throw in all the charges. A bounty of five-hundred gold pieces for whomever finds you as well."

"Look at you, Lothar. Moving up in the world, eh?" said Melkin, smirking.

Lothar grimaced. "That's one way to look at it."

"And your description says... five foot and three inches tall, shaggy blonde hair, and blue eyes. That's it. We do have some warnings here though—get ready: very violent, very dangerous. What incredible reporters."

Lothar chuckled. "They visually described most of the faul in the Shalin Empire; besides the height, but who can tell at a distance? I must say, though, nothing in that description is wrong, per se."

"And finally, you're up, Astrid. Four foot and seven inches tall, blue eyes, blonde hair past shoulders." Leina sighed. "You know, we can make fun of these all we want, but they are accurate."

"Well, they're not that specific," said Lothar.

"Right, but they must have interviewed people who know us. Astrid, did you look different in your sketch?"

"Of course, that was three years ago and my hair was only around an inch long."

"So they would have had to question the Pyantir guards. I'm just saying, it's unnerving," said Leina.

"No, you're right," said Lothar. "We suspected how deep this group is embedded but seeing it in action... you're right."

"You don't say. Anyway, back to your description, Astrid. You are being accused of assisting Lothar in his crimes. Only two-hundred gold coins on your head, I'm afraid."

"I'm devastated," said Astrid dryly.

"Are there any articles in the paper about us? I mean, I don't think most people really skim through the entirety of the wanted persons section of the paper," asked Galdur.

Good question. Leina flipped through the paper. "There's an article on page three that's about you being kidnapped. The window was smashed, guards saw Melkin enter the castle a few hours prior, then you two went missing. Pretty much what we expected. It really makes them look quite incompetent, though. The prince kidnapped from his own castle," remarked Leina.

"Indeed, but the public may pity Fareod for it," said Melkin.

"Let's see..." said Leina, flipping through the paper. She saw some articles about Galdur and Fareod when they were younger, Fareod's politics, and a small biography about Gladia. Leina saw no use in reading those out loud, so she closed the paper. "Nothing else useful."

She glanced over to Melkin, who had his gaze fixated on her. Would he take the paper from Leina and look through it himself? Read the articles that she skipped over? He averted his gaze, and Leina put the paper back in her bag.

"Am I missing something, or will talking to Thalen be far more difficult now?" asked Astrid, drawing out the words.

Lothar closed his eyes for a moment. "If he doesn't believe us, he could easily turn us over."

"And that's if we're even able to get an audience with him," said Leina. "Which is improbable."

"By Ryne, you're right. Let's just steal the records," said Melkin.

Leina shook her head. "No. Too risky to break into the vault of a Lord's castle. You know that."

"Well how else do you want to do it?" Melkin spun on his heel, facing her with angry eyes.

"We have time to figure something out!" she cried, failing to keep her composure under Melkin's impassioned outburst. She knew how delicate of a topic this was for him, but he had no right to yell at her.

"I'm not putting my fate in Thalen's hands again! You haven't lived under him!"

"Do you think I've never suffered?"

"You don't know Thalen. You don't know what you're asking me to do," he said in a low, dangerous voice.

"Well then maybe you shouldn't be here!" The five went deathly silent. She had gone too far. "I just think—"

Lothar stepped between the two. "We're stopping here."

27

ASTRID

Lunchtime was silent. Astrid didn't mind, except she was bored. She ached from sparring with Melkin the previous two nights and figured she'd better rest for a day or two. With nothing to do, she decided it could be interesting to skim through the old history book.

She walked up to Lothar. "Where'd you put the book? The true history one."

"In my bag," he said, a faraway look on his face. She rummaged through the bag and found the leatherback book, marveling once again at how slim it was. But, she supposed, most of the history in the giant tome they'd bought at the shop was true. This book only described the things that weren't told to the public.

She wondered who wrote such a thing; could their account really be trusted? The first few pages revealed that a human and a faul had compiled all the information they could about a decade after the war. Despite her current company, it still felt strange for Astrid—faul and humans didn't work together. However, they had done a good job, she had to admit. The book had records of several first-hand accounts by witnesses to the events it described. They corroborated the events written within the book so that it was regarded as the most honest history of the conflict ever recorded.

Of course, the respective governments wouldn't authorize the mass printing of the book, since it might have made their countries look bad. Publicity, secrecy, lies—she rolled her eyes at all of it. Half of the book was about the war itself and the other half was an even older history, referencing events that she assumed the governments wouldn't want their citizens to know.

Flipping to the war section, Astrid read more details than she'd ever heard before, including a chapter about the lives of each of the ten faul who had died. She scrolled through the names and recognized a few of them; their legacies lived on even when the stories of their true downfall did not. The most powerful of the bunch, Rowan Golanir, was a well-known name to her. Across the Shalin Empire, the Golanirs were considered to be one of the most powerful lineages of faul to ever exist. Their incredible power hadn't limited their lifespans at all, like it would for most faul. Rowan had no children before he died, and no others with the same surname were ever discovered.

"Let's move!" shouted Lothar. Astrid hastily put the book back in his bag and grabbed her own. Though her boredom had been relieved, the information she read weighed upon her mind. Despite the grim nature of the tales, she wanted to learn more about the lives of the fallen.

Turning her attention back to the present, she considered how they would obtain the records, and annoyance started growing within her. She supposed that Lothar brought her along for muscle power, but so far, they hadn't needed much of that. This whole espionage thing was draining and frustrating. Melkin was upset he couldn't stage a heist and Leina was trying to convince him that a diplomatic approach was best. Both ideas sounded tortuous to her. She accepted the reality that they couldn't just barge in and forcefully take the records, but she could dream.

"I don't want to get locked up for life or executed," stated Leina, breaking the stalemate between the two spies. "And if any of us are going to talk with Thalen, it won't be you."

Melkin sighed. "Yes, I'm aware. I don't like it, but I'm willing to hear you out . . . if you have a plan."

Leina grimaced, looking at the ground. "Well, I don't yet."

"So, let's see what we can come up with," said Lothar, ever the peacemaker. "We still have dozens of miles until we reach the castle, so there's no hurry."

The five fell silent. Astrid could think of nothing except pointing a spear at Thalen, but assumed the others were developing some sort of cunning plan. Something intricate and layered, surely.

"Galdur could go. Alone," said Melkin.

Or not. Still, the idea was simple and thus elegant, in a way. It could work, she supposed.

Galdur opened his mouth, but no words came out. His face grew red as he shied away from the group. "Well—um—Leina's not wanted either."

"But you have power that she doesn't," said Melkin.

"Not any real power, just as much respect as Thalen might give me."

"It may be the difference between him believing you or not." Melkin shrugged. "Or maybe not, but who's to say? Plus, if Leina went it would break her cover. If you pretended . . . yes, if you pretended that you were working with me for something, some end goal, then you wouldn't reveal anything. Deny the other three, as if we don't know anything about them . . . yes, that could work."

Leina glared at Melkin. "Don't make him do this."

"We cannot force the responsibility onto Galdur," said Lothar, stroking his chin.

"Let him speak," said Astrid. Why did people always speak for one another?

Galdur stared at the ground for a minute, brow furrowed. "I'll do it."

"Are you sure?" asked Lothar.

"Yes," said Galdur, gritting his teeth.

"Well, what if Thalen says no?" asked Leina.

Melkin grimaced. "At least Thalen would have no good reason to arrest Galdur. Doesn't mean he won't."

"What exactly am I to do?" asked Galdur, taking a quavering breath.

"Don't reveal any more than you need to..." Leina began.

Astrid tuned out most of the rest of the coaching Melkin and Leina gave Galdur about his new solo mission. She didn't mean to, but she was tired and couldn't focus on the intricate details of the conversation that Thalen and Galdur were to have. Instead, she watched their surroundings. There really was nothing like the forests of Valea. Astrid could see why Melkin enjoyed climbing the towering trees.

She had lived in the north as a child. Not so far into the mountains that no trees grew, but the trees near her were often glazed over with a thin sheet of ice. Not so easy to climb. It certainly wasn't warm in Valea at this time of year, but it was better than her home. Of course, she usually had a fire to keep her warm there. She rubbed her hands up and down her arms, trying to bring warmth to her limbs.

A flicker of movement caught her eye in the distance causing her mind to snap back to the present.

"Just make sure you—"

"I see something," said Astrid, cutting off Lothar.

"What?"

She pointed in the distance, toward the brief apparition. "A flash of something. Soldiers, maybe."

"Soldiers?" cried Galdur with wide eyes.

"Leina, can you see further?" asked Melkin.

"Not through these trees."

"Let's pursue." Melkin began a slow jog forward, and the rest of them followed suit. The leaves crunched beneath their feet as they tried to catch up with the group ahead. "There! Yes, I see what you're talking about, Astrid." He slowed their pace but continued to lead the group in a jog.

"We're heading toward the border," panted Galdur. His eyes were still a bit wide in fear, and he traveled behind the other four.

"How far?" asked Melkin.

"Still a couple dozen miles. But if those are soldiers, that's where they're headed."

"We need a better look." Melkin kept them jogging for nearly a mile before the group of soldiers came into clear view for everyone.

"A mix of professional soldiers and armed civilians," whispered Leina once they'd all stopped and caught their breath.

"What does that mean?" asked Lothar.

"Just a regular border fight. Not a full-on attack. A strange occurrence this far from the border, but not unheard of."

Astrid breathed a sigh of relief upon hearing those words, as did everyone else. She started to walk again, but a hand held her back.

"Wait until they're out of sight," muttered Melkin.

Breathing with care, she remembered the state that they were in. These were soldiers, and they would not hesitate to arrest them. For years, she feared being taken prisoner by Valea at the border. Her status now would entitle her to a far worse fate than what she had endlessly dreaded for so long. When the soldiers could not be seen or heard any more, Astrid breathed a sigh of relief along with everyone else.

"Of course, since people are joining the soldiers so far from the border, that means they're angry. People are taking up arms against the Shalin Empire of their own free will," said Melkin.

Gods, she was glad to finally rest that evening. For once, she just wanted to sit and relax. She felt slightly reinvigorated by an idea she'd been mulling over for a while, though. Astrid planned to work on her little project after setting up camp. While hammering one of her tent stakes into the ground, she heard a yelp of excitement from Leina.

"What is it?" asked Astrid, peering around the tree. Leina was holding the pouch of teleium in her hand while Lothar stood a few yards away, a slight smile upon his face. Melkin watched from afar, his face stoic as ever.

"I . . . cooled the teleium," said Lothar, gesturing toward a small pebble of teleium on the ground. The coldest I could go. "It won't ignite now."

Galdur walked up to Lothar, looking between the faul and the piece of teleium. "That must have taken a lot of magic. Are you alright?"

"Right now, yes. One piece of teleium, I can do. Even a handful is probably fine. More than that, I'll be too tired to do anything after. I don't know what my limits are, but I feel like there could be some ... unsavory repercussions."

Astrid nodded, looking at Lothar with awe. "I see." She wondered what that was like, though, to have enough power to tire oneself out.

"Well, we have something," said Leina, her smile faltering ever so slightly.

"Indeed," said Melkin with a nod.

After Astrid finished setting up her tent, she sat down on a log and carefully used her dagger to trim off some twigs on a long stick. She breathed a sigh of relief, feeling the enduring pain in her legs vanish. Unfortunately, the soreness in her arms was only intensified by the repetitive, precise movement with her dagger. She felt Galdur's eyes watching as he sat down beside her.

"What do you want?" she asked. It came out more annoyed than she intended.

"Just wondering what you were doing. I can leave if you want to focus," he said softly.

"Nah, it's alright." She lifted the stick to inspect it. "I'm trying to make a spear for myself. A blunt stick won't be too much help in a battle, obviously."

"Are you really going to use a new weapon in battle? I mean, you only picked it up a few days ago." Was that concern she heard in his voice?

"It's better than the faul way of fighting. Most aren't strong enough to use a spear," she said, glancing at him. "It comes much easier to me than all this espionage stuff, anyway." She continued to scrape off some of the stick's imperfections before standing to test it out. After deeming it acceptable, she sat back down.

"Yes, that stuff is quite tiring isn't it," said Galdur, clenching his jaw. She felt somewhat comforted, hearing that Galdur also resented the work.

"Well, don't get too tired of it yet. Though I suppose Melkin would be happy if you just had to resort to killing Thalen."

Galdur chuckled, leaning forward. "I don't think he would really be happy. He wants his plan to work. It's quite brilliant, and he knows it."

"I can see a few ways it could go wrong," she said with a shrug.

"Sure, but we're going after a document that is one of seven in the nation. There is no flawless plan."

Astrid mumbled her agreement, picking up the throwing knife that lay beside her on the log. She had originally planned to 'borrow' one of Lothar's, but Melkin had given her permission to take one of his.

"Tell me, did you ever want to be promoted to sergeant?" asked Galdur, staring into the distance.

"No. Not at all. Lothar would always write to me about how much paperwork and planning he had to do. Of course, he loved it, but I think I would have hated it."

"Right, I feel the same. I suppose helping here isn't too bad, but leading a whole country . . . alone." He shivered and she felt pity well up within her.

"Don't be stupid, you won't be alone." She started carving a slit through the middle of the shaft at one end to make room for the throwing knife so it could act as a spearpoint. It was a delicate process; she didn't want to split the stick beyond repair.

"Yeah? You and Lothar are going to go back to the Shalin Empire, and Melkin's going to leave forever for retirement."

"Order him to stay."

Galdur chuckled, glancing at her. "I can't do that."

"You could, though. Listen, I barely know anything about Valea. But if you end this war, stop the needless slaughter, you'll be ten times better than any previous monarch. I'm serious." She put the spear down and looked into his eyes. "I've been in battle. It's just anger and anger and anger. My friends died in vain. When I returned home, the remaining soldiers thought it was all Valea's fault. Blinded by their anger, they refused to see that the fighting was for no reason at all. By Talen, I've got no idea if the Incantir will appease those people, but you've got to stop the war!"

"I agree with you, but I don't know if I can!"

"If you don't see the faul as the enemy, then you can! I've never had this kind of hope before, Galdur. Never felt like there was even the smallest chance that things would change. But now there is." She wanted to believe, she really did. "The faul don't hate you, they hate the fighting. They just don't know it yet."

"I'd like to believe that," said a voice from behind her. She turned to see Leina standing with her arms crossed. "I can't unsee the scowls when I escaped the streets of Nuwelke. I'll never forget how quickly the townsfolk turned on us and tried to burn and choke me."

"That's not exclusive to faul, and you know that," said Astrid. Leina continued to scowl. "What do you think would happen if I walked into a Valean town? Nothing good, that's for sure. I don't blame you for retaliating against those faul, yet doing so is why the fighting continues."

"But if everyone is so angry—"

"That's why we're getting the Incantir. We have no choice but to keep going."

"Ryne's sake, this won't be easy," said Galdur.

Astrid faced Galdur again, resolve burning in her. "I swear to Oberel, I'm not letting you give up."

"Nor will I," said Leina. "I don't know how I can help, but I'll do whatever is necessary."

"That's if I even become king, remember."

Leina nodded slowly, eyes unfocused. Then she turned to Galdur. "How far are we from Annister?"

"Fifty miles. We'll reach it within three days."

"How long till Fareod can gather his troops?" asked Astrid, glancing between Galdur and Leina.

Leina blew out a long breath. "Each province's militia has to rally together. Possibly . . . a week until he officially declares war."

"And I assume Orwic knows that Fareod will declare war?" asked Galdur.

Astrid nodded and sighed. "He has plenty of advisors and it doesn't take much investigation to figure out if Valea is summoning their military."

Galdur shook his head in wonder, a sly smile forming on his lips. "Right, so in three days we'll reach the castle. Then we have another three or four to find the Incantir, dethrone Fareod, and deliver the Incantir to Orwic, assuming that it does anything. What could go wrong?"

28

Galdur

How could he be this nervous already? As Galdur walked the streets of Annister, his heart hammered within his chest so ferociously that he was sure passing townsfolk could hear it. He comforted himself by remembering the gist of what Leina had told him a few hours ago. No one here cared about him or what he was up to—there was nothing to fear. He walked with his hood pulled over his head to conceal his identity, but he doubted any of these civilians would know him on sight anyway.

He had entered Annister through the path closest to the castle, but it was still quite the walk—enough time for his fear to make him sufficiently nauseous. He had walked through a mile or two of farmlands and sparse houses before coming upon the true city. Along the path, he saw the dilapidated ruins of the new Annisik Castle. The plot of land, overlooking the city from a slight distance, was strewn with rubble, having never been cleaned up. It didn't look like there had ever even been an effort to do so. Perhaps that was a good thing. A few people were camped within the rubble, using the solid stone as cover from the elements. It wasn't much worse than the small wooden houses that crowded Annister. Pity and anger stirred within him. Annister was a major trading city in Valea, so there was only one explanation for where the people's money had gone. He fixed his eyes upon the towering old castle, imagining that if he stared long enough, he could see Thalen through the thick stone walls.

There was poverty in Hileath, Kasperon, Falarak—everywhere really. But the sorry state of this city, the decrepit ruins of a slave-built castle, the lack of any color, music, or art, which so often crowded the streets of Hileath, spoke to its extreme plight. He'd hoped for improvement in the four years since he was last here, but if anything, the city was worse. The sound of a scream alerted him to a confrontation not twenty yards away. A man held a spear to a woman, who quickly surrendered a handful of copper pieces. The man retreated, observers went back to their duties, and Galdur walked on. There was nothing he could do.

When Gladia was queen, Galdur had sat in on many of her meetings. It wasn't rare that a representative from Annisik Province, oftentimes a citizen who had found enough money for a carriage ride, would complain about the state of the city. Though Gladia would listen intently to the complaints and express her sympathy, she would have to deny intervention in many cases. "I wish I could, but look, Jurith has been attacked again, and so has Preloc," she said one time. She felt guilty about it, he knew. But with the constant border fights, she had a limited supply of both money and time and was forced to abandon most of her Annisik projects.

The journey to the castle felt like an eternity. He still felt like he wasn't supposed to be here. Why was the castle so far away when he'd been walking for hours? Galdur looked at the sun and figured it had actually been less than an hour since he departed from beyond the farms. It was late afternoon, probably an hour or two till sunset.

As he got closer to the castle, he could see guards walking with lazy steps, their gazes unfocused and uncaring. Galdur suspected their very presence warded off any crime near the castle; there were plenty of unguarded areas to rob instead. A tall, strong fence surrounded the castle, tipped with thousands of spikes to prevent anyone from climbing it. At last, he arrived at the castle gates, guarded by four armored soldiers.

One of them lifted his head, eyeing Galdur. "Do you have an appointment with Lord Thalen?"

"No sir. I have an urgent message that he should be eager to hear," said Galdur, keeping his tone respectful. He tried to control his breathing, remembering the past three days of coaching from Leina. He should have been given this training years ago. Leina said he was a natural though, and he had to believe that. There was no other choice.

"You may have to wait. Lord Thalen dislikes unannounced visitors. You'll leave your weapons in the waiting hall and a guard will be assigned to accompany you in case your purposes are misguided."

"That's fine," responded Galdur in what he hoped was a steady voice.

"Welcome to the home of Lord Thalen," said the guard monotonously, beckoning Galdur through the gates. He walked through the small door to the waiting hall, gazing around at his surroundings. The only furniture or decorations in the room were stone benches, lined up in rows along the floor. A few citizens were already sitting, waiting to talk with Thalen. He took a seat a few benches away from them, noticing that a guard followed him and stood creepily behind the bench he sat on.

As the hours faded from one to the next, he began to fear it was too late at night. But while the sky grew darker, he knew that so close to winter, it wasn't actually that late. In the few hours that he had been there, only one other person had been seen. After only a few minutes of speaking to Lord Thalen, the lucky person was kicked out of the castle. Galdur swallowed, drumming his fingers along his thigh. He saw several rats run through the cracks of the stone, which were caked with dirt and grime. He could certainly see why Thalen wanted a new castle, but this one wasn't a lost cause by any means. With some maintenance, it could be fixed up to look like it had a century ago. Leave it to Thalen to overspend on his own comfort then have it be blown up.

Some hours into his waiting, a guard from the throne room approached the one that stood behind Galdur and the two talked in a low voice. Galdur, with his back to the two, felt the hairs on the back of his neck stand up as their eyes surely watched him. At last, the throne room guard left, and his assigned guard stepped closer. "Hey, you. What's your name anyway?"

"Galdur."

"Galdur..." The guard narrowed his eyes.

Galdur felt some satisfaction watching him try to decipher if this dirty, ragged stranger before him was the prince of Valea.

"Lord Thalen will see you now. Leave your spear here."

He obliged, and after subjecting himself to a pat down, was allowed to make his way up the staircase to the throne room. Two guards stood at the entrance and parted to let him in. Half a dozen guards lined the room, spears at the ready. For the first time outside of paintings, Galdur looked upon Lord Thalen. He had long, sleek black hair, quite like Leina's, and a short black beard, very unlike Leina. His tall, slender figure had a laid-back demeanor, yet his sharp eyes focused on Galdur, unrelenting in their glare.

"And what is *your* name," asked Thalen, taking a sip from his goblet.

"Galdur Ravinyk," he stated, pulling back his hood. While the guards showed signs of surprise, Thalen only continued to stare at him, eyes narrowed.

"Last I remembered, you were kidnapped. By that spy, Edaireth. What are you doing here?" asked Thalen, tapping his fingers against the side of his goblet.

"Lord Thalen, the accusations in the paper are false. Melkin Edaireth did not kidnap me. Rather, we have joined forces and are attempting to secure the safety of the country in these trying times," he stated, standing tall and keeping his voice level. Silence penetrated the room.

Thalen's lip curled into a sneer. "What a lovely declaration. Now, if you've nothing else to say, you can be on your way. Next time, pour your heart out to someone who cares. I'm not begging the monarchy to clear your friend's name."

Galdur willed himself to calm the burning in his cheeks. Ryne, he had to get to the point. "No, no! You see, to protect the security of the kingdom, we need access to the guard records."

"The guard records? Why, if ever a demand so obviously villainous was made of me."

"It's true! We need those records to exploit a weakness in the Shalin Empire's army. If we are successful, your province will find itself free from threat for many years."

"And I suppose the papers are wrong, that it's all a misunderstanding, and that there's no possible scenario in which Edaireth, upon learning that his crime was discovered, forced you to demand the guard records from me. And most certainly for a use other than the seemingly noble one you preach."

Galdur was struck speechless for a moment, his mind working furiously to devise a competent response. "Would you care to hear the full story? Ten years ago, a Hilean castle guard passed information along to the Shalin Empire in return for a small fortune. Shortly thereafter, he retired to a nice comfortable cottage away from the mayhem. The information he gave to the Shalin Empire has enabled them to break through weak parts of our border forces for the last decade. It's the key to their continued success, the reason we haven't crushed them yet. If we determine exactly what information was given to the Shalin Empire, we can predict their next move, and ambush their forces." The story made just enough sense to sound plausible.

"Well, you see, little prince, by law I am not permitted to just let anyone see those records. Why, if perhaps I did allow you to have my copy, and you used it against me, my reputation would be ruined," said Thalen with a soulless smile. "Or worse." Then, his face contorted back into a scowl, and he leaned forward in his chair, keeping eye contact with Galdur. "So, I ask again. What proof do I have that you're not being coerced into this?"

"And I ask you, do you want to retain your lordship, or be dethroned in this impending war?"

"I suppose there's one way... no, you wouldn't..." mused Thalen. Galdur wanted to press him on the matter, but he knew that it would only give Thalen the upper hand. He didn't need the slimy lord to know just how much power he held.

"If no compromise can be reached, I will take my leave. I wish you the best of luck in your kingdom's defense." He started to walk. Twenty feet from the door, fifteen, ten, five—

"If you would be amenable to a show of proof, perhaps you and I could work together," said Thalen in his usual silky voice.

Galdur turned around and fought a grin. "What do you have in mind?"

"First, I noticed that the papers also mention a Lothar Raiken and an Astrid Inaria. Where are they?"

"Never heard of them. Melkin trusts no one else with our mission."

"You're lying." It seemed as if Thalen would bet his life on this statement. *He has to be bluffing. Please say he's bluffing!*

"If you continue to berate me, Your Lordship, I am afraid that I shall have to obtain these papers in another province. Who knows if by then, it will be too late. I tell you; I know nothing of these people you speak of."

"Edaireth, then. That spy could be anywhere, slip in anywhere. I ask simply for *you* to bring him to me. If you still ask for these papers while your friend is in captivity, then you may have them, and the two of you can be on your way. If you do not, I'll have him arrested and you can go free," said Thalen, who was now showing a slight grin. It wasn't a horrible demand, Galdur realized, but would Melkin do it? Would he let himself be captured by his greatest enemy?

"Indeed, my lord. It shall be done."

"Excellent. Six of my guards will accompany you on your journey to find him and bring him back to the castle." Galdur turned away and started to walk toward the exit once more. Departing the castle dressed in his ragged clothing, with six guards flanking him, he figured he looked like a dangerous prisoner being led to their execution. Well, in all fairness, Melkin might kill him for this. Though the sky was dark now, he suspected there to still be a few hours until the moon was overhead.

A new fear brewed inside of him; what if his companions all appeared when he called Melkin's name? What if they weren't hiding? He hoped that there would be a lookout. If the journey to the castle was an eternity, the one back to the forest was the blink of an eye. He felt strangely calm, as if he was in control of the situation. As they traveled further out from the castle, though, he began suspecting Thalen had some sort of ulterior motive. After all, Melkin had warned the five of them, hadn't he? He shook his head clear of the thought, it was too late to turn back now. Before he knew it, they had reached well beyond the city edges and were now approaching the foliage where he'd left his companions. It was almost too dark for him to see, yet he made out some familiar landscape.

"Melkin Edaireth!" he shouted, feeling stupid. No one appeared. "Lord Thalen wishes to take you briefly into captivity! He must make sure you are not forcing me to ask for the records!" For a minute, no one answered. Then, Melkin's face appeared from behind one of the bushes. There was a fire within his eyes that Galdur had only seen once before—when Vallec was stabbed.

"Am I to go to his castle?" he asked, voice calm yet laced with a dangerous edge that Galdur knew all too well by now.

One of the guards spoke. "Indeed. Thalen wishes to personally question you."

"Why can't you question me here? I'm not forcing anyone to do anything for me."

"We're sorry, but it's Lord Thalen's orders." Galdur was glad to see that the guard actually did look apologetic about the situation.

The night air was silent, except for the occasional chirping of crickets as Melkin stared at the ground, stroking his chin. "Fine."

Though Galdur would never tell him, Melkin's voice sounded almost identical to Thalen's at that moment. He started walking toward them.

"No weapons," said another guard.

Melkin emitted a small grunt of frustration before unstrapping his throwing knife sheaths and storing them behind a bush with his spear. Then, after a search, he joined Galdur and the guards. Though Melkin appeared disgruntled to say the least, Galdur's fears of betrayal were washed away. If Melkin was going along with Thalen's request, surely the offer was fair.

Galdur walked in front of him, the two of them flanked by the guards. He could feel Melkin's angry eyes boring a hole into the back of his neck for the duration of the walk. A few hours to midnight, the eight of them entered the castle again under the pitiful glare of the castle guards. Like they had seen this before, and it never ended well.

Galdur saw his spear sitting in the same place as it was when he left it, though the waiting hall itself was now devoid of all visitors. They slowly made their way up to the throne room where Thalen sat in the exact same position as before. This time, however, he held a leather-bound book in his hands.

"Come here, Edaireth," he said with reproach. Melkin walked out from behind Galdur and stood a few yards to the side of Thalen, letting a spear be brought to his neck. The man whom Galdur had revered for years, the best spy in the nation, was at Lord Thalen's mercy. Galdur's pulse accelerated, past what he thought possible.

"Did this man force you to ask me for these papers I have?" Thalen showed the cover of the book, titled, *Castle Records: Hilean*.

"No, my lord."

"You speak the truth then, little prince," said Thalen softly, his face falling in disappointment. He looked over at the guards restraining Melkin. "Take him to the high dungeons."

"What?" cried Galdur. Melkin didn't dare fight against the spear pressed to his neck while his hands were tied behind his back. "As the prince, I command you to release him!"

Thalen laughed. "A command that I am in no way obligated to follow."

"You're a coward and a liar, a disappointment to all of mankind," said Melkin, staring into Thalen's eyes. The lord's face contorted in anger, and Galdur winced as a guard punched Melkin in the gut. Melkin doubled over, but quickly regained control and stood his ground. Thalen stood up from his throne, revealing his intimidating stature, and began pacing in front of Melkin. Galdur noticed that he had a slight limp.

"Melkin *Evarith*," said Thalen, emphasizing the surname, "I would have thought that *you* of all people would not dare speak to a lord like that." At the last words, Thalen leaned in, his face inches away from Melkin's, who stood unflinching.

"Oh, I dare. No one else will. Go hang yourself, you miserable, insufferable pig." Galdur had never heard Melkin speak like that, with the utmost loathing. Thalen drew his own dagger from a side sheath and swung, slicing Melkin across the face. Galdur gasped and inadvertently took a step forward. A guard to his side held him back gently, and Galdur turned to face him, a young man with fear in his eyes. The guard shook his head, and it was this, more than anything, that allowed Galdur to keep his composure.

Melkin was ushered out of the room, blood dripping down his face from a gash that looked surprisingly superficial for such a close-range swipe.

Thalen resumed his position on the throne again, flashing Galdur a sort of smile. "It's nothing against you, Galdur. I'm just doing my job, you see. He is a criminal—he must be taken in."

That was not the reason. Thalen wanted to be the hero, to be the one to capture Melkin Edaireth, the kidnapper of the prince. The chaos of the times, between Gladia's death and the coming war, made it likely that Melkin may not even stand trial; he may just be executed. And Thalen could do it simply for disrespecting him.

Clear your mind. Galdur repeated the phrase in his head, knowing he had only seconds to remember how to speak intelligently. He was here for the records. To peacefully obtain the records. Melkin, against all odds, had held up his end. Now it was time for Galdur to do the same.

"May I have the records now?" asked Galdur, gritting his teeth.

"Absolutely. I don't want them back, so destroy this copy when you're finished with it. I will maintain that it was stolen. So if you're found in possession, well, that's not my problem. Oh, and I'll need some payment for it."

"Show me the inside cover," said Galdur, walking forward until he was a yard in front of the throne. Thalen obliged, showing the signature that affirmed the copy was genuine. He resisted the urge to back away from Thalen. "How much?"

Thalen smirked. "Everything on you."

"I'll leave right now," threatened Galdur. Thalen said nothing, only raised an eyebrow in challenge. "Half of it," bargained Galdur, cringing at the desperation evident in his voice.

"Don't test my patience now, I'm not in such a good mood," said Thalen, taking another sip of his drink. Galdur doubted the assertion, seeing as Thalen had already won. He had already captured Melkin. Still, Galdur removed the pouch of gold wrapped around his upper-thigh, concealed under his cloak, and held it in front of Thalen.

"You have more," said Thalen. It was not a question, but a statement. A true one, at that.

"I don't."

"Would you like for my guards to search you?" asked Thalen. Such a search, Galdur assumed, would be as humiliating as possible, so he spared himself from the ordeal. With a sigh, Galdur unstrapped the other pouch of gold and proffered it. Thalen eagerly took both bags and handed the records to Galdur. "You may leave now."

Galdur turned away and began to walk. He didn't want to think. After descending the stairs, he glanced over to where he had sat hours earlier, but his spear was missing. He supposed Thalen had stolen that as well—why not? Then, a guard approached him, holding the familiar weapon in his hands. He handed it to Galdur, a mournful look in his eyes. The soldier lowered his head almost imperceptibly and closed his eyes for a brief moment. Galdur felt tears rise, but swallowed and nodded at this guard who had shown as much sympathy as he could.

Would it be so bad if this place was destroyed? Galdur walked out of the castle, pondering the idea. Could it be rebuilt as something better? If Thalen died in the war, would a greater power emerge, a more just leader? Was there any alternative while Thalen was still alive? He wasn't young by any means, but Thalen looked to be in good shape. He could well live another few decades. What was this mission for? To preserve a corrupted Valea? To preserve leaders like Thalen?

Changing the entirety of Annisik Province, or even just Annister, without Thalen's help, would take massive national change. It would be a difficult, time-consuming effort that the former queen of Valea couldn't afford. But Galdur . . . if he became king . . . if he and his companions accomplished the impossible . . . he might. Galdur imagined a Valea that wasn't defined by war, and he nearly smiled.

As Galdur walked the same path for the fourth time, he felt worse than ever. He shivered in the cold night air and mourned the impending loss of all his mother had fought for. He loathed the brother that had caused it all to fall apart. He lamented the loss of a friend whom he'd not had the chance to forgive. Somehow, in his anger, he'd forgotten all that Melkin had done for the continent of Anzelon. Tears fell down his face.

Would the records he held even help them locate the Incantir? Had Melkin sacrificed himself for nothing? The likely truth resonated in his mind, willing him to give up, to simply stop walking. In the back of his thoughts, though, there burned a fiery image of not just a better Valea, but a better Anzelon. It fought against despair, against his plea to lie down and fall into oblivion. And because of it, Galdur walked on. He would see that future.

29

MELKIN

"Let go of me, you bastard!" Melkin shouted, twisting his arm out of the guard's grip. He didn't know why he bothered fighting. He didn't care. There were dozens of guards between him and the castle exit. Even if he made it that far, there were more in the city who would capture him in an instant.

Still, he savored the fiercely burning anger inside of himself and the strength it lent him. He'd shown incredible self-restraint, Melkin thought. He ought to have been awarded a medal for it. But now that Thalen had given the records to Galdur, nothing could stop his rage. No one held power over him anymore.

As soon as the guard's grip came free, another one replaced the tight hold on Melkin's wrist. He felt the sharp bite of a dagger pressed to his throat, but the guard withdrew in surprise as Melkin laughed. "Go ahead. Kill me. Do it. What's that? Oh, I know you bastards want your little public execution, don't you? That's right..."

The guard leaned in close to Melkin's face. "Shut up! We... we'll torture, you, alright? Just shut up! You're making things worse for yourself!"

"Just throw me in the cell!"

"Fine!"

The guards dragged Melkin the last few feet into the tower prison and kicked him into his cell. He fell on the floor and scrambled back up, but the cell door was already locked. Then, a brilliant idea surfaced in his mind. "Thalen should burn in a fire for the next thousand years!" he shouted at the top of his lungs. More insults and slurs left his mouth as he hit the iron door repeatedly with his boot, causing a deafening racket. Soon enough, guards reappeared outside his room.

"Stop this noise!" one cried. Melkin responded by punching him in the face through the bars. He shook his hand out from inside the relative safety of his cell, grinning despite the pain.

"Listen here!" shouted another. The soldier opened the cell door and shoved him against the wall, pushing the blade of his dagger into Melkin's upper arm. "You think Lord Thalen wants to hear all this?"

"That's kind of the point—"

"No! So, who does he take his frustration out on? That's right, *us*." The guard leaned in closer, his mouth inches from Melkin's ear. "You think we agree with him? You think we want to torture people? No, we don't have a choice. So shut up, or I swear we'll give you a real reason to scream."

Would they really? Melkin studied the small collection of guards blocking his cell door. These young men and women, did they have it in them to torture people? Time to call their bluff. He smirked. "I'll consider it."

"You'll do more than that," said the guard. He pressed the knife harder against Melkin's arm. He winced, determined not to cry out as his blood began to trickle down the blade. Well, at least one of them had it in him.

"Fine."

The guard relented. "Now, do we have to gag you?"

"No."

"Are you sure? Because if we have to come back in here, you know what'll happen."

Melkin rolled his eyes. "Yeah."

The guards left, some with hesitation and others with obvious relief. Melkin sat on the floor of the cell, head in his hands. Blood dripped from the cut on his face and arm, but what did it matter? He would die here in this miserable room, in this miserable province. Left to rot for eternity.

No, how could he forget the fate that awaited him? He'd be led into the square tomorrow morning, where a throng of people would watch from the stands, their houses, and the tops of buildings. Years ago, he'd been one of those people, watching the executions with a blank expression. He knew exactly what it would look like. A rope would be tied around his neck, pulled taut, and then the box beneath his feet would be kicked out from under him. He might even see Thalen's sneering face as he breathed his final breath.

30

Lothar

"I see someone!" whispered Leina, motioning for Lothar and Astrid to come look.

Lothar peered through the bushes but saw nothing. He turned back to Leina and Astrid, shaking his head. "One person?"

"Yes, too tall for Melkin though. It's Galdur." Though Leina's tone was relieved, her eyes were bloodshot and wide. Lothar strained his eyes, but even the bright moonlight could not enhance his vision enough, exhausted as he was. Eventually the vague outline of a figure appeared. As it got closer, the shadow grew and became more distinct. Astrid began to inch out from behind the bushes, but Leina put her arm out to stop her. "Wait. We must make sure it's safe—that there's no one following him. Just wait," she whispered. "Stay hidden."

"It's just me," Galdur said in the general direction of the tree line. He was close enough now that Lothar could see the book and spear he carried, and there was no one visible behind him. *Good enough.* Lothar left the cover of the bushes; if Galdur was lying, they were done for anyway.

"Where's Melkin?" asked Leina, coming out from behind the bushes with Astrid. Her eyes darted around, looking for the spy, but landed on Galdur's strained expression.

"He's..." Galdur sniffled and cleared his throat. "Thalen took him prisoner." In tears, he fell to his knees, the leather book and spear dropping onto the grass below. Lothar crouched down beside the prince and put an arm around him, knowing in his heart that Galdur's grief was about more than Melkin's capture.

During the past few days of easy travel, Galdur had kept it together. He had even made lighthearted jokes and had insisted on focusing on negotiations with Thalen instead of healing from his recent loss. The wound was not healed, though, Lothar knew.

A quarter of an hour later, Galdur had calmed down enough to tell them what had happened. He explained how Thalen had gone back on his word, sending Melkin to the high dungeons. "An—And we've given up all our money for a stupid book!" lamented Galdur, between sobs.

"Look at me." Lothar met Galdur's red, tearful eyes. "We're going to get Melkin back."

Galdur's lips still trembled, but a glimmer of hope shone in his eyes. "How?"

"We just will. As for the money, we all have some in our packs; there's more than enough for food and any other supplies we might need," said Leina as she picked up the spear and book.

"Oh. I forgot about that."

"It's still an hour till midnight, so let's get some sleep. We'll break him out... a few hours after midnight?" suggested Lothar.

"Why not now?" asked Astrid, pacing around with her spear in hand.

"They'll expect retribution, so the best we can do is pick a random time in the middle of the night," said Leina.

Astrid shrugged. "I can stay up to watch, then."

"Thanks," said Lothar with a yawn. He was exhausted from worrying all night. When Melkin had taken off his weapons and agreed to the terms, Lothar thought he had gone insane. He and Leina had agreed that the circumstances were incredibly suspicious, and that Melkin had to have known what was going to happen.

On the half-mile walk back to the tents that the three had set up while Galdur and Melkin were gone, Lothar began thinking up rescue plans. By the time they reached the campsite, he had an idea, which he figured he would share with the others after a brief rest. Lothar approached his tent and crawled inside, falling asleep quickly in spite of the cold, hard ground on which he lay.

"Wake up," said Astrid. Lothar felt a hand nudge his shoulder. He was sure he'd only been sleeping for a couple minutes, but that was the least of his worries now. He forced himself to open his eyes fully, but the black night did nothing to help him wake up. Groggily, he stood up outside his tent and yawned. The other three stood there, watching him blink the sleepiness out of his eyes.

"You could slap him," suggested Leina, looking at Astrid, then back at Lothar.

"What? What did I do this time?"

"Nothing, just to wake you up," said Leina with a shrug and a smirk.

"I'll pass, but thanks for the offer," he retorted. Lothar shivered in the cold night air and considered warming himself with his magic but thought better of it; he couldn't risk tiring himself out.

"Does anyone have a plan?" asked Galdur.

"Yes." Lothar took a deep breath and explained what he'd thought of before going to sleep. "And if we have any fire ash, Astrid and I could rub it into our hair to make it a bit darker."

"Yeah, I made a fire earlier," said Astrid. She walked over, grabbed a handful of ash, and began to rub it into her hair.

Lothar did the same, coughing as some entered his lungs and mouth, leaving a foul taste on his tongue. "Good. I'll need the three of you to keep a lookout while I rescue him. If you have to, fend off any guards. Let's pack up and take all our stuff; we don't know which direction we'll be exiting the city from."

With a real plan in place, anticipation began to build in Lothar. No one spoke of the numerous ways in which the plan might go wrong. After all, they had no other choice.

Leina confirmed that, in the moonlight, the ash in his and Astrid's hair looked quite convincing. As they walked the path to the city, Lothar could see the distaste on Galdur's face; this was the fifth time he walked the same route. Though Leina had suggested entering in intervals, the four ended up walking into Annister together per Galdur's guidance. "Merchants and traders go through here all the time, so it's not suspicious. Together, we're less likely to be robbed as well."

Every sound that hit Lothar's ears made him tense up—danger felt close, but he couldn't see it. People scurried along streets, their wild eyes darting between Lothar and his companions. A scream echoed from some alleyway every now and again. Even so, he swallowed his fear, glad his companions were by his side, weapons at the ready. Most of Annister was dark; only a few candles lit the dark streets from the windows in the homes of those who dared show their presence.

As Lothar stumbled on yet another crack in the old cobblestone and dirt walkway, he felt a tug at his pack, and spun around. A man darted away, slipping into an alleyway between two houses.

"Bastard!" whispered Leina, rushing up to his side. Lothar realized he had drifted a few yards back, to the rear of the group. Far back enough for an attacker to go unnoticed. Lothar checked the unstrapped pocket on his bag and counted the gold; a few coins were missing.

"It's fine." He didn't want to cause a scene and draw attention to them. The man probably needed it anyway. Closer to the castle, Lothar and his companions retreated into an alleyway, out of sight of any civilians or guards.

"Where's the prison?" he whispered, leaning closer to Galdur.

"The highest tower."

Lothar shuffled over to the street again and spotted the tower, but not the metal bars that Galdur spoke of. "We have to go around to the back."

"You can't guess where the bars are?" asked Galdur.

"Guessing isn't accurate enough." The four of them entered the street again and started walking to the opposite side of the castle. They kept a large distance from the menacing fence, avoiding the guards that patrolled the streets near the gate. Even Leina was quick to agree that an interrogation by the Annister guards could end up dooming them all. At the back of the castle, the four hid in another crevice between buildings, about a hundred feet away from the tallest tower.

"Keep a lookout for guards," said Galdur. Astrid nodded, positioning herself closest to the open street.

Lothar sucked in a breath. "One problem. I see three holding cells, three sets of bars. Do you know which one Melkin was in?"

"No. I—I was hoping he might show himself."

Lothar pressed his lips together—the solution was simple. "I have an idea." He summoned magic by muttering in the ancient faul language and instantly heated the inside of the prison cells up enough for Melkin to notice. A few seconds later, Melkin appeared at the window of the topmost prison.

"You should see his face right now," said Leina with an amused laugh. "Confused, and a bit pissed." Lothar wondered how she could joke at a time like this; they needed to stay focused.

"The gate is on the other side of the castle," muttered Lothar. "How in Talen's name is he going to get out?"

"Maybe he'll climb to the roof?" suggested Galdur.

"No, he'd be easily spotted," said Leina. "Worry about it later—we have to go."

Lothar focused his eyes on the window bars and took a deep breath. He would have to focus an extreme amount of heat in a very small area, from over 150 feet away. Tuning out the sounds of the city around him, he let his mind know nothing but those iron bars. With another quiet call of magic, he sent heat into the metal and two bright white specks appeared on one of the bars. In his mind's-eye, he saw the iron become white-hot where the bar met stone.

To Lothar's relief, Melkin grabbed the center of the bar and ripped it off almost immediately. Lothar ceased channeling and took a moment to catch his breath. Melkin disappeared from the window, presumably setting the bar down quietly. Lothar was glad that he hadn't simply dropped the bar on the ground; the noise would've alerted the guards.

"Astrid, Galdur, take our bags and go. I know how to get him past that fence," said Leina. "Go straight away from the castle and into the woods if you can. When Melkin gets out, we'll be running for our lives. We can't have bags slowing us down."

"We can't take them all!" whispered Astrid.

Leina retrieved something from Melkin's bag before strapping it up and handing it to Astrid. "Take all except for Lothar's and mine, then," she whispered.

Astrid and Galdur nodded, walking away briskly.

"Get the other bar off," ordered Leina. Lothar concentrated once more, but he felt the magical connection slipping from his mind. Even after thirty seconds, twice the time it had taken to melt the first bar, the second remained rooted to the stone.

"Kaima, please!" gasped Lothar, persisting with all his effort for another fifteen seconds until the metal finally melted where it met stone. His magic had been far less precise this time. Melkin grabbed the bar again but let go within an instant. Lothar winced as the sound of the bar clattering to the stone floor of the cell, carried all the way to him. Melkin doubled over, clutching his right hand.

"Talen's sake," gasped Lothar. The heating had taken far too long—would Melkin be able to use his hand for the decent?

"Cool the rest of the bars! He'll hurt himself if he goes through!" Right, how could he be so stupid? Lothar concentrated—not as hard as before—and cooled the ends of the metal bars that he'd left embedded, hoping it would be enough. He heard shouts of alarm from nearby guards who had heard the sound. They gathered in the windows of neighboring towers and on the stone pathway below, pointing at the figure climbing out of the topmost prison cell. Melkin was eighty feet from the ground when the toll of an alarm bell sounded from the top of another tower.

"What do you plan to do?" Lothar asked with bewilderment. He couldn't see how Melkin wouldn't be recaptured or killed now; their plan had been dependent on Melkin not making any sound. Leina opened the pouch she'd taken from Melkin's bag and poured some small rocks into the palm of her hand.

"By Talen! You really mean to—"

"Have a better idea?" she asked with a grin.

He didn't respond, just imagined the dozens of ways in which her plan could go wrong. Of course, it left one or two ways in which the plan might go right. That was better than their odds right now.

Guards rushed into Melkin's prison cell, but he was far out of reach, already halfway between the window and the ground. They called for crossbows to be brought out from the armory, and a few rushed back inside the castle. Melkin had to hurry. Lothar noticed that he was shifting his weight to his left side, using his injured right hand as little as possible. *How hot had the center of the bar been?*

"Thirty feet," muttered Leina from her crouch at Lothar's side. In another twenty, the guards would be able to reach Melkin with their spears from the ground. They had obviously realized that too and were gathering below him. Leina sprang from her hiding place and ran toward the fence.

"Hey!" shouted a guard as she reached the fence and dumped her handful of rocks by the base. Melkin was twenty feet from the ground. As Leina ran from the fence, Lothar waited for her signal—he didn't want to hurt her.

"Now!" she cried. Lothar obliged, summoning Kaima's magic once more. A deafening blow hit his ears and a flash as bright as the sun momentarily blinded him. Guards were thrown back and shrapnel embedded itself in bodies and objects surrounding the fence. The unhurt guards dragged their wounded companions away from the gaping hole in the fence, wide enough for several people to walk through at once. Fifteen feet off the ground, Melkin let go from the side of the castle and rolled to break his fall. Lothar was surprised that he'd remained on the wall during the explosion and didn't seem to be critically injured by any shrapnel. Melkin sprang to his feet, lithe as ever.

"Go!" shouted Melkin, running toward them through the destroyed fence of Annisik Castle. Lothar turned and sprinted, knowing that both Melkin and Leina could easily catch up. Indeed, a few seconds later, they appeared by his side. Lothar glanced behind—pursuing guards were only a few yards behind the three.

Lothar ran for his life—he had no energy left to stop any of them. It felt unreal, as if he might wake at any moment and find himself elsewhere. Only his all-consuming terror kept him running.

Cries echoed from the guards behind him, the bell kept chiming, and people were crowding the streets to see what the commotion was all about.

He looked down, imagining a spearpoint appearing through his stomach and felt a renewed burst of energy fuel him. *Thank Talen!* The guards must have been slowed by their armor, else Leina and Melkin would have surely been forced to leave him behind. As the three of them gained distance from the guards, Lothar felt his terror give way to desperation as he gasped for air and his legs began to feel like they were on fire. Any more of this and he'd trip over himself and ruin everything.

"I can't... keep... this pace!" he shouted. The guards chasing them were around forty yards away now.

"We can slow down once we reach the farms!" replied Melkin.

"Just a bit?" bargained Leina. Melkin nodded, and the three lessened their speed, keeping pace with the group that chased them, yet not allowing them to gain any more ground.

"Look out!" cried Melkin, pointing to a guard that had appeared from an alleyway ahead of them. Even if the guard was unarmed, Lothar suspected that in his current depleted state, he was helpless. Luckily, Melkin grabbed Leina's dagger from her sheath and ran ahead where he quickly wounded the guard, who hadn't even had a chance to fight back.

Each second of the next few miles felt like a year. Lothar kept glancing around, looking for soldiers he had no way of fighting off. The rough cobbles of Annister threatened to trip with every footfall until finally, the crude paths gave way to worn dirt trails. The paths branched out into the farmlands, but the rolling wheat fields were not tall enough to conceal their whereabouts. Still, Lothar looked behind once again to see the guards had fallen even further behind.

"Can we rest?" begged Lothar, feeling as though he were about to collapse.

"No," said Melkin, but he did slow the pace a bit. Now that the threat of immediate death wasn't looming over them, Lothar found it even more difficult to maintain their pace. His lungs burned and his legs were nearly numb from the exertion. Even worse, Leina and Melkin seemed only moderately uncomfortable.

Melkin looked around, his brow furrowed. "Where are Astrid and Galdur?"

"They went ahead to carry the bags. I don't know where," said Leina. "I told them to find a hiding spot."

After several more miles, or maybe only another hundred yards, the farmlands gave way to forest. They had to climb over foliage and thick bushes, but at least they weren't running anymore.

"Hey!" called Astrid from behind a tree. The three stopped in their tracks and followed the faul—Astrid and Galdur had found a steep drop-off that led to a patch of forest concealed by the sprawling roots of towering trees. Lothar stumbled down the hill and laid down on the cool earth to catch his breath.

When he sat up, Melkin was pacing and shaking his head. The other three were hunched over their bags, taking stock of what they had.

"What's wrong?" asked Lothar, still trying to calm his lungs.

"You—I—You came back for me?" His gaze darted between the four of them, and Lothar got the strange feeling he expected them to disappear, for it all to be a dream.

"What?" asked Galdur incredulously, turning around from the bags to face Melkin. Leina and Astrid did the same, glancing between each other and Melkin, confused expressions on their faces.

"Why wouldn't we?" asked Lothar.

"I . . . was captured."

"So?" asked Lothar.

"I never . . . the risk . . . why would you?"

"If we're caught on a mission, no one comes to save us," said Leina softly. "It's how both of us have operated since we were eighteen."

A silence hung in the air. Galdur stood up and faced Melkin, putting a hand on the spy's shoulder. "Never once did *any* of the four of us consider leaving you there. Never."

Lothar silently rejoiced at Galdur's forgiveness of Melkin. Then Melkin's eyes focused on Lothar. They were doubtful, unsure. "It's true."

Astrid nodded her agreement.

"Not even you?" asked Melkin, looking toward Leina.

"No."

31

MELKIN

They decided they would rest for the night in the alcove, since he, Lothar, and Astrid were all exhausted. He hadn't slept at all after the guards had ended his obnoxious racket. As he sat, staring at their tiny fire, he thought about his companions. The shock that they had rescued him still hadn't left.

"Are you alright?" asked Leina. She eyed the blood on his arm and face. He examined his right hand more closely; a piece of shrapnel or stone must have cut his burned palm, for blood was seeping from the wound. At least it didn't really hurt right now.

"Yeah."

Leina handed him some clean bandages and her waterskin. Gritting his teeth, he washed the wounds and bandaged them.

"You at least got the book, right?" Melkin asked, looking at Galdur. At the sudden silence, he realized the other four must have been talking, but he hadn't registered the conversation. Galdur nodded, holding up the leather book.

"Good. I suppose one of you will keep watch?"

"Sure," said Leina.

"Thanks." He lay down on the ground, neither able nor willing to set up a tent at the moment; he was too exhausted. Within seconds, he was out.

The blinding sun beamed down on Melkin, waking him from his dreamless sleep. Shading his eyes, he sat up and blinked, adjusting to the brightness. His four companions were already pouring over the records, talking in hushed voices. Their eyes darted to him as he stood.

"He's finally awake," teased Astrid.

"*You* only got up half an hour ago," argued Leina, turning to Astrid with a grin.

He felt more refreshed than he had in several weeks. "Thanks for letting me sleep."

"We're trying to find who our mystery man is," said Lothar. Melkin went over and kneeled beside the book. He looked at the list of names that ran down the pages, some with one or more symbols beside them.

"What do the symbols mean?" asked Melkin.

"It's a way of storing information about the guards. There's no key in the book, but I know it by heart. A dot means they're retired, a closed circle means they were killed while serving, an open circle means they committed a crime while serving, and a star means they were either given or overheard critical information," explained Galdur. "It goes for both the servants and the guards."

"Thalen gave us both?" asked Melkin. That would indicate unfathomable generosity from the man.

"It's one book. Guards and servants are both employees of the Hilean province government, so their records get stored together," said Galdur.

"Why look at the year 1087?" asked Melkin, checking the date at the top of the page.

"We don't really know where to start," said Leina. "The book lists the guards by when they were hired, and we don't know how old the guard was when the event happened.

"We thought we would look for an older one. If they died soon after, the location of the Incantir would remain lost to history. So far, none with a star, though," said Lothar.

"Just looking for a star isn't going to help us," muttered Melkin. "Else the Incantir would have likely been found by now."

Astrid leaned back against a tree and sighed. "So how *will* the records help us?"

Melkin flipped through a couple of pages, noting the retirement dates of all the guards. "Go through the years and write down the names of guards who served during 1145."

"That could leave us with hundreds, maybe a thousand, even. It's throughout the entire province," lamented Leina.

He shrugged. "What else can we do? I have some writing supplies, assuming we still have my bag?"

Galdur nodded, handing the satchel to Melkin. He sifted through it, finding a roll of parchment, a quill, and a bottle of ink.

"Planning on keeping a diary?" asked Lothar.

Melkin smirked. "Never know when it could be useful, like now."

"Touché." Lothar took the writing supplies and sat down with the book.

Melkin walked a few paces away from the others and gingerly unwrapped the bandage from his right hand, revealing a charred palm, surrounded by red, blistered skin and dried blood. He winced as he flexed his fingers. Even a slight breeze caused sharp, burning pains to shoot through his hand.

"Are you alright?" asked Leina, appearing beside him.

Melkin swallowed, gritting his teeth as he covered the wound again. "Probably. It didn't hurt too much when I was going to sleep, but now... I don't think I'll be able to use a spear or throw knives. We'll see."

Leina nodded; she had a faraway look in her eyes for a moment. Then, she stared at him. "You knew it was a trap, right?"

Melkin stared at the sky, wrapping his cloak around himself tighter with his left hand. "Of course."

"And you still went along..." she muttered. He nodded pensively and turned to see Leina's concerned expression.

"You would have done the same, I hope."

"I would have." The two stood there for a moment, each lost in their own grave thoughts.

Galdur turned toward Melkin; he was sitting a few yards away with Astrid. "I never told them what you said to Thalen." Lothar lifted his head in curiosity and looked at Melkin. All eyes were upon him now.

Melkin tried to smile, but all that appeared on his face was a grimace. "I shouldn't have. I could have been executed on the spot. It's technically a crime to insult, disobey, or upset a lord or lady in their home. Most would ignore it. Some might deduct some pay or flog the servant if they're feeling cruel, but . . ." He trailed off. "Galdur will recount the conversation, if you all want."

Halfheartedly, Galdur retold the entire conversation that occurred when he and Melkin had entered the throne room. Melkin reached up and touched the gash on his cheek, which had closed overnight. It wasn't too painful, but seeing Thalen wield a dagger in front of his defenseless self . . . it had scared him. As Galdur reached the part where Melkin insulted Thalen, he grimaced despite the satisfaction he remembered feeling when he spoke the words. His companions laughed with enthusiasm, making him wonder if they really understood how close he'd come to death.

"Come on Melkin, you shouldn't regret that!" laughed Astrid.

"Maybe in a few weeks I'll look back on it with humor, but right now . . ."

Their faces fell a bit, dampening the mood. Lothar walked over to him and nodded. "That's alright. But it's over now."

Melkin nodded and swallowed, remembering the fear he felt in that moment. He hoped he hadn't given Thalen the satisfaction of showing it. Still, Thalen speaking the word "Evarith" into his ears would perhaps haunt him for a long time.

"Do you remember the rest of the conversation with Thalen?" asked Astrid eagerly.

Galdur told the rest of the story from when he entered the castle, to when he left the second time. Impressively, he didn't seem to paraphrase much. Even better, Melkin didn't think that Galdur knew how well he had handled the situation. "It could have gone better, but I guess we're all here now," finished Galdur.

"Impressive. I taught you well," said Leina with a smirk.

"Really? We lost all our money, though."

"Why else would we have sent you in there with all of it?" said Leina. "We still have... fifty gold I think, so it's alright. I noticed something else, though. Thalen spoke your last name?"

Melkin sighed. "Indeed, he did. I underestimated him. He must have seen my name in the paper and done some research. In fact, I think that when I rescued Gladia from the ruins of the new castle, he must have noticed me. That, along with the fact that Galdur said I was working with him, prompted Thalen to investigate his records while Galdur was fetching me. All he had to do was put the pieces together. Edaireth is similar enough to Evarith, so he found the name in the criminal records and related it back to me."

Lothar raised an eyebrow. "Really?"

Melkin smirked. "You're that surprised?"

"Not that you committed a crime, but that you were caught."

"Well done. It was my parents whom he found in the records. My father was fired from his job when I was a child, and we were left without money. So, they stole food and got caught. And executed. Thalen was the one to make the verdict."

"He rules on crime in the city?" asked Lothar, his eyes wide.

"All the barons do."

"I thought he was a lord?" said Astrid.

"He's both. The lords of provinces can choose to either appoint someone or appoint themselves to be the baron of the capital city. So, Thalen made the verdict. I assume I was also reported as missing once I left Annister at sixteen, so he might have seen that as well. His resources stretch far and wide—I should have known he'd put it together."

Melkin took a shaky breath. He had told no one this story. Come to think of it, there were a lot of things he had never told anyone. The four were looking at him with sympathetic eyes.

"By Talen," said Lothar. "I'm so sorry."

Leina stepped forward. "I swear if I had known, I wouldn't have—"

"It was a long time ago. We have the records. It's done now. I got some sort of twisted revenge, I suppose."

"How are you alive?" Galdur asked softly.

"I began to steal after that, of course. Except *I* was never caught," said Melkin. "I had a house at least."

Galdur walked up beside him and stared into his eyes. "I was thinking—I had a lot of time to think while going back and forth to the castle—that my mother never had time to work on Valea because of all the border stuff going on. But I might. I swore to myself then, and I swear to you now, Melkin, that I will try to do something. I will try to make Valea better."

"I appreciate that, Galdur. I really do," said Melkin softly, recalling the construction of Annisik Castle, the friends he'd lost, the executions. "I really do."

"Alright, I'm finished," said Lothar, blowing the ink dry on the parchment that Melkin had given him. Though he felt some sort of relief from telling the story, he was glad for the change in subject. "Rock really isn't the best writing surface." Melkin shuffled over to the paper and scanned the names. His companions did the same for a few minutes, reading down the list.

Galdur sighed, shaking his head. "Why did we think this would work?"

"I'm actually surprised that there's only a few hundred," said Leina. "Each town seems to have at least a few, and there are plenty of towns in each province."

"A lot of them are just civilians granted some basic power by the baron," explained Galdur. "Not officially registered."

One of the names had a star next to it. Melkin stared at the entry, furrowing his brow. "Has anyone heard of this one?" His companions all shook their heads.

Lothar shrugged. "He's dead. We could go to his home."

"Of course he's dead," Astrid said with dry sarcasm.

"We don't have the time to guess anymore," said Leina.

Lothar sat back against a tree, defeated. "What choice do we have?"

"What if . . ." muttered Leina, deep in thought. "He could have hidden it himself . . . No."

"Not himself, but perhaps not with a guard either?" suggested Melkin.

Galdur started, leaning in. "A servant maybe? But why?"

"A servant... The guards would have known about the torture and all, but a young servant wouldn't have," reasoned Melkin. "The king might have just told them to go and hide a rock somewhere. They probably would have done it without further direction or questions because the order would have come directly from their king."

"I can take over and record the servants' section," said Leina, picking up the quill and flipping to the second half of the book.

Melkin nodded. "Yes, do that." The four left Leina to it while they packed up their belongings. A curiosity stirred inside of him, and he stood up, reaching for a throwing knife with his left hand. Immediately, his companions were alert.

"It's fine, I just want to see something." He drew his left arm back and released the knife at a nearby tree. It hit slightly off his target spot, and barely stuck before falling to the ground. "Well, that's not ideal..." he said. He tried to use his right hand, yet the pain from the burn was too great to grip the knife.

"Well, he's useless, guess we should have left him in jail," laughed Galdur. Melkin thought back to when Lothar had broken him out of the jail in Harolin; it seemed like so long ago. He'd convinced Lothar to join him by claiming he had important knowledge, and that Lothar might be saving lives if he let Melkin out. Now though, his companions knew everything, and they were more than capable of defending themselves. What use did they really have for him anymore?

"We're joking!" cried Lothar. Melkin realized he'd been scowling and softened his brow.

Leina looked up from the book. "Is everything alright?"

"Yeah, I'm fine. Sorry I just..." he trailed off, not really sure what to tell them. Galdur stood up and walked over to the tree, pulling a knife from his sheath. He drew his arm back and hit the center of the tree from five yards away. "Nice job."

Galdur turned to Lothar. "Have you been practicing?"

"A little," said Lothar sheepishly. He stood a little over two yards from the same tree and stuck it almost in the center, near Galdur's dagger.

"Can I try?" asked Astrid, grinning. Lothar handed her a knife and she gave it her best effort, unfortunately hitting the tree with the handle instead of the blade. "I'll probably just stick with close combat."

Melkin jumped back as a crossbow bolt struck the center of the tree between the daggers. Leina sat with her crossbow, a wide smile on her face. She raised an eyebrow at her startled companions. "Beat that," she challenged.

"Right. Now do it again," taunted Melkin. Crossbows took precious seconds to reload. If the user was running, forget about it.

"Don't have to. I'll be gone by the time they get to me. By the way, I finished writing down the names."

"Great, let's take a look," said Lothar, kneeling by the papers. Melkin and the others followed, eager to see the list of names. There were around twenty of them; not as bad as the guards, but not good either. While guards might be spread out through the entire province, government employed servants were typically only in the castle.

"I recorded the ages as well," said Leina. "But I hoped a name might stand out to one of you two." They shook their heads.

"Three of them were under twenty," remarked Melkin.

Leina nodded. "And the next youngest was twenty-eight."

"Wouldn't a younger servant be more likely to spill any secrets?" asked Lothar. "Perhaps he went with an older one."

"I don't think so. The servant instructors are extremely strict, so most of the new servants are extremely subservient and professional. After a few years, they learn that they won't usually be beaten or reprimanded, so they're a bit more relaxed, more outspoken," explained Galdur. "Unless they're under Thalen."

"Was this king anything like Thalen?" asked Lothar.

"King who?" asked Leina.

"King Gorrik. My great grandfather. No, I think he was a fair ruler to his own people. He doesn't have much of a reputation outside of everything in 1145."

Melkin nodded. "So back to these three. Is there anything else written about them?"

"None of them have stars, of course, but here are their entries," said Leina, passing the book to Melkin. "One has a clean record, one died while serving, and the other one committed a crime."

"In their first couple years, even," said Melkin. "That seems strange."

"It is. An open circle doesn't only mean they committed a crime, it means they were fired for it," said Galdur. "Unfortunately, the specific crime will be in another book."

Astrid scoffed. "That seems inefficient."

"That's the point."

Lothar sighed, backing away from the book. "Could Gorrik have told her to hide it, then fired her so she wouldn't tell anyone else?"

"Maybe..." said Leina, peering over Melkin's shoulder at the book.

"I don't think he would have brought more attention to it than he needed to," said Melkin.

Leina pointed at one of the entries. "The book does say that the one who died in service died in 1147, two years after the event. That's quite young. Suspicious, even."

"What are their names?" asked Galdur.

Melkin squinted at the small text. "Alethia Shanik, the fired one, and Daerus Falknir, the dead one. Well, they're both dead, but you know what I mean."

"And the third?" asked Lothar.

"Just a stableboy, stayed employed until he was sixty-seven. I don't think he has anything to do with this."

"Where do we go, then?" asked Leina. "We have records of both of their old houses, right? Should we go to Shanik's or Falknir's?"

"I think the open circle would have attracted the attention of anyone searching for the Incantir," reasoned Galdur, "So my vote is for Falknir. Where did they live?"

"Shanik lived in southern Starren Province, around five hundred miles away. And before he died, Falknir lived right on the western coast, a little over a hundred miles away."

"Shanik is out of the question anyway, then," said Lothar.

Leina closed her eyes in frustration. "But at our pace, so is Falknir."

"Not necessarily," said Galdur, pulling out the map. "See here, the Palzar river runs about a hundred and fifty miles parallel to the border until it hits the start of the Western Province, then it curves up before continuing west. It's the reason why this city is where it is. We're northeast of the city, and the Annister port is located at the very southeastern part of the city. It's only about ten miles from here, but if we don't want to cut through the city, it'll be far longer—and through forest."

"It runs westward?" asked Lothar.

"Yup."

"So, with a good wind and a proper sailboat, we could make it to the coast in less than a day," said Melkin.

"Great!" exclaimed Leina. She clapped her hands together and grabbed her pack.

"How do we get a boat?" asked Astrid quietly. The four were silent for a minute.

"Buy one?" suggested Melkin. "Fifty gold should be enough."

"Oberel!" swore Astrid.

"What is it?"

"We never took the gold from Leina and Lothar's bags."

"So how much do we have now?" asked Melkin.

Galdur walked over to the three remaining bags and rummaged through. "Twenty gold in total."

"Might be enough for a small boat. If we're lucky," said Melkin.

"Wouldn't there only be large trading vessels in the docks?" asked Lothar. "I don't think they can be crewed by five."

Galdur stroked his chin. "No, the Palzar has lots of tributaries and smaller rivers that one of those ships couldn't sail through."

"Well, we won't know until we get there," said Melkin.

"I suppose we're betting that this guy has descendants, and that they even live in the same place," remarked Astrid. "He *did* die at 21."

"We have no other options," asserted Melkin. "We're reaching that dock tonight."

32

ASTRID

By sunset, Astrid wished for nothing more than to rest. Her companions looked downright miserable. Even Melkin, who had worn a determined expression upon his face for the past few hours, seemed fatigued. But the grueling walk was not the only tiring thing they endured. Throughout the day, they had feared capture or recognition, despite always keeping a significant distance from the city's borders. It was not rare, Galdur told them, for guards to patrol so far outside the city.

The port was located a few miles from Annister, reachable through heavily trodden paths. Of course, the constant danger posed by guards forced them to walk the long way around. Now, though, the docks came into view as they reached what Galdur claimed was the largest port in the province. The riverbank sat about a hundred feet below the city and sloped upwards until it reached farmland.

Astrid had only sailed a few times and had never paid much attention to how it was done. She assumed that sailing with a hundred soldiers was different than four, but that was about the extent of her knowledge. "What kind of boat are we looking for here?" She squinted to see the port with more clarity. There were over two dozen docks lined up as far as Astrid could see, each with one or two ships tied to it.

"Those two in the center are the biggest vessels that could travel on this river. There's probably a third that's out somewhere," said Melkin.

"Why do you sound so... educated on the matter of boats?" asked Galdur. "Do you take a class on that in the academy?"

"Not as far as I know," laughed Leina. "I must have been sick that day."

"No, when I was waiting for something, *anything*, to do at the Akarist, I found some books in the storage room that were mildly entertaining. One of them was on boats and nautical warfare. I would have read the others but... Anyway, the three boats on the far right look to be about thirty feet long with one mast. I don't know what they're called, but they're the ones we want. It's a simple, shallow vessel without any enclosed rooms. They're supposed to hold about half a dozen people, and I'm more familiar with them than any other suitable ship."

"Can you sail it?" asked Galdur, raising an eyebrow at Melkin.

"Probably. I'm more worried about purchasing one and how to get the money. We don't even know if the owner will sell it."

"I would assume that it's owned by Thalen," muttered Leina.

"But he won't concern himself with whether it can be sold. That's the boatmaster's job," explained Melkin.

"I suppose I'll go," said Galdur. "Maybe they'll give me the boat."

Astrid sighed. "Let's hope so."

Lothar sat down on the grass, stretching his legs. "We'll stay here." The three of them followed suit as Galdur began the short walk down to the docks.

Astrid gazed out at the river and the steep bank on the other side. The setting sun reflected on the water creating a mesmerizing glitter. She didn't know the exact number of miles they had walked, but they had kept a relentless pace for over eight hours through the dense forest. If all went to plan, the five could rest on the way to the western shore, carried by the current of the Palzar river. Her eyes drifted closed as she imagined what it would feel like to be in the swaying boat all night.

"Are you sleeping?" asked Melkin with raised eyebrows. She jolted awake, sitting up.

She yawned and rubbed her eyes. "No? But if I was, how long would I have been asleep?"

"About thirty seconds."

"Figures." Astrid yawned again and grasped the spear by her side. Even in its crude state, it felt comforting to have it close by and ready. She felt like she was betraying her majoril and auxlar daggers by taking up the human weapon. But, as Leina said, it was just a weapon. Just wood and iron.

"Do you two think you would ever come back here?" asked Leina, who sat in front of Astrid, facing away.

"Astrid and I? Why would we come back to Annister?"

"Not Annister, Valea." Leina sounded almost wistful as she stared out at the docks and the bending river.

They were silent for a moment. "I hadn't thought about it," admitted Astrid. "If I wasn't persecuted upon sight, then yes. I think I would enjoy seeing more of Valea."

"I would say the same," said Lothar. "Why?"

"Just wondering."

"What about you two?" asked Lothar, looking at Melkin and Leina.

Leina shrugged. "Same, I suppose. My last experience in a Shalin town was . . . not promising. I *would* come back if that were not the truth, though. It's sad."

"I don't know." Melkin opened his mouth as if to elaborate but closed it. Astrid looked at him, but he remained silent.

Leina snapped her gaze toward the docks, setting a hand on her crossbow. Astrid followed her line of sight to see Galdur jogging toward them, and readied her spear just in case he was being pursued. Soon enough, it was clear that Galdur was simply out of breath, all was fine.

"They'll sell it, but it will cost thirty gold," he reported, panting. "That was the lowest I could get their price down."

"You revealed your identity?" asked Lothar.

"Of course. She still wouldn't just give it to me."

"I'm not surprised. She could get fired for offering special prices because of your status," said Leina.

"We could steal it, I suppose." Astrid threw out.

"The gold or the ship?" asked Galdur.

"Either," she said with a shrug. "Not that I know how, but..." She lifted a brow and looked at Melkin, who, Astrid was surprised to see, actually seemed to be considering it.

"We have a better chance of stealing the gold and getting away with it than the ship," said Melkin. "Dock security can be intense."

"Yes, there were three guards patrolling," said Galdur.

"So, we should steal the gold?" said Lothar.

"I don't like it," said Galdur. There was silence as the five considered their options. Astrid had seen the state of the city, the beggars and the thieves.

"No," said Melkin. "I can't let us steal from the people of Annister. Any sizeable sums of gold in the castle will be kept under higher guard than the boats, so that leaves only the shopkeepers and life savings of the people. We'll have to chance it, stealing the boat."

"I agree," said Lothar. "But how *do* we steal it?"

"Still working on that. Did you see how it was tied up?"

"Two thick ropes, and there are a few guards patrolling the port," said Galdur, sitting down.

Astrid thought for a moment and attempted to channel the cunning she'd learned from being around Leina and Melkin. "We still have twenty gold, right? We could bribe a guard."

"The other guards might see," said Melkin. "We can't risk that."

Lothar smirked. "I have a plan that might work. We'll need a crate."

An hour later, Astrid sat sealed inside of a cargo crate, wondering how everything in her life had led up to this point. She could have been a simple guard in Pyantir but *no*. She had to listen to Lothar. She had to go on this insane mission where her almost nonexistent espionage skills were in use more frequently than her strength. With a sigh, she tried to shift around in the cargo crate, to no avail. Of course she couldn't move. Lothar, only a few inches taller than herself, couldn't fit. And of course, this was the largest cargo crate they could find. Her legs would start cramping soon.

Astrid swallowed, wondering if her fear stemmed more from the cramped crate or from the task that came after the crate. Likely both. She stopped herself from gasping as Galdur and Leina set the crate on the ground, jostling her slightly.

"We'll buy the ship. Can I load my cargo now?" asked Leina, presumably to the boatmaster.

"Pay first."

"I only have twenty on me now. My partner is coming later with the rest."

"Another besides him?" asked the boatmaster.

"Yeah. He's bringing more cargo, so we'd like to get this one loaded up."

"If we're not ready to leave when he gets here . . . well, it won't be a pretty sight," added Galdur.

"Fine. But you two must stay here in this shack with me until he comes. And give me the twenty gold."

"Sure." The coins clinked on the countertop.

Astrid braced herself and felt her crate picked up once more by Galdur and carried gently out of the room.

"I'm keeping an eye on you two," said a voice, presumably a guard.

"We'll be no trouble." Galdur placed the crate on the deck of the ship. Retreating footsteps followed. Then she was alone. Leina had advised that she wait until the guards changed. Unfortunately, she neither knew the time, nor when the switch was to occur. So, she waited for something . . . anything.

"Where's my relief?" asked the guard. She tensed up in fear; was he talking to her? With a shake of her head, she took a deep breath. *What a stupid thought.*

"I don't know. That fellow is always late," said another guard.

"Forget it. I don't get paid enough for this—my kids need me. You'll back me up if I get reprimanded?" The complaining guard's voice sounded close, probably only a few dozen yards away.

"Yeah, go home."

"Thanks."

She heard the guard walk away from the port, his steps growing faint until she couldn't hear them anymore. Oberel was on her side. She breathed a heavy breath in relief, but stopped mid breath when she heard the remaining guards, the sound of their feet growing and then waning twice before she breathed easily again.

Hopefully it was pitch black outside by now—she needed to time this just right. She slid one of Melkin's throwing knives from her sleeve and into her palm. A vision flashed through her mind in which she accidentally sliced herself with it, screamed in pain, and was immediately caught. But fortunately, Astrid thought, she wasn't *that* much of an idiot. She maneuvered the knife to the top of the crate, cutting through the string that bound it together from the inside.

Astrid listened again for footsteps or any other indication that a guard had come near her boat. When she didn't hear anything, she used her free hand to open the top of the crate without a sound. Then, a patrolling guard walked closer. She was almost certain he could hear the beating of her heart and tried to remain as still as possible. *How in Talen's name do Melkin and Leina do this all the time?* If she was seen, she was dead. If she made a noise, she was dead. She wanted to burst out of the crate and run away while she still could. But no, she couldn't.

After the guard passed by, she stepped out of the crate and ducked down behind it, concealing herself. Galdur and Leina had chosen the furthest boat, so she only had to hide herself from one side. With shaking hands, she closed the crate so that it looked exactly as it had before. The only sounds breaking the tranquility of the silent night were the footsteps of the guards, their crackling torches, the rushing river, and the creaking of the wooden boats as they bobbed on the water. She looked around the boat and spotted six oars, some ropes for the sail, and a few other empty cargo crates. She crawled toward the ropes that anchored the boat to the deck, wincing as the planks creaked beneath her. Astrid didn't dare look toward the nearest guard—she didn't want to know if he'd noticed, didn't want to know how close to death she was. Slowly, she undid the tight knot that held the boat to the dock with clumsy, shaking fingers. When it finally came loose, she gently placed the end of the rope in the water and braced herself as the boat swayed in the Palzar current. She held her breath, petrified, waiting for a cry of alarm. None came.

"Sorry, I ran into some issues," said a voice. Hurried footsteps approached the boat and Astrid couldn't help but glance in their direction. The newly arrived guard was bent over and panting, right in front of her boat.

"You always run into some issues!" cried the other guard. "Areval is a fine guard. You're going to get him in trouble someday. He can't cover for you. He has a family to tend to!"

"I didn't ask to be assigned right after him! Before this, I worked six hours at the shipyard. It's not my fault we had to stay late. I can't lose that job."

Astrid turned her attention away from them and crawled over to the other rope ten feet away. Thankfully, the sides of the boat were high enough to partially conceal her.

"Alright, I'm sorry. Have a talk with Areval if you can. He'd appreciate it."

"I'll try. Ryne, I'll be dead if I lose *either* job."

As she tediously picked at the tight knot holding the boat to the dock, Astrid prayed this guard was not the one to tie it. The two men were now quietly chatting, breaking the silence that had previously reigned. The free end of the rope splashed into the river. She winced at the sound, then fell lightly back onto her hands as the boat inched away from the dock. Summoning the courage to move, she looked out at the water; the boat had a clear path out of the port. Oberel was truly on her side—no, they all were. The oars would attract too much attention, so she allowed herself to drift.

Once her boat had been carried out of port, she looked back to see the newly arrived guard drop his spear and run to the edge of the dock.

"What the—" cried the newly arrived guard.

"Don't! The current will sweep you away!" said the other guard, grabbing the first to prevent him from swimming after the boat.

"What's going on out here?" asked the boatmaster, running onto the docks with Galdur and Leina. "You two did this!"

"We didn't do anything!" cried Galdur.

"Useless guards! You must have seen an intruder!"

Leina ran onto the dock and grabbed the rope. "Look! The end of these ropes came free!"

"Came free—That foolish husband of mine!" exclaimed the boatmaster. "Where is that bastard?"

"What should we do, ma'am?" asked the reprimanded guard.

"If it hits the coast, board it and bring it back!"

"I can't sail!"

"Nor can I!"

"Just hold it to the coast, then! Only you! No one else may leave their posts! I'm sending a messenger to the ports further downstream. Lord Thalen is going to kill me!"

Astrid floated downstream along the right-hand side of the river, using an oar to keep her distance from the coast. She tried to keep her head low and out of sight while listening intently for any chasing guards.

"Who are *you* all?" asked the guard from the dock. Astrid whipped her head around, looking toward the voice, but unable to see anything. She prayed Melkin hadn't killed the guard—there'd been enough death on this mission. A few minutes later, she heard the muffled voices of her companions and squinted. Finally, she saw moving shadows jogging along the coast, keeping pace with the flowing river. She paddled closer to the riverbank as the five approached.

"Don't come too close!" cried Melkin. She was two yards from the coast. "That's it, now straighten up so you're going parallel to the coast." She turned a bit, now around four yards from dry land. Melkin had coached her on how to do this part, but even he didn't have any experience on a boat.

"Keep it there. I'm coming on." He backed up a few paces and sprinted toward her, leaping onto the boat. As it swayed dangerously, Astrid threw herself to the other side of the boat, balancing out the weight. Though tipping the boat would almost certainly guarantee a death sentence in the frigid waters, Astrid was simply glad to not be hiding anymore.

With each new member coming aboard, the swaying grew calmer until, finally, Leina jumped onto the ship with hardly any impact at all. With all members now on the boat, Melkin hoisted the single sail on their tiny craft, propelling it to almost double its previous speed.

"You're welcome," Astrid said as she sat on one of the rowing benches. "What did you do to that guard?"

"He just knocked him out," said Lothar. "Talen, I can't believe this worked!"

"We're not in the clear yet. They'll try to get the boat back," said Melkin.

"But now we can rest. We'll row in the morning, but floating on the river overnight will give us plenty of rest so that we can row the last stretch in the morning." Lothar kicked out his legs and leaned back on the bow, looking very pleased with this turn of events.

"Or," said Melkin, a grin on his face. "We can have two on night watch, and they can both row. Lothar, you got some sleep earlier while waiting with me." With a long groan, Lothar walked over to the bench and picked up an oar.

Astrid resigned herself to sleeping on the bare wooden planks of the ship and using her collapsed tent as a sort of mattress. Despite her previous exhaustion, she found it hard to sleep amidst the rocking of the boat and pent-up energy she had after the heist. But as exhilaration gave way to fatigue, Astrid fell into a deep sleep.

The gray morning sky surprised her—she had not been woken for night watch. Her relief was short-lived, however, for it was the coldest day of autumn so far. She shivered, awake now, but wishing to slip back into sleep. With a grunt of pain from her sore legs, she stood up from the hard, wooden floor of the boat and stretched her stiff muscles. Astrid looked around and saw Leina and Galdur manning the boat while Melkin and Lothar slept.

"Morning," she said to Leina and Galdur. The two of them jumped at the sound of her voice. "Do we have any food left?"

"No, I forgot to mention that before we sailed. Not that we could have bought food in Annister," said Leina. Astrid nodded in resignation and woke the other two. "Dangerous to show our faces anywhere, really," continued Leina. "Will you take over? My arms are tired."

"Sure." Astrid picked up an oar, sitting beside Galdur and dragging the oar through the water, trying to match Galdur's rhythm. Behind her, a thud sounded as Lothar tumbled to the deck.

"Ugh . . . I'm not too fond of this thing," said Lothar as he struggled to stand up.

"How about you come sit and row instead, then?" teased Astrid with a grin.

"We'll be at the shore by the end of the day if there are no slackers," said Melkin. "What's the rest of the river like, Galdur?"

"Slower than it was when we left port," said Galdur, eyes focused on the skies. To her, they looked alright. Overcast, but no sign of rain. "The current is nice here, but it may slow down."

"As long as I don't have to hide from any more guards, I'll be happy. You two must be crazy, doing that stuff as your job," she said, pointing from one spy to the other.

Leina smirked. "And worse."

"Very true. Oh, I snagged a newspaper from a farmer while we waited for you three," said Melkin. He sat down and pulled out a paper from beneath his cloak. "I think you all may find it interesting."

Lothar gave him an incredulous glare. "*That's* what you slipped off to do?"

"What does it say?" asked Galdur.

Melkin glanced at him with narrowed eyes. "I'm getting to that," he said, flipping the paper to the front page and showing them.

Emperor Orwic Calls for Negotiations, King Fareod Yet to Agree.

33

Galdur

"I can't believe that old bastard called for negotiations," said Lothar, pacing the deck.

"Take all that energy and put it into rowing," said Melkin. "And don't fall into the water." Reluctantly, Lothar took a seat, picking up an oar and dragging it through the water.

"Remember, Fareod doesn't have to agree to negotiate. He may just declare war," warned Galdur. "As far as I know, he has nothing to gain from negotiations."

"But now we know Orwic doesn't want war," said Lothar.

Galdur thought that over for a few moments. Perhaps if he became king, he could work *with* Orwic instead of against him—it would certainly increase the chances of creating peace with the Shalin Empire. That was a strong 'if,' though. Unfortunately, he and his friends would probably be dead or imprisoned in the next few weeks.

"How old is Orwic?" he muttered to himself. "How long has he been emperor?"

"Around seventy years old, but he's only been emperor since Empress Persec died. She was his niece. So . . . around fifteen years," explained Lothar. "Why?"

"I was just wondering," he said. "People change, you know? But if you say he's been against Valea for his entire rule so far, I wonder what his motives are in trying to negotiate."

"I really don't know. It seems out of character," said Lothar.

"Can I take a look at that paper?" Melkin handed it over, and Galdur rifled through it, looking for anything that might hint at Orwic's reason. "I wonder if he plans to attack Fareod at the negotiations," mused Galdur.

Lothar gave a small grunt of disapproval.

"If there are no obvious motives for this, we have to look beyond our instincts," reasoned Galdur.

"I know, I just don't think Orwic would do that."

"You didn't think he would call for negotiations either," pointed out Leina.

"I know . . ."

"How do you know Orwic anyway?" asked Galdur, looking away from the paper.

"I . . . well, the news and such . . . I suppose," said Lothar.

"Which is famously accurate?" said Galdur with a grin. The other four smirked; the papers certainly hadn't been very valid lately.

"Yeah, I suppose you're right," said Lothar with a sigh. "But by your logic, Orwic also could have had a change of heart."

"Sure. We just don't know right now."

"Enough speculating. What else is in there?" asked Melkin, pointing at the paper.

"Right." Galdur continued to scan it, skimming several irrelevant articles before finding an important one. His eyes widened as he read the title and scanned the article. "Looks like Fareod has appointed a sort of second-in-command." He looked up at his four companions. "His name is Gillan. That's the one who—"

"—saved us at the Akarist." Melkin looked at Lothar with a solemn expression.

"Why would Fareod have to appoint someone to do his bidding?" asked Leina. "Isn't he king?"

"If Gillan is so high up in the chain of command, why was he setting bombs in the Shalin Empire?" muttered Galdur.

"Well, I'm sure Gillan isn't second to Elvine or anything," said Melkin. "Or at least, he wasn't before his appointment. Most of their recruits looked really young, in their twenties, but—"

"Calling me young, Melkin?" asked Lothar innocently.

Melkin glanced at Lothar, a smug grin on his face. "Don't you all live shorter lives? So it's kind of like you're somewhere in your thirties."

"Ouch." Lothar pouted and pretended to look hurt.

"Anyway, most of them wouldn't have that leadership quality to them yet. Older people are more respected, since they're wiser." Melkin glanced at Galdur. "No offense."

Galdur shrugged. "Nothing I can do about it."

"But Gillan looked to be in his early forties, much more suited to authority, especially since Fareod is only nineteen."

"That makes sense. Do you think that's why he appointed Gillan in the first place?" asked Leina.

"Possibly. Fareod can't be everywhere at once. Appointing Gillan gives him another person to carry out orders. And it's another Talwrek planted deep inside the Valean government," reasoned Melkin. "Anything else in the paper?"

"There are lots of articles in here about preparing for war." Galdur began to list out some of the events described in the paper. "The military getting called to Hileath, civilians stocking weapons, armor blacksmiths getting paid to speed up production, and so on. Unsurprisingly, it's no secret what Fareod plans to do."

"Hopefully, once we get where we're going, we'll find more information," said Lothar. He frowned, tilting his head. "Which is where, exactly?"

"Kasperon, the capital city of Kaspea, the coastal province. In the book, there's an address that we'll find once we reach the city," said Galdur.

Astrid sighed. "We don't even have any money though, do we? Will we be sleeping on the streets?"

Melkin grinned, reaching into his bag and pulling out a handful of gold. "I stole it all back from the boatmaster."

Leina shook her head in wonder, smiling. "Of course you did."

Galdur flipped to the back of the paper, dreading the stories he might see there. "Of course... Leina, they say you're now a traitor. The same caliber as Melkin."

"What?" cried Leina. "But my plan—"

"I know," interrupted Melkin. "We'll just have to be careful."

"And fast, presumably," said Lothar. "Give as little time as possible for guards or Talwreks to recognize us."

"Which is why we must put all our energy into rowing. We're reaching Kasperon by nightfall!" exclaimed Melkin. He stood by the mast, watching the river ahead and calling commands. Galdur knew he couldn't row efficiently with his injured hand and suspected Melkin was trying to make himself useful.

Occasionally, icy water would splash onto his hands when he hit the water roughly with his oar, and soon they were numb with cold. Grateful for his warm cloak, Galdur refrained from complaining as they traveled miles and miles down the river. To distract himself from the cold, he gazed out at the landscape, which changed from forest, to plains, to the towering Venerath Mountains as the hours passed from one to the next.

"That's it, right there!" cried Galdur, rushing to the front of the boat. He leaned on the edge, pointing at the white spire of Kasperon, the most notable landmark of the city.

"We've reached it?" Astrid exclaimed excitedly.

Galdur smiled, watching the magnificent city come into view. "Yes. Welcome to the western coast of Anzelon."

Sailing into the docks of Kasperon with a stolen boat could have been troublesome, even if news of their crime hadn't reached the city yet. As such, they decided to tie up the boat a mile or two from the city with some of Melkin's spare rope and stepped onto dry land once more. As the orange and pink sky began to darken, the five finally entered the city.

Galdur yawned and rubbed his eyes, loath to leave his cot. The thin blankets and scratchy sheets were infinitely more comfortable than the cold earth and rough ground he'd slept on for the past few weeks.

Melkin had insisted on purchasing the cheapest rooms despite protests from the rest of the group. *Perhaps it was a good thing.* If he were lying in one of the more luxurious beds, it would have taken nothing less than direct intervention from Ryne himself to make him leave it.

He sighed and sat up, throwing off the blankets and lacing his boots. The five of them had been so filthy that they'd bought new clothes before heading to the largest inn in Valea to blend in with the other travelers in the busy port city. When the group had entered the inn wearing clean garments, in one of Valea's greatest and richest cities, he had been able to ignore how dire their situation really was, for a little while.

As he stepped out of the inn, into the crisp autumn air and bustling streets, Galdur smiled. He'd almost forgotten the sheer beauty of the city from when he last saw it seven years ago. Kasperon was almost void of the ubiquitous inner-city grime and dirt that he knew from Hileath. In spite of the prevailing fish smell, it was easily Galdur's second favorite place in Valea.

He'd always admired the brick streets and tall stone buildings crowding the inner city. It bustled with citizens hard at work, hawking their wares to all kinds of people—families, travelers, guards, and nobles alike. Though Galdur kept his hood pulled over his head, most people around him did the same, keeping their faces hidden from the biting wind.

He tore his gaze away from the magnificent structures and walked toward the meeting spot Melkin had described to them the night before. A fear had grown in his mind that one of his companions would be caught and arrested overnight, but when he finally found the meeting spot, he breathed a sigh of relief at the sight of his well-rested friends. Galdur took a seat next to Lothar who sat with his head down, hood concealing the mop of blond hair on his head. A few minutes after Galdur sat down, Melkin, Astrid, and Leina stood without a word and began making their way to the northern sector of the city. In another minute, Galdur and Lothar followed. Half a mile of walking later, the two of them rejoined their companions in a narrow alley between houses.

Melkin pointed just beyond the group. "Around this corner should be Falknir's home."

"What's your plan?" asked Galdur.

Melkin shrugged. "Figured you'd go knock on the door and ask."

"You said you'd think of a plan last night," grumbled Galdur. "That's the best you could come up with?"

"This guy lived here a hundred years ago," whispered Lothar. "You expect to find anything?"

"We might," said Melkin.

"Fine." Lothar turned to Galdur, looking into his eyes. "Just be careful."

Galdur nodded, not too keen about the situation. He didn't like the idea of banging on a random person's door and asking for information.

"We'll be just around the corner if you're in danger," assured Astrid.

Galdur took a breath, cleared his throat, and turned the corner to see a wooden door that looked centuries old. With a glance behind him to make sure no one else was within earshot, he rapped on the door three times. A moment later, an older man, maybe in his late fifties, opened it.

He eyed Galdur up and down. "Morning. Who are you?"

"I'm looking for a man named Daerus Falknir."

The old man's brows drew together and looked thoughtful for a moment before responding, "Haven't heard that name in some time. Who are *you*, though?"

"I'm . . . a historian. I read that Daerus Falknir was involved in an old scheme and wanted to learn more."

"Well, I don't know how you found this house, but he's been dead for a long time. I don't know of any scheme."

"Did he live here?"

"Yeah, a long time ago. But I don't know where he went."

Galdur raised an eyebrow in surprise. "So, he moved? He didn't die here?"

"What? Oh, I—I suppose so . . ." The man sighed. "Yeah, my grandfather talked about a man who was in a hurry to leave. He sold the house to the first person who showed interest and left in the mid

'40s." The man glanced back inside the house, tapping his foot on the wooden floor as if his breakfast was getting cold.

"Thank you so much. Have a nice day," said Galdur with a small wave.

"You too," said the man gruffly, shutting the door.

His companions all faced him with varying degrees of grimaces as he reappeared around the corner.

"Well, that was somewhat informative," said Leina.

Melkin nodded and rubbed his forehead. "We need some indication of where he went, though."

Leina stared at the ground. "Do you still have those writing supplies in your bag?"

"Yeah, why?"

"I have an idea."

Why was he the designated negotiator? *Ugh.* Galdur knew exactly why, but he nonetheless hated the answer. It didn't help that he could see Leina's annoyance, her frustrated glances every time someone brought up the fact that she'd been called a traitor in the newspaper. She obviously wanted to be here, doing what he was doing. He would gladly switch places if he could.

"A debt?" The baroness of Kasperon looked at him with concern in her eyes.

"Yes, My Lady."

"He's been dead for a century, and you want to collect money from his . . . what, Grandchildren?"

Galdur couldn't be mad at her incredulous tone; he *was* making a ridiculous demand. "Yes. I've been paid a considerable amount for this retrieval." He handed her the stack of papers. "Take a look at these."

She sighed, rifling through the first few pages and handing them back to Galdur. The papers were, of course, forged documents that he and Leina had hastily written. The baroness sighed and turned toward a servant beside her. "Get me the housing records."

A few minutes later, a servant appeared with a thick book and started rifling through it. "So . . . Falknir. Fanir, Famral, Falknir. Yes, the Falknirs lived right here." He pointed at a map of the city and showed it to Galdur.

Of course, it was the house to which they'd gone only hours prior.

"Wait, look at that," The baroness pointed to something in the book, out of view from Galdur.

"Ah, yes. It seems that Daerus Falknir bought a house along the coast, some . . . fifteen miles down from the city, in 1146. A year before his death."

"There you have it," said the Baroness, closing the book with finality. "Ryne's sake, I don't even know if he had children. How important could this be?"

"I really don't know, My Lady, I'm just the collector. It seemed important to my clients."

"Well, good luck I suppose. Next!" she called, beckoning the next person into the meeting room. It was a good thing he hadn't been to this city since he was ten, or else the baroness might have noticed she was talking to the crown prince. Galdur turned away and left the throne room, praying to Ryne that no one would recognize him as he walked past the people waiting to speak with the baroness. The many guards he passed seemed to be examining him while he walked down the flights of stairs that wrapped around the inside of the Kasperon Spire. He hoped he was only being paranoid.

After emerging from the building, he quickly walked in the direction of his companions who waited a mile away. As the four came into view, Galdur finally breathed a sigh of relief; it had all gone according to plan.

"You got the address?" asked Melkin.

"More or less. It's fifteen miles down the coast." He pointed in the vague direction. "So, if we keep walking that way, we'll eventually find it."

"Alright then," replied Melkin. "Leina got us a couple maps, so we should hopefully be able to find it. One shows Kaspea, the other is a map of the city."

Galdur nodded. "Let's get going, then."

"Oh, and we bought more food," said Lothar, holding out a bag of dried fish in front of Galdur. "Can I see that newspaper, by the way?" Though not his favorite food, Galdur eagerly took the bag, hungry as he was. He handed the paper to Lothar and chewed on a piece of salty fish. The faul scanned the 'wanted' section, furrowing his brow at increasing intervals. "Is it at all possible that the Talwreks and Fareod genuinely think Leina is spying for them, and wrote otherwise so she could keep her cover?"

"That's an interesting idea . . ." Melkin shrugged. "I suppose it doesn't really matter, though."

"If we can *all* keep under the radar, that would be preferable," said Leina. "But if it comes to it, well . . ." she trailed off.

Galdur heard shouts coming from across the block and the group turned to watch. A horde of people were gathering around a vendor stall, reaching for newspapers.

"Another edition already?" said Astrid, eyebrows raised.

"It would seem so. News travels fast in Valea, though, and all the major cities have printing centers," said Galdur. "Let's get a copy and leave." He walked away from the others, pushing through the crowd and grabbing a fresh copy before retreating away from the throng of people. As he glanced at the page, his stomach dropped—it was impossible. His four companions waited for him, their eager faces anxiously awaiting an update.

They needed to go, though. "Let's get moving down the coast. It's already noon, and we have to get to that cottage," he said.

"What does it say?" asked Melkin, trying to peer at the paper.

Galdur glanced around—something about this square made him uneasy. He felt too visible. He checked the paper again, making sure his eyes hadn't played a trick on him. Indeed, as he scanned the headline and listened to the cries of joy and of outrage around him from the people of Kasperon, the unthinkable seemed to be true. He turned back toward his rapt companions. "Fareod accepted the negotiations. They're in eight days, on the eleventh."

34

Informant

He walked down the street, watching left and right for the criminals that scattered the streets of Kasperon. Though travelers often suspected there to be no crime in the opulent city, he knew otherwise. Still, there was little to do that day. He sighed, wishing the sun would strike the horizon, signaling the end of the twelve-hour long shift. It wasn't like he hated his job; he was just particularly tired and bored that day. Alas, hours remained until he could be with his wife and children.

As a respite from his boredom, he walked by the Spire of Kasperon, always a favorite area of his. Though the building wasn't as large as Kaspea Castle, located a few miles down the river, it was infinitely more remarkable. The white marble spoke volumes about the power of the baroness and the wealth of the city.

"You dropped this," said a voice from behind him. He turned to see another city guard holding a folded slip of paper.

"Ah, so I did. Thank you, sir." After slipping into a less crowded street, he opened the slip of paper and read. His heart skipped a beat—it certainly wasn't what he expected. He continued to walk, mind working furiously to process the short bit of information. If they were going down the coast, they would end up at the south side of the city—there was plenty of time to reach them. He almost smiled; if it had been too late in the day, his disappearance would look suspicious. As it was, he was allowed to patrol anywhere he wished to in the city. Quickening his pace, he followed the most important trail of his life.

After only a short walk, the smell of fresh food and fish filled his senses as he scanned one of the southernmost city squares. *They should be somewhere around here.* People began shoving in front of him as they scrambled to get the day's edition of the newspaper. He shifted to the side to avoid the energetic crowd and smiled at the beautiful news that was so commonly reported nowadays.

His gaze fell upon a group of people in the distance, also avoiding the flock of people around the newsstand. He ran through the checklist in his head, matching their physical features to the ones he had memorized. It all checked out. He swallowed, almost afraid to report now. But their presence in Kasperon had been expected. And the descriptions matched what he'd been told. He turned away, resisting the urge to run to the inn where his superior was.

When he reached the inn, he marched into the brightly lit hall and up to the back of a man at one of the few tables. He planted the end of his spear onto the ground to make his presence known.

The man held a hand up, pausing the conversation between him and his friends. He turned around, brief recognition flashing across his face. "What?"

"We'd like to question you about a recent robbery. You're not a suspect."

The man rolled his eyes at his companions, then looked up with a bored stare. "Ugh, fine."

The two left the inn and retreated into a more secluded area.

"They're here." The words felt strange as they left his mouth.

The man's eyes widened. "Where?"

"They're going south."

"By Talen . . . I'll take it from here. Good job."

"Thank you, sir."

35

Lothar

"I don't like the looks of them," said Astrid. "They're eyeing us."

Two people in the distance were walking toward them and staring as they made their way down the coast. One of them had a bit of a limp, but they were still fast approaching.

"They might just have a question, might want directions," said Leina.

"I hate being around so many humans. I feel like I'm about to be recognized at any moment," Lothar complained.

"I'll do the talking, alright?" said Leina.

Melkin nodded, looking back at Astrid and Lothar. "Just relax."

"Thanks, that helps a lot," Astrid said with an eye roll.

"Not much more I can do."

As the two came closer, he and Astrid drifted to the back of the group, shielded by the humans. Lothar kept his head down, not daring to look up at either man.

"Good day, do any of you know where I could purchase a fishing boat around here?" asked the man with the limp. Melkin opened his mouth, but said nothing, only narrowed his eyes at the man.

"Indeed," said Leina from beside Melkin. "If you head closer to the city there are some for sale by the docks."

The next few seconds passed in a blur. The man looked past Melkin, presumably eying the beach for any indication of boats. An instant later, Melkin drew a knife with his left hand and grabbed the man around the neck with his right arm, putting the knife to the man's throat. The second man immediately turned and began to sprint away.

"Get him, Leina!" shouted Melkin.

"What—"

"Just do it!"

Leina aimed her crossbow and shot. Lothar flinched, glancing away as the bolt lodged between the man's shoulder blades and he fell to the ground. Leina dropped the weapon, mouth open in horror at what she'd just done. For a single moment, all six were silent.

"Melkin, you'd better explain right now!" demanded Lothar, turning his attention back to the insane scene he'd just witnessed.

"I will . . ." said Melkin through gritted teeth.

"What did I do?" cried the man. He winced as Melkin's blade pressed into the skin under his Adam's apple.

"You know exactly what you did, you lying scoundrel!" Melkin looked back at Lothar and the others. "Three years ago, he stabbed me!" he shouted.

Lothar stood there, stunned, waiting for a reaction from the captive man. *Has Melkin lost his mind?*

After a pause, the captive exclaimed, "No—It can't be—You're dead!"

Melkin leaned in, speaking into the man's ear. "Not quite."

"I should have cut your head off."

"I could say the same. Why did you attack me?"

The man laughed against the blade. "You really think I'd tell you?"

"Oh, you will," said Melkin, pressing the knife just a little deeper. Lothar's pulse quickened as a bead of blood collected on the knife.

"Melkin," pleaded Leina. Lothar averted his gaze, dread filling him. *Please . . . no . . .*

"Long—Long live the Virtue Guided . . ." gasped the man. With that, he drew a knife from his boot and plunged it into his own chest. Lothar gasped and jumped back. Mouth agape, Melkin dropped the man and he fell to the ground, dead.

"By the deities!" cried Astrid. Her face was ashen, surely mirroring his own shock.

"Let's go. We don't want to be found here," said Melkin as he backed away from the body.

No one else moved. Lothar tried to erase the horrific scene from his mind, but it burned bright—he suspected it would for a very long time. Finally, he found enough sense to begin walking, prompting the others to do the same. "Explain."

"Three years ago, Queen Gladia sent me on a mission. Another spy had heard rumors that there was some evidence found in Starren province relating to the death of the last empress of the Shalin Empire."

"Queen Persec?" interrupted Lothar.

Melkin shrugged. "I suppose. Anyway, supposedly Starren scouts had recovered some information on a mission, but Gladia hadn't been given a copy of the reports, so she sent me to investigate."

"Was Persec's death suspicious?" asked Leina.

Lothar nodded. "We don't like to admit it, but yes. First of all, there was an assassination attempt around a year before she died. She was poisoned and only barely survived, though she ended up making a full recovery. Afterwards, it was reported that she was never quite the same, intent on peace to a mad degree. Fifteen years ago, she journeyed to the border to witness the fighting and was never found again. She got caught up in a skirmish in which over a thousand died."

"No body was found?" asked Leina.

"No." Lothar stared at the ground, stroking his chin. "The investigators assumed she had died in battle..." Lothar's mind focused on the portrait of her from Imar's study—he could envision it coming to life, like he had seen the empress alive in person. But he hadn't.

"On my way to Starren, I was ambushed in the middle of the night, stabbed in my side. I stabbed my attacker's leg and got help from a nearby town. When I returned to Hileath, I told Gladia what had happened, and she decided to drop the issue since others were more pertinent."

"Why did he... kill himself, then?" asked Galdur.

"I—I'm not sure. I thought he could be a Talwrek. I just wanted to interrogate him... not kill him."

Lothar found himself lost in thought. Virtue Guided... something about it seemed so familiar. "He *is* a Talwrek!"

Galdur furrowed his brow. "What? He said Virtue Guided not Talen's Guided. Isn't that what 'Talwrek' means?"

Lothar nodded. "Yes, I may have forgotten some of the old language. It does indeed mean that, but I think it has a lesser-known meaning as well, without the religious connotation. Virtue guided, as the man said..."

"But the man I killed," said Leina, snapping her gaze toward Melkin. "You knew who *he* was, right?"

"No, I had never seen him before."

"What if that man I killed was just a civilian? You had me kill him over a suspicion?" cried Leina.

Melkin turned toward her and closed his eyes for a moment. "I'm sorry. I truly didn't want you to bear that burden. If I had the crossbow, the skills, I would have done it. But listen to me! If that man had alerted anyone, we could be captured or worse. Even if he wasn't a Talwrek, he could have been a bandit. We've come so far—we can't put the life of one person over the safety of the mission."

Leina looked into his eyes and nodded. "I'll consider it to be you who pulled the trigger."

"Absolutely. Now, what puzzles me is why the Talwreks ambushed me all those years ago. What did they gain from my not investigating in Starren province?"

"Maybe... uh... I—I can't think of a reason," said Galdur, throwing his hands up in frustration.

"Back to the name though, these Talwreks must think they're doing something virtuous, right?" said Leina.

Astrid sighed. "I guess?"

Lothar shook his head. "It just—It doesn't make sense."

"None of this does," said Melkin. "But we must keep going. If we get the Incantir, we might not need to understand all of this. We'll do everything we can, as fast as we can, and it'll have to be enough."

"Nice recommendation, Melkin," Lothar teased. "And an uplifting one, at that. I'm surprised."

"I'm full of motivational advice," said Melkin in a monotone voice.

Some hours later, Galdur called for a halt.

"I think it's this cottage here," he said, pointing at a small, stone house just beyond a steep embankment near the water. He was looking back and forth between the map and their surroundings.

"Are you sure?" asked Leina.

"No, but there's only one way to find out." Lothar looked around for some sort of cover, but the flat beach offered no place to hide them. Thus, when Galdur knocked on the door, they all stood beside him, hoping that if they were recognized, they could defend themselves from whomever opened the door. After a lengthy minute and some shuffling sounds, an elderly man opened the door. "Who are you lot?" he asked, eyes darting between the five of them.

"Did Daerus Falknir live here?" asked Leina. The man went slightly slack-jawed, and his eyes burned with recognition.

"What do you want?"

"We—We were wondering if we could have a few words with you. About the tragedy in 1145. About the Incantir."

"1145 . . . Ryne . . . Better come in."

He limped his way over to a table in the cozy cottage and sat down with a sigh. "Make yourselves as comfortable as possible." The five of them crowded in and sat around the table and on the mismatched furniture near the fire or, in Melkin's case, leaned against the wall.

"I'm Daerus Falknir's son." After a pause in which the old man took a deep breath, he asked, "What do you wish to know?"

Lothar was rapt; this could finally be it. The Incantir might be here.

"When did your father die?" asked Melkin.

"Around fifty years ago. He was seventy-something years old."

"We have servant records here. They say he died in service when he was twenty-one," said Melkin.

"I know. The records are wrong." The old man smiled wryly. "Shall I start with that?"

Although lengthy pauses followed each sentence spoken by the old man, Lothar held on to each word.

"Yes. Please do," said Leina, who sat nearest him at the table.

"Excellent. Forgive me . . . I must take a moment to remember. Strange, isn't it? How one can forget the most crucial information at the most crucial of times." Lothar watched as the old man stared blankly into the distance for a long moment before he began. "King Gorrik. He asked a servant girl to hide it."

"The Incantir?" asked Galdur.

Falknir nodded. "Yes . . . Alethia Shanik. She . . . refused to. She and my dad were both young, but she understood what it would mean to hide it. She was born in Hilean province. She didn't know anywhere outside of Hilean, and Gorrik demanded that it be hidden far away. She refused. For that, Gorrik laid false charges upon her and exiled her to a remote section of Starren province. Not officially exiled though, just strongly advised, you see. Or threatened, I suppose. He couldn't ruin his reputation by executing her on such charges, so he had a spy poison some of the food in her new home. She died about a year after she was exiled."

"How do you know this?" asked Lothar, leaning forward.

"My father . . . he went a bit crazy after the incident. He devoted his life to finding the facts, and then he told me everything. He was relentless. Anyway, after Shanik refused the mission, Gorrik moved on to my father. He grew up in Kasperon, knew people out west, knew the paths out here. And he was loyal. So, he agreed."

"Where did he hide it?" asked Melkin, staring eagerly into Falknir's eyes.

"Ah . . . before I tell you . . . I'd like to hear *your* story."

"It's long," warned Lothar.

"I've waited for a long time. I can wait some more. I will say though, I'm surprised to see two faul here. Raiken and Inaria, is it? I've read the papers. But, like so many other things, I assume that they're false. Or twisted. So . . . tell me . . . why are you here?"

The five took turns recounting every detail they could remember, for the man insisted upon it. Perhaps it was reckless, but they had no choice, and Lothar was confident they could take the old man if it came to it. After two hours, they were finally silent. Surprisingly, the old man had seemed attentive throughout the entire story, his sharp eyes always focused on whomever was speaking.

"Incredible... Thank you, my friends. Galdur... I trust you are not like Gorrik?"

"I should hope not. I would never *wish* for war."

"Gladly then, I shall recount the rest of my father's tale. I know that you... Melkin... would like for me to simply tell you the location... but I think you shall enjoy the story.

"While being a servant at the royal castle, Daerus was engaged to a young lady in Hileath. When he returned here to Kasperon, to hide the Incantir, he brought her with him. They purchased this cottage, then convinced his mother to move in with them. He loved his fiancée, my mother, dearly, and he left her a note that she was to open if he was ever killed or didn't write to her for over a year. Then, Daerus went back to serve at the king's castle. During that time, Gorrik ordered Daerus to never tell another soul of his mission, or where he hid the Incantir. Daerus agreed, but Gorrik became increasingly paranoid, as he had with Shanik, and eventually had Daerus arrested.

"In prison, Daerus begged to send Gorrik a message, and the guards eventually allowed it. Daerus wrote that if he was not set free, his story would get out and there was no way for Gorrik to prevent it. However, if Gorrik gave him a small sum of gold, Daerus would swear to leave, never come back, and never tell a soul. Gorrik agreed, and for extra precaution, reported that Daerus had contracted an illness and died. No one ever thought to question Daerus about the Incantir. He returned home and my mother gave birth to me soon after."

"You must be almost a hundred years old, then," Galdur said with wide eyes.

"Indeed. I have lost count, but it is around that. Well, my father returned triumphant, but the incident ate away at his very essence over the years. He'd sworn to never tell of it, but after nineteen years, he broke down. He told me, my mother, and my grandmother everything he could remember.

"He told us that the voices haunted him. He was young when the capture and torture of the faul occurred and hardly knew what was happening at first. Strange, small people were brought to the castle. He was naturally curious and eavesdropped on every conversation he could. He talked... relentlessly... about the screams he heard. He only knew about half of what had happened by the time it was over. Well, after telling us, he asserted that he couldn't be at peace until he knew the full truth and started leaving us for extended periods of time. Once, he went for a year, somewhere in the Shalin Empire, searching for information about the dead faul. The work... to him it was healing. Uncovering the facts that had escaped him during his nineteen years of silence became the most important thing to him. He learned more than what the history book you all retrieved says."

"So, he knew everything?" asked Melkin.

"Quite possibly. And though he wanted to, he couldn't alter the history book as a dead man. In fact, he said that I was to keep the information after his death. He didn't say when, if ever, to reveal it, but I think the time is right." Falknir leaned back, resting against his chair.

Silence reigned in the cottage for a long while. Lothar stood up, eager to stretch his legs, and stared out the window. Out of the corner of his eye, he thought he saw movement near the cottage. He blinked and looked closer, but nothing was there. He shook his head and turned back toward Falknir.

"Do you know anything about Rowan Golanir?" asked Astrid.

"Who's that?" asked Melkin.

Falknir sat forward in his chair again. "I'm not surprised you ask. The Golanirs were one of the most powerful magical families in the Shalin Empire. Rowan was one of the murdered faul in 1145 and with his death, the line of Golanir was lost. Apparently before he died, he called a name. When my father looked at the Golanir family tree, he found that it was the name of his sister, Revina Golanir. Now, my father had to dig quite deep for this information, but somehow, he found out that she married and took her husband's name."

"I can't believe... such a well-known name across the Shalin Empire, and his true story is lost," mused Astrid.

"Why would Revina take her husband's name? That's frowned upon in cases of powerful families," said Lothar. "Why erase any trace of the Golanirs?"

"Well, she was rightfully concerned that the Golanirs would be targeted by humans—eradicated. It was her disguise, which worked well, since obviously the line survived."

Lothar frowned, feeling as though he was missing something. "What do you mean?"

"Her new last name. It's why you asked in the first place, right?" said Falknir, furrowing his brow.

Lothar glanced at Astrid, but she looked as confused as him.

Glancing between the two, Falknir raised his brows, his ancient face showing genuine amusement. "Ah, I see. What a coincidence, that you all don't know."

"What was her new surname?" asked Lothar. He felt like the air had grown heavy with anticipation as he waited. Falknir looked at him, a wide grin spreading across his face.

"Raiken."

36

Leina

"We'll soon be on our way," said Leina. "It's getting late, and we have a war to stop." She looked over at Lothar who was staring at the floor with a faraway look.

"Will you tell us where he hid the Incantir now?" asked Melkin, leaning on his spear with his good hand. An eager fire still burned in his eyes.

"Yes... certainly. It is buried on an island a few miles out from the coast. I've never visited myself, but my father left a little map. Hold on a moment." The old man stood up and walked over to a lockbox. He pulled on a chain around his throat, revealing a key that had been hidden beneath his shirt. With shaking hands, he unlocked the box and produced a square of cloth. He held it out to Leina, and she slowly took it, marveling at the hand-sewn outline of the island, and the two stitches that marked where the Incantir was hidden.

"Do you have a boat?" asked Astrid.

The old man grimaced. "Two. Buried beneath the sand on the beach right in front of my cottage—I haven't had need of them in ages but didn't want them to be stolen. I have some shovels behind the cottage which you can use. I don't know how far the island is from the beach, but if you go straight out, you should reach it."

"Thank you," said Leina. "For everything." She offered a hand, and the man shook it firmly.

"I've done nothing but keep knowledge. It's you five who I should thank. I'll be dead soon whether your plan works or not. But I don't want this country to fall, corrupted as it is. Please, save us all."

"We'll try," said Melkin. With that, they filed out of the cottage and found a half dozen shovels tied to the shed in a bundle near where they needed to dig. Everyone but Melkin began to dig; Leina had noticed that he still struggled to grip objects with his right hand. He'd only rowed for a few hours along the Palzar river, using the crook of his elbow to brace the oar and his good hand to row.

The blinding afternoon sun reflected on the water, shimmering as the waves crashed on the shore. For once, urgency was not at the front of their minds. Eight days to find the Incantir and make it to the negotiation grounds felt like plenty of time to Leina.

"The Golanirs..." said Lothar, almost to himself.

"Well don't get too cocky," said Melkin. "I'm sure the bloodline has been quite tainted by now." Lothar laughed and the group relaxed a bit.

"Still, I wish we could keep talking to him. I'd love to hear about everything else he knows," said Lothar.

Leina tilted her head, a slight smile creeping onto her lips. She didn't know why, but the same desire had struck her earlier. "You know what? So would I..." She dug her shovel into the sand again, her arms burning. Thankfully not as much as they had in the Dalyuben mines, though.

A thud resounded and they all looked to see Astrid's shovel hitting something. They redoubled their efforts and uncovered the old wooden planks of a rowboat, their dirty, sandy surfaces blending in with the beach that buried them.

Melkin motioned for everyone to stand back as he and Astrid gripped the boat. With a grunt of effort from both of them, the boat rose from the beach, showering them all in sand. Leina coughed violently, expelling the grit from her lungs. She took a long drink of water, then examined the boat.

"It looks well preserved, I suppose," said Melkin. Besides the dirt and sand that still caked the boards, it seemed void of imperfections to her. Soon, they had extracted the other boat, as well as eight oars that were buried in a similar fashion. They packed two of the shovels in the boat, assuming they would have to dig for the Incantir, and each grabbed an oar.

Leina took a boat with Melkin and Astrid, while Lothar took the other with Galdur. They paddled swiftly, anxious to reach the distant island. As she had suspected, Melkin tried to help for a few moments, but gave up.

In the hour it took to reach the island, Leina felt deep satisfaction at the strength with which she pulled her oar through the water. Not easy by any means, but with Astrid's vigorous training over the past couple weeks and all the rowing she'd done on the Palzar, there was a noticeable difference from before.

Once on the sand with the rest of her companions, Leina stretched and looked around at the island. It was very small, with only a few patches of grass and sickly brush. Anticipation built within Leina as the five set off across the island, coming closer and closer to the Incantir.

Ten minutes later, on the far side of the island, Leina gestured at the sandy beach and sparse grass that lay around them, eyes darting back at the map to confirm. "It should be hidden . . . somewhere around here."

"Where?" asked Astrid.

"Well, it's not like there's much to go by," said Leina.

"I guess we'll just get to digging," said Astrid with a shrug.

Galdur blew out a breath, looking at the vast area in which the Incantir could be buried. "We could be here all night."

Leina gestured at the sky. "At least we have time."

While Astrid and Galdur worked, the other three had no choice but to wait. Leina sat down on the beach, facing the western sun. Her legs were weary from travel and the afternoon sun was warming after rowing through freezing water.

Something stirred within her, though—sadness, was it? That they'd all likely be dead soon? Or, more frightening perhaps, that the continent would be torn to shreds soon. How ever far they'd come, she knew they still had a very slim chance of success. On the other hand, it was quite the miracle they were still alive and maybe the miracles would just keep coming. Leina sighed, staring out at the setting sun as Lothar took a seat beside her.

"What do you think is out there?" he asked.

"I don't know. Other continents?"

Lothar leaned back on his arms. "Maybe we're just a small island... somewhere in the world."

"I've heard stories where people sail out there, never to be seen again," said Melkin. "I've thought about such a fate before."

"You'd sail out there?" asked Lothar, looking at Melkin.

He shrugged. "As I said, I've only thought about it. Probably not, though."

"Would any out there care if this continent was torn to shreds by war?" Leina asked softly.

"Who can say?" said Lothar. "Maybe Talen knows."

"Maybe..." said Melkin.

"You all should really get some sleep while we work," suggested Astrid. Leina shrugged; she didn't feel the least bit tired. Though her aching body begged for sleep, her grave thoughts kept her awake.

"Something's here!" cried Galdur two hours later. Leina turned around and saw that great swaths of the land had been excavated. Galdur was grinning as he carefully dug with his hands. The other four gathered around, kneeling beside the deep hole. Something had become barely visible under the sand. Its surface was jet black, plastered with geometric grooves and bumps.

"It's warm. There's an energy exuding from it," said Lothar in awe. "I can't believe..."

Galdur continued to gently uncover the orb from the sand. The overall shape was almost perfectly spherical, despite the surface imperfections.

"It's like their souls... their very essences are in here," said Astrid.

"They are," said Lothar. He picked up the sphere and beheld it, a slight smile upon his face.

Leina took a breath, imagining what Lothar felt in the moment. *What was it like to hold the soul of your ancestor?* She shuddered, not really wanting to know the answer.

"Why does it look like that?" asked Galdur. "Surely the king didn't have an old ominous ball lying around."

"I would assume that it started out as just a regular stone, then the essences inside changed it. Again, we don't experiment with this kind of thing in the Shalin Empire, so we don't know anything about it."

"We have to go now," said Melkin, wrapping his cloak tighter around himself. Despite the urgency in his words, the man had a smile on his face. They put the Incantir in the boat with Astrid, Leina, and Melkin.

"You know, you should really take my spear, Astrid," said Melkin as they began to paddle back to shore. "I can't use it right now anyway."

Astrid chuckled. "It's a little tall for me."

"You can cut it," said Melkin with a shrug. "But as is, it'll still work well for you."

"Well in that case"—Astrid laid her paddle down inside the boat and unstrapped her majoril dagger sheath—"Take this. I like using a spear better anyway. You should have a real one-handed weapon."

Melkin grinned, glancing at Leina. "I guess the joke is on me. After all these years . . ."

Leina smirked as Melkin strapped the weapon around his hip. Though it *was* poetic justice, she would have preferred him to be able to use his best weapon.

The sky was almost pitch black by the time the shore came into view. The moonlight was so faint that Leina could hardly see the cottage that sat upon the beach. Her pulse once again increased as they rowed the boats onto dry land and stepped on shore—it was so quiet. The surroundings felt wrong for some reason. *Why?*

"Take the Incantir, Astrid," whispered Leina, handing the orb to her. "Conceal it, just in case."

Astrid looked up at her with a quizzical expression. "Why not you?"

"You run faster." It wasn't a lie, but it wasn't the whole truth either.

She squinted and focused on a point instead of the surroundings in general. A tree—a shape behind it. A small hill—something peeking out above the crest. A patch of grass—a figure pressed to the ground. They were here. Probably dozens, if not more. She steadied her breath and averted her gaze.

"Is everything alright, Leina?" asked Melkin in a whisper. She felt sure he sensed something was wrong, but he didn't have her eyesight.

She wished she had the time to explain. "I see something in the distance. I'm going to check it out."

"Don't be gone too long," said Lothar.

"I'll go with you," said Melkin.

She looked dead into his eyes. "Trust me."

He hesitated for a second before nodding and turning back toward Lothar. She started walking, heart hammering against her chest. When she was sure her companions could no longer see her, she raised her hands above her head and approached a group of staring figures, confused expressions on their faces.

"My companions are ashore. They suspect nothing."

"Who are you?" asked a female. "Keep your hands up."

"I'm Leina Kierth. I've been following Edaireth, Raiken, Inaria, and Prince Ravinyk as they attempt to foil your plans."

"Which are what?" asked a man's voice.

She swallowed and tried to conceal her heavy breathing. "To start a war. For a new day to dawn." She wasn't really sure what she was saying, but it had to be enough.

"Elvine!" the man whispered. "Come here."

A woman quietly approached. "What is it?"

"Supposedly, this is Leina Kierth. She claims she is spying upon our prey."

"How do you know about us?" asked Elvine.

"I read some documents that Fareod left out. Melkin invited me and I went with him. I've sent Fareod updates about my mission. Listen, I told my companions that I was just looking at something I saw in the distance, so they'll get suspicious if I'm gone too long."

Elvine thought for a moment. "You could be useful. I'll have you speak with Fareod once we get to the negotiation ground. You'll stay with us right now, and I'll watch how your friends react. Then, perhaps we'll come to an agreement."

"Understood. They have the Incantir."

"Excellent. I had hoped as much," said Elvine with a grin. She tapped the arm of a human next to her, and he did the same to the person beside him. Within ten seconds, all the Talwreks were alert and started moving toward the water, closing in on three sides.

"Leina?" called Melkin. The sound startled her, but she kept pace with the Talwreks. Elvine then whispered to a faul next to her, who started to mutter. *What could he be doing?*

With a sudden deafening boom, the cottage was blown to bits. She clamped her hands over her ears, the sound of the bomb almost deafening. Orange fire lit the night sky, revealing the presence of the Talwreks as they cornered her friends. Falknir had still been in there. Leina breathed in and out, fighting to hold herself together. If she came apart now, they would know. Leina fought for control over the raging emotions coursing through her, knowing she had to pull this off—her friends would die if she didn't. She would die if she didn't.

Astrid shielded her eyes. "What the—"

"Get back!" shouted Melkin as soon as the Talwreks became visible in the firelight from the explosion. Her friends were staring at the cottage in shock. Galdur had fallen to his knees and Astrid had her hands over her mouth in a silent scream. Melkin's eyes widened at the sight of Leina with unbound hands, walking side by side with their enemies.

"I'm sorry Melkin, your journey ends here," she said, contempt in her voice. She saw out of her peripheral vision the weapons drawn by the bombers, how her companions were trapped with the sea behind them and danger all around. She met Melkin's eyes for a few seconds, praying he would understand. At once, he turned his head toward his companions and whispered something. Their expressions hardened as they scanned their attackers, looking for a way out.

"I should never have trusted you, Leina," he growled. "You were always weaker than me and now... you've succumbed to the enemy."

Leina laughed. A cold, unnerving sound that she had perhaps learned from Melkin. "You're wrong. They were never *my* enemy. Your strength has gotten you nowhere."

37

Astrid

Astrid looked around frantically, trying to keep her wits about her. If Leina could pull off this façade, then they would at least have a chance if captured. However, if the four managed to escape, Leina would be taken by the Talwreks. Astrid was sure that she had considered both possibilities.

Melkin stepped forward, glaring at Leina. "So it was *you* who—"

"Of course it was. You really shouldn't have joined forces with someone smarter than yourself. You never could see past your own pride."

"Hand over the Incantir, and you all can go free," said Elvine, cutting off the exchange. Astrid recognized her from the speech she'd given near the mines. "Resist, and I'll use my other plans for you."

Astrid was shocked at how calm she sounded—almost like Elvine was sorry she had to do this. Astrid shook her head—they had to get out of here. She resisted the urge to pat her cloak pocket and give away the location of the Incantir.

"We don't have it," said Galdur.

"Oh yes you do. Your friend told us." That unnerved Astrid, a different fear than the one she'd felt when Falknir's cottage was blown up with him inside. But she also understood that the Talwreks would find it once she and her companions were captured and unable to defend themselves. All Leina did was give information that made her look trustworthy. Astrid gripped her spear more tightly and tried to control her breathing.

"Or perhaps she lied." Elvine put her dagger to Leina's neck. Melkin turned around and glared quickly at Astrid, Lothar, and Galdur.

"Kill her then. She is a traitor," said Melkin, his voice lathered with hatred. Astrid kept her face as blank as possible. From where he stood, Astrid could tell Melkin had tried to hide them from the Talwreks' view. Perhaps this time, his untrusting nature was warranted—Astrid was sure her face betrayed her true emotions. Elvine pressed her blade against Leina's throat and Astrid could see fear in Leina's usually cool face.

"Well then . . ." said Elvine, letting the dagger hang by her side.

Without warning, Melkin shouted, "Go!" and took off running. They followed him, sprinting toward a spot on the right side of the cottage remains, a spot that had fewer Talwreks around it. Melkin struck out with Astrid's majoril dagger, plowing through the Talwreks who were unfortunate enough to get in his way. Five Talwreks blocking their escape quickly fell beneath Lothar's powerful magic.

"Aim to capture, but don't let them get away!" cried Elvine. Cries echoed around them, and chaos erupted as the bombers came to their fallen companions' aid, closing in on Astrid and her friends.

"I can't use magic!" cried Lothar in surprise. A soldier ran for him, but Astrid was too far away to get to him in time and Galdur and Melkin were fending off their own attackers. Lothar drew a knife and threw it, hitting the soldier right before he would have been stabbed. Astrid ducked beneath a spear thrust and stabbed upward with her auxlar dagger, catching the man in his gut. "Go!" cried Melkin again. They were past the majority of the Talwreks. They could make it if they ran faster than any of their pursuers, and if none of the Talwreks had crossbows.

Midstride, Astrid felt her legs go limp. She hit the ground hard, unable to break her fall with her useless arms. Looking around, she saw the other three had similarly collapsed, struggling against the spell with panic in their eyes.

"Good girl. Try to keep them all down, okay? But make sure that the humans stay down," spoke a woman. Straining against the magic, Astrid flexed her fingers and her wrist. With great effort, she was finally able to use her elbows and shoulders. Her arms were free.

"Keep the blondes from using their magic," said another voice.

"Yeah," responded the voice of a boy, a young boy. She couldn't see, but she remembered the children that Elvine spoke of at the campsite. Astrid cursed her lack of foresight—they should have expected this.

She focused on her legs, trying to use them. Two soldiers physically started to restrain Melkin and another came for Galdur. She struggled and the little girl using her magic to keep Astrid from moving emitted a grunt of effort. *Break free. Break free.* She repeated the phrase in her mind, refusing to let anything else consume her thoughts. Her leg moved slightly. Another grunt from behind. Astrid planted her hands on the ground and pushed up, letting out a scream of effort.

At once, the magic broke from her. She jumped onto her feet and spun, slamming into the girl. Her companions immediately started trying to break from their captors, buying her the time she needed to sprint away. Unable to resist, she looked behind and saw that all three of her companions had been restrained and tied up.

"Get her!" cried a voice. A crossbow bolt shot past her, and Astrid yelped.

She prayed to all the gods. She had always made the annual offerings to all five deities—not as seriously as others like Lothar, but wasn't it enough? Another shot flew past her. Her foot hit a rock, but she regained balance and focused solely on running. When she couldn't hear her pursuers anymore, she slowed her pace just a little. She knew they were there, but she could barely see where she was going, and to twist an ankle would be deadly. It was still a fast jog, and Astrid knew she could keep the pace for a number of miles.

She didn't want to think the grim thoughts and sadness that consumed her, but she could no longer ignore the persistent questions attacking her mind. Where to go? What should she do? Could she find help? Was there anyone whom she could trust? Then it hit her, and she felt relief ease her mind.

The capital city of Valea. Three streets down from the academy. Fourth house on the left.

38

MELKIN

Though he'd tried to resist, obviously, there was nothing he could have done with a knife to his throat. The three of them were tied up and stripped of all weapons. Then, Elvine ordered for them to be searched. Melkin hated to admit it, but they were being treated quite well, except for Lothar, who had to be gagged at all times.

He prayed that Astrid wouldn't be caught; he'd seen the few who chased after her and predicted she'd be able to defeat them. She had to.

"It's not on any of them!" reported a Talwrek after searching the three of them.

"The female!" shouted Elvine in frustration. "She must have it!"

"She's long gone by now. Three are chasing her," said the Talwrek beside Elvine. She stared at the ground and Melkin wondered what she was scheming now. This was the leader of a group that had been operating, undetected, for years. He did not doubt her cunning.

"Let's stay here for now. I don't want to leave before they return with the girl, dead or alive, and we all need some rest," she commanded. "As for you three, you'll be under watch for the night, of course."

Melkin nodded, at a loss for words. It had happened so quickly—he couldn't keep up. It seemed the other two couldn't, either. He resisted looking at Leina, who stood with unbound hands, her weapons taken from her. Funnily enough, he wanted her reassurance. He wasn't quite sure if she had a plan past just remaining free. Questions raced through his mind. What did she write to Fareod? Did he believe her? Were the newspapers really trying to keep Leina's disguise? *Could there be*—he almost didn't let himself believe it. *Could there still be hope for Anzelon?*

39

ASTRID

Half an hour later, Astrid stopped. She couldn't run forever, and neither could they. Within moments, her first two attackers came into view—faul. As they approached, the male threw a gust of wind at her, but she recovered quickly and swung her spear toward his head. He ducked, barely avoiding it, and she followed the trajectory of her spear, spinning around and bringing the tip lower so that even as he righted himself and tried to move away, she sliced him across his thigh. Astrid stabbed him in the foot, and he let out a blood-curdling scream.

Astrid turned to the female who had finally come close enough for her to disarm. Pity stirred in her heart for the poor faul. Astrid was better—*far* better, and she felt no desire to cause her the excruciating pain that came with a stab wound. She easily avoided the faul's majoril dagger and grasped her left hand with her own, twisting her wrist until the dagger dropped and Astrid shoved her to the ground. The blast of light that momentarily blinded her did nothing to stop her from easily kicking away the faul's other dagger and restraining her while the male groaned in pain from beside her.

"Just relax. I'm not going to kill you," she said, looking back at the young faul—she couldn't have been over twenty, and she looked terrified.

"You—you're not?"

Astrid thought for a second. "Maybe..." The faul's eyes turned wild and terrified once more. "Wait—no, I'm definitely not going to kill you. Might knock you out, though."

"Please, let me tend to my husband. I just want to stop him from bleeding out."

Astrid sighed. "You won't follow me?"

"I swear it on Talen."

She released the female, keeping a close eye on the two docile faul. She watched the female retrieve medical supplies from her pack and apply pressure to the wounds. They didn't look life-threatening to Astrid, so after taking all the money from their packs, she continued to run onwards. Once she was sure that the two could no longer see her, she stopped again, waiting. She had seen three people chase her and figured they were all good at tracking. Better to take down her attackers now. After a moment of complete silence, she saw movement.

A man, about fifteen yards away, was running toward her at full speed. She swallowed, readying her spear. He was tall and muscular, likely adept at fighting. She ran a few steps toward him, meeting his incoming strike with a two-handed block. With a shove of her spear, the man backed away a pace, and she stabbed toward his torso but received a block. *This is just like sparring with Melkin, only with slightly higher stakes.* The man was good, worryingly good.

"Why—why does a worthy soldier such as yourself hinder our efforts?" asked the man as he huffed from exertion. She backed off, catching her own breath and making note of the differences in his fighting style from Melkin. He was less purposeful with his swings but put more force behind each one.

"What efforts?" Again, she blocked an overhead swing and their spears clashed. She felt his enormous strength push against her and was forced to retreat a few paces. The growing fear heightened her senses.

The man lunged toward her legs. "For peace!"

She swiftly dodged and thrust at his side, but her recovery was far too slow. His spear grazed her shoulder and pain lanced through her. "Peace? You want war!" She stumbled back and clutched her shoulder.

"Surrender and come with me!"

"No!" she cried. Retreating backwards, she tripped on a rock and fell backwards on a spot of sandy ground. The man towered above her.

"Please surrender!" he cried, pointing the spear at her. "Or I'll have to kill you!"

Astrid had no time to respond, she was busy talking to someone else. A certain someone to whom she rarely spoke. As the ancient faul prayer to Kaima left her lips, she cast sand into the man's eyes, swiped his spear away from her and rolled onto her knee, jamming her spear into his leg. He collapsed to the ground with a cry of pain and started crawling toward her.

"You'll see! You'll see in the end!"

"Get away!" she cried, clambering to her feet. As the man began to rise, Astrid swung her spear at his head, and he fell once more to the ground. She rushed up to him and checked for a pulse. Remorse and relief hit her in equal waves—he was dead.

Astrid leaned on her knees, out of breath and shaken. It had been close. She was safe. But how to reach Hileath in time to save the others? And of course, she also had to know for certain where her companions were being taken. A somewhat reckless plan formed in her mind. The Talwreks were between her and Kasperon, so she might as well stop by.

Astrid grabbed the man's pack and rummaged through it, finding a map, food, and more money. Content, she wandered away from the body and found some bushes for cover. She laid down, falling asleep within minutes.

Long before the sun emerged, Astrid started her journey back to Kasperon. She prayed the Talwreks had stayed near the beach to rest for the night. Glancing around, she realized this was the first time she'd ever awakened in the middle of nowhere, with no one to talk to. Her nerves were on edge; she was constantly aware of everything happening around her. Was this how Melkin became so paranoid? Even more troubling, the Talwreks had to be less than ten miles away, able to ambush her at any moment. She took a breath; it was pointless to worry right now. Not when she had a job to do.

An hour later, the camp of over fifty people was in sight, less than a mile from the shore. She hid behind some trees, a hundred yards from the Talwreks. Her heart pounded inside her chest—why did she think this would go well? It was impossible to hear from so far away. *Melkin and Leina would do this without a second thought.* Motivated by that idea, she crept closer, now only forty yards from the camp. She could only hear bits of conversation but shuddered at the thought of going closer. Then, they started moving. The creaking carts, stomping of the horses, and clattering of weapons cloaked her presence as she drew closer still. Now, thirty yards from the rear of the group, thirty yards from her tied up companions—she listened.

40

MELKIN

Melkin woke up a total of nine times during the night. He kept track by making a mark in the dirt with his shoe because he'd had nothing better to do. A few times, the shooting, burning pain in his palm woke him, and other times, it was a noise from one of his captors. Fear, exhaustion, and exhilaration perpetually filled him.

After all the Talwreks were awake, Elvine permitted a soldier to cut the bonds wrapped around his, Lothar's, and Galdur's feet. She warned them of painful retribution should any of them try to escape or attack, but Melkin pondered how far she'd go. Melkin assumed the three of them were part of her plan, so they wouldn't be killed, but he wasn't keen on being tortured. Plus, he was surrounded by forty weapon-wielding soldiers. There was no hope for escape.

"Alright Talwreks, let's depart! Keep two guards on each prisoner at all times!" shouted Elvine.

Melkin glanced at Galdur and Lothar, meeting their grim stares. None of the three seemed to know what to think at the moment. What could they think about? After the journey was well under way, Elvine drifted to the rear of the group, walking beside them.

"This one, right?" she asked, pointing at Lothar. "He's a Golanir?"

"That's what the old man said," said another Talwrek. "And you saw what he did to those five." They weren't dead, but the five that Lothar had injured the night before weren't likely to be fighting again in the near future.

Elvine raised an eyebrow. "Actually, this might be better than the Incantir."

"To Orwic, he's a traitor," warned the Talwrek.

"He broke a minor criminal out of jail. That's nothing compared to being the last of the Golanirs," said Elvine, still looking at Lothar.

"You want to kill him?"

"Maybe... I'll let you know when I decide."

"Will you let us know as well?" asked Galdur.

"Perhaps, Young Prince," said Elvine with a smirk. She then turned to Melkin and Lothar with an amused smile. "Oh... I remember you two. And to think, I saved your lives."

"You were listening to our conversation with Falknir, weren't you?" Melkin was disgusted with himself for not checking their surroundings, for letting his guard down.

"Indeed. See Leina, he does have some brains," cried Elvine, grinning. He finally allowed himself to glance at Leina. In that moment, he hated how good she was at disguising her true emotions. Her face showed no comfort, no pity, no evidence of their two-year long friendship.

"Yes, it would seem that he does. Pity they are of no use now," said Leina with a smirk.

"Why do you want war?" asked Galdur.

Elvine turned toward Galdur, a grin still upon her face. "Well, it's obvious, isn't it?"

None of them answered. Melkin blinked, a radical idea forming in his mind. Too insane to be true, right? But maybe...

"Well, I assume you know my former identity?" asked Elvine with a dramatically raised brow.

Melkin and Galdur looked at each other with confused glances. All of a sudden, Lothar began struggling against his gag, eyes wild and afraid.

"You have something to say?" asked Elvine, gesturing for his gag to be removed.

Lothar coughed as a faul removed the slimy wad of cloth. Other Talwreks moved closer, holding their spears and daggers at the ready while they walked. "You—you're Empress Persec. Emperor Orwic's niece."

Elvine laughed and clapped. "Nicely done, my friend."

Galdur sucked in a breath. "Ryne's sake..."

Melkin hated how good-natured Elvine sounded; her innocent tone making venomous words sound friendly. He thought over the revelation; it wasn't shocking. As adept a leader as she was, he'd expected her to have had experience, perhaps as an earl or an official. The 'dead' empress was an interesting turn, but did it change anything?

"'Ryne's sake,' indeed," said Elvine. "You know, I'm disappointed you only discovered this *now*. I mean, you got the history book, you got the servant records, talked to Daerus Falknir's son, and found the Incantir, but still couldn't put two and two together? Anyway, that's where I'll start. I spent my entire time as empress trying to stop the skirmishes and ease the tension. I came to power at age fifteen, and I 'died' when I was thirty-one."

"Sixteen years isn't that long," said Galdur. "Not for a monarch. Or emperor."

"Of course, but I saw no progress toward peace. I knew that if I searched for it, I could have found the Incantir, but that wouldn't have appeased my people. I visited the battlefield many times and found only hate there. There are two types of people, my friends—two types of soldiers who come back from the border. Those whose hate only grows for the other race, and those whose hate grows for war itself. The former just keep the violence growing but the latter make up much of my group here. We have many members; some lost their friends in the skirmishes, some lost family, and some even lost themselves. They all went home and found no sympathy for their loathing of war. 'Some land here, some money here, what does it matter?' my people asked. They received excuses and shallow answers. 'Well, they disrespected Talen and the deities, they look different, they have a different form of government. They're savage brutes who can't do magic, thus Kaima hates them...' Well, those answers obviously didn't please them, so here they are. I asked the same questions, received the same answers."

"How were you able to organize the Talwreks when you were supposedly dead?" asked Galdur, shaking his head.

"Ahh... When I was twenty-eight, a young faul became apprenticed at the military headquarters after having lost his family in the war. For years, I had no one to speak about peace with, since my family dismissed my opinions. This faul though, was more than eager to discuss it, and he became my main advisor, though never officially. After the assassination attempt against me sixteen years ago, I knew I could not solve the problem through legislation. The people... they had to be forced to accept peace. So, I poisoned the young faul's master and arranged for him to become the replacement, my new domestic historian."

Lothar's gaze snapped to Elvine's, his eyes full of anger and regret. "Imar..."

"Yes. The first member of the Talwreks. We planned everything out before I faked my death. I expanded his scope of power, and when I disappeared, he covered my tracks by controlling information throughout the empire. Without him, we never would have succeeded."

Lothar's face was pure anger. "I—you dare—do not speak—"

"Do not speak of the faul who dedicated his life to our cause? Oh Lothar, he would *want* to be spoken of in this way. This was his greatest wish." Her smile was genuine, as if she really were recalling the memories of an old friend.

Lothar narrowed his eyes, fixing them upon Elvine's. "Fine. Speak of him as a traitor, then."

"Well, that depends on what you call a traitor. Melkin, you're a spy. You've betrayed people's trust. You and the prince defied the will of Fareod, your king, by hiding the Incantir from me. And of course, Inaria and Raiken are both traitors to the Shalin Empire for leaving their posts. Aren't we all traitors? What makes you any better than Imar? Why should *you* be able to speak ill of him?"

The three were silent. Melkin felt his heart pounding in his chest, but no words came to him—nothing that would erase his guilt. He *had* betrayed people. He *was* a traitor. They had all fought for what they believed in, including Imar. "What did you want with the Incantir, if not peace?" asked Melkin.

"Oh, nothing too special. Just to anger Orwic by destroying it in front of him. To make him and his people declare war. And of course, I couldn't let you have it, couldn't let you disrupt the plans I have so carefully laid out."

Melkin clenched his fists in frustration. "Why *not* use it for peace?"

"Anzelon is too far gone for that. No, relations between our countries can never be improved. The only way to stop it, to end the constant fighting, is to start over."

"You're wrong," Melkin said.

Elvine shrugged. "Orwic is a cynical old faul, and his heirs are no better. I can do a lot of things, Melkin, but I can't fix that. Galdur, I know you don't want war, but are you fit to rule? Can you control your raging, seething country? I doubt it, talented as you might be."

"So instead, you mean for one country to completely destroy the other?" asked Galdur.

"Absolutely. A new continent, where people aren't constantly losing their loved ones to a pointless, childish battle. A stronger country, ruled and inhabited by the superior race."

"Which is?" asked Galdur.

"I've no idea, only time will tell. But Anzelon will be a place where a ruler can focus on improving their people's lives, not keeping their borders secure or fueling a deadly fire. Why have a continent inhabited by two groups who hate each other, when that simply doesn't have to be the case?"

"More will die in the war than they ever have in the skirmishes," said Galdur.

"Are you sure? What about in another hundred years? Two hundred? Who knows when the battles would end on their own. And what about those in the meantime who live without those whom they love? Those who live in poverty? No, despite the cost in lives, Anzelon will be happier. In the ages before 1145, do you think Valea and The Shalin Empire ever coexisted peacefully? Of course not! The hostility created by the Incantir, by those ten faul who fell under Gorrik's torture..." Elvine shook her head, a pleasant smile on her face. "My friends, it is a gift. It will bring peace. We will create a better world."

Galdur shook his head, clenching his jaw. "You're out of your mind."

"I don't really care what you think, young prince."

Silence fell over the group. Melkin shook his head, processing the information. Her deep insanity seemed reasonable at a glance. He looked up, meeting Elvine's still kindly gaze. "That's all well and good, Elvine, but why tell us? You're going to kill us, aren't you?" asked Melkin.

"Two reasons. *You* don't necessarily need to die. The other two probably will, though I may be able to imprison the prince. And I figure you have a right to know. After all, you've come quite far. You've probably figured out by now that we were roughly tracking you all as best we could and discovered all of your impressive achievements. Would you rather die knowing the truth, or not?"

41

ASTRID

She couldn't waste any more time, she had to move. Though she tried to calm herself, each breath quavered in her chest. Almost everything that Elvine had said was true to her. The kind of people whom she would have found solace with a year ago . . . they were all here. Her three pursuers all probably had similar stories to her own. Was Melkin's mission truly idealistic beyond reason? Had she created an illusion of hope to escape the depression that had consumed her from her service at the border?

It didn't matter though, did it? Whether or not she believed in her friends' plan, she couldn't leave them there. Surely the slaughter of hundreds of thousands was wrong. Not to mention Elvine's plan to execute Lothar. Leina had given her the Incantir, trusted her with the group's most precious object. She couldn't fail them now. Resolve stirred in her as she drifted further back from the group and turned north.

After three hours of light jogging, she reached Kasperon again. It was later in the day than she wished, but there wasn't anything she could do about it. During the journey, she had thought about the timing of her mission. From the map she had, it looked like the Palzar river ran up by the negotiation grounds. If she reached Hileath on the seventh, she could make it to the grounds by the ninth, a day before the negotiations between Fareod and Orwic. She scanned the city outskirts; the seventh was only an attainable goal if she could find a horse. Finally, she spotted a stable in the distance, located in a less-traveled area outside the city.

She pulled her hood further down over her face and approached the man preparing food for the horses. "Can I purchase a horse?"

He turned around, flashing a grin. "Sure." The man stepped a few paces back, glancing between the six horses in the stables before looking back at her. She stared at the ground and pulled her cloak tighter. "There's no need to hide, you know. Anyway, this one looks to be about the right size for you," he said, pointing at the smallest horse. "She's got some good endurance, too."

"How much?"

"Ten gold."

"I'm two silver coins short." It was all she had been able to get from her three pursuers the night before.

"I'll take it. What's your name?"

She dropped the coins into his outstretched palm. "A—I'd rather not say . . ." He looked at her with a raised eyebrow. She cursed her own stupidity as she walked past him to mount the horse, but a tug from behind, pulling her hood down, stopped her in her tracks. Rage and fear filling her, she spun around and pointed her spear at the man's throat. Instead of cowering, as she expected him to do, he laughed and raised his hands in the air. A real, friendly laugh.

"A faul, eh . . . Well, I was just wondering. Business is business. I'll not tell a soul," he assured her. She wanted nothing more than to scream at him, to rant that he could have ruined the fate of the continent, but she didn't. Astrid had to trust him, at least in this. After a final glare, she pulled her hood back up, checked over her horse, mounted bareback, and tried to focus on staying atop the horse. Bracing herself for a long, cold journey ahead, she set off toward the capital city of Valea.

42

GALDUR

Galdur's legs ached as he traversed yet another mountain. The sights that had left him mesmerized from the river were now the bane of his existence. At least everyone seemed to be struggling with the hike; they'd left their horses and carts with a rancher before starting their journey through the mountains. Galdur had suggested that they take the long way around, but Elvine was quick to scoff and insisted they trudge through the mountain range instead, all on foot. At least his exhaustion and aching legs almost kept him from focusing on the nauseating dread that constantly filled him. Almost.

With a sigh, he brought himself back to the present. To his left and right, the three of them were flanked by guards at all times. At least only Lothar was prohibited from speaking, but the faul seemed miserable. Elvine had considered letting Lothar walk without a gag, but decided against it since they were in such an open space. The best part of the whole ordeal, if he could call it that, was that none of them had to take night watch.

"When do we hope to reach the negotiation grounds?" asked Galdur, turning toward one of the Talwreks.

"Well, it's the fifth now, so hopefully we'll cross the mountains by the end of the sixth. There we have horses and carts waiting for us, so it should only be another couple of days until we reach the grounds."

"Thanks," he said, out of habit. Melkin glared at him, but he just shrugged. He understood Melkin's desire to be a thorn in every Talwrek's side, but Galdur couldn't summon the energy to be annoying.

Melkin sighed, glancing about. "Well, Galdur, you said you wanted to see Valea, all the places on your maps. Is this what you meant?"

Galdur looked around at the glorious mountaintops. They stretched from below the Palzar, past the border, to around a third of the way up the Shalin coast. He closed his eyes and ignored the pain in his feet and legs. He had never seen this view, and he likely never would again. He wasn't in captivity, he wasn't facing death, he was with his friends. He opened his eyes and let a slight smile creep onto his lips. It was incredible.

"Yes. Yes, it is."

43

VALLEC

Vallec sipped his morning coffee and flipped through the newspaper, taking note of the silence that lay outside his house. He hadn't quite become used to it—the sounds of the bustling city had surrounded him for as long as he could remember. Over the past weeks, he'd seen many young men and women join their battalions and regiments, preparing for a war they may never return from.

Still, no one had thought to draft Vallec himself. He smiled—that was one benefit to having been stabbed. Or possibly, no one in Taleek's brigade had been called to battle. There were around a hundred that had been left behind from this year's Akarist, but Vallec didn't know if they had been drafted. As for him and Atlia, the only surviving military members of the Akarist, he wasn't even sure that the public knew they were still alive. He hadn't thought about that before. For weeks, his thoughts had been focused on his old companions, not on any small article that might mention Atlia or himself.

Ever since the first paper mentioning the five, Vallec had been on edge, dreading that the next paper would tell him they'd been captured—or were killed. News of the queen's death had been almost as bad, but as long as Melkin lived, he had reason to hope Valea would be alright. It was strange, really. His last moments with the other five had been anything but hopeful or kind. Now though, he placed his full faith in them. He had to.

Vallec had told them he would return—in fact he'd sworn it—but he had no way of knowing where they were, which was quite a good thing. The paper about the negotiations puzzled him; he'd considered making his way up to the old meeting grounds, but he had nowhere near enough information to risk his life like that. Besides, he had told Melkin where he would be. He smiled, remembering the mix of shock and laughter that consumed him when he discovered Evarith had lied about his name. A surprise, and yet not surprising at all. He hoped Melkin had become a better leader since he'd last seen him.

He continued to rifle through the newspaper, finding articles about war preparations and supply shortages. Swallowing his fear, he flipped to the wanted section and found it to be mostly the same as before. Now though, they were also suspected of stealing a boat in Annister. Ryne's sake, *Annister*. If they had a boat, that would take them even farther out west. Miles and miles away from Hileath and the negotiation grounds. He sighed, hoping they knew what they were doing.

A knock on his door broke his concentration. A brief hope flashed through him that it was Melkin, though he didn't know why he was so eager for him to return. He stood up from his kitchen table and opened the door to a small, hooded figure.

"Who—" started Vallec before the person looked up at him and pulled their hood back. "Astrid!" he cried.

"Can I come in?" she asked. Her voice, which he vividly remembered as apathetic and rough, was now kinder, but he took note of the distinct quiver in it. Most concerning of all, her lips looked slightly blue, and she was violently shivering.

"Y—yes of course," he said, beckoning her inside. He hurriedly put another pot of coffee on the boil while she sat down.

"It's w—warm in here," she said, dragging out each word. He ignored his desire to start bombarding her with questions and fetched some clean blankets from the closet.

"Here." He draped the blanket over her. "I'm making hot coffee, but it'll be a few minutes."

"T—thanks. It's Vallec, right?"

He laughed; their relationship hadn't exactly ended on a friendly note. "Yes."

Ten minutes later, they were both sitting, sipping hot coffee. When Astrid's teeth had stopped chattering, she leaned toward him. "We must reach the negotiation grounds before the morning of the tenth."

He felt his eyes widen with shock. "But that leaves less than two days. Where are the rest? Are they safe?"

She shook her head. "No. Not safe, but not dead either. Listen, we must go. I'll explain on the way."

He looked around for a few short seconds, contemplating the offer from Astrid, a faul whom he had found almost wholly unreasonable only two weeks ago. "What do I need?"

"Money. How much do you have? And your armor and weapons, of course. Is there a place to buy gambeson in this city?"

"I have a decent chunk of money stored up. What do we need to buy besides the gambeson?"

Astrid shivered and took another sip of coffee. "A boat so we can ride the Palzar to the negotiation grounds."

She showed him the map and he nodded. "A small rowboat, I suppose. You know, I always wanted to take the Palzar to the Akarist. But Taleek insisted it was too dangerous, that it would be too easy for anyone to sabotage us. I suppose Melkin thought the same when he journeyed to Hileath and back—"

"Vallec!"

"Oh. Yes, I should be able to afford a boat," said Vallec, grinning.

"Excellent," she said, taking another sip, then grimacing. "Talen's sake, do you people always drink your coffee black?"

44

Galdur

As the meeting grounds came into view, Galdur recalled seeing them on their way to the Dalyuben Hills. Then, he hadn't cared too much about examining the structure. Now, he couldn't look away. There was a tall, elliptical outer wall, about fifteen yards high which had only two entrances he could see, one on the south side, and the other on the north.

Only around twenty of their captors remained, the ones that were clad in real soldier's armor. Before they entered, the faul separated from the group, leaving the human Talwreks to lead the prisoners through the southern Valean gate. Before entering, the three of them had their hands bound in front of them. At the entrance, they presented paperwork confirming the validity of their presence, paperwork that was surely falsified. Inside the first gate, a campground of sorts had been set up. Tents plastered the grass and Valean soldiers walked to and fro, tending to their armor, fetching water, and cooking dinner. The inner wall was lower, around ten yards tall, and a great deal smaller than the outer wall. As they were led through the camp, they received suspicious and confused glances from the soldiers. Then, a Valean soldier unlocked the inner gate, and their group was allowed to enter the inner grounds.

The entire premises were symmetrical, split down the middle between Valea and the Shalin Empire. On the far Valean side of the grounds, a stone building was embedded into the inner wall. Wide steps led up to the roof of the building. Galdur figured they served as both a means to reach the roof and places for the king and his advisors to sit. In the center of the inner grounds, there was a large stone discussion stage. According to a book he'd read on the architecture of the grounds, this is where the debates themselves took place.

One of the Talwreks stepped forward and knocked on the door to the stone building. A wave of dread and nausea hit Galdur—he knew exactly who would appear at the door. Soon enough, his fears became reality as his older brother stood in the doorway, glaring with contempt at Galdur.

"Ah, our prisoners," said Fareod Ravinyk. He crossed his arms and stepped down from the dais on which the building stood. "The fifth?"

"She, ah, got away. We haven't found her," said one of the Talwreks.

"I see . . ."

Galdur couldn't take it; he was either going to explode or faint. He now understood precisely what Melkin felt at Thalen's castle. "Murderer!" he shouted, feeling his face flush with his anger. In an instant, a dagger was pressed to his throat. Fareod looked at him disapprovingly and gestured for the guard to let Galdur go.

"That's no way to talk to your king, little brother. I could have you executed for that, you know."

Galdur was too angry to speak—it was all he could do to listen without attacking Fareod.

One Talwrek grabbed Leina's arm. "This one says that she was spying on these prisoners. Elvine wanted to see what you thought before trusting her or killing her."

Fareod raised his eyebrows. "Yes, of course. You remember the letter, right?"

"We weren't sure if she was an imposter," explained the Talwrek. Galdur blinked. Had Fareod been fooled? Was Leina truly a spy in his eyes?

"No, she's definitely Leina Kierth. I'm sure she has plenty of valuable information for me."

"Yes, Your Majesty."

"Now that that's settled, you may take the rest to the prison. I have something special planned for them," said Fareod with an evil grin.

In a daze, Galdur, Lothar, and Melkin were led back to the outer grounds and to a trapdoor. He climbed down the ladder with hands still bound in front of him, and the three were locked into a cell. Lothar looked thoroughly depressed; he'd had the gag in his mouth removed only a few times over the journey to eat or to talk with Elvine. His eyes pleaded with Melkin and Galdur for help.

"Can you see about getting that removed?" shouted Melkin as the Talwreks left the dungeons. They made no indication they'd heard. He sighed. "What is it, the eighth?"

"I think so. The negotiations will take place on the tenth, so that leaves us some time to . . . well, sit here. Do you think Fareod actually believes Leina—"

"I don't know. I hope so. He might be trying to manipulate her, make her think that she's won so she'll divulge information somehow? I'm not sure."

An hour later, a Talwrek reappeared in the dungeons. "Elvine says his gag can be removed, but if he does any magic—"

"She'll torture us?" asked Melkin.

The Talwrek smirked. "Too predictable?"

"Maybe, but we'll take it."

Lothar nodded as well. The man came into the cell, cut the gag off, and even removed the bounds around all their wrists. Lothar coughed, spitting out the cloth and panting. "Finally. Gods, I hate that." He sighed and looked at Melkin and Galdur. "It's going to be a long wait until our execution."

"Would you like to get gagged again?" asked Melkin with a smirk. The trapdoor was opened and closed again, leaving them alone in the prison cell.

"I'll pass, but thanks for the offer."
"Anytime."

45

ASTRID

"After that, I bought a horse and rode it without stopping until the night of the sixth. It then refused to go on, so I ran the rest of the way here. Luckily, I'd slept during part of the day, so I had enough energy to get to your house."

The two made a good team, Astrid had to admit. Both she and Vallec were strong and could row all day.

"So, what do you suppose we do?" asked Vallec after a pause.

"Well, I hoped you might have some ideas. But seeing as you're a Valean soldier, I figured you could sneak into the outer grounds." As it happened, Vallec owned a book about the old Akarist. In it, he found a map of the negotiation grounds, which was quite useful in their scheming. It also reminded Astrid of the oaths that Galdur had explained all those weeks ago and which would soon be made again. The soldiers would swear not to attack unless it was for self-preservation or to protect their nation's officials.

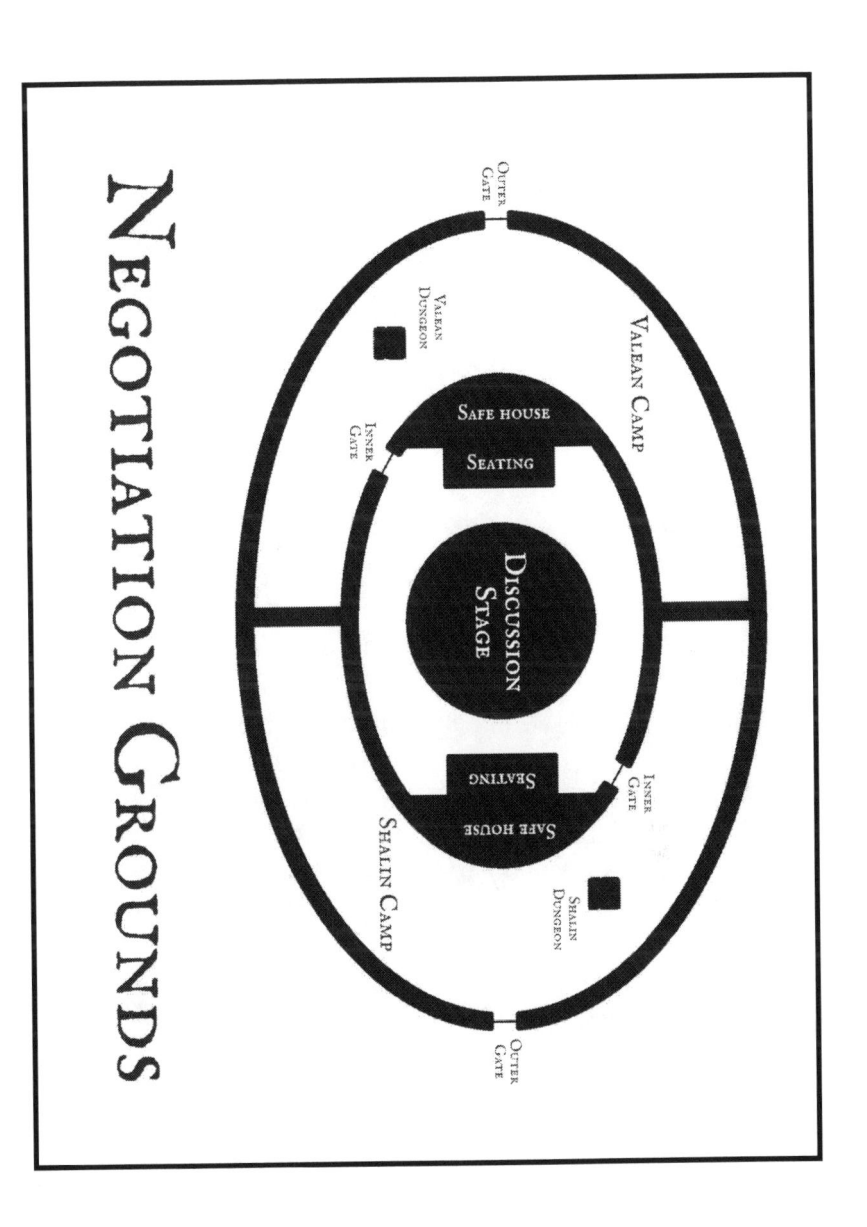

Negotiation Grounds

"The Akarist castle was blown up, so perhaps the same will happen here," suggested Vallec. "Maybe just one side."

Astrid nodded, pushing down the fear that her friends would be blown to bits. "Okay, so that's one possibility. Back in Kaspea, they were discussing a possible assassination."

"Could be."

"We *need* to figure out exactly what they plan to do."

"Perhaps you could sneak behind faul lines?" suggested Vallec.

She thought for a moment. "Maybe. This gambeson is better than nothing, but it's not identical to the official military version."

"And if the Talwreks are orchestrating this thing, they're sure to be all over the negotiation grounds. We could try to gain information, and if needed, save the other three."

"If needed?"

"Well, you say Leina is free. Hopefully she can take care of it. Remember though, if things get dire, we must at least save Galdur. And the Incantir."

Astrid ran her hand over the Incantir in the pocket of her gambeson suit. She could feel its warmth even through the thick cloth. "We certainly won't be able to sneak past the inner gate."

"I know. Perhaps one of us can steal a key? Or if we make it in time, we can sneak in during the night of the ninth."

"I suppose we'll just have to see what happens."

Vallec grimaced. "I'm not too fond of that plan."

"Blame Leina. I learned it from her. At least we might give them a chance." Her voice, she knew, sounded less than certain.

46

Leina

Leina quickly recovered from her shock, remaining straight-faced while Fareod ordered her friends to the dungeons. He turned his attention back to her.

"Now, we must have a conversation in private. I am eager to hear of your findings."

"Are you sure you want to be alone?" asked a Talwrek.

"Absolutely. Now off with you," said Fareod.

The Talwrek pressed her lips together. "Elvine would not approve."

"Elvine is not the king. Now leave us. Come, Leina."

Fear flashed through Leina's mind as she obeyed this young man's command. She couldn't fool herself into believing she had any power in this situation; despite his age, Fareod was king. He followed behind her and locked the door. At the sound, she resisted the urge to try the door handle, to make any effort to escape. Her fear accelerated her pulse and she fought to maintain a blank expression.

"Sit down," said Fareod, gesturing toward a chair before leaving her alone and going up a staircase to her right. She took in her surroundings, a small stone room kept comfortably warm by a central fire. She sat in one of the four wooden chairs around a table with some silverware and plates on it. There were no windows, and the door could be barred by two wooden planks. This was not only a place for the king and his friends to stay before the negotiations; it was a safe house in case anything went wrong.

Fareod came back downstairs. "Apologies, I had to make sure no one else was here," he said with a smile and took a seat across from her.

She folded her hands across the table and looked into his eyes. "What do you wish to know, King Fareod?" she asked, keeping her tone flat. She waited for him to make the first move, to reveal a shred of his intentions. As she stared at him, she noticed some of Gladia's features in Fareod. The high cheekbones, pointed chin, and familiar mannerisms that she hadn't consciously taken note of before.

"I want your help, Leina Kierth." He handed her a small, unmarked black book.

She glanced from the book to his tired eyes. "What's this?"

"It's my account, my diary. The Talwreks don't know about it. The short version is that"—He sucked in a breath, averting his gaze—"I don't want war anymore."

She stared at him in shock, failing for several moments to come up with a response. "Anymore?"

"I just want to stop the Talwreks now."

"And why is that?" asked Leina, keeping a cool tone. Could he be lying? Or might the odds have tipped in their favor?

"They sold me their ideals by arguing that when I inevitably became king, my reign would never be peaceful. My people would always resent that I could not tend to their every need, for there simply would not be enough money to go around. But if I helped them, then there was a chance I would rule over the greatest kingdom in the history of Anzelon. Those seemed like good odds to me, since I believed I would win—humans would win."

"What changed your mind?" asked Leina.

Fareod sighed and rubbed his face, glancing at Leina with a pained expression. She could not pity him, though—not after what he'd done. "After I... killed... my mother... they mentioned something about killing Galdur. I asked why they would have to do that, and they said that in case I died, the crown had to go to my cousin, Esadora, instead of him. They've taken her in and raised her since she was eight."

"What's your point? You know you're a part of their plan. It's only natural that they would have a backup. And you knew that it wasn't Galdur."

"Yes, I know, but that was just the beginning. I was haunted by the death of Gladia—"

"As you should be." She couldn't help it.

Fareod sighed. "Really, Leina, I should think you wouldn't stoop to pettiness right now."

"You don't know me. I've never answered to you."

"I wasn't completely an idiot back then, you know. I knew all the castle staff. I heard how my moth—Gladia spoke of you. But anyway, I kept thinking about Gladia and how she wanted peace, and how she thought it was possible. She really did. And of course, Galdur ran away with you and Melkin and the faul, and so he must have also thought peace was possible. Well, suddenly the plan that had been sold to me as revolutionary and brave seemed like the easy way out, the cowardly path."

"Why do you need me? You're the king. Have them executed and don't obey their plans."

"If only it were that simple, Leina. You probably know how deep it goes." He sighed, resting his hands on the table. "If I were to do that, even if I killed Elvine, I don't know which guards and servants are corrupt. One way or another, I would be poisoned, they would kill Galdur, and Esadora would become queen."

"Why haven't they already done that if you're not totally aligned with their plans?"

"They don't know, obviously. But picture this: the queen, her son, and his brother all assassinated within the span of a month—chaos. Better to just have me rule and force me to appoint Gillan. I don't want them to kill Galdur. I was the one to ask Elvine if he could be put in jail instead of killed."

"You're still a terrible man," said Leina, gritting her teeth and looking down at the table.

"Sticks and stones. Will you help me?" asked Fareod. "Or would you rather I just accept the path I chose when I poisoned her? That I throw you in prison like the rest?"

Leina stared into his eyes for a few moments. They were full of regret and anger. Anger directed at himself, most likely. "What do you need me to do?"

"That depends on what happens in the next two days. You'll be by my side for the negotiations. I don't know what Gillan has planned, but it can't be good. Nowadays, everything is told to me on a need-to-know basis. Maybe it always was."

Leina thought for a moment. He was obviously in over his head and didn't know what needed to be done. What option was there besides helping him, though? She couldn't plan this out—she would have to listen and keep watch constantly to find her opportunity to get her friends out and, if possible, stop a war from happening. She met Fareod's eyes and nodded. Then, her gaze fell once more to the black book in front of her and she held it up. "Can I take this to Galdur and the others?"

"That's why I gave it to you. I don't know who will live through the ninth. If either he or I die, well, I think he'd want to read it beforehand. To know the truth."

47

ASTRID

Two hours before dawn, Astrid approached the northern entrance of the grounds. Two guards stood outside the gate, blazing torches in their hands. She crouched down in the tall grass and moved toward the side of the outer wall, almost between the two camps.

In Hileath, Vallec had bought her two daggers and sheaths. She would have preferred a spear, but she had no way to carry it up a wall. After removing her boots and clipping them to her belt like Melkin had explained, she began to climb the rough, eroded wall. She hadn't practiced much with Melkin, but he had told her, in detail, what climbing a wall was like. Though the cracks in the stone were large and plentiful, climbing to the top was no less intimidating than staring death in the face.

At last, she sat perched atop the wall, relieved no cries of alarm had been called. She looked down—now came the descent. Swallowing her fear and letting out a slow breath, she briefly envied Vallec. He had decided to just wait until the soldiers were going to and from the fortress, gathering supplies in the morning, then he would slip in. But as she touched down on the grass completely unnoticed, her envy vanished. While her eyes had accommodated to the dark night, the bright torches next to the guards' faces surely obscured any movement in the distance. Yes, this was quite a bit better. Silently, she slipped behind a bush, put her boots back on, and waited until morning.

As dawn approached, a bell rang several times. It was loud enough to wake everybody on the entire grounds; negotiations would surely commence shortly. Each camp held around a hundred soldiers, who all started to wake and begin their daily tasks. Astrid emerged from behind her bush and started walking as though she had a purpose. Less than a minute into this façade, she felt as if every pair of eyes was staring at her and looked around for some way out. Her eyes fell upon the trapdoor. After looking around discreetly, she opened it and crawled down the ladder, not daring to look back. It was the prisons of the Shalin grounds marked on the map she and Vallec had studied. Thankfully no one was down here—she needed to think in silence. What was she supposed to be doing? Right, gathering information. How would she... interrogate one of the Talwreks, even if she recognized them? They would attack her far before she could lead them down into the prisons.

An idea began to take shape and she felt the corners of her mouth quirk up in relief. She left the prison and glanced around the camp, eventually finding a face she recognized from the beach in Kaspea. A few seconds later, Astrid was able to make eye contact with her and looked away. Attempting to appear inconspicuous, she again retreated into the prison and stood by the entrance, heart hammering. The trapdoor opened.

"Hello?" She stayed pressed up against the wall, waiting for the door to close. "Who's there?" Surely the girl could hear her heart, right? Then she shut the trapdoor, holding out a dagger as she descended the ladder. Astrid grabbed her arm and pulled her down to the floor, taking her dagger and resting a knee on top of the girl.

"Where is Esadora Ravinyk?" asked Astrid.

"She's not here," gasped the faul.

"So, you know her?" asked Astrid, putting more of her weight on the girl. She was silent. If this bomber knew about Esadora, it meant they had Esadora on their side. If their backup plan for Fareod wasn't here, then Elvine must have something destructive planned. A bombing on either the Shalin or Valean side.

She and Vallec had discussed their assumption that the Akarist bombing was for shock value. Both sides were destroyed and both sides were angry. This would be more precise. A Shalin bombing would anger her people, but a Valean one would make more sense if Esadora was absent.

Astrid leaned in, her face inches from the faul's. "Where are the bombs?" The girl's gaze darted around, but she didn't seem confused. *There are bombs!* Then, the Talwrek sucked in a breath and Astrid quickly clamped her hands over the faul's mouth, muffling her scream. She hadn't thought about that. If she questioned the faul any more, she would alert anyone who was near the trapdoor. Swiftly, she knocked the faul out with the hilt of her dagger and stood up, considering her next move.

48

Lothar

After what could have been a full night or only a minute's worth of sleep, Lothar woke once more on the cold stone floor of the prison cell, covered in sweat. Exhausted as he was, his mind protested sleeping away his last moments in this world. He sat up, panting, as he tried to decipher the time of day. There had originally been a torch lit in the prison, but that had burned out last night, and Lothar couldn't remember if any daylight had shone through the door in previous days.

"Trouble sleeping?" asked Melkin.

Lothar jumped at the voice a foot away from him. He breathed a sigh of relief, glad Melkin too was awake. "I wonder why. I can't believe I'm saying this, but I prefer the blindness of the Akarist rubble to this."

"Ah yes, I have a similar sort of feeling. I also have the distinct memory of being quite annoyed with you then, Lothar."

Lothar grinned, somehow momentarily forgetting their plight. "The feeling was mutual."

"I'm trying to get some sleep here," muttered Galdur, who was presumably curled up on the floor nearby.

"Of course. I forgot, you have a big day ahead of you," said Melkin. Lothar could practically hear the smirk in his voice. "You'll want to be nice and well-rested for your execution."

Lothar chuckled. "Weren't you the one who was preaching positivity? I seem to remember you threatening to gag me again."

"Oh yes, that *was* me, wasn't it? Do as I say, not as I do."

"Wonderful sentiment," murmured Galdur. Lothar was sure that he was still thinking about the diary. Leina had taken it back on the ninth so that no one would see prisoners with it. Since reading it, Galdur had scarcely talked about anything else. He ranted for hours about Fareod's wickedness, how one change of heart could never excuse the murder of his mother. Lothar didn't blame him.

"So, this is what the dungeon of the Akarist was like?" asked Galdur.

"Basically. Except we weren't in the cell, right?" said Lothar.

"No, we were almost at the door," said Melkin. "Then I saved you from some rubble."

"I seem to remember saving you from heat exhaustion as well."

"I would have been alright."

"I highly doubt that."

The three were silent for a moment. For some reason, Lothar looked back on his time buried in rubble with some sort of fondness. Maybe because his escape meant freedom rather than execution.

"Is it morning yet?" asked Melkin.

"I was wondering the same," said Lothar.

"I guess we'll just have to wait until someone comes for us," said Galdur. "Enjoy our down-time until then."

Again, the three were silent. Lothar pondered the fate that awaited them once more. How would they do it? Hang them?

"Ryne's sake!" cried Melkin, slamming a fist on the stone.

Lothar jumped, snapping his head up to face Melkin. "What's wrong?"

"What's wrong? Everything's wrong for Ryne's sake! We're all about to die horrific deaths and we're just waiting here! Doing nothing!"

"We're all scared. We're all furious. There are a thousand things that could be going better right now, but there are just as many that could be going worse. Astrid and Leina got away, and Leina's less than a few hundred yards away. They will do everything they can, and presumably, so will Fareod," said Lothar, resting his head against the stone wall and trying to convince himself to believe his own words.

"I know . . . I just . . ." Melkin sighed.

"Plus, Elvine might let you live," said Galdur.

"My death is not what I fear. No, I dread that you two die and Elvine's plan comes to fruition. After today, either Valea or the Shalin Empire may be torn to shreds! Or both! Ryne, I just hate sitting here and waiting, it's driving me insane!"

Lothar put a hand on Melkin's shoulder and sighed. "You know, Galdur said you weren't religious, but if Ryne isn't smiling down on you for everything you've done, well . . . that seems improbable to me. I believe that if *I* die, Molaib will give me a good afterlife. Don't you see everything we've done?"

"Yeah, absolutely nothing as of now."

"You're wrong. We've tried to save thousands of lives, and there's a sliver of a chance that we might still succeed. I choose to believe that matters," said Lothar. "Why did you survive the Akarist? Was it luck? Or was there something else there? That was a question I asked myself a few weeks ago. Out of all of the people there, you and I were the ones to survive."

"That's . . . that's something," admitted Melkin.

"It sure is," said Galdur.

"I know. Maybe we were spared by chance, I'm willing to admit that. But then again, maybe not. So, I'll sit here for another few hours and hope that it wasn't. After all, why would I have survived that just to die here?"

"I—I just don't think I can convince myself of that," said Melkin.

"I understand. To be honest, Melkin, I think I'm just as afraid and angry as you are right now. For Talen's sake, I don't want Valea or the Shalin Empire to be destroyed—for hundreds of thousands to die. In spite of everything, though, I'm glad to have met the two of you." A tear ran down his face. "I—I never thought I would ever work with humans, much less become friends with them or trust them with my life."

"Likewise." Galdur embraced him, and Lothar felt more tears run down his cheeks. "Who would have thought the prince of Valea would become close friends with faul? It's unheard of."

Lothar choked back a sob. "Not anymore it isn't."

"I'm glad to have met you, Lothar," said Melkin.

A bell rang, signaling the start of the day. Lothar wiped the tears from his face.

"No more waiting then," said Galdur.

"Indeed," replied Melkin. Lothar could swear he heard his friend's voice shaking.

Five minutes later, the trapdoor was shoved open, and several guards descended. One entered the cell and gagged Lothar again. He loathed the rough cloth filling his mouth, but at least it couldn't last too long, right? They were then led out into the daylight and had their hands bound behind their backs again.

"Ah!" cried Melkin, struggling against his bonds to try shielding his eyes from the glaring sun. Lothar squinted, glancing around the campsite for a hint of what was happening. The inner gate was unlocked for the soldiers to enter the negotiation grounds. They would be standing on either side of the seats for the king and his advisors, Galdur had told him and Melkin. After the Valean soldiers had entered, the gate was locked once more, leaving Lothar and the others still on the outer grounds.

"You'll go in when it's time," growled a guard in Lothar's ear. He didn't know if he was a true guard or a Talwrek. He supposed it didn't matter. They had all been branded as traitors anyway.

"My side is ready, Emperor Orwic," he heard Fareod say.

"And so is mine," said Orwic. "Let the negotiations begin."

"We propose that you give reasons for why you would declare war," said a Shalin advisor, presumably taking the floor. "And then we may come to an agreement."

"Though you should know that if demands are too high, we are also fully prepared to declare war," said another Shalin advisor. A pause as the advisors took their seats again and a Valean advisor stepped up. No—it was the voice of Gillan.

"Let it be noted that I am speaking on behalf of King Fareod as his second-in-command."

"Your role is noted," said the Shalin Advisor. "Now, the reasons."

Certainly. I think it would be best to show you." The gate was unlocked and the three were led through. As his pulse accelerated, he felt like he was suffocating. His gaze darted around the inner grounds to the dozens of Shalin and Valean advisors. As he stepped onto the stone stage, he envisioned the weathered bricks running red with blood. The thought made him shudder. His guard brought him to the right side of Valea's half of the stage while Melkin and Lothar were led to the left. True fear showed in their eyes, fear that surely reflected his own. Hope flared within him as he noticed Leina was seated beside Fareod.

"What's this?" shouted Orwic.

Gillan grinned, stepping forward with outstretched hands. "If we set aside the matter of bombings of the past few years in Valea, and the destruction of the Akarist, there is one more grievous act that your country has committed!"

"How dare—"

"This faul here, Lothar Raiken, poisoned our queen! Queen Gladia is dead because of him!" Lothar felt his eyebrows shoot up; that was news to him.

Orwic himself now stepped on the stage. "Even if that is true, which I highly doubt, we did not send him to do such a thing! He is a criminal, even in our country."

Gillan flashed a conciliatory smile. "Right, of course. He broke this one out of jail, Melkin Edaireth. Edaireth is a castle spy and thus knows every inch of our royal castle. He would have known how to access the queen's food and which poisons to use—all of it. The two worked together. We have witnesses of Lothar in the castle. Perhaps you branded him as a criminal simply to hide that it was your country who killed our queen. Or maybe you didn't. It doesn't matter. For decades, nay centuries, your people and government alike have committed atrocities against the innocent people of Valea. That is why you must be destroyed. You yourself, Emperor Orwic, may have no intention of harming us, but your people certainly do, and there's nothing you can do to stop them."

The Shalin Empire was silent for a few moments as Gillan's booming voice reverberated throughout the grounds.

"Why is your prince also on the stage then?" asked a Shalin advisor.

"He made an assassination attempt on King Fareod. He is also up here for another reason, though—"

"So, this is it then? You'll kill Raiken, Edaireth, and the prince? And then what, declare war?" asked Emperor Orwic.

"Possibly, possibly. But I have one solution for you, Emperor. One way in which we might come to an agreement." Gillan's grinning face turned serious. "It involves the renouncement of a thing you faul dearly treasure. Sort of a . . . peace agreement and a warning all in one. But before I tell you, there's one more thing you need to know." The guard beside Lothar handed him a rock. He stared at it in confusion. His mind was numb; fear had consumed all rational thought.

Orwic stepped forward. "What?"

"Lothar Raiken. He is the last of the Golanirs."

"The Golanirs have already died out!" proclaimed an advisor.

"This here is the great-great-grandson of Revina Raiken, whose maiden name was Golanir. Her brother was Rowan Golanir."

"It can't be . . ." said Orwic.

"It absolutely is. Go ahead, Lothar Golanir," said Gillan. Lothar stared at the rock in his hand with wide eyes. *Talen, no. It can't be. How could he have been so stupid? Maybe he thought that Elvine, a faul, wouldn't do it. But he was wrong.* He heard cries from the faul soldiers. An outrage—just what the Talwreks wanted. He stood now in the same position as his renowned ancestor.

Orwic jabbed a finger toward Gillan, his face flushed. "If you make him perform elentac, it will be unforgivable. You don't know what you're asking, human!"

"Remember your oath," said Gillan, looking around at the guards. Lothar looked up; Melkin and Galdur had daggers held to their throats. Lothar could see a bead of blood had dripped down Melkin's neck. The guard beside him untied his gag—they knew he would have to call his magic.

"Gillan, please. We can have peace; we can work together! If this faul really did kill your queen, you may execute him. But you may not do this."

"Oh, no. This is how your people will know not to trifle with us. This is how we will create peace, Orwic."

"You're hopelessly misguided! Please, I beg of you!"

Gillan was silent. All eyes were upon Lothar as he held the stone. Surely all of the faul expected him to refuse this process. He would, right?

He looked back at the young prince he had come to know over the past weeks. Galdur was their only hope. The Talwreks would find a way to start a war between Valea and the Shalin Empire whether Lothar performed elentac or not. Only Galdur, as king of Valea, could have a chance at stopping it. He, along with Melkin, would be tortured to death should Lothar not go through with this. If nothing else, he could stall for time by following Gillan's orders.

Magic was his one gift, he had told Galdur. Could he give it up to save Anzelon? If he had to die either way, would elentac really be much worse than hanging or beheading? Even as he tried to convince himself, he knew it was a lie. Elentac would be far, *far* worse. Nothing might come of it, either. He might rip himself to pieces, drive out his very being, for no reason at all.

"We need not declare war," offered Gillan, "once justice has been served."

"Call it off. Call it off and we may have peace," said Orwic dangerously. "This is not justice."

Long ago, it seemed, Lothar said he wouldn't perform elentac for anything. But as he stared at his captive friends, both of whom could be dead within seconds, a strange, unheard-of question rushed to the front of his mind: Would he do it for everything?

49

LEINA

She watched the scene unfold with horror. Fareod had given every bit of speaking power to Gillan—or perhaps it had been taken from him. As the man ranted, Fareod's face remained flat—he seemed to be mentally elsewhere. She could do nothing but watch as her friends were led to the stage and the talk between Orwic and Gillan commenced. The setup was perfect. There was no time for evidence, and the Talwreks certainly had many guards who would lie about seeing Lothar. Orwic probably thought that Gillan was ignorant or simply insane for demanding such a thing to initiate peace. It was all calculated, though. Gillan didn't intend to come to an agreement; he wanted conflict.

She leaned in, her face inches from Fareod's ear. "Do something!"

He jumped, broken from his trance. "I—uh—do what?" Sweat was dripping down his face—the idiot was petrified.

"Stop this! You're the king. Call it off," commanded Leina in a hushed tone as Orwic pleaded with Gillan. What was the point of being by Fareod's side if he wouldn't do anything? All of a sudden, Lothar fell to his knees; a blazing bright red aura cast out from him.

He was muttering, his face reflecting pure agony. *He's going to die.* The thought echoed in her mind, paralyzing her for a few precious seconds. Every voice from the Shalin Empire cried out in horror and anger. Swears, slurs, and pleas of mercy were thrown at the humans.

"I can't . . . or else Elvine will—"

"Elvine wins if you don't do this *one* thing!" growled Leina, tears freely falling down her face—she couldn't watch. "Have you really turned away from the path you took?" Fareod whipped his head around to the stage.

"Stop! Release them!"

The guards lifted their daggers from the necks of Melkin and Galdur, and Lothar immediately stopped channeling his magic into the stone. The red aura disappeared as he dropped to the ground. Leina rushed from her seat and onto the stage beside Lothar. His face was calm now, and she hastily grabbed his wrist and checked for a pulse. Slow, but it was there.

The guards by Lothar stood confused, neither hindering nor helping her. She spun around, taking in the chaos of the scene. Individual soldiers from all around the grounds began to emerge from their ranks—Talwreks. With dread, she remembered the oaths. She and her friends were as good as dead without any extra help. She whirled around—a faul was running toward her, daggers drawn. Leina scrambled to her feet, weaponless. The guards still did nothing. "Do something!"

"We can't attack!" said one of them.

"He's not a soldier!" cried Leina, pointing at the approaching faul.

"Neither of you are protected by Fareod."

Leina's gaze darted toward the stands, but Fareod was engaged in an argument with Gillan and unable to help her. "Give me your dagger!" shouted Leina. The soldier glanced at his companion before obliging. The realization that this was her first fight to the death only occurred to her as she parried the faul's first strike. His two daggers weaved in and out and Leina struggled to keep them both in sight. The faul was nowhere near as good as Astrid, but she had only the one dagger to defend herself with. She backed up a step and hit Lothar with her heel. Retreating was not an option. She would die between her attacker and Lothar, or she would best him. He jabbed at her side, and she parried it away, opening him up to attack. She lunged in but was blinded by a flash of light. She felt his dagger slice into her torso and doubled over in pain, barely dodging his next attack. The faul then stumbled back, blood soaking his tunic from her earlier lunge. Taking advantage of the moment, she grabbed and twisted the faul's left hand, evading his auxlar dagger and stabbing him in the chest, piercing through his gambeson layer. Dead, he fell to the stage.

"I'm... an official! A spy of the castle! Protect me!" gasped Leina, trying to remain standing. The pain was overwhelming, and the guards were just *watching*.

"Not technically. You ran away."

"I was sitting right next to Fareod! He trusts me! I'm his top spy!"

The two guards looked at each other, silent for a moment. She pressed them. "I'm... trying to save... an innocent, tortured faul... for Ryne's sake!" A man started to run toward her from the sidelines. Tall, clad in plate armor and handling a giant spear. "Please..."

Her legs gave way, leaving her collapsed on the stage beside Lothar. She put more pressure on the wound, wincing as the agonizing pain grew more intense. The two guards stepped in front of her and fought the incoming man until he too fell to the stage. Turning her head, she reached for Lothar and felt his pulse again—it hadn't changed. *Please, please don't let him die.* She unlaced her jerkin and saw her tunic soaked with an alarming amount of blood. She fought to hold more pressure on the wound.

Shouts echoed from all around her. In the cacophony of unfamiliar voices, she was able to pick out a few she recognized. Melkin, Fareod, Gillan, Galdur, and... was that Vallec that she heard? No, it couldn't be. She must have been hallucinating. *Stay awake. Stay awake.*

50

VALLEC

Vallec strode around the campsite, finally in his comfort zone. It had been simple, really; all he did was wait until the morning bell rang and the soldiers departed to gather wood and water. With the outer gate unlocked, he walked in, clad in the official Valean uniform. Vallec knew how these sorts of things were run; he had accompanied Taleek on every single one of his Akistaria missions. He approached a man digging through a pack of supplies. "Where are the spare weapons? My dagger broke, some shoddy thing from the north."

"There's an armory tent on the right side of the right inner wall," said the man, not looking up at Vallec.

As he walked to the armory tent, the negotiations commenced and Melkin, Galdur, and Lothar were led from the prisons onto the grounds. He fought the urge to yell out to them and instead focused his attention on reaching the group of tents by the wall. The first few were soldier tents, but the fourth had a sizable stash of weapons. He stored several daggers and two sheaths of throwing knives in a pack he'd brought. Sure, he looked ridiculous carrying a bag in full plate armor, but perhaps observers would believe he was fetching supplies for someone. In the current circumstances he wouldn't be questioned. The guard by the inner gate held a key in his hand as the negotiations progressed. He could do nothing but wait. His pulse accelerated as Gillan and Orwic debated, and he realized what the Talwreks' plan entailed. Silence fell on the whole group. Then, everything erupted into shouts and cries of injustice, especially from the faul.

Finally, a booming shout demanding the prisoners be set free rang in his ears—Fareod's voice.

"Open the gate!" shouted a Valean commander.

"Yes sir!" As soon as the lock clicked, Vallec ran through, along with several other guards. His gaze fell upon Galdur and Melkin, hands bound in front of them, cowering back against the inner wall. He glanced around, spotting a 'soldier' running toward his helpless friends with a drawn sword. Vallec sprinted, spear in hand, exhilaration coursing through his veins. Would he be too slow?

Melkin put himself in front of Galdur, awaiting the incoming slash that never came. A moment before the sword came down upon the two, Vallec struck it aside and countered with a stab toward the man's gut. Vallec pulled his spear free and the man dropped to the ground just before another swung his spear down at Vallec's head. He easily deflected it and bashed the end of his spear into the young man's armor plates, pushing him off balance before stabbing between the plates.

After ensuring no more attackers immediately threatened them, Vallec dropped his pack on the ground and drew his dagger, cutting the bonds on Galdur and Melkin. They each retrieved throwing knives and a dagger from the pack and strapped them on. Vallec stood in front of the two, concealing their freedom as much as possible and watching for more attackers. He was a guard, after all. He felt his skin grow hot and his armor begin to burn and looked around for the culprit. A faul had snuck up on him. Clad in only gambeson, he knocked her to the ground with a nonlethal strike to her torso. As she groaned in pain from her likely-broken ribs, Vallec sucked in a breath of air, cooling his body as much as he could.

"Kill the prince!" shouted a female voice from somewhere within the grounds. He turned to find the source, but she was nowhere to be found.

"Vallec!" cried Melkin.

He spun around, looking for enemies. "What?"

"You're . . . here!"

Vallec laughed, relief filling him though danger still lurked nearby. "So I am. I swore I would be."

51

ASTRID

Astrid shook her head—she had a better plan than luring Talwreks into the dungeons and assaulting them. As the negotiations began, Astrid left the dungeon and the unconscious faul behind. She jogged around the campgrounds, looking for a familiar face. Finally, she found another Talwrek from the beach. In an instant, she drew her dagger on the boy—he was younger than her by the looks of him. All eyes turned toward her at once. The practical approach.

"Where is the bomb? Tell me now!"

"I don't know . . . w—what you're talking about!" said the faul, cowering back and looking around frantically as she stepped forward. She heard the hesitation; he'd tried to conceal his slip-up. Soldiers surrounded her, yet no weapons were brought to either her or the Talwrek's throat. They stood back, watching the confrontation. The Talwrek made no attempt to either attack her or kill himself, which was a good start, she figured.

"Listen, if you tell me, it will all turn out, alright? You'll have your peace, you just won't have to die for it! That sound like a good deal? Come on, don't lose hope when you don't have to!"

Seemingly gaining some resolve, the young faul stepped forward. "Listen to what's going on out there! There is no going back!"

The word elentac rang out, but she couldn't focus on it. Vallec would save them—he said he would. Astrid lowered her dagger and stepped forward. "It's never too late! Not if you help me. Right now. You're surrounded by people—soldiers that don't want to die. Tell me! Now!"

His wild, darting eyes eventually steadied and met her own. "Valea's side. I don't know where, I swear. She doesn't tell us!"

Astrid turned around to face all the shocked faul. "Move!" She sprinted through the throng of soldiers, arriving at the inner gate. Shouts and screams echoed from the inner grounds—a fight had broken out. She yanked the gate, but the heavy iron door remained shut. "Isn't there any way to get this thing open, for Oberel's sake!" Swiftly, the guard with the key unlocked it for her and she burst into the inner grounds. Leina was lying on the stage next to Lothar, guards defending the two. Vallec, Melkin, and Galdur were defending themselves from any Talwreks intent on eliminating them. Astrid sprinted up to the three, heart pounding.

"There's a bomb... Valea's side. Vallec, go look for it, I'll take over." She leaned on her knees for a second, panting.

"On it!" He checked for attackers once more before sprinting away.

"Astrid, you're here!" cried Galdur, grinning in spite of the danger they were in.

"Wouldn't miss it for the world." Then, two attackers sprang from the crowd of soldiers. "Watch out!"

A woman and a faul sprinted toward the prince. Galdur threw a knife at the faul and hit his shoulder while Astrid moved in from the side to engage the woman before she could reach Galdur. She had come to loathe fighting dagger against spear, but she defended herself against the skillful warrior until Galdur came to her aid, splitting the woman's focus. Between them, they were able to disarm and wound her.

Astrid picked up the woman's spear, noticing that the true guards from both sides were standing around, horror plastered on their faces. Neither Orwic nor Fareod, nor the guards themselves were in direct danger, though. Astrid spotted a group of Talwreks gathering at the Valean side—around a dozen, drawing their weapons and pointing at the three.

"Incoming!" shouted Astrid

Melkin glanced around, his eyes focusing on the wall behind him. "Climb!" he shouted at Galdur.

"I'm not leaving you two!" Galdur shouted back.

"Just go!" cried Melkin. With a pained glance between the two, Galdur removed his boots, sheathed his dagger, and began the climb. Three faul from the Shalin side sprinted at Melkin and Astrid, daggers out. The all-too-familiar sensation of air leaving her lungs hit her, filling her with panic. The furthest of the three faul was muttering, and Melkin threw a knife at him, freeing her from the spell. Gasping for air, Astrid engaged the closest faul while Melkin took on the other.

"They're coming!" shouted Melkin. The dozen Talwreks that had gathered began sprinting toward them from across the inner grounds. Astrid and Melkin easily defeated the two faul, leaving them wounded on the grass. She breathed a short-lived sigh of relief, dropping her spear and kicking off her boots. "Let's go!"

She and Melkin began to ascend, not daring to look back at the horde of Talwreks pursuing them.

52

Melkin

Halfway up the wall, Melkin let go with his right hand to lessen the agony and look back at the fighting scene. Fareod and Gillan had ceased their shouting, presumably because Gillan was directing the Talwreks now. Fareod was sitting, petrified, on the steps again. The Shalin soldiers had formed a circle around Orwic and his advisors, but no one threatened the emperor. Earlier, he had heard Elvine demand that Galdur be killed, but he didn't see her.

As the pain in his right hand grew unbearable, so did his regret for climbing this wall in the first place. Yet as he looked down at the dozen Talwreks crowding the wall below, he felt relief fill him. Melkin climbed faster than the other two, reaching the top before either of them did and resting for a moment on the five-foot-thick wall. The thin, flimsy prison shoes worked quite well for climbing, he found. Astrid came next, grunting with exertion as Melkin helped her to the top. Galdur was close, one hand on the edge. Melkin blinked as a flash of something passed in his peripheral vision and Galdur cried out in pain. He peered over to see a crossbow bolt embedded in the side of Galdur's calf. *Ryne's sake*. He leaned over the edge and grabbed Galdur's wrist with his good hand while Astrid grabbed the other. Melkin grunted in effort as he and Astrid hauled Galdur over the ledge, trying to ignore the scream of pain that left the prince's lips. The man who shot was reloading—they had to go.

"What now?" gasped Galdur, examining his leg.

"I don't know. I'm watching Fareod, waiting to see what happens." Melkin grasped the arrow shaft and broke it in half. Galdur yelped but stayed still. "Leave that in for now—we'll deal with it later," said Melkin. From the arrow's position, he could tell it hadn't hit bone.

He focused his eyes on the steps. "It's Elvine!" She was descending the inner wall, above the Valean safe house. Once she reached the roof, she sprinted down the steps, a dagger in her hand. Melkin knew what was about to happen an instant before it did. Elvine thrust her dagger through Fareod's back. As the king gasped in pain, she turned and retreated up to the roof.

"Fareod!" cried Galdur. "Oh, by Ryne!"

"Come on, let's go!" shouted Melkin. "See if we can reason with Orwic!" He stood up and started running behind Astrid and Galdur, toward the Shalin section. Less than halfway across the inner grounds, he was nearly tossed off the wall by an intense gust of wind. The three flattened themselves against the stone, grasping at the cracks and crevices to keep themselves from falling.

Four faul had climbed a rope secured to the top of the wall and were blocking their path to Orwic and his advisors. The faul were advancing and would soon be able to engage them in close combat, with magic on their side. Suddenly, the stones grew hot beneath Melkin.

"Oberel!" swore Astrid.

"Stay down!" cried Melkin as he drew two knives from his sheath. There was no way he could throw so far from his prostrate position. He prayed that he could aim with his almost useless left hand and his right one in agony. If there was a time for luck, it was now. He burst up from behind Astrid and Galdur, throwing a dagger from each hand with as much force as he could muster. As soon as he released the two deadly blades, he was swept off his feet by a strong gust. He grasped the edge of the stone wall but failed to find a foothold. After the grueling climb up, his right hand now refused to hold on any longer, leaving him dangling by only his left. There was still no foothold to be found. Had his luck finally run out? Had he served his purpose? He was exhausted from the earlier climb, from the fighting, from everything. *Please, Ryne, let Astrid and Galdur be safe*, he thought as his left hand gave way, and he plummeted to the ground.

53

VALLEC

Vallec rushed back through the gate to the outer grounds. "There's a bomb somewhere here on our side! It's probably going to have blue powder on or near it. Find it! And don't touch it!" Having nothing better to do than listen to a complete stranger, the guards sprang into action. Vallec himself started searching in the tents, in the prison, all around the grounds. Would it just be some powder on the ground like Melkin had seen at the Akarist? No... it was probably something they wouldn't just be able to shovel out. Hopefully it would be obvious enough to find.

Agonizing minutes later, the search was still fruitless. He ran back through the inner gate to see what was happening; the shouts and screams had been unrelenting for the entire search, and he was growing increasingly worried.

He spotted Astrid, Melkin, and Galdur atop the wall and breathed a sigh of relief. Galdur had a crossbow bolt through his leg, but other than that, they seemed relatively safe. He rushed to the steps and gasped at what he saw; Fareod had a dagger in his chest. Other soldiers were tending to him, but they parted for Vallec. He felt like he was channeling Taleek's authority, copying the mannerisms that Vallec himself had always admired.

"He's not dead yet..." said a soldier with a hand on Fareod's wrist. It was hopeless though; Vallec had seen enough death to know that nothing would help.

"I..." mumbled the dying Fareod, "relinquish...my...power."

The words made no sense to Vallec; this was not the Fareod that Astrid had described. But that didn't matter anymore—the words could save his friends. He sprinted to the roof of the stone building overlooking the red-stained negotiation grounds and sucked in a breath. "Defend your new king! Defend Galdur Ravinyk!" He then rushed down on stage beside Leina and Lothar. He kept yelling, "King Fareod is dead! Defend King Galdur! Hold true to your oaths!" There were probably more Talwrek spies on the grounds, but Vallec doubted they would reveal themselves—every soldier of Valea was bound to protect their king. They wouldn't try to kill Galdur, at least.

"Vallec!" cried Leina weakly. She was sitting on the ground, holding her stomach.

Vallec kneeled beside her and sucked in a breath. There was a lot of blood. "Listen to me, Leina. Don't give up. I've seen people come back from worse."

"Like...yourself?" asked Leina, holding the wound.

"Exactly."

"I found it!" shouted a voice from behind him.

"Guard her!" cried Vallec to a group of nearby soldiers.

"I don't know if we can..." said one of them.

"She's one of King Galdur's spies, you *have* to." After a moment of indecision, Vallec dropped his spear and picked up Lothar in his arms. He was quite light and alarmingly unresponsive. The soldier had cried out to him from between the stairs and the stone wall of the building. There, a group of soldiers were crowded around a hole in the ground. "Move!" They parted for him as he knelt by the three-foot hole, at the bottom of which laid an iron box. "Do you know if it's fixed underground somehow?"

"Yes, sir. We dug around it a bit and there are pieces of metal buried deep under the earth. It would take hours to remove it." Vallec stared down the hole, guessing the explosive was precisely measured and placed so that it would kill everyone in the Valean camp, but leave the Shalin camp and the emperor alive.

"Lothar, come on, talk to me," he said, laying him on the ground. He clamped a hand over Lothar's wrist and found a weak pulse. Gently, he grabbed Lothar's shoulders and tried to sit him up a little.

"Vallec?" asked Lothar weakly, eyelids fluttering open. "What are you doing here?"

54

GALDUR

"Melkin!" cried Galdur as his friend's hand disappeared from the top of the wall.

"We have to move!" shouted Astrid, jogging forward to engage the two remaining faul. Galdur couldn't make himself look over the edge—they had to keep going. He threw a knife at one of their attackers and the stones immediately cooled down as he hit his mark. Astrid defeated the last faul while Galdur limped in agony, and she ran back to assist him. With one arm over Astrid's shoulders, Galdur felt the pain lessen, and the two began to make their way over to Orwic's side of the grounds.

"Here, take it," said Astrid, handing him the Incantir. "They need to know *you* found it." Galdur nodded and grasped the invaluable artifact. He tried to ignore the pain in his leg as they traversed the top of the wall. He had heard Vallec shout that Fareod had died and that he was now king but hadn't yet processed the words. He did notice, however, that no more crossbow bolts had been shot at him. It seemed that the Valean soldiers were protecting him now.

They were almost close enough to call down to Orwic. A few faul advisors spotted them and gestured to them, whispering to Orwic. The crowd of guards around the emperor led him up to the roof of the stone structure, only five yards below Galdur and Astrid.

"Emperor . . . Orwic!" he shouted.

Orwic glanced around, rage on his face. "What in Talen's name is going on?"

"Our monarchy has been infiltrated by those who desire only war, only destruction. But no more! Fareod was corrupted by these people, but I am not. And I would like to offer you something." He hoped his voice held some sort of authority, or a hint of confidence he was sorely lacking at the moment. "Emperor Orwic and all the peoples of the Shalin Empire!" He held the Incantir high. "I offer you the Incantir as a gesture of peace. I offer it to right past wrongs, though such things can never truly be undone. I offer it so that we can finally live in harmony. Do you accept this gesture?"

"Can it really be . . . ?" said Orwic with wide eyes. Three faul below began muttering, and Galdur released the orb to gently swirling air currents which carried it down toward the emperor.

Suddenly, the object was swept from its path. Galdur whipped his head around to find that another hand had taken the orb. Elvine. She stood in the center of the stage, Gillan next to her, as well as two more faul—at least one of whom must have been an air wielder. The Valean and Shalin armies, including Emperor Orwic himself, rushed to surround them.

Orwic's mouth dropped open. "Persec? By Talen!"

"What a lovely reunion," said Elvine. "And before you think about taking this, just know that I can blow this place up on a whim. Try me."

55

Vallec

"Can you do magic?" asked Vallec, gently shaking Lothar.

"Talen . . . I can barely move . . ."

"Lothar . . . you have to. There's a bomb right next to you. If Persec decides to, she could blow up the entire Valean side, as well as the inner grounds. You have to disable it."

"Can't we all just move?" mumbled Lothar, his eyelids drooping.

Vallec gently shook him awake again. "No. Persec is right there, in front of these stands. We can't move now. If she decides Emperor Orwic won't declare war, then it's over."

Lothar sat up with Vallec's help and looked down the hole. "That metal box there?" He nodded and turned his attention back to the emperor and former empress.

"Persec, my niece, why would you do this? King Galdur gave me the Incantir. We won't have war!" cried Emperor Orwic.

"You won't declare war?" she asked.

"No!"

"But will you prevent the battles? Will you heal the relationship between faul and human?"

Orwic was silent.

"Vallec. I can do it." Vallec whirled around, watching as Lothar took a deep breath and started muttering. He looked calm, at peace, even. Vallec couldn't even tell if he was actually doing anything; the faul's eyes were closed as he sat next to the hole, his lips moving almost imperceptibly.

"Why stay on the brink of war, when it can all be over?" asked Persec.

"Give me the Incantir!" shouted Orwic.

A soft thud sounded from behind him; Vallec looked behind and saw Lothar had collapsed back onto the grass.

"Did you do it?" asked Vallec, kneeling beside Lothar.

"Yes." Lothar's eyes closed and he fell unconscious again.

"Check for a pulse!" Vallec whispered to the nearest soldier. He peeked out from behind the stairs to glimpse the confrontation.

"If you refuse to declare war . . . then I must take matters into my own hands."

"He's alive," said the guard behind Vallec. He nodded and braced himself for an explosion. Sweat dripped down his face in rivulets and fear hung heavy in the air as all expected to be blown to bits at any point. Prayers to Ryne were muttered from soldiers asking for a good afterlife and for the safety of their families.

Vallec knelt and put a hand over the hole and quickly withdrew it as the intense rising heat touched his palm. No explosion came.

"What!" cried Persec, spinning around to look at the Valean side. "I—What is—?"

"You three faul . . . are under arrest!" cried Orwic.

"And so is Gillan!" shouted a voice from the top of the wall. Galdur. Vallec emerged from behind the stairs and squinted, seeing Galdur and Astrid. Where was Melkin? He rushed back through the inner gate and ran along the perimeter of the inner wall, finding a body a few feet from the separating wall between countries.

"No . . . No!" He kneeled beside the unmoving body, grasping Melkin's wrist.

"Vallec . . ." said Melkin in a weak voice. "I'm alive . . . my legs . . ."

Vallec let out an enormous sigh of relief. "Broken?"

Melkin managed a small nod. Worry shone in his eyes. "Vallec... are they okay? What's going on?"

Vallec grinned, tears running down his face. "It's going to be okay. Persec and Gillan were just arrested. Emperor Orwic has the Incantir."

Melkin grinned, and then winced. "Thank you, Vallec. I'd be dead without you. Again. By Ryne, I heard how you commanded those soldiers. Taleek... he would be so proud of you."

"He believed in you too, Melkin. He's smiling down on both of us right now."

56

GALDUR

Each time Galdur glanced at his leg, he instantly turned away. Somehow, the pain was only mildly agonizing if he couldn't see the wound. He was sure it would get worse later, but that wasn't important now.

"I'm sure he's fine," consoled Astrid, placing a hand on Galdur's shoulder as the two sat atop the wall, waiting for a rope to be secured for the two of them.

"He fell from ten yards!" cried Galdur, wincing as his leg continued to pain him.

"There's nothing we can do about it."

Finally, the rope was secured, and the two made their way down. Once they reached the top of the Shalin building, faul and human soldiers alike surrounded them, all trying to ensure the two were safe.

"Is Melkin okay? What about Lothar? And Leina?" he asked the soldiers. He received only deflections and shrugs before Vallec arrived, panting.

"They're all okay," he reassured Galdur.

He breathed a sigh of relief and turned to Astrid. "We . . . did it."

"I know..."

Tears began to form in his eyes. He shook his head in disbelief. His mind was numb—it was all a blur. He went from traitor and prisoner to king in... how many minutes? He looked at the sun; it was still early in the morning, so the whole event couldn't have been that long.

"King Galdur, you need medical help. Now!" said a guard beside him.

"Have the others received help already?"

Vallec nodded, looking around impatiently. "Yes, they're all being helped by medics. Lothar was given to the Shalin medics after he passed out from disabling the bomb. Galdur, he's right. You need to get that wound treated."

"Where is Emperor Orwic?"

"He and his advisors are talking in the safe house, debating what to do. From what I heard, you two will reconvene tomorrow for final negotiations," said a faul soldier.

"Where is my brother?"

Vallec swallowed, looking behind for a second. "He's not dead yet. He relinquished his power and was taken to a medical tent. He's not going to make it."

Galdur winced at the pain in his leg, but steadied his breathing, meeting Vallec's gaze. "Take me to him."

After a few torturous minutes, he arrived at the entrance to one of the tents. Ducking inside, he saw Fareod lying on a blanket, a gaping wound in his chest.

"Galdur... come... here..." mumbled Fareod. Galdur kneeled beside him as best he could. "I'm going to die..."

Galdur nodded. He remembered kneeling by Gladia's bed when she was first found to be ill, Fareod beside him. "Fareod..."

"I'm sorry," muttered Fareod. He closed his eyes; his breathing was slowing by the second.

Though the walk here had left him with no clue as to what to say to Fareod, it now came to Galdur in a rush. "Thank you, Fareod. Without you, my friends and I would be dead and Anzelon would be in turmoil. You've done a truly honorable thing—that is undeniable. For your actions, Ryne might even grant you a good afterlife. But I do not forgive you, my brother."

Fareod nodded his head almost imperceptibly. "I deserve nothing more."

The next morning, a guard woke Galdur for the final negotiations. Only a few were awakened for this meeting, since neither he nor Orwic had requested any advisors. With just a party of five guards helping him walk to the negotiation stage, the place felt ominous and eerily quiet. Guards had toiled all throughout the previous day, tending to the injured, counting the dead, and removing the bodies. Still, blood stained the grass and stone stage on which Galdur walked, adding to his unease. He sat in one of two chairs center-stage, arranged by guards the previous night. "I'm tired," he complained with a yawn. The soldiers around him laughed.

"Me too, King Galdur," said one of them.

A short while later, Orwic arrived with his five guards, and he sat down a few feet from Galdur. He had never seen the emperor up close before. He had a small, silver beard and shoulder-length silver hair. His face was stern but kind.

"Emperor Orwic," greeted Galdur.

"King Galdur," Orwic said in return.

"Let's keep this short. I want you to *not* declare war, to recall all your troops from the border, and to work with us to strengthen the relationship between our nations. I will do the same."

"You know, King Galdur, a month ago I would have only agreed to the first. But now . . . I submit to all three. If nothing else, to prove the terrorists who invaded your country wrong, I suppose. Do you really think our people can come to accept one another?"

"Slowly, but yes. I do believe that. Astrid Inaria and Lothar Raiken both helped me find the Incantir. I have and would trust my life to both. And as much as I hate to use this example, the ones who infiltrated both of our countries—yes, both—were a large group, made of hundreds of faul and humans alike. If they can do it . . ."

"I see. Later, you or another from your group must recount your story for all to read. I have no doubt it will ease the tensions, at least a little. The Incantir... it's a thing of legend. I just don't know if my people will be able to see that you are not your..."

"Great-grandfather."

"Yes. And then what happens when you or I die? Does another come along and undo all our progress?" asked Orwic.

"I hope not, of course. I have an orphaned cousin that was under Persec's wing, and she was next in line after me, but hopefully she is never crowned. I don't plan on dying anytime soon. No, all we can do is our best while we rule. Can you teach your heirs acceptance? Forgiveness?"

"Maybe..." said Orwic, stroking his beard. "My son is thirty years younger than I, but I may be able to bring him around. I assure you, though, I am in good condition for my age."

Galdur grinned. "Excellent."

"Where do you plan to start?" asked Orwic.

He thought for a moment. "I'll make it legal to travel between countries without having explicit permission from either the ruler or their officials. Faul can live in Valea if they please, and humans in the Shalin Empire. Don't get me wrong, I do not intend to merge nations. I will rule how I wish, and you may rule how you wish, but the people need to accept one another as rightful inhabitants of the continent."

"You make a strong case, Galdur. I do hope that you are not too optimistic about the chances of reconciliation."

"So do I, Emperor Orwic, so do I. I must ask though, what made you change your mind? Lothar told me you hated humans."

"I did... a while ago. I'm sixty-seven right now. Only recently, did I consider the possibility that we might not have to fight endless battles. Persec talked with me about that a lot. Her own parents had passed, so she naturally turned to me to discuss political matters. I disregarded her opinions; she was young, and I considered myself wiser than she. After her disappearance, we all thought that she'd been killed by humans, amplifying our hatred toward them. But then... I started thinking about how her words could still hold true even in death. After all, the actions of one human might not define all of them, even if she was killed by one. But I didn't think my people would hear it."

"They may not have. But the Incantir is the first step in a long and hard path that we must take toward true peace. The people will know the truth, and then they may come to accept it."

"Agreed. You know, I'm curious about something." Orwic gestured to the ten guards around them. "Have any of you ten fought at the border? Answer truthfully to these questions."

"You may answer that. And honestly," said Galdur to his five. Eight of the guards raised their hands.

"Before . . . this whole ordeal, how many of you wanted the battles to end?" asked Orwic. Four kept their hands up. "And now?" Slowly, all ten raised their hands. Maybe they were lying, but maybe not, thought Galdur.

Orwic grinned, and Galdur followed suit.

"There is hope," said Galdur softly.

57

MELKIN

SIX MONTHS LATER...

Melkin sat in the same room that he had lived in for the past four years, at the same desk where he used to peruse files and papers before his real missions. Next to him was a fresh stack of documents that Galdur had so graciously assigned to him: guard records, servant records, incident reports, everything. Melkin had complained *one time* about being bored, and now...

He sighed as he took another paper from the stack and scanned the information. All the servants and soldiers in the kingdom had been subjected to a background check to ensure the Talwrek ideology was eradicated. Of course, the remnants typically tried simply to hide their past and go on with their lives. After all, their ultimate goal of peace was now well on the way. New laws for attaining citizenship to both countries had been created recently, and as such, a substantial number of humans had gained citizenship in the Shalin Empire and vice versa. He couldn't attest as to the treatment of such immigrants by the commonfolk, but their existence was a good sign.

The door opened behind him, but he didn't turn around, only continued to stare at the reports on his desk.

"I could have been an intruder, you know," said Leina.

Melkin shifted in his chair, facing the doorway. "I'd be done for either way. Come in."

Leina took a seat on Melkin's bed and grinned. "They're arriving tonight."

"Are they now?" asked Melkin, raising an eyebrow. "And who else?"

"There's going to be a banquet and party with a group of faul. Soldiers, servants, and whomever else Emperor Orwic decided to send."

"Anything important happening?"

"Probably not. It's just a celebration for the completion of the Akarist memorial. And it's been five months since the last major border skirmish. Anyway, Galdur has requested our presence downstairs," said Leina.

"Why?"

"To give you enough time to get down there before the celebration. Come on." She beckoned him forward. "Plus, our friends are arriving a bit before the others."

Melkin sighed and smiled weakly, grasping the cane by his desk. Slowly, he stood up from his chair, bracing himself on his left leg and his cane. Sometimes he forgot about it; his right leg didn't really hurt, it just couldn't support any weight. He was grateful for Leina's patience as he hobbled over to the door and down the hall. "I ask for the thousandth time, why does this castle have so many stairs?" he grumbled, making his way down to the first floor.

"Petition Galdur to rebuild the royal castle," said Leina, grinning.

"Yeah, that would go over well," said Melkin. "Ryne, it smells good! How many people did Galdur invite?"

Leina chuckled, jerking a hand out as Melkin nearly slipped on one of the steps. "A lot, if I remember correctly. His aim is not to scare the people of Hileath, but for there to be a good number of faul roaming the streets, checking out the Valean shops and such."

Finally, they reached the bottom of the stairs, where a few servants were setting the banquet tables. "They're almost here" cried Galdur excitedly from around the stairs. He rounded the corner and beamed at Melkin. Though the two lived in the same building,

Galdur didn't usually come to the second floor, and Melkin rarely left his room. Galdur motioned for the two guards beside him to back up so he could approach Melkin.

"It's great to see you down here," said Galdur, putting a hand on Melkin's shoulder.

"I'm glad *you're* happy. All I can think about is going back up, but that's a problem for later tonight, I suppose," said Melkin with a small grin.

"King Galdur, your visitors are here!" announced a guard, pushing open the doors that separated the lobby from the great hall. Melkin leaned on his cane, trying to peer around the corner. Then, Astrid and Lothar came into the great hall, flanked by six Shalin soldiers. Melkin watched as Galdur strode toward them and embraced them both, followed by Leina. Melkin smiled at the reunion, but a forlorn feeling was building up inside of him. Lothar spotted Melkin and looked him over, his elated face falling at the realization.

"Come now, I'm no ghost," joked Melkin, starting to hobble over to the door. Astrid saw Melkin as well and had a similar reaction to Lothar. "I'm lucky to be alive."

"Let's talk somewhere a little . . . quieter," said Galdur, leading them into one of the lounge rooms. "You may leave us," said Galdur to his two guards.

"King Galdur, are you sure?" asked one of the guards, glancing at the faul.

"Yes, I am. I won't tolerate such insinuations about my friends. I'd be dead without every one of them. You may stand outside if you wish," said Galdur, closing the door firmly behind him. "Sorry about that. They don't really mean it; it's just how they've been conditioned."

"It's okay," said Astrid. "I'm sure that won't be the worst of it."

"That's not really my point," said Galdur, taking a seat on a couch. "But I appreciate the positivity."

"I don't think I've ever been in one of these," observed Melkin as he sat in one of the chairs, easing off his right leg.

"You live here," pointed out Astrid.

"*Supposedly*," said Melkin with a shrug. "So, I assume you're not a criminal anymore?" he asked, looking at Lothar.

He laughed. "No. Astrid and I recounted the whole story to Emperor Orwic and his advisors. He was quick to drop all charges and publish our story to the public."

"Then you're a sergeant again?" asked Leina excitedly. Lothar's face fell and Melkin felt dread consume him—he knew what Lothar would say.

"My magic never returned to me after . . . that day," said Lothar, shaking his head. "I don't know how it worked, but something about the elentac and then cooling the telium afterwards . . ."

Lothar had been unable to perform magic the day they left the negotiation grounds, but Melkin had thought that perhaps he just needed to rest and recover, that his powers would soon return.

"What *have* you been doing, then?" asked Galdur.

Lothar shrugged. "Not much. To have any government position, including the military, one must be able to use magic. I'm a terrible fighter without it anyway, unlike Astrid. Orwic gave me some money and said he would have made me one of his advisors, but the magic requirement obviously made that impossible. He didn't think altering a long-honored tradition would be a good idea right now."

Galdur nodded. "Probably a wise move. At least there aren't any such rules here, though."

"I'll probably end up in some job that doesn't use magic. Maybe a craftsman, but my skills leave much to be desired. It is what it is. What are your plans, Melkin?" asked Lothar. "Same as they were before your injury?"

Melkin appreciated the blunt nature of the statement. "My left leg healed quite well, and my right hand has lost a bit of feeling, but it still works. So yes, after a few more years of saving up money, I still plan to buy a house on the beach and fish for food." Galdur shot him a glance, but Melkin said nothing about his reservations.

"What have you been doing in the meantime?" asked Astrid.

"Going over guard and servant background checks, looking for Talwrek affiliation. Riveting, right? And if I find anything, Galdur has to send someone *else* to investigate. Obviously." He could not keep the bitterness from his voice. Lothar nodded; he was the only one of the four to look him in the eyes. Melkin, of course, wished Lothar could still use magic, but appreciated that he understood.

"What about you, Astrid?" asked Leina, breaking the silence.

Astrid grinned. "I'm back in the military, and they're allowing me to use a spear. No more fights at the border. Just taking care of any domestic threats and doing guard work. Five months ago, with the help of an informant, we found where the rest of the kidnapped orphans were being kept. We were able to take them back to the castle and now homes are being found for them. Only a few of the older ones really understood the Talwrek philosophy, so they're receiving help for that brainwashing as well. I'm just so glad that I can be in the military and actually be doing something useful."

"Same here. I'm Galdur's personal spy now," said Leina, her face bright with excitement.

Melkin felt a pang of sadness at that statement. Though four spies lived in the castle in Gladia's time, he had been considered her main spy. He tried to purge the memories from his mind, though; tried to forget who he had been when he was whole.

"—making sure that no one plans to assassinate Galdur, trying to track down Esadora, who continues to evade my searches, and keeping tabs on any remnants of the Talwreks. I run a team now," explained Leina.

The door creaked open, and a guard entered the room. Galdur raised an eyebrow and turned to face them.

"Sorry, King Galdur, but the rest of your company awaits your presence."

The banquet and celebration that night was wonderful; it lightened Melkin's heart almost as much as seeing Lothar and Astrid again. The twenty-five civilians with their twenty-five guards were to stay for a week in Hileath. Their occupations ranged from musicians, to dancers, to writers. They would be staying in the city to explore the Valean culture while imparting some of their own. Melkin didn't know how successful that endeavor would be, but he placed his faith in Galdur's foresight, and presumed it would be a step in the right direction.

Over the coming days, Melkin found himself constantly yearning to walk around Hileath with the faul—Lothar and Astrid especially. But, unable to do so, he stayed in his room and poured over more documents. It had been three days since the faul had arrived, but he had hardly seen them after the banquet. A knock at his door brought his mind back to the present.

"Come in," he said, turning around. Lothar appeared in his doorframe. "Is something wrong?" asked Melkin. "Why aren't you exploring the city with everyone else?"

"I'm allowed to go where I please," said Lothar, leaning against the wall near Melkin. "It feels like it could have hardly gone better, doesn't it? Half a year ago."

"Indeed," said Melkin, glad to be talking with Lothar again.

"You and I both came very close to death. And yet here we are."

Melkin nodded, keeping a flat expression despite his racing pulse. His thoughts that had consumed him for the past six months—were they finally being voiced? "Here we are."

"I have scarcely been happy since then. I'm glad to be alive, but to everyone else, I died. The last of the Golanirs died. Now I'm simply a weak, magic-less faul. I don't know what to do, where to go . . . who to be."

Melkin nodded. "You know, Galdur offered me the money to buy a house, but I declined. I'm not sure if I can live by myself in the middle of nowhere anymore."

"Is that what you really want?"

Melkin paused. A part of him remained true to his former longings and yearned for the life he could now never have. Yet another part of him wanted to remain with his friends, to support Galdur's hopes and dreams for the two nations. "I don't know. But I don't want this either. Even if I didn't have to work, I would still want to be doing something useful. Remember when we came to an agreement at the border? When we both proclaimed our passion for our jobs? I want to be an actual spy again—more than anything. This work . . ." He gestured at the stacks of paper on his desk. "It's killing me. What about you?" Melkin felt on the verge of tears; he hadn't wanted to worry Galdur or Leina with these feelings, but Lothar understood. He'd lost part of himself, too.

"I went back to Imar's study while I was figuring out what to do. I want to be a sergeant again, but it wouldn't be the same without Imar. He was like my father, my closest friend. There's no one for me in the Shalin Empire besides Astrid, but she's busy. I've talked to her about this, and while she understands, she's just a soldier. I don't know what I want anyway..." Lothar averted his eyes, but not before Melkin could see tears forming. "Elentac is such a forbidden process... people part for me in the streets and pity me, but they don't talk to me."

Melkin grasped his cane and stood up, embracing Lothar. "It'll be alright. By Ryne, I don't know how, but it will."

"I hope so, Melkin. I hope so. Talen's sake, I'm so glad that you're here."

On the morning of the seventh day, Melkin was again working on his files. There was to be a final banquet before the faul left tonight, and Melkin planned to attend. Then it would be back to normal again. For how long, though? Months? Years? Decades? He didn't want to think about it right now.

"Melkin?" said a servant from behind him.

"Yes?" he asked, not looking up from his table.

"King Galdur has summoned you to the meeting chamber." It must have been something important; Galdur wouldn't make him climb to the fourth floor unless he had to. Melkin nodded and limped out of his room.

"Would you like help?" asked the servant. "Or company?"

"No, thank you. I'll be alright." After ten minutes of limping, he made it to the familiar chamber and entered. A confusing mix of emotions filled him as he remembered the last time he was here.

Galdur and Lothar were seated at the table, awaiting his presence. "Some eight months ago I was told in this very room that I would be going to the Akarist, you know," said Melkin, sitting down in the same seat he had back then. "This better be important—I had to climb all the way up here."

"I think you'll find it to be exactly that. I have a question for both of you. I was going to spring it during the banquet, but I decided against that. Too much pressure, too many people," said Galdur.

"Way to be cryptic," said Lothar dryly. "The anticipation is killing me."

"Yes, yes, I'm getting to it," said Galdur. "I've created a new position in my royal court. It's an official ambassadorship, available to be filled by any citizen of the Shalin Empire. I also haven't filled the last spot on my panel of advisors, and apparently that needs to be rectified shortly. I'd like to offer the position of ambassador to you, Lothar, and the position of royal advisor to you, Melkin."

Melkin stared at Lothar, speechless for a second. Then, he turned to Galdur, whose face was stoic. "What do these jobs entail?"

"They're both the exact same, except the ambassador can't vote on small issues. That's a little too radical of a change right now. It's a mix of paperwork, speeches, traveling by carriage to different cities and reporting back, advising me on all sorts of issues, researching said issues, proposing laws, dealing with mail, and more. Until we can relocate the advisor rooms, you'd both have to stay in one of the castle towers, though—sorry Melkin."

A long silence reigned in the meeting room. Melkin stared down at the table, considering the proposal. "It's not my dream job. I've always sort of liked gathering information and not worrying about what happens with it."

"I know. But think of it this way," said Galdur. "When you go to cities, you have to talk to people, maybe do a little eavesdropping as well in order to bring me the peoples' opinions. I know it's not what it was. It can never be. But I think you might enjoy that. It's a big part of the job, and you get to go all over Valea."

Melkin nodded. A chance to work closely with Galdur and perhaps Lothar, too. He turned toward the faul. "What are your thoughts?"

"Before you make *your* decision," interrupted Galdur, "know that it will be hard. The people won't like it, I presume, even though you have no *real* political power besides influence over me. I wrote to Orwic about this though, and he approves. He even said it was a great idea, and he plans to create a similar position that obviously doesn't include the current employment requirements."

Melkin could tell he was trying to remove himself from the situation, to not pressure them into a decision. He was using that authoritative, factual tone he'd recently learned.

Lothar placed his hands on the table and sighed. "I'm open to it. Quite open to it." Then, a grin broke out on his face. "But I'm not sure I would want to unless I knew someone else on the panel. Knew them quite well, actually."

"I was thinking the same," said Melkin, for once not forcing the smile that came to his lips when thinking about his future.

"So, you'll accept?" asked Galdur.

He was gradually failing to conceal the excitement in his voice.

"I accept your offer," said Melkin.

"As do I," said Lothar.

"Wonderful!" Galdur shot up from his chair in excitement. "I'll announce it tonight." He cleared his throat. "You two are dismissed and may go on about your day. Once it is official, rooms will be made ready for the both of you."

Galdur left the room as Melkin once again struggled to stand up. Lothar was waiting for him.

"You go on ahead. I'm going back to my room anyway to get some more work done," said Melkin.

"No more work," ordered Lothar. "I came here expecting to see you, Leina, and Galdur. But you've been locked away in your study this whole time. How about a walk? Just around the grounds?"

"Why? I walk at about a mile an hour."

"Do you think I care? It's morning, we have all day. It doesn't hurt to walk, does it?"

"No, it's just slow."

"Will you join me, then? Please?"

Melkin matched Lothar's cheerful expression. For the first time in six months, he felt extraordinarily good. "Alright then."

Acknowledgements

Writing this book was . . . quite the experience. A frustrating, rewarding, tiring, beautiful experience. Perhaps my junior year of high school was not the best time to dedicate hours upon hours of my life to a novel, but who's to say? In any case, it wouldn't have been possible without the support and encouragement from those closest to me.

    I would like to express the deepest gratitude to my wonderful family. To my mom for listening to my senseless ramblings about the plot of this book and for her unwavering support throughout the writing process. She read each draft of the book and provided invaluable feedback from first concept to final proofread. To my dad, who, despite his dislike of fiction and fantasy, was always happy to discuss writing, editing, and publishing with me. To my brother, who gave me constructive criticism from the start.

    I am greatly indebted to my good friend Saturniidae Guethler, who worked for many hours on the cover and map, was second to read the novel, and without whom, this project would have been extraordinarily more difficult and costly.

I thank the following close friends who listened to me rant, day after day, about the various aspects of creating a book: Maggie Moran, Abbie Heath, Alethia Brown, Ruby Howland, AJ Scott, and Efi Prevezianos. They all gave me their support as I descended into slight madness during these past ten months.

Finally, to my readers, thank you for your support and kind words.